**Acclaim for the fabulous
and for author Jan**

"Stoddard tells a thrilling story . . . that features not only a unique and powerful family but a magnificent edifice filled with mysterious doors and passageways that link kingdoms and unite the universe." **—Publishers Weekly**

"A real treasure . . . Without question, *The High House* is one of my favorite books of the year."
**—Charles de Lint, Magazine of Fantasy
and Science Fiction**

"The language is rich and whimsical, poetic and lyrical in a style one doesn't see often these days. . . It's a mixture of epic fantasy, high adventure, and conceptual capriciousness. Evenmere is what you would get if you dropped the Winchester Mystery House into a giant mirror maze, and left it alone for a few decades."
—Michael M. Jones, Green Man Review

"Like its predecessor, *The False House* is part adventure tale, part allegory and all delight. It is high fantasy at its finest, peopled by characters so vivid we long to be able to step into the pages and join them for tea. It is the stuff from which classics are made."
**—Elizabeth K. Burton
The Blue Iris Journal**

Other Books by James Stoddard

THE HIGH HOUSE

THE FALSE HOUSE

THE NIGHT LAND, A STORY RETOLD

Evenmere

JAMES STODDARD

Ransom Books

Visit www.james-stoddard.com to learn more about the author.

To contact James Stoddard email evenmere@gmail.com

Cover illustration and design by Scott Faris
www.fariswheel.com

Edited by Betsy Mitchell www.betsymitchelleditorial.com

A Ransom Book
Printed in the United States of America.

First Printing: November 2015

10 9 8 7 6 5 4 3 2

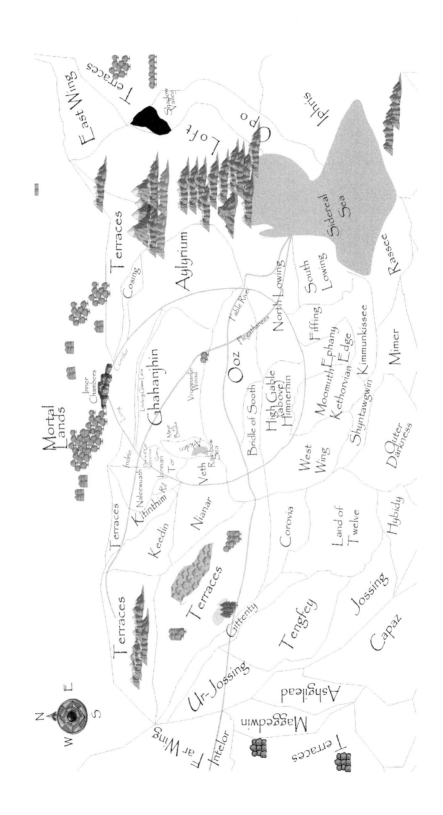

THE INNER
CHAMBERS

Coal House

Boiler

Engine House

Store Room

Scullery

Kitchen

Kitchen Court

Larder and Pantry

Servery

Kitchen Entrance

Servant's Stair (from Day)

Housekeeper's Room

Still Room

Store Room

Woman's Work Room

Servant's Hall

Brushing Room

Foot-man's Room

Housekeeper's Corridor

Men's Corridor

Women's Stair

Butler's Bedroom

Gun Room

Odd Room

Butler's Pantry

Back Stair

Cloak Room

Entry

Servery

Butler's Corridor

Library

Main Entrance

Porch

Gentlemen's Stair

Entrance Hall

Dining Room

Book of Forgotten Things

Transverse Corridor

Drawing Room

Morning Room

Main Stair

Yard Entrance

Yard

Picture Gallery

Gentleman's Chamber (Mr. Hope's Office)

THIS TALE OF FIGHTS AND FLIGHTS
AND POETRY MEN
I DEDICATE TO MY SON:

WILL

LONG MAY YOU RUN

ACKNOWLEDGEMENTS

Writers write novels mostly in solitude, but novels become finely-honed only with the help of others. I am deeply grateful to my wife, Kathryn, First Reader of my books and my heart. Also to Lon Mirll and Kreg Robertson for their priceless critiques, without which this would not be the book it is today, to fan and friend Dr. Robert Finegold, a fine writer in his own right, for his invaluable insights, and to Scott Faris for his friendship and beautiful cover design.

To have the opportunity to work again with Betsy Mitchell, who edited both *The High House* and *The False House*, is a gift beyond hope. Good editors show writers ways to make their books better; Betsy is one of the best.

I owe an endless debt of gratitude, one I should have acknowledged long before now, to Terry Waldren, who made many things possible.

Also thanks to fan Erin Shoemate for allowing me to use her Wonderfully Cool Name. Erin and I have met only through correspondence, so any actions or personality traits given to her namesake in no way reflect those of the real person.

Finally, many thanks to those who have written over the years, asking for a third novel about Evenmere. They provided the encouragement that made this book happen.

Walking up a road at night, I have seen a lamp and a lighted window and a cloud make together a most complete and unmistakable face . . . Yet when I walked a little farther I found that there was no face, that the window was ten yards away, the lamp ten hundred yards, the cloud beyond the world. Well, Sunday's face escaped me; it ran away to right and left, as such chance pictures run away. And so his face has made me, somehow, doubt whether there are any faces.

—*The Man Who was Thursday* by G. K. Chesterton

The Poet of Vroomanlin Wood

Jonathan T. Bartholomew made his way up the narrow stair toward the great attic of the infinite manor known as Evenmere. His lantern cast dim shadows on the wooden steps and unpainted walls. He trembled as he went, and could not stop trembling. *If I can delay it for the first minute, there is a chance. If I can survive for sixty precious seconds . . .*

He reached the top and paused. No winds disturb the attic; the pelting rains are never heard within. It is set apart, as if outside time and space. Jonathan peered into the dimness, listening to a silence broken only by the rhythmic creaking of the floorboards.

Like breathing, he thought. *That's right. The old serpent's hot breath.*

He took a dozen paces forward, his boots making prints on the dusty boards. He paused, certain his presence had already been detected. This was the beast's kingdom; nothing occurred in the attic without its knowing. Even if the creature were far from the stair, miles away in the depths of the immeasurable garret, distance meant nothing within its own realm; it could reach him in the twinkling of a moment.

It likes to play with its prey, torment them like a great big tomcat with a mouse. Maybe that will buy a little time. It all depends. If it recognizes me, that might be good. Jonathan frowned. *Or it might be as bad as bad can be. Terrible bad.*

A low rumbling arose, a throaty growl increasing in volume until every board in the attic resonated with it. The vibrations reached Jonathan's feet, shaking his whole body, filling his chest with a pulsing pressure. He thrust his fingers into his ears. On and on it rolled, growing louder and louder; and when it was as loud as he thought flesh could endure, it increased even more. The pounding was in his head; the vibrations toppled him to his knees. And still the intensity grew.

He rolled into a ball, gritting his teeth against the pain. *I'm gonna be shaken to bits without even getting the chance to talk. Going to be pieces of Jonathan everywhere.*

The roaring abruptly ended. He groaned and lay gasping for breath. Bracing himself against the floor on his slender, ebony hands, he rose unsteadily to his feet.

Sixty seconds. If I can last long enough to get its attention. Maybe I better say something, before it swoops by and gobbles me up.

From out of the darkness a massive tail, thick as a tree trunk, slammed against the floor in front of him, sending him bouncing across the boards like a tossed coin. Head spinning, body aching from innumerable bruises, he crept on hands and knees to retrieve his lantern, which had rolled a few feet away. He raised the lamp.

A tyrannosaurus of unspeakable proportions stood before him, its head large as a house. It reared its colossal frame into the attic heights, licking its lips with serpentine tongue, its rows of yellow teeth sharp as spears, its scent the overwhelming odor of reptile. Saliva, dripping from its open mouth, fell hissing to the floor. It bent over Jonathan and roared.

The entire attic shook with its force. Jonathan could only cover his ears and squirm beneath the power of its awful trumpeting, certain he was about to die.

The dinosaur ended its blaring cry. Its head was less than ten feet away, its terrible jaws so close Jonathan could see the red, festering sores on its gums.

"Who is this dark morsel, scarecrow thin, who dares enter the attic of the Last Dinosaur?" Jormungand rumbled, its voice deep as a foghorn. "Speak! Tell me your name, the name of your kin, the name of your station."

Before Jonathan could answer, the dinosaur leaned even closer, so near its fetid breath enveloped him. Its cold, unblinking eyes narrowed. "Why, if it isn't the famous Storyteller. Aren't I the lucky one."

Jonathan drew a deep breath, and slowly, cautiously, climbed to his feet. He gave a low, theatrical bow, and without straightening, lifted his eyes toward the dinosaur's face. "Most folks call me that, but I prefer going by Jonathan T. Bartholomew. At your service."

"You will indeed be served," Jormungand replied. "With butter if I can find it. I have noticed you off and on for centuries, Jonathan Bartholomew, wandering from country to country, the perpetual tramp, the eternal hobo, spreading your jaunty little stories to lighten the heart and warm the inner soul. I can't tell you how long I've been dying to eat you."

"That's right," Storyteller said, trying to steady his voice. "That's right. But before you do, tell me, do you like living in this big ol' attic?"

"A question. But you aren't the Master of the house, and I am not required to answer."

"That's true," Jonathan said, "but since there's just you and me way up here in the dark, and so much time to spend with nothing to do, why not tell me? Besides, I don't ask it for my own gain, nor for yours, so it's as if it's not really a question at all. More like a presumption waiting for a testimonial."

The dinosaur stood eyeing the man, its head weaving back and forth, its heavy breath pumping in and out. Finally, it said, "I do not enjoy it here. I was imprisoned ages ago by Those even I may not defy."

"It must get dreary dull," Jonathan said, "all these centuries up here alone. I can just imagine you, dreaming of long-denied battles, struggles from the days of blood and breaking bones, when you were Cyclops and Grendel and Dragon slaying warriors by the thousands, longing for the time when you can make your escape and slip away to do all your old mischief. Raisin' Cain; makin' trouble."

Jormungand's head lifted higher. "That is well-said. I do have a dream, a grand aspiration of being free again, a vision of a single, united world where all humanity suffers equally beneath my dominion, without respite, without hope. I dream of burning fields and wasted cities, victims scrabbling through the wreckage under the light of a million cold and distant stars. I dream of children orphaned, of the old and infirm left to die, of deadly plagues and torrential floods, of massacre on an indescribable scale, armies slaughtered by the millions, the smoke from the pyres blotting out the sky. I dream of cracks in the earth leading to the molten core, planets sundered from their orbits and whole suns extinguished. I dream of destruction as art and myself as the master artist." Jormungand gave a groaning sigh. "Yes, I have a dream."

"Poor beast. Is there nothing else in your heart?"

"Only that. But we each must have our little fantasies. And who are you to enter my domain, the country of the Last Dinosaur, offering pity, seeking to touch the pain of he who *is* Pain, he who knows that none of his dreams will ever come true? Would you dare give comfort to Despair? What stupendous ego!"

"I didn't come to offer pity, old worm, for there's nothing in you it can touch, but only to tell a story."

"What kind of story?"

"One you already know."

"Why should I listen to something I have heard before, and why should you slink up here to tell it?"

"Because it must be told, and only in hearing it can you understand the necessity for its telling."

"Mysterious and abstruse. How philosophical. How wise. I don't like abstruse. I think I will eat you, instead." Jormungand opened his jaws, preparing to strike. Jonathan's heart fluttered.

"You could do that," the man said quickly, shaking a slender, ebony finger at the monster. "You could have me for a snack. 'Course, I wouldn't be much, the smallest tidbit, the tiniest morsel for that great big appetite of yours, that endless craving, that terrible hunger no amount of flesh can slake. That's right. Better, wouldn't you think, to eat me after you and I have passed the time with a good yarn, after we've whittled down a few moments of eternity? Neither for your amusement nor your edification, but simply because it's what I came to do?"

Jormungand eyed him for endless seconds. Finally, the behemoth closed its jaws and gave a heavy nod.

"Very well. Begin your little recitation. Every moment it diverts me delays your death. Think of yourself as the Scheherazade of the attic. But don't expect a thousand nights, or even a thousand seconds."

"Mighty fine," the man said, wiping the sweat from his brow. "Mighty fine."

Beneath the dinosaur's very fangs, Storyteller reached into his backpack and withdrew a worn, woolen blanket. He spread it carefully on the floor and sat cross-legged upon it, his lantern by his side, its beams catching the planes of his dark face.

"I will begin at the beginning," Jonathan T. Bartholomew said.

Beyond Jonathan's wildest hopes, the dinosaur stood silent as a child, listening.

As every youngster knows, Storyteller began, *and many foolish adults refuse to believe, Evenmere, the High House, is the mechanism that runs the universe. Its lamps must be lit lest the stars fail; its clocks must be wound lest Time cease. The Master of the house must maintain the Balance between Chaos and Order so the warp and weave of existence does not unravel. The Circle of Servants aids him in his task; and the White Circle Guard and the myriad rulers of the countries within the mansion help maintain his authority.*

But a most peculiar stranger has appeared in the halls of the mansion. He has traveled many miles through the corridors and halls of Evenmere, driven by a need few can comprehend. Perhaps he doesn't quite comprehend it himself, but it will lead him to perform terrible deeds. And in the doing, he and others like him will shake the foundations of the house, and with it, the entire universe . . .

As the Poetry Man made his way through a tapestried hallway of the High House, he trailed his hand along the wall, laughing in delight at the cool touch of the oak paneling. His eyes sparkled with pleasure. "I can feel the proximity of stone. It is very near."

Since heeding the call of the Wild Poetry he had traveled the house, spreading the word, sharing it with whoever would hear. With his verse and the tiny chameleon who whispered from its position on his shoulder, he had been drawn through Ooz and West Wing and the green corridors of Gittenty. From there he had passed into the winding passages of Tengfey, which are adorned with carvings of astronomers and leprechauns.

He now stood at the border of Jossing, a blue antechamber unguarded save by double doors flanked by marble wolves. On the lintel were carved the words, *Welcome to Jossing, Land of Stone.*

He flung the doors wide, sending them rattling against the walls. A balding clerk, seated at a desk in the small chamber, started at the sound and stood in alarm.

"Fear nothing, friend," the poet said, "I've come in peace today. To spread all cheer to Evenmere, and to your happy kin."

With a strangled cry the man fled the chamber, spilling quill and ink in his haste.

The poet laughed. He did not know why those he met feared him, nor did it concern him; his business was only with those who desired his gift.

Leaving the chamber, he entered a short corridor. Following the sound of the clerk's receding footfalls, he turned onto another passage with walls covered with mosaics depicting distant mountains.

After a time, the passage gradually widened. The mountains on the mosaics slowly grew closer; the carpet changed from gold to dusty brown, with patterns like veins of ore scattered across it. The light, which issued from louvered openings in the ceiling, lessened until he proceeded through twilight. In the dimness his eyes seemed to betray him; the rock patterns on the walls and floor appeared to be real stone protruding into the passage.

To his delight, he became aware of the noise of gravel beneath his boots. Kneeling, he ran his hand over the ground, which was no longer carpet, but bedrock. He retrieved a rough limestone shard, tossed it in the air, caught it, and let it fall clattering against the stones. Just ahead the ceiling was higher, and escarpments descended from it, giving the passage the appearance of a narrow gorge. Desert vegetation—cactus and yucca, long-stemmed wild grasses—grew between the rocks; stone columns supported the ceiling. He grinned. He had heard that Jossing began this way, the house melding into a country of rolling canyons. Countless lands lay beneath the eaves of Evenmere, and he intended to spend the rest of his existence spreading his gift to as many as possible.

Moving gracefully among the boulders, he wound along the

corridor, gradually ascending, singing as he went:

Earth and Stone
Earth and Stone
Massive mountains
Caverns deep
Molten deserts
Underground
Where the heart
Of granite sleeps

As he sang, he felt the power of the earth welling within him—like calling to like—filling him with its strength. The source of his poetry was that of high crags and subterranean pits, molten mantles and mountain peaks. It was that kinship to Jossing which had drawn him here.

The clerk must have contacted his superiors, for a dozen soldiers came scrambling over the rocks, pistols drawn.

"Halt and state your business!" their captain ordered.

"I've come to see the Thaloddian Arch," the poet said, raising his hand, "and to parlay with your decemvirs."

The captain aimed his pistol and fired. The bullet whined toward the Poetry Man, but a gray light pulsed from his hand, sending it veering away.

A hail of gunfire followed. The gray radiance expanded to surround the poet's frame. He laughed as the missiles ricocheted around the gorge.

Knives drawn, the men charged. The Poetry Man raised his arms, and the earth beneath them rose in answer, erupting in an undulating wave, scattering the soldiers across the hall, leaving them broken and moaning.

Without a backward glance he continued on his way, softly singing, "Earth and stone, earth and stone . . ."

Within the hour, he approached the High Mount of Jossing. The passage had sloped upward throughout his journey, and with it the marble roof, lifted by row upon row of columns until it formed a vaulted chamber vast enough to encompass the mountain before him. The mount was an artificial construction, an alabaster pyramid rounded by design, as if by the rain. Halfway up its peak stood the Thaloddian Arch, a granite expanse stretching across one side of the mount. Beyond the arch, at the peak, rose the swirled domes and towers of the Palace of the Decemvirs.

Robe flapping, the poet hurried along the steep stone steps, making his way up the dizzying height. A company of soldiers had formed beneath the arch, and down from the manor behind them strode the ten regal decemvirs, clad in silver and sable, their dark cloaks flowing at their backs.

The Poetry Man reached the level beneath the arch, a flattened expanse covered with tessellated tile. The arch curved thirty feet above his head, a granite band wide enough for ten men to walk abreast. The line of soldiers stretched beneath it, barring his way. He waited where he was.

The warriors directly before him stepped stiffly back, opening a corridor through which the decemvirs strode, six men and four women, tall and majestic. The eldest, silver-haired and keen-eyed, spoke first.

"Who are you?" The decemvir's voice was deep and commanding. "Why are you here? And why do you shroud your face in mist?"

"Do I?" the poet asked. "I did not know. My name is unimportant. I came because the poetry of your country calls me. I have seen, you see; I have found the ecstasy, hidden in both earth and stone. Do you hear its calling? Do you want to come with me?"

"From the hour you crossed our borders we have felt . . . something," the decemvir admitted. "A force, great as this mountain and far older. Perhaps old as the earth itself. That is why we came to meet you, to discover what it means."

The poet raised his index finger. "Know, o children of the canyons, that I have touched the deep-earth's core. I bring you the essence of rock itself, the primal source of all that is stone. The strength of caves and towering peaks. A gift of stone to the people of the stones. Come with me, and accept the glorious bounty of the Wild Poetry."

The decemvir hesitated, but the youngest of his fellows stepped forward, his eyes alight with excitement. "I will go!"

"Do not be hasty, Tycamber," the eldest warned. "We cannot trust such power as I sense within this stranger."

But the young man's eyes danced all the more. "I trust what

I feel. It's everything we've ever wanted! Not just stone, but Stone Incarnate, not just earth but Earth herself!"

"Who else will join me?" the Poetry Man asked.

The decemvirs exchanged glances. Sweat beaded their brows; their faces were hungry with longing.

"I have never felt such desire," one of the women cried. "It makes me want to desert both life and duty. I cannot bear it. Leave us, whatever you are, while I can still resist."

The poet turned to Tycamber. "We will leave, but the ecstasy goes on. There is no escape from the power of which I partake. Many are its forms and myriad its callings. The Song of the Earth for you and I, but for others, rhapsodies equally enchanting."

The Poetry Man could feel the energies rising inside him, wave upon wave, the quintessence of all that belonged to the earth. It emanated from him, surrounding him in a widening aura.

He clasped Tycamber's shoulder. The man gasped at the touch as the force swept through him. Eyes dazed, grinning in joy, he began walking down the hill at the poet's side.

"Wait!" the elder decemvir ordered. "We will not allow this, Tycamber."

"A Lord of Jossing has accepted my gift; so that which is released cannot be contained," the Poetry Man called over his shoulder. "Those who reject my prize must be overwhelmed by it."

The gray light radiating from the poet surged outward, undulating like water. It swept along the mount, passing over the rocks. Whatever it touched, whether plant or animal, it transformed into stone. Like a wildfire it rushed down the mount, snaking along the corridors and canyons of Jossing, filling all that country with its enchantment.

It passed among the soldiers, who screamed as it touched them. Their eyes grew gray, their limbs stiffened, leaving them forever locked in marble form.

The poet glanced back. The decemvirs stood, as they would stand through the ages, monuments to their past glory, their nobility etched in lines of stone.

The wave passed over the arch, and the span grew harder and even more massive, until it could not bear its own weight. As the poet and his new follower reached the base of the mount, the arch collapsed in a shower of granite.

"A shame," the Poetry Man said, "but the earth will not be denied. Come, my friend, we must spread the Wild Poetry to all of Evenmere."

The bedazzled decemvir did not once look back.

Near the end of the day, the upper supports above much of Jossing fell in on themselves, leaving a gaping hole in the endless roof line of Evenmere. By that time, the poet and his disciple were far away.

An hour before the Poetry Man confronted the decemvirs of Jossing, Carter Anderson, Master of Evenmere, Keeper of the Seven Words of Power, Holder of the Master Keys, the Lightning Sword, and the Tawny Mantle, stood within the wide halls of Indrin, gazing at the tall windows above him, where sunlight streamed through air heavy with dust motes and the promise of beckoning spring. A central marble column with gilded capitals supported a vault of Oozian intricacy; stenciled decorations interspersed with panels of Morris wallpaper covered the walls. Statues of ancient Gwyve—plumed warriors, athletes, and lolling women—peered down from alcoves beneath the vaultings, and a stained-glass window twenty feet in circumference overlooked a gallery at the chamber's end. Outside the windows, cotton clouds swam through an ocean-blue sky, and a yellow bird on the outside ledge assaulted a pecan shell with its beak.

Scaffolds were strung across the room, and men in brown aprons covered them like beetles, hoisting tools and wires up and down their rungs, installing the telegraph lines intended to eventually connect the entire White Circle.

Standing beneath the gallery, Lord Anderson closed his eyes, fingertips lightly touching the wall, searching for the forces of Order and Chaos, listening for the Balance. Before the telegraph project began he could not have done this, would not have known what to seek; but he was well practiced now. He saw the two opposing forces as colors within his mind: Order, white and pure in planes and straight lines; Chaos, shimmering many-hued, perpetually changing its form. He searched the wall, eyes still shut, sensing the flow of energies, seeking a place where a hole could be drilled. But at every point, he saw that the slightest change would corrupt the Balance.

He called the Head Architect to him. "Doonan, we cannot drill through this wall. No hammer must touch it."

Doonan, dressed in his customary blue robes, stroked his handlebar mustache thoughtfully, eyes bleary from lack of sleep. "Are you certain?"

Carter glanced at the man in irritation. "Would I say so if I weren't?"

"Sorry, sir," the architect said stiffly. "It's just that I thought we had the go-ahead. The next nearest spot is half a mile north. We'll have to reroute the entire section."

"I am aware of that. Are there any other options?"

Doonan thought a moment. "Could we take the lines beside the gallery on the east and bring them into the side chamber? It would cost us half a day's work, but it would save at least some of our labor."

The two men strode to the wall leading to the side chamber. Lord Anderson sought the Balance again and marked a place on the paneling. "This will work. Drill right here." He clasped the architect's shoulder. "Forgive my testiness. I'm not angry at you, but at myself for overlooking the problem. We are all tired."

"That we are, sir. That we are."

As Doonan walked away, Carter turned to find William Hope, the Butler of Evenmere, waiting to the side, hands behind his back, lips pursed in a soundless whistle, a round-faced man wearing a dark sack suit and black bowler.

"A bit miffed, are we?" he asked.

"I never would have started this project if I had known that every nail affects the Balance. Remember how easy it was in the outside world? Grab a sledgehammer and tear down a wall?"

Mr. Hope laughed. "But a wall there wouldn't affect the fabric of the universe. Understandable, it taking so long."

"Four years and only a third done! But that's not why I'm frustrated. I checked that wall six months ago. I know I did. How could I have missed it? It's as if the Balance has changed."

Mr. Hope shrugged. "You've had a lot on your mind. But think! Ancient pharaohs are known for their pyramids; you will be remembered as the Telegraph Master, the Caliph of the Singing

Wire. I have your lunch set out on the Greensward. A breath of fresh air will do you good."

Carter laughed ruefully. "Lead on. Telegraph Master? More like Baron of Boondoggles. Did the pharaohs have advisors to keep them in their place?"

"Yes, but they executed them regularly. A regrettable policy."

The two passed through the hall, down a winding stair, and along wainscoted corridors exiting onto a long commons fragrant with lilacs and newly mown grass. The porches and balustrades of Evenmere surrounded them on every side. A marble fountain stood in the center of the square with water foaming from the mouths of carved dolphins. Close to the fountain, on a picnic blanket beneath a stand of cottonwoods, sat Carter's wife, Sarah, their five-year-old son, Jason, and Enoch, the Windkeep of Evenmere. The sun shone bright, the air blew cool; Sarah gave Carter and Mr. Hope a happy wave.

"Look, Daddy. I found a bug!" Jason shouted, holding up a jar, his hand clasped tightly over the lid.

"What color?" Carter asked.

"Green."

"Bugs and lunch should never mingle," Sarah said. "Put it away. I'll not have it nibbling the salad."

Jason had the dark hair and the cheekbones of his mother, but Carter's blue eyes and straight nose. Carter thought him a handsome lad, quick and intelligent—but beyond that, a miracle on legs—for he and Sarah had once despaired of ever having children. To him, Jason was a fragile vault with all the world's hope locked within. Sometimes, it took his breath away.

Carter turned to Enoch, who rose to meet him. The two exchanged warm handshakes. "I didn't know you were in this part of the house," Carter said.

"I have to see to a water-clock in Lippenhost," Enoch said, "so I thought: why not drop by and find out how the telegraph is going?"

"Lippenhost?" Mr. Hope said. "I'm unfamiliar with that one. I thought I knew them all."

"I usually leave it to my apprentice," Enoch said, "but I think it's time I checked it. The truth is, all these years I still can't tell you what it does."

"You could let it run down and find out," Carter suggested.

Ignoring the humor in Lord Anderson's eyes, the Windkeep shook his head, his Assyrian curls bouncing with the movement. "That might not be so smart. The trouble with Time is, you let it stop, it's hard to start it again."

Carter clapped him on the shoulder. "Which is why I'm glad you're on the job. Stay and eat with us."

Of all the servants, Carter loved Enoch best. He was burly and brown as a giant oak and easily as ancient, having by his own admission seen three thousand years, though his jet-black hair and jovial nature gave him the appearance of a man in his late fifties. As a boy, Carter had often followed him on his rounds to wind the various clocks that maintained the flow of Time, and the Windkeep had indulged him like a doting uncle.

The three men joined Sarah and Jason on the blanket, and from the picnic basket Mr. Hope produced a feast of poached turbot with lobster sauce, steamed carp forcemeat served in anchovy butter, and salad of pike fillets with oysters. The meal went splendidly, except for a rough patch when Jason would not eat his carp.

Carter glanced across the commons. Hard rains had recently torn scores of leaves from the cottonwoods, and a gust of wind sent them flurrying through the grass. Lord Anderson studied their motion, a bite of pike hanging forgotten on his fork.

"Is something wrong?" Sarah asked.

Carter withdrew from his reverie, looked at his fork as if seeing it for the first time, and ate the morsel. "I was just thinking. Have you given much consideration to movement?"

"I consider all my moves before I make them," she replied, "but in what way do you mean?"

"It's like those leaves stirring in the wind while we sit still. There is a mystery there, as if all of life could be understood if only we comprehended their motion. Both Order and Chaos are represented—the leaves blowing at random, gusted by haphazard winds, yet the winds are part of a vast world system, chaotic in manner, but following a complex, orderly pattern of interactions. Order and Chaos working together to create reality. When I first became Master I understood so little. I thought it was about wielding the Seven Words of Power and the Lightning Sword, like some cowboy gunslinger in the American West. Only later did I begin to comprehend the relationship. Now, I could sit for hours thinking of the movement of a twig floating down a stream, the fluttering of an eyelash, the tapping of a branch against the panes."

Sarah reached across the blanket, plucked a leaf from the grass, and handed it to Carter. "What do you see?"

He turned the leaf over by its stem. "A pointed, tear-shaped object, nearly but not quite symmetrical, darker on one side than the other, with capillaries filled with chlorophyll. Order and Chaos again."

"No," she smiled sweetly. "It is a leaf."

"You mock me," he replied, grinning back.

"I do not, sir." And he saw she was suddenly serious. "In your brooding on the Balance, do not forget the beauty of the leaf itself. Don't go from me, Carter."

"Have I been absent?"

"Not in body. Oh, I understand. You see things other men can't. You feel the whole house breathing around you. It is intoxicating. A week ago I saw you standing in the hall, gazing at a Morris tapestry as if it were the Holy Grail."

"I suppose I do get wrapped up. It's just—"

"I know," she kept her eyes on his. "But it is my duty to rouse you from your reveries, to show you the world, the sun, and your own son, all Chaos and little Order at this stage of his life, who should be seen merely as a small boy."

Carter grinned ruefully. "Have I really been that bad? What do you say, Enoch? Has she bagged me?"

The Windkeep shrugged. "Being the Master is a troublesome business. Sometimes you lose track of things."

"A diplomatic answer," Carter said. "What of you, Will?"

"You *have* been a bit intense of late," Mr. Hope admitted.

Lord Anderson leaned back on one elbow on the blanket. "Even my butler condemns me, and he with a degree in law. I can but surrender and promise to do better."

Yet Carter wondered whether he could. The Balance was always with him now, as it had not been in the early days. Sometimes, in the dark of the night, the responsibility he carried for the whole of Existence seemed unbearable. He spent far too much time worrying about it.

The last few days had been especially difficult. He kept sensing something—some disturbance at the farthest reaches of consciousness. It was like the problem with Doonan and the wall: a vague sense of things going wrong.

Jason, having apparently decided to disagree with the tone of the conversation, abruptly rushed into his father's arms, spilling his dinner. By the time everything was set right, the talk had turned to other topics. When dessert ended, Carter rose to go back to the telegraph.

He had taken less than a dozen steps when a searing pain swept through the center of his head, a jolt so powerful it brought him to his knees. An involuntary shout escaped his lips, and blackness momentarily covered his vision.

By the time he could see again, Enoch knelt beside him, Sarah stroked his face, and Mr. Hope stood close by.

"What is it, love?" Sarah was asking him.

Lord Anderson's breath had been driven from his lungs, and it took a moment before he could reply. His voice came in a half-whisper. "The Balance . . . something has happened. Some part of the house has been destroyed." He sat down in the grass, breathing heavily. "I'm all right. A moment."

When he was stronger, Enoch and Sarah helped him up. Leaning on their shoulders, he closed his eyes and opened himself to the Balance, searching for the source of his pain. He could feel it, far to the west.

"Jossing," he said, straightening his shoulders. "We must go at once. Will, you come with me. Sarah, contact the White Circle Guard. Tell them we need men and medical teams. The disaster is unprecedented."

After a few moments' discussion and some additional instructions, they were ready to go. Carter clasped his son to his chest.

"Papa, you're hugging too hard," Jason said.

"Because I love you so much."

"How quickly our lives shift," Sarah said. "One moment we're enjoying a picnic and now this. Like the leaves in the wind, stillness and motion."

"You always listen," Carter said, "even when I babble."

"You never babble," she replied, kissing him on the lips.

It took Lord Anderson and his butler three days of hard travel to reach Jossing. They journeyed down the Long Corridor to the train station at Indrin. Dawn, peering over the roofs and towers of Evenmere, found them waiting in a wide quadrangle, listening to the roar of a yellow locomotive streaming out of an opening in the south wall. The ancient train was the only one in all the known regions of the house, with passenger cars just wide enough for one row of bench seats. Upon this narrow conveyance, Carter and Mr. Hope sped along a skinny lane, with a high roof above and long windows flashing by.

At first, winding its way between the chambers, the locomotive went little faster than a pony's pace, but upon reaching straighter passages its speed increased, and the condition of the rails became apparent. Between the jostling, Mr. Hope leaned over and shouted above the rattle, "I now understand the expression: *I've never felt an earthquake, but I've ridden the Innman train.* I hope we're not shaken to butter before we get there."

Hours later they reached the rail yard at Innman Tor, a wide, open field surrounded by the house. They stayed only long enough to stretch their legs and board two companies of the White Circle Guard. The soldiers' pearl armor glistened in the glow of the car's electric lamps. The train, now heading east, swept back into slim corridors. The locomotive rolled through Ril, Kitinthim, and Keedin, popped out like a mole from its burrow onto the vast courtyard surrounding the farmlands of the western Terraces, and traveled from there to the station at Gittenty, where the travelers and soldiers proceeded on foot through Tengfey until they reached the entrance to Jossing.

Throughout the journey, Lord Anderson and Mr. Hope had speculated on who was responsible for the attacks. There were many factions within the High House, but the main threat were the members of the Society of Anarchists, an organization whose goals bore little resemblance to its name. The anarchists were not so much anti-government as anti-reality. They wished to gain control of the mechanisms of Evenmere in order to use them to reshape the nature of Existence, to end all pain, suffering, and death. A seemingly laudable ambition. But Carter, like the Masters before him, doubted it was possible for humans to remain human in such a reality.

The anarchists were the likely suspects, but how they could have accomplished such destruction was unknown.

Leaving Tengfey, Lord Anderson and the soldiers opened the double doors into Jossing—and stepped out of comfortable halls into a region of utter destruction. Blue sky stretched overhead through a miles-wide hole where the ceiling had collapsed, leaving the mountains of Jossing exposed to the sun. Crews of soldiers, civilians, and the firemen of Ooz sifted among the rubble, looking for victims. Volunteers had poured in from all the neighboring countries. Mr. Hope gasped at the enormity of the wreckage; hollow despair gripped Carter's heart.

The next few days were a blur. Lord Anderson did what the Masters have done since the beginning of Evenmere, rallying the people of Jossing, who had lost their leaders with the destruction of the decemvirs, arranging for men and materials, and demonstrating that even in chaos, the High House stood firm. All of Evenmere had been stunned by the attack, and messengers and emissaries came from the surrounding countries, seeking information and reassurance. Carter attended constant meetings and public appearances, getting little rest and less sleep, while Mr. Hope, conducting interviews and collecting evidence, sought to learn everything possible about the nature of the perpetrator of the crime.

And always Lord Anderson was asked the same question in different forms: *What will the Master do to stop those who committed this atrocity? And what will keep them from striking again?*

It was the duty of Chant, the Lamp-lighter of Evenmere, to ensure the stars of the universe always burned, a charge he accomplished by keeping certain lamps in the great house lit. He had a boyish face and a boyish smile, but the gray at his temples bespoke middle age. (He was actually in his second century, long-lived as are some members of the Circle of Servants). A bit of the gentle rogue lay upon him, and his eyes were rose-pink. By nature a poet, he liked to quote Stevenson, saying his duties as Lamp-lighter consisted of "punching holes in the darkness."

Two days had passed since the attack at Jossing, and the news had rippled through the house. Only his responsibilities had kept the Lamp-lighter, who held a degree in medicine, from rushing to lend aid. Instead, with a pensive heart, he had finished replenishing the oil in the green lamp beside the Ionian candles at Riffenrose, and was on his way back to the Inner Chambers, when an urgent message from an old friend forced him to divert his course to Vroomanlin Wood.

Any time he journeyed through this part of the High House he enjoyed spending time in the wood, which grew in a thirty-mile-square courtyard consisting of hundreds of interconnected walled gardens open to the air, no chamber greater than twenty by twenty feet, with stone paths winding through the vegetation. An endless variety of trees grew within the forest, but the predominant species was the *oto*, a sparse-leafed, twisting growth that gave the wood an especially bare appearance in early spring, when the trunks looked like gnarled ballerinas cast in bronze.

He came to the place where he was to meet his friend, where grew The Men Who Are Trees. The Men Who Are Trees were each about ten feet tall, with a single human head sprouting from their topmost branches. Yellow beetles lay in dead piles at their trunks; wood ants gnawed their barks; sap oiled their waxen faces. Seated before them on a gray stone bench, Chant withdrew a red leather volume of poetry from his pack and began to read, his voice echoing off the stone walls. At first, The Men Who Are Trees cursed the Lamp-lighter in their hollow voices and flailed the air with the hands that grew from the ends of their branches, but they soon quieted as if listening, their limbs waving in the breeze.

Throughout that evening Chant read to them, closing the book only when the last rays of the sun no longer shone on their strained faces. For half a minute The Men Who Are Trees wept, then closed their eyes and fell quiescent as flowers folding for the night; and the Lamp-lighter climbed into his bedroll and fell asleep, lulled by the wind in the branches.

He was awakened at dawn by the wailing of the creatures, an alarm more abrasive than any rooster. The Men Who Are Trees fear fire above all else, so he ate a cold breakfast and read aloud from his book again. Once more his bizarre audience soon ceased their railing, save for an occasional anguished cry.

After an hour he was interrupted by a tapping sound behind him. Turning, he discovered a blind man approaching, dressed in robes like a monk, a hood pulled over his eyes, his cane clacking along the stone path.

Chant rose, bowed to the trees, and said, "We will continue when next I return."

Again they quietly wept before becoming still, while he placed the book in his pack and turned to the newcomer. "Nighthammer! At last! *Well met, old friend, on this far shore, we two who never dreamed to meet again.*"

"*Beside the ocean's roar we stand,*" Nighthammer replied, finishing the verse, "*and clasping hands, we laugh to scorn those bitter tongues of idle men who said it never could be so.* Reading to the vile vegetation again, eh? Why do you waste your time?"

"I think it relieves their suffering."

"*If* they truly suffer," Nighthammer said. "They may be no more intelligent than parrots. *His numbers, though they moved or seemed to move in marble and in bronze, lacked character.*"

As if in answer, the nearest of The Men Who Are Trees, a raven-haired fellow with hollow eyes and a twisted scowl, gave a dreadful roar.

"Perhaps they think otherwise," Chant said, "or at the least don't care for Yeats."

Nighthammer grinned. "Coincidence. They have existed in Vroomanlin for ages, and are nothing more than plants resembling men. You spend your valuable time seeking to comfort them, while they revile you the next time they see you."

"My friend, true compassion never depends on the reaction of those who receive it. I enjoy my time in Vroomanlin, and I like reading poetry. A few hours spent reading to trees is a small sacrifice. I brought you a sandwich. Come sit beside me and tell me why your message was so urgent."

Nighthammer made his way to the gray bench, feeling along with his cane. As he sat down, Chant handed him a small bundle wrapped in paper. Nighthammer smiled and placed the parcel in a pocket of his robe. "I will come to the point, for there is little time. A month ago, my brothers and sisters in the Colony of Blind Poets began leaving Vroomanlin Wood, lured away by the call of a new and dangerous power. They are all gone now; only I remain. Others will soon hear the siren song: the romantics, the artists, the musicians. I suspect you have already sensed it—touches of joy or sorrow in unexpected places? A special enchantment in the starlight? Storm clouds reeking of terror and awe? Have you felt it?"

The Lamp-lighter moistened his lips. When he spoke, his voice was low, almost conspiratorial. "On the night of the new moon, I stood in the twilight preparing to light the lamp beyond the Yard. For the barest second, I felt the utter, unalterable *horror* of the impending darkness, a surging sea of emptiness breaking against the shores of existence. The feeling was excruciatingly intense, unlike any fear I have ever known. I lit the lamp with the haste of a frightened boy, but drew no comfort from the flames, which appeared equally terrible to me—the essence of fire itself, burning, cleansing, destroying, too dreadful to bear. I fled back across the Yard with as much speed as my pride allowed."

A long howl from one of The Men Who Are Trees echoed among the gray walls, making both men start.

"How long have we been friends?" Nighthammer asked.

Chant frowned in thought. "Over twenty years, I suppose. Why?"

Nighthammer turned his face toward the sky and smiled. "I have enjoyed our conversations, our talks of books and poems and dreams. We have whiled away many pleasant hours. I regret losing that friendship."

"Must it be so?" Chant asked.

"It must, for circumstances force me to admit that I am an anarchist."

Filled by the emptiness of sudden loss, Chant was momentarily silent. "I see," he finally murmured.

Nighthammer groped until he gripped the Lamp-lighter's shoulder. "I hope you do. I was assigned to Vroomanlin a decade ago by the Society of Anarchists to engage travelers in conversation and learn what I could, especially from you."

"Why tell me now?"

Nighthammer sighed and folded his arms, hugging himself as if against a chill. "Matters have not gone well for us since the death of the Supreme Anarchist six years ago. There has been growing dissension which reached a peak recently when a number of members broke from the main body. This group, which we call the Radical Anarchists, obtained access to the new power of which I spoke, through the discovery of a mystic volume. Apparently, the first signs of its use appeared at the College of Poets at the University of Aylyrium. Those who wield it call themselves Poetry Men."

"Your former colleagues?"

"Some of them, though other poets have come from all over the house. Rumor has it their very words can drive men mad. At Jossing, we have now seen what they can do."

Chant raised his eyebrows. "*The woods decay, the woods decay and fall . . .* Your story fits the description of the poet who appeared there. What can be done?"

"We believe the Poetry Men can be defeated only by finding the source of their might, an ancient tome called *The Book of Verse.* But we have also learned they will soon attempt to recover a companion volume hidden within the Mere of Books. If they obtain it, we believe they will become nearly invincible. The Society has sent me to you because only the Master of the house has a chance of stopping them."

Chant raised a wry eyebrow. "The Anarchist Council wanting the help of the Master of Evenmere? There's a tickle for my fancy."

"Believe me, we come to you as a last resort. We are afraid, my friend, as we have never been before. When the Poetry Men first appeared, we sent ambassadors in a futile attempt at parlay. Upon finally making contact, we found the goals of the cult members, who possess neither leaders nor any form of organization, both unfathomable and intransigent. Two of our envoys, men wholly dedicated to our cause, joined the Radicals on the spot, and four others were slain. Only one survived to report back to us. Later that week, a squad of our best attacked a single Poetry Man in North Lowing and were annihilated to the last man. Armed might cannot stop these people. We have tried, and been sorely punished for it. Their only goal appears to be destruction for its own sake."

Chant sighed. "*They brought me bitter news to hear and bitter tears to shed.* Very well. I will take you at your word. We *have* known each other a long time, so I might as well admit I knew you for an anarchist from the very beginning."

Nighthammer sat upright, twisting his cane in his palm. "You knew? How?"

"I had you investigated. One mustn't be too careful. Our agents discovered your anarchist associations, along with your real name. I never gave you any information of value, and occasionally, when necessary, fed you false details. It allowed us to capture the Sullenbode spy ring in Ooz several years ago."

It was Nighthammer's turn to sit speechless. "But you sounded surprised when I told you."

"I knew only the most desperate situation would force you to give yourself away. I too have valued our conversations. I . . . regret our charade cannot continue. You are really blind, aren't you? I have always wondered."

Nighthammer gave a grim chuckle. "As a mole. I lost my sight trying to learn to build bombs. Wasn't very good at it. Will you give me over to the authorities?"

"You are already a known anarchist. Sitting in a wood listening for information is hardly a crime. But now that things are out in the open, I wish I could convince you to renounce your creed. Our friendship could continue."

Nighthammer shook his head sadly. "Regretfully, no. The universe that blinded me needs to be changed. I may sometimes disagree with our methods, but not our goals. We will not rest until Existence itself has been altered."

"And I regret we have no more time to sit and chat of books. I must get a message to Lord Anderson at once. Clasp my hand, old friend. I shall miss you."

"And I, you."

With a heavy heart, the Lamp-lighter rose and strode away. But he hesitated at the opening of the quadrangle to watch Nighthammer make his way in the opposite direction, softly tapping his cane against the bark of the trunks, his hood pulled over his eyes, while The Men Who Are Trees squawked like belligerent monkeys.

The Relay System of Evenmere, with outposts every four furlongs, allows messages to be sent through the house with marvelous speed by runner, bicycle, and—across the broad fields of the Terraces—horse and carriage. By late that same evening, Lord Anderson had received Chant's letter, and he and Mr. Hope were back on the train to Innman Tor, from whence they would head to the Mere of Books. Depending on what happened there, they might then travel to the College of Poets at the University of Aylyrium, where Nighthammer claimed the Poetry Men had first appeared.

"I hope we are doing the right thing," Carter said, over the clattering of the wheels. Night had fallen behind the distant walls of the Terraces, and the electric lamps sent shadows flickering across the yellow seats and sides of the car. The compartment was mostly empty, and this was the first uninterrupted moment for either of them since their arrival at Jossing.

"There's no help for it," Mr. Hope said, "even if the information did come from an anarchist. We can't trust him, but we can't ignore it, either."

"I like none of it," Carter said. "We're too much in the dark. Did you contact the guard?"

"I sent a message to Marshal Japth in Ghahanjhin, but even if they leave at once, they'll be at least a day behind us."

"Just as well. The whole house is on the edge of panic. It will give us a chance to investigate without the sight of soldiers stirring everyone up more."

They spoke of the armies and militias mobilized throughout Evenmere, the governors clamoring for action, the displaced victims, the threats of political unrest, all this on top of their other responsibilities: the telegraph, their neglected duties in the Inner Chambers, the rebuilding of North Lowing (in which Carter's brother, Duskin, had some part), Fiffing's rejoining the White Circle the year before, all the details of administering the limitless house. The men had become fast friends over the years, and Carter enjoyed Hope's optimism and unorthodox approach to legal matters, while the butler appreciated Lord Anderson's imperturbable calm, his solid logic, and his gift at making rapid decisions.

They journeyed through the night, dozing in their seats for lack of a sleeping car. By early morning, they stumbled blearily off the platform at Innman Tor and passed through double doors, leaving the open field of the rail yard for carpeted chambers.

The pair journeyed throughout the morning and afternoon,

traveling not down corridors, but through pillared and ornate rooms with white wall-carvings of ferns, acorns, and human faces no larger than fists. Deer, unicorn, and gnawling heads hung on the walls beneath dark-oak ceiling arches. Etched spider-monkeys loomed from the architraves.

One of Carter's greatest joys was in traipsing through Evenmere, guided by his inner maps, knowing yet never *exactly* knowing what lay around the next corner. But on this day he was too worn by worry and travel to appreciate the journey. Not so his irrepressible butler, whose duties often prevented him from leaving the Inner Chambers; Mr. Hope hurried bandy-legged behind his Master's long strides, eyes gleaming with excitement, asking questions about portraits and statues and architectural terms.

By early evening they reached the edge of the Mere. The borders were unguarded save by a bronze plaque, posted above French doors, proclaiming *Welcome to the Mere of Books, Owned by the People of Evenmere. Quiet, please.* On the handle of the door hung a crooked sign with *SHH!* neatly printed in large letters. Carter turned the brass knob and led the way into a tiny room filled with dark shelves of books and the heavy odor of paper. Doorways on either side opened into similar snug chambers. Signs were posted here and there, with messages such as *Please do not re-shelve volumes*, and *Help is available at the Main Desk.*

"I actually know little of the Mere," Mr. Hope said, keeping his voice low, "besides the fact that its Pilot is a member of the Servants' Circle. The histories seldom mention it, or when they do, describe it only as a small region, too tiny to call a country."

By a casual reference from Enoch during Lord Anderson's third year as master, Carter had learned of the Circle of Servants, a group of men and women who served the Balance: the Seneschal of the Deep, the Queen of Shadow Valley, the Smith of Welkin Well, twelve in all, including Chant the Lamp-lighter and Enoch the Windkeep. Within his or her own domain, each possessed mastery over the fundamental forces of the High House, and by extension, those of the universe. When Carter had first learned of them, he felt he was no longer alone in his struggle, but part of a society of allies. The reality had proven otherwise. The members of the Circle were often aloof, eccentric, or dangerous. Still, he wished he had known about them from the beginning; it would have made his first years easier.

"You will think the Mere heaven, as much as you love books," he said. "I've only been here twice before, but Chant comes through regularly. He is friends with Pilot Abershaw, an amiable old man concerned solely with maintaining the library. I've met him, but at the time he and his sailors were too busy for much conversation."

"Why the nautical titles?"

"You will soon see. I won't ruin the surprise. A wonderful place, always fire in the hearths, cakes and steaming cups of cider on the credenzas, and beautiful volumes on every side. There is only one strict law; the books may never be removed."

"A shame," Hope said, eyeing the contents of the nearest shelf. "I had hoped to borrow some volumes for later perusal."

"No, you don't," Carter said, taking his friend's arm. "Once you get started, I'll never pry you away. We need to find the Pilot."

"You know me too well." Hope chuckled, glancing wistfully from shelf to shelf. "It's hard to concentrate with so many books around."

They passed through several small, carpeted rooms with reading tables tucked into comfortable nooks and blue-stained glass adorning the shelves. The gas jets burned low, sending slow shadows swaying across the oak paneling. The Mere seemed to enfold the men, drawing them into its butter-rum serenity.

After a time they heard murmuring, which they followed until they found a pair of boys clad in gray shirts and caps, crawling along wooden ladders, dusting the shelves.

"Pardon me," Carter said.

One of the lads climbed politely down from his perch and said in a voice scarcely above a whisper, "Yes, sir?"

"I am Lord Anderson, Master of Evenmere, seeking Pilot Abershaw on a matter of urgency."

The boy's eyes widened. "Master Anderson! Is there trouble in the Mere?"

"None I know of," Carter said, smiling. "I need the Pilot's advice."

"The Pilot is unavailable," the lad said, "but I'm sure the bosun would see you."

"He will have to do."

"I'll take them, Slith," he said to the other boy. "If you will follow me, sirs."

The lad led through a winding way, ascending and descending, gliding between the rows of books.

"What is your name, son?" Mr. Hope asked.

"I'm Nuth, sir. I dust."

"An important task in such a large library," Hope said.

"Yes, sir. I was trained in Kitinthim by the Guild of Dusters and Burnishers. Next year I'll be allowed to polish floors. But I hope someday to be a librarian on the Pilot's staff. I like to read. I've read everything about you, Lord Anderson."

"Have they written books about me?" Carter asked, surprised.

"Oh, yes sir, about your father and you, and the seeking of the Lightning Sword and the Tawny Mantle, and how you tamed the dragon in the attic and put down the rebellion at Veth. I've read it all."

"I must see these books sometime," Carter said, "and perhaps speak with their author. I have done several things, but domesticating Jormungand isn't one of them. He's untamable. Besides, he's a dinosaur, not a dragon."

"He doesn't breathe fire?"

"Well . . . he's an unusual dinosaur. But I never go to the attic willingly. It's too dangerous, even for me, and no one else, especially a young boy, should even consider it."

"I wouldn't, sir."

"What do they teach children in school these days?" Carter muttered to Hope, as they passed through another doorway.

Nuth led up a flight of stair to a landing with a single bookcase. Sliding a volume aside, the boy uncovered a hidden knob and swung the bookcase inward on brass hinges.

"This way, sir."

"Why a secret doorway?" Carter asked.

"We've little defense here, sir. The passages were made ages ago to provide a way of escape in case of an attack. These days the bosun uses them for his office."

The library had spilled into the hidden corridor, for the travelers entered a passage containing still more shelves and books. After several minutes of winding their way, they reached a room occupied by a heavy, bearded gentleman of middle age, wearing sailor's-cloth trousers and a serge frock. A book entitled *Tautology and the Topgallant Sail* lay open before him.

"Bosun L'Marius, sir," Nuth said. "The Master of Evenmere has come."

The bosun glanced up and rose with military rigidity, extending a hand. "Lord Anderson! I recognize you from your portraits. 'Tis a surprise! To what do I owe the honor?" His voice was deep, but he spoke in soft, library tones.

"My pleasure," Carter said, taking the bosun's firm grasp. "I wanted to speak to the pilot, but the boy says he is absent."

"He is, indeed, but if you'd care to wait, he's due to return in no time at all, certainly before the end of the week."

"I'm afraid the matter is pressing," Carter said, smiling at the idea of living where one thought nothing of waiting a week.

"Perhaps I can help. Before I was bosun, I served as Head Librarian, and am well informed in most matters of the Mere. Pray be seated." L'Marius indicated two worn Morris chairs. "Nuth, bring tea."

Carter cast his eyes over the room. Paintings of sailing ships, clustered together in Victorian style, covered one entire wall. A chart hung askew behind the bosun, displaying the flags of the countries in Evenmere. A map of the Mere occupied another wall, drawn in ornate style with the words *Here There Be Bookworms* sketched in the margins beside drawings of silverfish and weevils. On the battered desk sat a brass sextant, a worn copy of *The Boats of the Glen Carrig*, and a wooden nutcracker in the shape of a panda.

Mirth twinkled in the corners of L'Marius' blue eyes, as if he were privy to some private jest. His nose was large and bulbous; dark veins ran like estuaries across his left cheek, vanishing into the jungle of his black beard. Carter told the bosun what he knew.

"So these Poetry Men are seeking a secret book?" L'Marius asked, hand to chin. "Do you know its nature or title?"

"Our informant did not say," Carter said, "except that it is an object of power."

"Hmm." The bosun tapped his forehead, as if trying to start his brain. "There are hundreds of legends written about the Mere. Such a fanciful place—all these books, the great writings of so many—it lends itself to tall tales. Upon first thought, I recall a reference within *Nameless Horrors*, but that book is mostly concerned with specters haunting the halls . . ."

L'Marius rolled his heavy fingers thoughtfully along the desk. "*The History of the Mere* chronicles the exploits of every pilot since Tompalhoost and the founding of the first library, which was actually in Kitinthim. I seem to recall a story within it that might be relevant. A moment."

L'Marius strode across the room and withdrew a volume from a corner bookcase. He consulted the index, scrawled something on a piece of paper with the stub of a pencil, and unclasped a small silver key from a chain around his neck.

"Nuth, I need you to find this book. Be quick, and don't lose the key."

The boy, having just finished serving the tea, took the paper and key and hurried from the room.

"It shouldn't take long," the bosun said. "'Tis nearby, locked in Special Collections. And speaking of collections, while he's away, let me show you my own."

The bosun picked up a long box from beside his desk.

"Ever since I was a lad," he said, "I have acquired the buttons off naval uniforms. I have quite an assortment, including a brass one from Admiral Thornbeam's dress uniform, worn just before he fought the Battle of the Sidereal Sea. Let me show you."

L'Marius selected a button and held it aloft. "The very one. And not just a lower button either, but a collar button. Think of him, Lord Anderson, perhaps fingering this while giving commands that would change the course of the battle. Amazing, isn't it?"

"Truly extraordinary," Carter said, while Mr. Hope nodded gravely.

To the Master's relief, before the bosun could launch too far into the details of his hobby, Nuth returned hefting a heavy, black book.

"Here it is, sir."

"Ah, good." Seizing the volume, L'Marius consulted the index and thumbed his way deep into the pages. He glanced up, beaming, his nose red with delight.

"It seems I'm still navigator enough to steer my way

through the shoals of my memory. This may be exactly what you want! An extraordinary tale. Let me see. Let me see."

He scanned the page. "According to this, over six centuries ago, during the captaincy of Pilot Lessingham, John Kenton was the Master of Evenmere. Though renowned for saving the house during the Great Famine, Kenton was so overwhelmed by his responsibilities he refused to marry, believing he had no time for a family. He lived in terror of perishing prematurely without passing his knowledge to his successor. Apparently his butler was unreliable as well. At that time, some scholars working out of the Mere were trying to catalog all the knowledge of the house. Driven by obsession, Kenton gave them maps of the Secret Ways. He told the uses of the Master Keys, the location of the doors of Darkness and Entropy—all the secret lore save the Seven Words of Power. The scholars inscribed the information in a book and gave it into the keeping of the Pilot of the Mere."

"Dangerous knowledge, indeed," Carter said.

"Shortly thereafter, the Master perished, as Masters sometimes do. The new Master must have seen some use in the book, for he sealed it in its hiding place with a Word of Power, where it has remained ever since."

"Does the account indicate the book's location?" Mr. Hope asked.

L'Marius placed his finger on a line of text. "It is a place deep within the swamp."

"Swamp?" Hope asked.

L'Marius strode to the map of the Mere. "The Mere is divided into four quarters. The Cozy Rooms, where we are now, are situated in the South and West. If you travel east or north, you find The Waters. Journey far enough into The Waters, and you reach the Thought Marsh. Beyond the marsh is the underground sea, and beyond that none know. The Mere has many unexplored regions, places even I daren't go except from dire necessity."

"The Thought Marsh." Hope said. "An odd name. Is it really a marsh?"

"Indeed," L'Marius replied. "No one knows how it got its title, but there is an old saying that if you are lost in Thought in the Mere of Books, you are lost in a real place."

"Sounds like a dreadful pun," Carter said. "Can you take us

to the book?"

L'Marius gave a grin. "Am I not the Bosun of the Mere? I know the swamp better than any save the pilot himself. We can go at once, if you'd like. I'll have Nuth ready a boat. I only wish I had time to show you more of my button collection."

"Perhaps on our next visit," Carter suggested.

They finished their tea and set out. L'Marius led them through winding corridors lined with every sort of book, going deeper into the Mere, finally following narrow, ill-lit passages. Carpet gave way to cobblestone floors, wood paneling turned to rough-hewn stones that made the corridor seem a cave. The hollow echoes of the men's footfalls fluttered between the walls. A brackish odor filled the air. The bookcases were also of stone, with shelves starting three feet off the floor.

After a full hour the passage began sloping downward, and the travelers soon found Nuth waiting beneath the dull green flames of a gas lamp, water glistening at his feet. A red boat, scarcely larger than a canoe, lay by his side. The boy leaned against a wall, reading a pamphlet. Noticing the travelers, he quickly returned the tract to its place on the shelf.

"Is she prepared, lad?" L'Marius asked.

"Aye, sir. I've waders for each of you and a lunch basket at the stern."

As the men donned the heavy wading boots, Nuth lit a lantern hanging from a pole at the boat's bow and released the vessel from its moorings. Despite his girth, L'Marius stepped easily into the boat. Carter and Hope followed less gracefully, their weight making the vessel stammer.

"Shall I come to row, sir?" Nuth asked.

"Not necessary, my lad," the bosun replied. "I've stroked many a mile. Let the second-mate know where I am gone, though, so he doesn't fret. A fretful man, the second-mate."

"Aye, sir. And is that all, sir?"

"Hmm? Ah, just this," L'Marius reached into his pocket and tossed a coin the boy's way. "A bit of reward for a job well done."

"Thank you, sir!" Nuth called enthusiastically, leaping away up the passage.

Taking the oars from their locks, the bosun propelled the

boat with even strokes. The lantern's glow revealed the rough walls to either side, but beyond the circle of illumination the water before the travelers lay in absolute darkness. The noise of the oars echoed between the walls.

"I didn't expect *this*," Hope said softly. "And see, there are still bookshelves on both sides."

"Mostly grim volumes here," L'Marius said, "though none so loathsome as those within the marsh itself, where you can find not just the *Krankenhammer* and *The Book of Eibon*, but the dreaded companion volume to *The King in Yellow: Regrets of the King*. The Pilot carries a scar on his left thumb, seared there from merely touching its spine."

"Books housed in darkness with water all around?" Mr. Hope asked. "How do they survive?"

"Through the work of the Book Dryers, whose task is to preserve the publications within the Waters. We'll probably see one of their boats. But they handle only the volumes outside the marsh; those within do not require any care, even if men courageous enough to grasp them could be found. They sustain themselves. 'Tis said the anarchists gained much of their power reading those books."

"Why not move them to a better place?" Carter asked.

"The Mere of Books isn't like that, you see," L'Marius said. "It was above-ground in the beginning, a white-marble fountain and pool surrounded by the library. Well-lit, no darkness anywhere. 'Twas the darkness of men's minds created the marsh, and the books gravitate to the part of the library that suits 'em."

The walls abruptly fell away from the range of the lantern, and the changing echoes told the men they had entered a large cavern. The roof, now lower, was visible in the lantern light.

"This is the actual Mere," L'Marius said.

"Are all the books of a disturbing nature?" Mr. Hope asked.

"Oh, no. There are lots of mysteries and adventure novels, things like that. Some good reading, long as you don't fare too far into the marsh."

"There are forces at work around us," Carter said, the hairs on the back of his arms standing up. "Chaos and Order, and—most especially—Entropy. It is very strong here. The Mere has more to do with the Balance than I ever imagined."

"The human spirit," L'Marius said, "that's what it's about. Cities and countries, physical objects—these are ephemeral. Words and ideas, they have a tangible reality. When towers tumble, the words remain. Troy is gone, but Homer lives on."

Carter glanced at the bosun. Sitting at the oarlocks, gazing into the darkness, the man seemed more bard than sailor.

They soon spied a Book Dryers' tubby craft, brightly lit with seven orange lanterns, crewed by ten dryers in gloves, helmets, and yellow slickers. As the vessel slipped slowly along the wall, the dryers removed the books one at a time, working in assembly-line fashion, the last man replacing each volume on the shelf.

"I would like to see the process more closely," Mr. Hope said.

"I fear I am pressed for time," the bosun said, giving a careless wave to the members of the crew. "Other duties require my attention. But perhaps if our mission goes well, we can stop on our return."

"It must be a miserable job," Carter said, "spending so much time in the dark."

"It is oppressive, and their duties require deep concentration. Theirs is a battle against Chaos. A book must never be lost to the waters. They work in shifts, each man laboring only every other day, three days per week, and are well compensated."

To quicken their pace, Mr. Hope manned an extra set of oars, and thereafter he and Carter took turns rowing. The water remained still, a stagnant, reeking pool. Moss hung along the walls and from the stone roof. They passed intersecting channels and followed tributaries of varying widths, twisting and forking in many directions. Even with the help of his inner maps, it would require hours of study for Carter to make sense of it, yet the bosun navigated with obvious ease.

Black trees appeared, like cypress but with slimy leaves white as mushrooms. Pale tangles of vegetation protruded from cracks in the walls. Carter wondered how they survived without sunlight. Featherless, eyeless birds, large as pelicans, flapped silently between the branches.

"We are in the Thought Marsh now," the bosun said. "Keep your hands out of the water. The serpents are poisonous."

"Have I mentioned my dread of snakes?" Mr. Hope asked, peering suspiciously along the gunnels.

"You wanted an adventure," Carter replied.

"I want nothing serpentine. Is this the sort of thing you normally do when you travel?"

"At times. The house is full of strange places. But I will be glad to be done with this one. I don't like the feel of it."

"Perhaps I have undervalued the importance of research," the butler said. "I would prefer to be back in my office just now; but I suppose I'm breaking some unspoken rule, speaking of my terror. I will try to refrain."

"There's the spirit," Carter said, giving an encouraging smile. "An out-thrust jaw and a brave stance—you'll feel better for it."

Inwardly, Carter felt no more courageous than his friend. The darkness was nearly complete, though a foreboding glow, like will-o'-the-wisps, danced in the distance. The only sounds were the slapping oars and the unsteady drip of water from the overhanging trees, a sticky dew that covered the travelers' faces and garments.

As they moved farther into the marsh, a green scum appeared upon the water, which the boat parted in its passing. Bloated, bone-pale lily pads dotted the surface; blood-eyed frogs peered between pallid rushes. Fire-flies, emitting a ghostly green glow, drifted above the pool. Stinging gnats swarmed the men's faces, forcing Carter and Hope to constantly defend themselves. The bosun, protected by an ointment offensive to the creatures, gave no heed; nor did he apologize for failing to provide protection for his guests, but kept up a good-humored chatter about the marsh's eccentricities. With some irritation, Carter realized the man was enjoying detailing its dangers.

Four oppressive hours later, they stopped rowing long enough to eat a cheerless meal of cold beef and bread. After swallowing a dozen of the gnats covering the food, Carter tossed the remainder into the marsh, where something immediately pulled it beneath the surface. Mr. Hope followed suit, while L'Marius ate his with a good appetite.

"Adds protein, my good fellows," the bosun said. "Adds protein."

They rowed on, Lord Anderson and Mr. Hope miserably

hungry, L'Marius humming a tune.

At last they came to a stone pillar rising from the water, etched with the crest of the Inner Chambers: a triple-towered castle with an armored hand wielding a sword rising from the topmost turret. Beneath, half-hidden by moss, were inscribed the words *Gainsay Who Dare*. The men rowed to an embankment facing the edifice, which proved to be a stone pier obscured by vegetation. L'Marius lit a second lantern, and they scrambled onto the pier. Beyond it stood a granite door with a rusty lock.

"I haven't a key for that," Carter said.

"I do," the bosun said, withdrawing a large ring of keys from his pocket. The lock turned remarkably easily, but it took the strength of all three men to open the heavy door, and even then they could draw it back only a few inches. Fetid air, the scent of a crypt, struck Carter full in the face.

L'Marius led the way, forcing his bulk through the opening. "This way, gentlemen."

They stepped through a passage into a rectangular chamber, also of stone, bare save for another door against the far wall. Carter could feel energy emanating from the door, warm as a flame against his face, a force which could only have been created by a Word of Power.

"You were right," Lord Anderson said. "This door is sealed."

"Can you get inside?"

"The question is, do I want to?"

"Isn't that why you came?" L'Marius asked.

"Perhaps not. Since we now know the door is secured, our best course may be to leave it alone."

"Assuming the Poetry Men have no way to open it," the bosun said. "You said they'd discovered a new source of power."

"It would take power indeed to overcome the Word Which Seals."

"I'm merely a bosun," L'Marius replied, "ignorant of the high matters of the Master, but I know there are many forms of energy within Evenmere, and I give the devil his due. Evil can be powerful."

"There is another consideration," Mr. Hope said.

"You're thinking what I am," Carter said. "You and I have

faced what Master Kenton most feared. Both my father and the previous butler died without passing on the Master's knowledge."

"If we had the book," Hope said, "we wouldn't always be struggling to uncover the mechanisms of the house. It might supply information that could mean the difference between life and death."

"We should at least investigate," Carter said. "I suggest you step out of the room, gentlemen, while I unseal these doors. The manifestation of one of the Words can be dangerous."

After his companions departed, Carter closed his eyes, seeking within himself with practiced ease, bringing his concentration to bear. Gradually, the Word Which Seals, which can also be used to unseal, rose from the darkness behind his eyelids, the letters burning with fire in his mind's eye. The Word grew until it loomed before him, its heat pulsing against his brow. He brought it to his throat, poising it there, releasing it only when he could hold it no longer.

Nargoth!

It roared from his lips, filling the entire chamber. He felt the seal on the door resist, then quaver and break.

He opened his eyes. A moment later, the bosun peered cautiously into the room.

"Are you well, Lord Anderson? It sounded like the whole world's cannons firing at once."

Carter swayed unsteadily. Sweat beaded his brow. "The level of released power is variable according to the need. That was a . . . particularly strong display."

"It was, indeed," Mr. Hope said, squeezing back into the room behind the bosun. "You've cowed the entire swamp."

"No more than I cowed myself. I've never tried to break another Master's seal before. Proof the Words of Power exist outside the wielder's will. Whoever secured the door may be long dead; the Word he used isn't. I think I should enter by myself."

"We can't desert you now," L'Marius said.

"Your bravery is appreciated, but there are times the Master must walk alone. We have nothing more than a reference in your book to tell us what lies beyond the door. You should both return to the boat, where there is light."

Carter lifted the lantern and drew his Lightning Sword. The

jagged blade glowed golden. He pulled at the iron ring on the door, but the stone resisted his strength. The bosun lent a hand and together the two dragged the door wide, revealing an ascending brick stair. A puddle lay at its foot, apparently made from water seeping up through the stones. With a nod to his companions, Carter began to climb.

The passage was old. Runes lined the walls, suggesting that whatever lay within had been interred with great ceremony. The shells of beetles crackled beneath Carter's boots. Stories of mummy's tombs rose to his mind; he felt his pulse throbbing at his wrists. Though he tried to turn the fancy aside, he could not help thinking that opening what another Master had sealed might be a criminal act. But a crime against whom? The ancient Master? The house itself?

Carter started as a black and gold snake slid down the steps. It hissed and darted into a crack in the bricks.

He came to an upper chamber, empty save for a stone dais supporting a large, leather book. Striding to it, he examined its cover, but it was blank. He touched it and quickly withdrew his hand; it reeked of Chaos. He opened it to the first page. In a thin, handwritten script were inscribed the words: *The Book of Lore.* He instantly decided to take it with him. Whatever was within it was powerful, and would surely be safer in the Inner Chambers than left to lie in a lonely cave.

"Are you certain you want that?" a voice whispered from the darkness.

Carter shouted in surprise and whirled, his Lightning Sword at the ready. Raising his lamp, he discovered a side-alcove previously hidden in the shadows. Within it, an eight-foot serpent twined around the barren, petrified trunk of a tree thrusting from a breach in the wall. Its eyes glowed yellow, its fangs glittered diamond-points. Its body was thick as the neck of a pony. A pair of large spectacles rested on the bridge of its snout.

"One shouldn't take what one doesn't own," the serpent hissed. "Bad luck, bad manners, bad form."

"Who are you?"

"Just a bit of snake left in the darkness like an old shoe, waiting through the centuries for someone to appear so I can question his motives."

Carter gripped his sword tighter. "Why shouldn't I take the book?"

"Because it ought not to get out. Lots of secrets in there. Things your average, everyday person doesn't need to know. Sealing doors, unsealing doors, opening passages into Abysses and Deep Knowledge. Have you read Temunte's *Eclipse of Doom*?"

"Yes."

"Come closer. It's difficult to hear you."

Carter drew forward only a step, keeping a careful distance from the serpent's maw. "I said *Yes*."

"Then you know Temunte believes Evenmere is a metaphor for the universe. He asks two relevant questions, one of which is: Why does the house reflect so closely the cultures of Europe? Do you recall his answer?"

"He had several theories."

"I'm sorry. I didn't catch that. I'm very old."

Carter took another step closer and raised his voice. "Essentially, if Evenmere is a metaphor for Existence, it should reflect the cultures of that Existence. But he was mistaken; though the European model occurs nearest the Inner Chambers, the cultures become more diverse the farther one goes from the center of the house. What has this to do with the book?"

"Impatient, aren't we? I'm getting there. I spend decades waiting for you and you can't give an old serpent a paltry half-hour? No justice in the world. Temunte's second question was: If there is life on other planets, as common logic suggests, why are the people of Evenmere human? Why not another species altogether, or a blend of species? What was his answer?"

The serpent slithered to the top of the tree where it could look down on Carter, its eyes made huge by the spectacles.

"That the human race is archetypal for all races everywhere," Carter answered. "But even he admitted the answer did not satisfy."

"And what do you believe?" The serpent wove its head back and forth in an almost hypnotic motion. Carter found it increasingly difficult to look away. With a force of will, he drew his gaze to the floor and watched the reptile from the corners of his eyes.

"Since I am speaking to a talking serpent, I assume other

races *are* represented."

"SSSSophistry!" the serpent hissed. "Talking or no, I am an earthly snake, as the Tigers of Naleewuath are merely tigers."

"I believe every facet of Existence is expressed in the house," Carter said, "but since the peoples of other planets are separated by a great gulf, so too are those in the High House. Travel far enough into Evenmere and you may meet more bizarre forms of life. One day I hope to discover the truth for myself. But enough of this! I am the Master of Evenmere. If the book belongs to anyone, it belongs to me. Tell me what it has to do with Temunte."

"Excellent credentials. But to make myself clear, I must tell you a tale from before the making of the book, a story from long ago, in the time when Tharmaldrun was king—"

"I will hear no tales." He loathed being alone with this creature, who was surely some type of guardian.

"It will only take a moment. It was in a day long ago. There was drought upon the land and—"

Carter heard the faintest noise behind him. He whirled as a second serpent struck. Reacting instinctively, he brought his Lightning Sword in a downward arc to block the blow. Something hit him hard in the chest. Without stopping to see what it was, he turned back to the first snake, which extended itself from the branch, striking downward. The Word of Power that Carter had prepared from the moment he met the viper sprang to his lips.

Falan! The Word Which Manifests. A golden wave of force hurled the reptile against the wall.

In one continuous motion, Carter whirled back to the second assailant. The serpent's severed head lay at his feet. It was that which had struck him. He glanced at his chest to ensure the fangs had not penetrated his coat, then returned to the first snake, who lay writhing, glasses broken, eyes blinking, half-blind.

"Now you will answer," Carter said. "Who are you? Who set you here to protect the book?"

But the serpent glared and said, "Ashes, ashes, all fall down." Flames abruptly licked it, consuming it instantly, leaving only a pile of ash.

Hands trembling in the aftermath of the battle, Carter glanced around the chamber for further danger. The room was empty. He turned back to the book.

"You really should leave it alone."

Carter dropped to his knees and pivoted, bringing his sword above his head in anticipation of another assault. The serpent, or one identical down to the spectacles, had returned to its treetop perch. Wrapped among the branches, it stared at the Master.

"What are you?" Carter demanded.

"I could ask you the same thing. Don't you think 'Guardian of the Universe' a presumptuous title? Suggests a touch of delusion. Maybe you're simply a madman in an oversized house."

The serpent slithered from the tree, and as it did it grew, nearly doubling in size by the time it reached the floor. It said no more, but advanced with marvelous speed, tongue forking, fangs gleaming. With one hand occupied with his sword, Carter was forced to drop his lantern in order to seize the voluminous book. Tucking it under his arm, he retreated toward the top of the stair. The monster continued to grow until it filled half the room. Its bulk sent the discarded lantern rolling across the floor, where it struck a wall and went out, leaving only the faint glow of the Lightning Sword for illumination.

As the viper coiled to strike, Carter reached the stairwell. He leapt down it, coat flapping behind him, and landed several steps below. Lurching from side to side, overbalanced by the heavy volume, he stumbled, missed a step, caught himself against one wall and continued running. Behind him, he heard the noise of the serpent's massive head colliding with the sides of the doorway.

With the hissing of the reptile at his back, Carter took the steps two at a time. Reaching the room below, he found L'Marius awaiting him in the dark.

"The door!" Carter cried, dropping the book to thrust against it. "Help me, man!"

Aided by the dim glow of the Lightning Sword, the bosun rushed to Carter's side, where the two hurriedly pushed the door shut. The Master rapidly raised the Word Which Seals into his mind, even as the body of the serpent slammed against the door, sending painful shudders through the men's arms and shoulders.

"Stand back!" Carter ordered.

Lord Anderson now had to use the Word Which Seals on an object he was physically touching. He had never tried it before and could not predict the result, but there was no time for hesitation.

No sooner had the bosun withdrew than Carter spoke the Word.

Nargoth!

The rising power seemed to emanate from his face. When it struck the door, he gasped in pain as a force like twin hammers struck the backs of his hands. He fell to his knees, momentarily blinded by the agony.

As the blackness cleared, he dared to look, expecting to find smashed pulps at the ends of his wrists. He gasped again, this time in gratitude. His hands were whole, though stiff and tingling with pain. With some effort he used them to retrieve his Lightning Sword from where he had dropped it.

A silence filled the room. No sound came from behind the door. Carter turned to find L'Marius crouched on the floor, his hands clasped to his ears.

"Sorry," Lord Anderson panted. "There was no time to get you out."

"I'm all right," the bosun said. "You?"

"Better than expected."

The two men got to their feet. Bending down, L'Marius picked up the heavy leather volume. "You found the book."

"Yes. Where is Mr. Hope?"

"Waiting outside."

"Probably hurrying to see what caused the noise. I'd better reassure him."

Carter squeezed through the crack in the outer doorway.

"Will? Where are you? I'm fine, no harm done." Carter hoped he was right; his hands, numb from the blow, were stiff, almost useless. He sheathed his sword, which he could scarcely grasp.

The lantern glowed beside the boat. Carter walked to the edge of the pier, but saw no sign of his friend.

"Where is he?" Carter asked, as the bosun pushed through the doorway.

"He was here a few moments ago."

Puzzled, Lord Anderson turned a slow circle. There was little to conceal a man, though it was impossible to see beyond the lantern light.

He turned back toward the bosun. L'Marius held a gun aimed directly at Carter's heart.

In the split-second that the weapon erupted, Lord Anderson dodged to the right. Searing pain jolted his side. His knees gave way, sending him tumbling off the pier into the marsh. The water was black and ice-cold. He swallowed a mouthful and came coughing to the surface.

Scarcely had he cleared his lungs than the bosun appeared on the dock above him, preparing to fire again. The Master dove. Bullets sped like arrows past his head. He plunged deep into the murky depths, floundering along the edge of the pier, trying to distance himself from his assailant. At last, when he thought his lungs must burst, he rose.

He had passed thirty yards or more along the pier. The bosun, now in the boat, was holding the lantern high, searching for him. This continued for several moments, while Carter clutched the dock with his benumbed hands, keeping to its shadows. He was weakening; he must be losing blood. He wondered how long he could remain conscious. He tried to summon a Word of Power, but was unable to focus.

At last, after what seemed an agony of waiting, the bosun turned from his search and paddled away, leaving Carter in complete darkness.

He tried to pull himself onto the pier, but his vitality was gone. He sought to summon the Word Which Gives Strength, but his concentration failed. He seemed to be watching himself from a distance, as if it were someone else. The waders L'Marius had given him had filled with water, dragging him down. His fingers lost their grip. He slipped below the surface. He knew he was dying, but could do nothing about it. *Sarah*, he thought. *Jason*.

At the last second, before darkness took him, he thought he saw a golden glow like a star in the water above him, and a man rowing a boat.

Now I am dead, he thought. *And the ferryman comes to take me home.*

Assault

Carter awoke to find himself lying beneath warm sheets, in an oak-paneled room with a tall bookshelf built into one wall. Beside him sat an old man with a Roman nose, a strong jaw, and a lithe body belying his age. He wore a green uniform with gold buttons and braids, and the sunlight passing through the lace curtains of the single, octagonal window made his gold-green eyes almost luminous. A locket in the shape of a scarab beetle hung from a chain around his neck; a green admiral's hat sat by the foot of the bed.

"Do you know where y'are?" the man asked, in a Westwing accent.

Carter cleared his throat with difficulty. "Pilot Abershaw. Did you find Mr. Hope? Is he alive?"

The gentleman smiled. "Safe and sound. Your assailant beaned 'im with an oar, bound 'im, and hid 'im in the shadows beyond the pier. No permanent damage."

"Thank God! I was certain he was dead. Of course, I thought I was, too. Before everything went black I remember seeing a light from a raft."

"That was the lantern from m'ship."

"How did you ever find me?"

"I was looking for you. Few things occur within the Mere without m'knowing. I sensed something amiss even before you arrived. I knew enemies had infiltrated; I knew when you entered the portals. But I was far downstream, lured away from the Cozy Rooms by other business. It took several days to get back. The man, L'Marius, who claimed to be my bosun, was an imposter." The pilot's voice grew low. "The bosun himself is dead."

"I'm sorry. If L'Marius spoke the truth, your bosun had been with you many years."

"Since he was a boy." The old man's eyes grew bleak. "I should've gotten here sooner."

Though Carter had spent little time with Raven Abershaw, he held the man in high esteem. The Pilot of the Mere of Books could sense the currents within the Mere, the passing of the waters, the dancing of its shadows. He knew the locations of its secret passages and possessed unexpected knowledge as well, such as the names of the Seven Words of Power.

"The false bosun was doubtless an anarchist," the pilot said. "The deception was well managed. The office within the secret corridor where you were taken is never used, and the connecting corridor allowed him to lead you to the boats without encountering m'people."

"That explains why the bosun avoided the Book Dryers. What of the boy, Nuth, and his companion—I have forgotten his name—they said they were dusters."

"There ain't any Nuth working in the Mere. He and his accomplice were part of the deception. From what I've been able to piece together, so was the history they fed you about the book you found, *The Book of Lore*. Mr. Hope and I spent much of yesterday and today searching for references to it. I had never even heard of it before, which is odd; I know as much about the Mere as anyone living. We finally discovered a mention of it in annals dating back to the second century. By that account, it's ancient, perhaps old as Evenmere itself, and was written long before Master Kenton's time. No one knows who penned it, but one of the Masters did seal it in that chamber. That much is true."

Carter felt a flush spread across his face. His voice grew cold. "What is this book?"

"A powerful weapon for our enemies. You should've consulted me before entering the marsh, but it makes no difference now. The thing is done."

Lord Anderson fell into stunned silence, stung by

Abershaw's just reproof. Events had happened too quickly, and Carter's judgment had suffered for it.

"I was played the fool from the beginning," he finally said, "starting with the poet at Vroomanlin Wood. With their talk of anarchist factions, he and L'Marius maneuvered me into delivering the very book they warned about! Everything is clear now—the bosun's seeming unintended cruelty, Nuth lingering to be paid for his part. Why, L'Marius even showed me his button collection! How he must have laughed behind his sleeve! What an actor he was!"

"A small part of what he told you is true," the pilot said. "I've learned the Society of Anarchists has split into two factions. But which group seized the volume?"

"It might have been either one. That book should have been burned long ago."

The pilot shook his head. "Once a book reaches the Mere, there are always ramifications to destroying it. The Mere of Books represents the thoughts of the worlds. That's why part of it is a swamp, for ain't the thoughts of humanity akin to a marsh, filled with twists, turns, and backward loops? Each volume adds to the total of human learning. Placed together they form a vast tapestry. Some can be taken without causing harm, but remove the wrong support and the whole structure crumbles." The pilot cleared his throat. "You must be starved. Would you like something to eat?"

The mention of food made Carter realize how hungry he was. "I would, indeed. You've said nothing about my wounds, and I am afraid to ask. I'm not in pain, but I remember being shot at least once."

"Twice, though one only nicked your leg. Our doctor removed them both, and I used what power I possess to promote the healing."

"I owe you my life."

"Each of us owes somebody something, there's no doubt about that. You rest now. We'll have some grub for you momentarily."

After Raven Abershaw departed, Carter inspected his side and thigh for injuries, and found them not only whole, but totally without scar. He lay back in wonder. Abershaw's power to heal was an ability unknown even to the Master.

Hope appeared moments later, carrying a tray of food. "At your service, sir," he beamed. "And glad to see you looking hale."

He set down the tray and the two shook hands. "I'm relieved to see you looking anything at all," Carter said. "We've been played for a pair of buffoons."

"Honest men are always at a disadvantage, but I prefer being counted in their number. Marshal Japth's men arrived several hours behind us, and I sent them searching for the mysterious bosun. Of course, they turned up nothing. Our enemy was well prepared. Japth also dispatched soldiers to Vroomanlin Wood to try to track down the blind poet. The question is, what should our next course of action be? Do we continue to Aylyrium University and the College of Poets?"

"Even though the information came from Nighthammer, it may still be true," Carter said, "and it's our only clue. I will go there as soon as I am able, but I want you to return to the Inner Chambers. Research everything you can about *The Book of Lore* and *The Book of Verse*. We have to find the source of the Poetry Men's power before they strike again."

Lord Anderson rested through the afternoon, but by evening felt well enough to join the pilot and Mr. Hope at supper.

Toward the end of the meal, Abershaw excused himself. "I must be gone the rest of the evening. This afternoon it came to me that a yellow book lying on a dusty shelf in a lower basement needs be fetched to the Mere, else we will lose some brilliant exposition on the habits of bumblebees."

"I don't suppose bees will vanish from the earth if you fail to find it?" Carter quipped.

Oh, no," the pilot said, "no danger of that." He frowned. "At least, I don't think so."

Still weary from his ordeal, Lord Anderson was about to turn in for the night, but Sarah and Jason appeared at nine o'clock, having traveled two days to reach him. Sarah uncharacteristically rushed into his arms and wept, while Jason, accompanied by a nurse, waited in some confusion behind.

"There, now," Carter said quietly. "I have distressed you."

"Mr. Hope sent word you were shot but alive, then followed with a message of a miraculous healing. I didn't know what to believe. I have been brave for Jason's sake—"

"I am well, as you can see."

Jason broke free from his nurse and rushed impatiently to his parents' side. "Papa, why is Mommy crying?"

Lord Anderson lifted his son into his arms. "Because she loves us both very much and has missed me. As I have missed you."

"Are we going to Aylyrium tomorrow?" the boy asked.

Carter's smile faded. Before the attack at Jossing, he had promised to take his son to the circus at Aylyrium, checking the progress of the telegraph as they went. "We shall see. For now, it is late."

They slept in Carter's chamber that night. Because Jason sensed their anxiety, they prepared a cot for him beside their bed. Carter slept fitfully, dreaming of falling roofs and the Balance staggering like a drunkard.

Jason found himself standing in a drab, gray passage, carpeted in brown, with gargoyle heads peering down from the molding. The house was silent, as houses seldom are, and he could not remember how he had arrived; his last recollection was of being tucked into bed.

"Am I asleep?" he asked. He pinched himself experimentally, discovered it hurt, and decided he was awake after all, despite the slight blurring at the edge of his vision.

Thunder rolled overhead, startling him, followed by the slow rush of rain on the eaves. The solitude frightened him, for his parents never left him alone in the great house. He wandered along the corridor, wishing for his father, wanting to call out but reluctant to do so, listening to the soft padding of his shoes on the worn carpet. The shifting shadows cast by the gas jets alarmed him, for they danced and bobbed, sending his own shadow puppeting across the wall.

The thunder roared again as he came to a gray door at the corridor's end. He halted, staring up at the ornamental brass knob, afraid to open it, afraid to remain in the still passage with its threatening shadows, very close to tears, feeling much younger than his five years.

He turned and saw his own shadow stretching long behind him, made tall by the gas jet beside the door. He flung his arms above his head and watched it do the same, the bones long and thin, extending down the hall. He flapped his hands and saw his shadow pelican-flap in turn. Momentarily delighted, he stamped his feet to see the shade tromp on its spindly stumps. He stood still to watch its stillness.

The shadow abruptly raised its hands to its mouth and pulled its face wider and wider, until it was an elongated mask, with red, shining eyes.

Jason shrieked in terror, rushed to the door, and clawed at the knob. It resisted his strength an instant before he pulled it open on screeching hinges. He fled down another gray corridor. Turning to look back, he saw his shadow following, no longer connected to his legs, but running along the wall and floor, long tongue protruding, head shaking, face still distorted.

Jason darted around a corner, shouting in fear. A clown stood in the middle of the hall, holding a wooden mallet and stake.

"Hurry, boy, hurry!" the clown cried, gesturing wildly. "Run past! I'll get it."

Many children would have been as frightened by the clown as the shadow, with his baggy clothes and flower button, white skin, red lips, red nose, but Jason had spent hours studying the circus books his mother had given him. He obeyed without hesitation.

No sooner had he passed the clown's position than he heard the thud of the hammer.

"Got it!" the clown cried.

Jason turned and saw the clown nimbly hammering the stake into the floor, his whole body rising with each stroke, while the shadow writhed in soundless pain. Though it twisted and bent, it was held fast.

The clown dropped the hammer and brushed his hands together to indicate a task well done. He removed his hat, allowing wild curls of red hair to spring out, and gave the boy a crooked smile and a bow. He was a heavy man, with deep blue eyes and red, oversized shoes.

"Just the lad I've been waiting for!" the clown said. "You must be Jason."

Jason watched the shadow warily.

"Oh, don't worry about that old thing. It just needs a bit of taming," the clown said. "We'll leave it here and go somewhere to find you a better-mannered one."

The clown gave another deep bow. "I am Mister Simular. The other clowns gave me that name in fun because I'm not like any of them. I am Mister Simular with a *u*, not an *i* because I ain't similar at all, you see."

"Are you a real clown?" Jason asked, beginning to recover from his fright.

"Am I a real . . . why, boy, do you see this suit?"

"Yes."

"Does it look like a real clown suit to you?"

"I guess so."

"Of course it does. And look at this face. Does it look like a real clown face?"

"Yes."

Mister Simular rolled his eyes. "There you are! It's the suit what makes the clown, I say. Wouldn't you agree?"

"Yes," Jason said, giggling.

"Then let's go."

The clown extended a red-gloved hand, but when Jason took it, it came loose at the wrist.

"Hey, wait a minute! Give that back!" Mister Simular took the hand from the laughing boy and feigned screwing it into place. Upon completion, he rubbed his hands together. "Here, try again."

Jason took the hand. "Now, we're off!" the clown cried.

"Where to?"

"To a special room to find the shadows. Do you mind if we skip? I like skipping."

They skipped together down the hall until the clown got out of breath and started fanning himself with an orange fan. As they walked, Mister Simular told jokes and riddles, asked questions, and sang snatches of funny songs. Jason laughed in delight, no longer frightened by the storm. They soon came to another door opening onto a curved stair, a gloomy way with ebony carvings of dark angels in alcoves to the side and green gaslights in carved skull sconces. Standing at the portal, Jason felt a touch of fear. He suddenly longed for his father.

"Here now, what's the forlorn expression?" the clown demanded. "Don't like the look of it, eh? Well, I don't neither, so never mind. It's the way we got to go to get to the special room, which is full of all sorts of wonderful things, including an entire circus."

"Will we see elephants?"

"Oh my, yes. We will see elephants and tigers and leprechauns! Have you ever seen leprechauns? Fantastic creatures, little taller than you and full of fun."

"Are they scary?"

"No scarier than me." The clown paused to give a mime-stare of surprise, hands outstretched. "But!" he cried, halting for emphasis. "You must beware their tricks. You must be more clever than they are, or they'll fool you. You must believe nary a word they say. But you needn't worry. I'll show you the ropes." From out of nowhere, the clown unraveled a foot of cord. "See, here's one now."

Jason laughed as only a child can. Determined to be brave, he took the clown's hand again, and they descended together past the staring eyes of the dark angels.

They journeyed a long time, until the boy grew tired. He was about to ask to rest, when they came to the bottom of the stair. A single, massive door with a heavy iron lock stood there, black as a moonless sky. A horned gargoyle peered down from the lintel. The clown drew a ridiculously large key, red with rust, from one of his pockets.

"This is a special key for our special room," Mister Simular said, giving a wink. He turned the lock with a quick twist, but struggled to open the door. At last, it swung wide, striking the wall with a boom.

"It's dark," Jason said. "There's something moving inside."

"It's bright once you get in. And you'll meet some wonderful people. Come on, I'll help you."

Jason gave the clown a trusting look, took a deep breath, and started forward.

A noise louder than any thunder shook the corridor, startling the boy so badly he closed his eyes and yelled in fright. When he opened them again, he found his father, dressed in his greatcoat and Tawny Mantle, gripping the clown by the collar, his eyes aflame with a terrible fury, the blade of his Lightning Sword pressed against Mister Simular's throat.

"Get behind me, Jason," Lord Anderson ordered, in a tone demanding obedience. The boy, afraid he had done something wrong, burst into tears and crept behind his father's legs. But his papa's attention was fixed on the clown.

"I used the Word Which Masters Dreams," Carter spat. "*I* control this dream now! Answer my questions or I'll cut your throat. Who are you? Why have you threatened my son?"

"Why, I was just taking him on a little trip," the clown replied, coolly. "He wants to see the circus."

Though Mister Simular was much larger than Lord Anderson, Jason's father slammed him against the wall as if he were weightless.

"*No man!*" Carter screamed in the clown's face, so loud Jason tried to stop his ears. "*No man* takes my child into that *Room of Horrors!*" For a moment the sword trembled, and Jason thought the clown's throat would surely be cut. But Lord Anderson seemed to master himself, for he spoke in a softer, but still deadly voice, "You have one more chance to answer my questions, or you die. Who are you and who do you serve?"

"I serve myself," the clown replied. "But you ain't the only one with power in the land o' dream." With a slight gesture of his left hand, Mister Simular abruptly vanished, leaving Lord Anderson grasping empty air. His face suffused with rage, he seized the ebony door and slammed it shut with a force that rattled the corridor.

Terrified by such violence from a father who had always been kind, Jason hid his eyes and sobbed. But powerful hands wrapped themselves around him, lifting him into a hug so hard the boy could scarcely breathe.

"Are you all right?" his father demanded, his voice trembling. "Did he hurt you?"

Jason could muster little more than a shake of his head, but it was enough, for Lord Anderson's voice grew steadier. "I'll never let anyone harm you. I swear. Every second we stay here increases our danger. It is time to wake."

Jason found himself lying on his pallet beside his parents' bed, in the chamber within the Mere of Books. Before he could call for his mother, his father's gentle hands clasped him.

"Papa, I had a bad dream!"

"It's all right," Lord Anderson told him, hugging him. "It's all right. It was just a nightmare."

"I want Mama."

"What is it?" Sarah asked, confused at being abruptly roused. Nonetheless, she immediately took charge, kissing Jason's forehead and cheeks, stroking his hair, bestowing the special comfort only mothers can give. He fell asleep in her arms moments later.

But Lord Anderson would sleep little that night. No sooner had Jason returned to slumber than he drew his wife into the outer chamber.

"This is dreadful," he said, his face ashen.

"Tell me," she replied, drawing her robe close about her, her eyes still dazed by sleep.

Carter had awakened to find himself within the shadowy, other-worldly country of Dream, a dangerous region the Masters walk only when they must. Whether it is really the place where dreams go, no one knows for certain, but the halls of Evenmere are replicated down to the last detail there. Carter had been drawn into the dream dimension by the danger to his son, a threat to the Master's family representing a danger to the house itself.

With his Lightning Sword drawn and the Tawny Mantle about him to cloak his movements, he had followed an unfamiliar corridor. Seeing his son and the clown standing at the threshold of the Room of Horrors, a chamber filled with unspeakable nightmares, he had spoken the Word Which Masters Dreams and seized the clown.

"Yet," he told his wife, "once the Word was used, I should have been able to prevent him from waking. Whoever he is, he wields considerable power. Power enough to transport Jason to the Room of Horrors by moving him in a dream."

"Could this power come from the stolen book?"

"I believe so. I suspect the clown was the same man who posed as L'Marius. Both were heavy, but not as fat as they looked. The bosun had a powerful handshake; and when I seized the clown, I could feel solid muscle under his garb. Our son is in grave danger. I thought the Room of Horrors destroyed."

"Perhaps Evenmere must always have a Room of Horrors."

"I know I've rarely spoken of it." Carter spoke vehemently, pacing across the room. "You don't know what it's like. The things I saw as a child—my boy must never go through what I did!"

"Shhh," she said, though her own eyes were frightened. "You will wake him. Certainly, we will protect him. But how?"

Carter sat at a table and ran his hands over his eyes. "The Inner Chambers would be safest. It has some proof against the anarchists' powers. I'll have a company of the White Circle Guard escort us there."

"But you were going to the College of Poets. Can that wait?"

Carter drummed his fist against the arm of the chair. "I can't leave him unguarded. Someone must protect his nights."

"Isn't that what our enemies want? To keep you occupied?"

"Of course it is. But how can I . . . wait, perhaps I can! While I sleep, I can return to the Inner Chambers and watch over him within the dream world."

"You will soon be exhausted."

"I won't. A paradox, I know, but I have always been able to walk the world of dream and wake refreshed. You mustn't allow him to sleep, except at night when I can be there."

"No naps? That won't disappoint him." She managed a smile. "Proof there is some good in everything. But I will feel helpless, not even knowing if his dreams are peaceful."

"I'll see to it that they are."

She went to him and they held one another. Carter felt himself relax in her arms. He took a long breath.

"There's no help for it," Sarah said, "but he will be dreadfully disappointed. We promised to take him to the circus."

"The circus?" It took Carter a moment to realize what she was saying. "It's too dangerous."

"Little boys don't understand the danger. He only knows he won't get to see the elephants."

It was with some dread that Carter and Sarah met with their son after breakfast the next morning. In such moments children have great power to discourage the heart, if only they knew. When told that other things had come up, he did not weep as they expected, but his eyes grew sad. And later Carter saw him lying on one of the couches in the Mere, weeping and murmuring, "I don't know why my papa always has to leave."

Stricken to the heart, Carter could not even bring himself to comfort his son, but went misty-eyed to Sarah. "I've recreated my boyhood in Jason. My father was often gone; I missed him terribly. Have I done no better?"

"A child lives for the moment," Sarah said. "At this instant he is sad. You spend time with him whenever you are home. He loves you very much."

But Carter would not be comforted. Though he and Jason were both brave when Sarah, Hope, and the boy had to depart in the company of the White Circle Guard, their eyes were mournful. Thus they suffered one another's pain.

Carter departed the Mere that same hour, making his way past the rosewood tables and oak shelves in a thoroughly black mood, remembering how the anarchists had tricked him into stealing the Master Keys as a child, then imprisoned him in the Room of Horrors. No matter how he tried to blot out the memories, he could never forget his time there—always in half-darkness, running from monsters, ghosts, every form of terror a boy could imagine. He still dreamt of it sometimes, waking Sarah from her sleep with his muffled cries. And Jason had almost suffered the same fate . . .

Following Carter's rescue, his father had sent him from Evenmere for his protection, an exile that had lasted fourteen years.

Despite the pain he had suffered, he did not hate the anarchists. Rather, he despised their doctrine, that strange mingling of compassion and murder, the ends always justifying the means. And he despised them for daring to strike at his son.

He knew their motives well; finding the Master difficult to capture or kill, they attacked his family to break his will. Like wolves, they employed the same hunting methods again and again.

The splinter group known as the Poetry Men, however, was a different matter. They no longer seemed to share the same goals as the Anarchists' Society. Save as a show of force, Carter could not fathom their destruction of Jossing. So far, it had not been followed by demands or ultimatums. What were they attempting?

Lord Anderson's fury grew as he walked, until at last he stopped, drew a deep breath, and reprimanded himself for wasting his strength in brooding. Such was the power of hate, to gnaw away the inner resources. He needed to focus on the task at hand instead of on endless fears.

The day went better thereafter, and he reached the guard post at Ghahanjhin before noon, where he was saluted by sentries garbed in silver and sable and given passage through that country. He did not travel into the interior, where lay Lamp-lighter's Lane, or even far enough to enter the Looking Glass Marches, but skirted along the southern border, traveling east toward Aylyrium.

He spent the day trekking through the halls and corridors of Ghahanjhin. By the end of the evening he reached regions where an hour often passed without his seeing another person. The solitude of the house entered him, a seclusion he found pleasurable, especially journeying, as he now did, through previously unvisited parts of Evenmere. The corridors changed from dark-paneled oak to Oozian variations of gilded French boiseries. As was common in Ghahanjhin, there were few windows, and Carter deeply regretted the lack of time that prevented him from viewing the skyline from the upper reaches, where the rose minarets and heavy modillions were reportedly exquisite.

Instead he padded over stone steps, always in half-shadow, often forced to light his lantern through the darker ways. As the evening progressed, a disquietude fell upon him, an indefinable apprehension. He was accustomed to traveling alone, yet now he fancied phantoms in every shadow. He reminded himself how much he loved the winding ways and empty chambers, the carpeted steps and paneled walls, the red rose in the blue-stained glass, but it did no good. His uneasiness grew, and by the time he stopped for the night before a mammoth fireplace in a marbled hall, he hurried to build a fire to chase away the darkness. The fender, sticking down like jagged teeth, reminded him of a gaping maw.

Once a small flame burned on the andiron he felt somewhat better, though it cast but a dim light through the great chamber. For supper, he roasted a potato on a spit. Supplemented with dried meat from his pack, this filled him well enough, and a few swallows from a flask of wine warmed him.

He could feel the immense silence on the floors above him, broken only by the creaking of the house settling for the night and the throbbing song of a cricket echoing in some distant hall. The thought struck him, as it sometimes did in such desolate places, that if he became ill or injured, he could die alone. Perhaps no one would even find his body. The logs popped cheerlessly in the flames; the smoke roiled upward. Above him, in the red glow, he could just make out the dim shapes of the brass ceiling tile.

The room was comfortable enough, with floral rugs, floral couches, floral chairs. He had slept in worst surroundings. But tonight he longed for his wife and son.

His reverie was broken by a noise from above, the dull, regular thump of heavy feet.

He sat up in his chair and glanced around the shrouded room, wondering who walked the deserted halls. Another traveler like himself? He had met many such in his journeys. Or perhaps someone seeking him, hoping to find him in a dark, lonely place. He glanced at his pocket watch—a quarter past eight. His son would be in bed by nine. By then, Carter had to be in the dream dimension.

He listened to the footfalls for what seemed a long time. Doors opened and closed. Silence fell again. The seconds passed into minutes. Just when he thought the stranger had moved beyond earshot, the slow treads came again, creaking the overhead boards.

Like someone walking on the ceiling, he thought. He traced the sound, left, right, left, right, shuffling from one side of the fireplace to the other, proceeding across the middle of the chamber. The shutting of a door. Silence. A distant pattering.

He strained to listen, his whole body tense.

Most likely a hermit, living out his years in these deserted halls. Probably more afraid of me than I of him.

The door at the far end of the room creaked open.

In one swift motion, Carter stepped away from the fire and backed into the shadows, drawing his Tawny Mantle about his shoulders; it lengthened, falling past his knees, covering him in its chameleon darkness. He clutched the hilt of his Lightning Sword.

The floorboards popped and creaked beneath the intruder's tread. Carter pressed himself against the wall, not daring to breathe.

A figure appeared at the edge of the flames, hovering between the border of light and darkness: a slender man, his face half-lost in shadow. He turned his head, surveying the room as if listening. Lord Anderson searched the gloom, trying to see if the intruder was alone.

"Lord Carter . . . Anderson," the man finally said, his voice soft and mellifluous. "Master of Evenmere. Keeper of the Master Keys. Owner of the Lightning Sword and Tawny Mantle. Wielder of the Seven Words of Power. I see you in the shadows; I espy you in the night. Pray come closer to the fire; let us parley in the light."

Carter drew his sword so smoothly it left its sheath without a sound. To his surprise, it did not emit its golden glow, but remained quenched, as if safety lay in concealment. By this, Lord Anderson suspected the man lied about being able to see him. Yet, how had he recognized him? Had he known Carter would be here?

"Who are you?" Carter demanded. As soon as he spoke, he stepped three paces to the left to avoid being located by the sound, in case the man carried a revolver. By keeping close to the wall, where the floor had the most support—a trick learned long ago— he prevented the boards from creaking.

"Once I had a face. Once I had a name. Now I am a Man of Verse, needing none, requiring none."

Carter strained to see through the obscurity. The man did appear faceless, for a mist streamed up, revealing only glimpses of his head: a chin, an eye, a shock of unruly hair. A reptile of some sort, with red, unwinking eyes, stole along his shoulder. Carter felt a chill at the back of his neck. He kept quiet, waiting for the other to speak.

When the silence had grown long between them, the intruder said, in his sing-song voice, "Perhaps you have heard of us. We were men . . . once." He gave a peculiar laugh, low and tonal as a flute. "We are more now. Would you like to hear? Would you like to see? Would you like to know what you can be?"

Carter remained still.

"I will tell you. We tapped into . . . a source of power. Archetypal force. Immeasurable, indefinable. Have you read Arkdeason's *Treatise on God's Puppy?*"

Carter took another step to the left, keeping his eyes on the intruder. The reptile on the interloper's shoulder crept down his arm, making its way to the floor.

"According to Arkdeason, there is an archetype for every kind of life, a master image from which plants and animals take their form. Thus a babe grows up to be a boy rather than a cat. God's puppy, the archetypal dog, the very soul of doghood, sits at his Master's feet, creating the mold for dogs everywhere."

The reptile, at least a foot long and resembling an iguana, slipped along the circle of light, moving toward Lord Anderson, its crimson tongue flickering in and out.

"What is the archetype of man, you might ask," the stranger said. "Are we dreams the dreamer dreamt, or cast-off toys from days of play? I do not know. But there are other archetypal forces. Water, fire, earth, and air! Grendel-beasts and dragons! Courage itself in corporeal form! And they exist not just in the human heart. We have touched them. We have seen music incarnate, heard words given flesh. So beautiful. So beautiful. Some of us were destroyed by it; we were each driven a little mad. And now we journey throughout Evenmere, sharing what we have seen."

Carter became aware of a distant throbbing somewhere within the house, created by engines he could not identify.

"We are bringing the archetypes to Earth," the Poetry Man said. "Not to tame. Oh, no, there is no taming them! We carry them like fallen stars in our hands, until they burn their way out, eating through the flesh, scalding us as they go, a terrible ecstasy. We have touched the infinite; we have seen the face of the Ultimate; and we will give this gift to all of Evenmere."

The reptile slid toward Lord Anderson, head held high, hissing slightly, its serrated teeth glistening. Carter relaxed his grip on his sword, letting it hang loosely in his hand. The throbbing had grown louder, filling his thoughts, making it difficult to concentrate.

"You have tasted it," the poet continued. "You tap into the Eternal whenever you use the Words of Power. But that is all you will ever know unless you join us. Listen to the Wild Poetry, Lord Anderson! Few have ever known its like; artists, poets, mathematicians, those we call geniuses, have glimpsed only a single spark. Come and take your fill!"

Carter kept his eyes fastened on the lizard, which was nearly within striking distance. The throbbing, ever louder, was indescribably exquisite, and in its measured beats he detected a single word. And that word was *Power*.

The battle Carter now fought had nearly taken him unawares, for he found he did want to give himself to the calling. More than once, using a Word of Power, he had recognized the way it made him feel—strong, almost invincible, terrible to his foes. He had trained himself never to misuse that might. Yet, as the sweet throbbing echoed through the hall, encompassing him, drawing him into its warmth, he wondered what it would be like to embrace even more power, to become one with it.

An almost unbearable breadth of emotions swept through him. He remembered his dead parents, the terror of being thrown into the Room of Horrors, the sight of Evenmere receding into the distance on the day of his childhood exile. Unexpected tears streamed down his face. If only he had possessed enough power, how he could have changed things! He closed his eyes, no longer able to look at the reptile.

"Listen to it!" the poet urged. "You lost your way once. That old wound, every old wound, can be healed. Only listen!"

But his foe had made his first mistake. Just when Carter felt himself going under, giving himself wholly to the calling, the poet had reminded him of his responsibilities. If Carter fell, there would be no one to stand between the Poetry Men and the rest of the house, including Sarah and Jason. At the thought of his son he gathered his will, pushing aside the armada of emotion. At once, he was aware of his danger.

He opened his eyes in time to see the lizard spring. He flicked his wrist upward, and his sword met the creature's leap with a roar of power, cutting it neatly in half.

Carter stepped into the light toward the Poetry Man. As if in answer, the pulsing grew to a ferocious volume, a spinning turbulence driving directly into his brain, tearing at his thoughts; no longer a temptation, but a weapon aimed at his core. It filled him, and his determination failed. He staggered and fell to one knee, mortal flesh overcome by immortal longing.

The poet stepped out of the shadows toward him. "You should not have slain my pet."

By the firelight, Carter saw the man wore an olive robe with a black question mark emblazoned on the front, but the streaming mist still hid most of his face. "You have rejected the calling, but it will not reject you! Such power will now break you." The man laughed softly. "A shame. A shame."

The pulsing rose, higher and higher, maddeningly loud, surpassing any volume Carter thought possible. He dropped his sword and clutched his ears. It was useless; nothing could drown it out. With one hand, he searched for his pistol, but could not lift it from his pocket. His breath came in gasps; he felt his thoughts disintegrating before concepts vast as galaxies, glories beyond expression, sorrows beyond solace. A terrible vision filled him; he seemed to be approaching a great and mighty Face, too wonderful and awful to bear, the archetype of Power in physical form. He had no doubt that if it manifested itself, its sheer presence would destroy him; and perhaps half of Ghahanjhin with him. Something similar must have happened at Jossing.

In desperation he sought anything that might block its coming, searching his innermost thoughts, where lurked the Words of Power. It was hard to concentrate with the throbbing all around, but at last a Word rose within his mind, its brass letters smoldering. He turned every vestige of his will toward it, inviting it in, asking it to use him as its instrument.

In response, it burst into golden flames. The Word Which Gives Strength. The heat burned away the beating pulse, creating a quiet space where he could think. With an effort, he brought the Word to his lips, held it there, and released it, his voice barely a whisper.

Sedhattee.

The effect was abnormally subdued. A fluttering ran around the room, small echoes in the darkness, yet Carter felt its energy rush through him, restoring his sense of purpose, causing the dreadful vision of the onrushing Face to splinter, blur, and fade.

Even the throbbing became more bearable.

In one swift motion, he scooped up his sword and lunged at his opponent, extending the full length of his body. The poet threw up his hands to protect himself, and a glow emanated from between his fingers, turning the thrust of the Lightning Sword with a flash of light and energy. Seldom had Carter seen his blade thwarted, and never by a creature of flesh and blood. But he had learned battles were often lost by the one who paused his attack, giving his enemy the chance to retaliate, and he struck three times in quick succession, a downward blow and thrusts to either side. The glow surrounding the Poetry Man's hands reacted to the assault as if alive, appearing wherever Carter struck, blocking the sword with a metallic clash.

A staff composed of light appeared in the poet's grasp. He used it like a hammer, striking at Lord Anderson's head, a clumsy swing displaying a lack of training. Carter parried and the weapons met in a cascade of fire. The staff fell upon Lord Anderson's sword with a weight that jarred his entire frame. Had the Poetry Man been a true warrior, Carter would have been beaten, for it took him a fraction too long to recover from the impact.

As it was, his assailant hesitated, and when the poet did attack again, he struck at the same place. This time, Carter braced himself as he parried. Even then pain shivered down his arm and shoulder. The Power the poet was funneling gave him strength far beyond his slender frame.

Lord Anderson stepped forward, feinting, striking wherever he chose. In a normal battle, he would have wounded the poet a half-dozen times; the man had the fighting ability of a child, making it easy to avoid his blundering jabs. But the Lightning Sword could not penetrate the luminous shield; and whenever the poet did force Lord Anderson to parry, the devastating impact nearly broke Carter's defenses. Still, by his enemy's expression, seen through the swirling mist surrounding his head, Carter knew his thrusts were having an effect, and he kept battering away, hoping to get past his foe's guard.

Even as he fought, Carter sought to bring a Word of Power to mind. Something about the pulsing made it difficult, as if the two forces warred with one another, but at last he envisioned the Word Which Manifests rising not out of darkness as was usual, but upon the tides of the pounding noise, like a ship struggling on the storm. With an effort, he brought it to his throat.

Falan!

A golden wave of force proceeded from Lord Anderson, meeting his opponent's shield with a deafening crackle. The shield held against the hammering wave, but as the power began to build, the poet gave a strangled cry.

Carter was abruptly sent hurtling across the room by a jolt so unexpected he did not at first realize what had happened. He found himself lying on his back, his sword fallen from his hand. He raised his head to see the Poetry Man thrown in the opposite direction. The convergence of the twin forces had created a backlash.

He crawled on hands and knees, retrieved his weapon, and stumbled to his feet. The Poetry Man had also regained his balance and refashioned his staff.

Carter drew his pistol and squeezed the trigger, two precise shots aimed at the poet's heart. The bullets struck the Poetry Man's defenses and vanished, not even causing the man to wince. Lord Anderson returned the useless weapon to his pocket. On tottering feet, the adversaries closed once more.

Carter struck with his Lightning Sword, danced back to dodge the return swipe, and moved forward, wielding his blade with the precision of a machine, never hitting in the same place, never giving his opponent a chance to counter, never allowing the poet to connect. Left side, right side, high, low, chest, head, waist, thigh. Again and again. But though he struck until his limbs were leaden, he could not break through.

He began to slow. He met his enemy's staff with a clumsy parry, the poet's weapon sliding down to the Lightning Sword's hilt, its tip an inch from Carter's face. He ducked just in time.

"One of us will break, Lord Anderson," the Poetry Man said. "I am willing to die to spread the Light."

Through the mist, Carter caught a glimpse of the poet's fanatic glare; the madman would indeed fight to the end. The Master retreated a few steps to catch his breath. His enemy followed after.

It would not serve Evenmere for Carter to perish this night, not when the other poets still threatened the house. He sought a path of escape, but his foe blocked the way.

Taking advantage of Carter's hesitation, the poet launched a furious assault. Normally it would have been ineffectual, but Lord Anderson was tiring. He turned too slowly to avoid the staff, and it slammed against his sword arm, sending him careening backward. Miraculously, he kept his footing, but the poet hurried forward, still flailing, giving no respite. Carter's arm was numb; he could no longer hold his sword, so he shifted it to his left hand. He had little skill in this fashion, but was still better than his opponent, and managed to parry twice against blows that shook his whole body.

He grew hot with anger at his inability to strike a telling blow. Again he marshaled his strength and launched a steady attack, keeping his foe off balance, striking at his face, forcing the poet to instinctively close his eyes. The nimbus surrounding the Poetry Man was wavering; the glow of the Lightning Sword had dwindled to obscurity. Carter wondered which of the two would fail first.

In the midst of his attack, a song arose, the rise and fall of a powerful bass voice, distant at first, but gradually growing nearer. It cut through the throbbing, which abruptly ended, the last echoes choking away. Carter retreated a few steps to appraise this new danger.

The Poetry Man stood wide-eyed, listening. With a snarl, he sprinted across the room and vanished into the corridor. Carter rushed to the threshold, where he heard his foe's steps echoing down the hall, followed by the slamming of a door.

His strength gone, he groped his way to a chair. The singing was closer now, near enough for him to catch the words.

> *Pass through the night-time*
> *Pass through the day*
> *Pass through the darkness*
> *Run far away*
> *Oh, yes chil'*
> *Run far away*
>
> *Hide in the meadow*
> *Safe in the corn*
> *Far from the danger*
> *Never alone*
> *Oh, no chil'*

Never alone

Envoys of mercy
Close by your side
They will be with you
There where you hide
Oh, yes chil'
There where you hide

The echoes of the last notes died away, followed by foot-falls along the corridor. Carter backed toward the fire. His sword-arm was nearly useless, so he sheathed the blade and drew his pistol, steeling himself for whatever approached. But instead of an attack, a man called from beyond the circle of the flames. "Hello. Hello. Is there room round the fire for everybody?"

Though the tone was deep and friendly, Lord Anderson kept his weapon leveled. He could feel his hand trembling from fatigue and the aftermath of danger.

"Present yourself," he ordered, still panting from his exertions.

A black man stepped into the light. He was unarmed, tall and thin, broad-faced and broad-nosed, wearing a gray top hat and a frock coat with so many colorful patches little of the original material remained.

"It's powerful dark here," the figure said. "Powerful dark. Whither do you wander, alone along the Ghahanjhin border?"

"I could ask you the same."

The man bowed at the waist, lifting his arms in a sweeping gesture. "I am Jonathan T. Bartholomew, singer of songs and teller of tales. Some call me Storyteller. Maybe you have heard of me."

"Storyteller? *The* Storyteller?"

The man gave a brilliant grin that wrinkled his broad nose. Despite his apparent age, his teeth were ivory white. "There is only one in Evenmere and that is me. I heard a terrible commotion and came to see what it might be. Do you mind if I sit?"

"Suit yourself," Carter said. "Your singing chased away a . . . bandit." Lord Anderson glanced at the place where the lizard's severed body had fallen, but only a dark stain covered the floor-boards. He shivered.

"My thanks," Storyteller replied in his deep, sonorous voice. He sat in a wing-back chair, and Carter sat down again too, so they faced one another across the hearth. Lord Anderson remained on the edge of his seat, gun ready but pointed away from the newcomer.

"This is nice," Bartholomew said, ignoring the weapon. "This is real nice. Shall I call you Carter or Master Anderson?"

Carter recoiled in surprise, but Storyteller laughed.

"Now don't you go gettin' agitated. The Words of Power gleam bright as diamonds inside you, and I have known too many of your predecessors not to recognize your fancy cloak and jagged sword."

"Call me anything you like, then," Carter said, bowing at the neck to avoid drawing close enough to shake hands. After the deception by L'Marius, Bartholomew's sudden appearance in these deserted quarters struck him as more than suspicious. He knew the man only by reputation and could not know if this was an imposter.

"A fine pleasure, Master Anderson. A fine pleasure."

Carter's breathing had eased; he was settling down from the combat. He tried to recall what he had heard about Storyteller. "It is said you have traveled the house for centuries."

Bartholomew grinned again, dark eyes glistening in the flames. He set his hat on a nearby table and scratched his head. "Well sir, I reckon it has been a few thousand years. I am old, that's true, perhaps the oldest person in all the house. I am the Storyteller, and I have traveled the great halls of Evenmere. I have stood in the gray corridors and counted the shadows by inches and known the whispering of the wind through the endless reaches; and I am part of the Balance and the Song of Evenmere. That's right. For I tell the tales to remind the house it has a Master who must see to its maintenance and the keeping of the spinning worlds. At times, men scoff and say the Master has no such powers. When that happens, I tell the Terrible Tales, those not meant for human sensibilities, such stories as are given only to me, and at first the scoffers smile, and then their smiles turn to scowls and their haughty faces fill with fear and their eyes with tears, and they throw themselves at my feet, hands over their ears, begging me to say no more. I always quit when they ask, and I tell them if a man has the power to tell a story too awful to bear, the Master has the strength to keep the suns in their courses. Thus, in my own way, I maintain the Balance between the Chaos and the Order, and the people of this great house allow the Master and his servants to pass, never barring the winding of the clocks, nor the lighting of the lamps. I am Storyteller, the joy and terror of Evenmere."

"I . . . see," Carter said, impressed despite himself.

"But it nears nine o'clock, Master Anderson," Bartholomew said, "and you have an appointment with a dream."

Carter leapt to his feet, eyes blazing, pistol raised. "How could you know that?"

But the minstrel simply grinned. "Now, now, Master Anderson. Be easy. Be eeeasy." He spread his hand in a fan as he said it. "I am not a bit of a danger. Storyteller sees into the heart, you know. That's right. He knows your fear for your son and can smell the dream-stuff around you, a fragrance like lemon custard. A sweet smell. You have recently been to the country of dreams. You have been and you have come back, and you must go again."

"How can anyone know such things?"

"Why, the Storyteller does. Didn't I say I knew of the Balance? I too have wrestled with Entropy. That's right. My kingdom is the whole house. All of Evenmere."

"Like myself."

"But different. You are the Master; the Storyteller sings the songs and tells the stories. The kingdom of songs is my realm."

Carter lowered his weapon slightly. "Perhaps that's why your singing interfered with the siren call of my assailant. You must have heard it."

"That's right. And you did the correct thing, Master Anderson, resisting the call of Power."

"Is there anything you don't know?"

"I know you must sleep now, so you can go protect the child. Storyteller knows that for certain. And I will sing to make you sleep. You do not trust me yet, but you must. Yes, you must. There is no time for anything else."

How strange it seemed afterward to Carter, that there in the darkness where Bartholomew could have driven a knife through his heart while he slept, he took the man at his word, for he found he *did* trust him. His spirit, his personality, everything about him, felt right. And the minstrel was correct; Carter had to reach Jason at once.

And so, as Jonathan T. Bartholomew sang a soft, cheerful song, Carter sat back in the chair, closed his eyes, and spoke the Word Which Masters Dreams. Immediately, he walked once more in the country of slumber.

Doctor Armilus

Through experimentation over the years, Carter had learned he could enter the dream dimension wherever he wished, simply by thinking of the place he wanted to go. Thus, when he passed through the gates of slumber, he did not find himself in the dream-equivalent of the room where he had gone to sleep, but in the gray mist of the Long Corridor beside the Green Door leading into the Inner Chambers. With a smile of satisfaction, he opened the lock with the Master Keys, passed through the small room beneath the servants' stair, and made his way down the men's and butler's corridors from the back of the house to the transverse corridor.

The Inner Chambers includes the front door of Evenmere, which looks out into the ordinary world. Except for being deserted, the dream version of the Inner Chambers was exactly like its counterpart in reality. Carter hurried up the stair to Jason's room and stood hovering above his son's four-poster bed. Since the covers remained in place, he assumed the boy had yet to be tucked in. He paced back and forth for a few moments, then forced himself to sit in the bedside chair.

In the country of dream, events happening in reality do not manifest themselves at the normal speed. Carter imagined the effect as waves on a shore, washing up bits of flotsam. As his eyes swept over the unlit beaded lamp on the night stand and the paintings of tigers on the wall, he was unsurprised to see wooden toy soldiers, fallen in battle, sprawled across the rug where none had been before. He glanced back at the bed to find the covers drawn back, and knew Jason was preparing for slumber.

The upper stories could not be easily reached by an intruder, so Carter descended to the main floor, where he made his rounds along the transverse corridor, through the entrance hall, drawing room, morning room, dining room and library, then to the yard entrance, the gentleman's chamber, and the picture gallery, where hung the portraits of the former Masters of Evenmere. Seeing nothing amiss, he continued through the butler's corridor into the servants' block, passing through each of the rooms in turn.

Finishing his rounds, he backtracked with the intention of returning upstairs, when a soft tapping attracted his attention. He followed the sound, which proved momentarily elusive until he traced it to the outside doors of the entrance hall.

Peeking through the blue-stained glass in the narrow fenestra on either side of the rounded oak doors, he glimpsed a tall figure. He considered opening the door and confronting whoever lay beyond, but thinking better of it, hurried back down the transverse corridor and slipped through the dining room into the servery, along the men's corridor to the housekeeper's corridor, and over to the luggage entrance. Through the large panes of glass bordering that door, he saw no one waiting on the other side. Withdrawing his Master Keys, he unlocked the door, stepped quickly outside, and locked it behind him.

The luggage entrance stood at the end of the ell formed by the servants' block. Carter could not angle across to the main entrance without being seen, so he slipped south along the wall, following it as it turned west, wholly hidden from the intruder's sight by the abutment of the entrance hall. Moving in swift silence, he reached the porte-cochère and peered from behind its fluted pillars. A heavy, broad-shouldered man in a black greatcoat stood studying the door, bowler hat tipped back on his head, humming a melody from Swaylone's *Branchspell* symphony.

Beside the man sat a beast, black as coal, its head a cross between that of a wolf and a horse.

The intruder began speaking in a strange and exotic language, and flames danced like fireflies across the surface of the oak doors, banishing the shadows beneath the porte-cochère. For several moments, the fires roared. But when the attack was spent and the flames exhausted, the doors remained unscathed.

"No luck there," the man said.

Carter drew his Lightning Sword in one hand and his pistol in the other. At the sound, the stranger whirled with amazing gracefulness for one so large. The beast also turned, and to Carter's shock, its eyes were a molten gold, without iris or pupil, as if poured into its sockets.

Without hesitation, he placed a single shot between those eyes. It staggered, collapsed, and lay still.

"A ton of dynamite wouldn't crack even a single pane of glass," Lord Anderson said. "I could open that door wide and unless you had an invitation, you could not step across the threshold."

The intruder gave a grim, brave smile. If the noise of the pistol had startled him, he did not show it. He had heavy jowls and wide, staring eyes of a pale blue. A short lock of blond hair protruded from beneath his bowler; a silver chain peeked from under his collar.

"Just the man I was looking for." His voice was rich and full as a dramatist's. "I am Doctor Benjamin Armilus, former dean of the College of Poets at Aylyrium."

"I recognize the name. You were arrested some time ago."

"For a time I languished in a prison in Ooz. But I wonder . . ." He indicated the pistol. "Is that necessary? Or do you intend to kill me, too?"

Carter ignored the question. "What was that animal?"

"I wish I knew. I assume it is a product of *The Book of Lore*. It has been my constant companion since shortly after I retrieved the volume from the Mere. I was surprised to discover it had followed me into the dreamland."

"You were the one disguised as the bosun?"

Armilus gave his half-smile again. "The very same. A good bit of work, that. I enjoyed our boat ride together."

"You bloody butcher!"

"Yes, well," Armilus glanced down at the ground, "necessity is the mother of assassination. I didn't want to kill you, but that is often the only way to stop a Master. I am the Supreme Anarchist now, Lord Anderson. Previously, I had fallen from grace in the Society for opposing some of our more overly ambitious plans.

Now I am returned, but to a party divided. I needed the book to counter the threat of the Radical Anarchists and their Poetry Men. I do not know where they receive their power, but it is a force too terrible to control."

"Strange words from an anarchist."

"I won't argue politics here. I have my responsibilities even as do you. We simply disagree. I need to halt the Poetry Men and reunite the anarchist party, so we can go about our business. To that end, you see me before you, walking the world of dream, trying to break into the Inner Chambers, a feat I never would have attempted until I read *The Book of Lore*. It is the most vile and dangerous volume in the world, one only men such as you or I should be allowed to peruse. Since I am blessed and cursed with a photographic memory, there are parts of it I fervently wish I had never read, sections that will haunt me for the remainder of my existence. But it was worth it, for its power now resides within me."

"What is its origin, since it was obviously not written by Master Kenton?"

"That was a necessary fabrication," Armilus said. "But I don't think I will tell you any more about it. No point in giving you information you might use against me, you understand. Do you know my objective in wanting to enter the Inner Chambers, Lord Anderson? I intend to steal your son."

At the confirmation of his suspicions that the doctor was not only L'Marius, but the clown, Carter gave a cry of fury and lunged forward, his Lightning Sword inches from the anarchist's heart, the weapon trembling in his hand, ready to slay.

With one rapid motion, Armilus batted the blade away, his naked palm striking its edge.

Carter hesitated in amazement. The sword, capable of slicing through steel, should have severed the doctor's fingers, yet he was not even nicked.

Hand still upraised, the anarchist said, "You have used the Word Which Masters Dreams, but it cannot master me. *The Book of Lore* has given me power within the dream dimension. I think you will discover you can't harm me here, any more than I can hurt you."

The doctor dropped his arm to his side and lowered his voice. "I have a proposal to offer you. If you agree to the terms, I swear to leave your son alone."

"Go on," Carter said, keeping his voice level to avoid betraying how Armilus' display had shaken him.

"My people need time," Armilus said. "Time to gather our strength. I want your promise that you won't interfere. Fight the Poetry Men, as will we, but leave us to our own devices, and I vow to trouble your dreams no more."

"You, the Supreme Anarchist asking for my help, wanting me to trust your word after everything you've done? Do you expect me to believe you're that desperate?"

"You wound me, Lord Anderson. Deception is not a bludgeon; it is an art. I fancy I painted some fine strokes in the Mere; but now the brushes are put away. Even anarchists must honor their agreements or lose credibility, and I have negotiated many treaties in the past. Nor will I lie to you about the poets. Neither you nor I control anything like the force used to destroy Jossing. Whatever their intent, the Poetry Men threaten everything the Society of Anarchists has worked for."

Carter studied his opponent. There was something compelling about the man. "You ask me to break my oath as Master."

"You are sworn to protect the manor. Nothing more."

Lord Anderson pondered only an instant. With a sinking sense of hopelessness, he said, "I cannot agree to such a pact. Either I am responsible for the entire house or I must abdicate all authority."

"You are making a mistake," the doctor said. "True, we are enemies, but enemies faced with a common foe. This isn't about ethics, but politics."

Carter gave a bleak grimace. "I am afraid, Doctor, I do not know the difference."

"Then I will be back until you do, or until I hold something so precious of yours that you cannot oppose me. Good evening."

Before Carter could react, the anarchist vanished, leaving him standing alone before the front door. The ghost of a growl sounded behind him, causing him to whirl. The body of the dark beast was also gone.

Lord Anderson entered the house once more, bolting the door firmly behind him. He drew a deep breath, concentrated, and spoke the Word Which Brings Aid. He waited for several minutes in the silent house before a low whistling drifted down the transverse corridor, and Mr. Hope appeared at its far end. The butler approached warily, his face noticeably pale. Seeing Carter, he asked, "Is this a dream?"

"Yes."

"You summoned me to it?"

"I did."

Hope gave an exhalation of relief. "That's good."

The two shook hands.

"Why were you whistling?" Carter asked.

"Because I was afraid. The last time I walked in dream was a terrifying experience."

"I hoped you would be the one who came. Is Jason safe?"

"Quite so. We have a guard on him every hour of the day and night. How goes your journey?"

Carter related what he had seen, including the attack by the Poetry Man and his encounter with Jonathan T. Bartholomew. "We now know the Poetry Men and the Radical Anarchists possess only *The Book of Verse*, while Armilus and *his* anarchists have the *The Book of Lore*. We need to circulate the doctor's description throughout the house, to try to capture him and his book, but the poets are clearly the greater peril. We've seen what they can do. Doctor Armilus, despite his villainy, appears rational."

"Even when he threatens the Master's son?"

Carter grimaced, wondering if this was how his father had felt when Carter was in peril. He cast the thought aside. "I'll tell you what I fear, Will." He felt the blood drain from his face as he attempted to put the idea into words. "The poet I fought, the words he spoke—he acted like he was trying to do me a favor. They have discovered the very essence of Power, and it has driven them completely insane. Unless we can find and end the source of that power, they will channel it until Evenmere, and the universe with it, lies in smoking ruin."

Hope licked his lips, and for a moment his eyes filled with dread. Then his jaw grew firm. "Well. That's what we're here for, isn't it? The reason we get to sleep in those soft beds in the Inner Chambers."

"That's why you get to sleep in them. Right now I'm dozing in a dilapidated chair in a cold, dank room with an unknown stranger keeping watch."

"True. But before we declare the poets wholly demented, keep in mind they attacked you, the Master of the House. That suggests method to their madness."

Carter barked a grim laugh. "It's a desperate situation when we take comfort in thinking our enemies might be slightly sane."

"I'll redouble my research on the Poetry Men and Armilus. I'll also try to find out about this Storyteller."

Lord Anderson glanced around the room. "I have another problem, one I hadn't considered. In this dream, I can't know when Jason wakes so I can end my vigil."

Hope removed his bowler and scratched his head. "There is a pretty paradox! But easily solved, I think. We could simply make the bed when he rises, I suppose, but to give you a clearer indication, why don't I move the lamp from the night stand to the dresser? When he sleeps I will return it to its original position."

"It's worth a try," Carter said. "Do you want me to send you back now?"

"I might as well stay and help you keep watch. It's not as if I'm missing any sleep."

"True; and I would like some company. These halls are so barren. Familiar, yet uncomfortable."

They made the rounds together through the night, until Hope abruptly vanished in mid-sentence, so Carter knew he had awakened. Going to Jason's room, he found the lamp moved. He breathed a word of thanks to his friend and commanded the dream to end.

The Master woke to find the fire still burning in the hearth and Jonathan Bartholomew sitting wide-eyed in his chair, as if he had watched throughout the night. The minstrel gave Carter a broad grin. "Good morning, Master Anderson. And how were your dreams?"

"Dreadful," Carter replied. "Thank you for keeping watch. You even stoked the fire."

"It grew chill in the small hours. But you are troubled. A bit of breakfast helps curb the fears of the night. Would you like some? I have oranges, bread, and cheese."

The mention of food made Carter realize how famished he was. "I would, indeed." He rose and stretched. Despite his vigil in the country of slumber, he felt refreshed, as is the way when the Master walks the land of dream.

Bartholomew did not ask what had occurred, nor did Carter volunteer any information, but as they ate, the minstrel said, "I think I will accompany you awhile, if it isn't any trouble."

"Surely you have other responsibilities?" Carter replied, uncertain how he felt about it.

Bartholomew gave a broad smile. "That's right. But I will tell you the truth, Master Anderson. I didn't find you by accident last night. No. I heard you were nearby and I was searching for you. Don't start lookin' troubled! I didn't tell you that yesterday evening because if I had, you wouldn't have trusted me enough so you could visit your son. I know who you faced in this chamber. I wanted to see you because these men of verse have caught my ear. They are, after all, trampling on my roses, if you follow me. Who is more likely to find them than the Master?"

"I see." He considered, wondering exactly who this man was. "How do you know so much? What can you tell me about these poets?"

"As the saying goes, the walls of Evenmere have ears. In my travels, I meet a lot of people and hear a lot of things. Most of what I hear doesn't matter, but the Poetry Men are different. I know no more than you do about them, but I want to see for myself. So Storyteller will come along."

"And what will you do when you find them?"

"Maybe I will ask them what they mean. Should we be off?"

Lord Anderson appraised the man, who sat, eyebrows raised, awaiting Carter's answer. He was likable enough, and there would be time to learn more about him from Mr. Hope's research. If he was as old as he claimed, he was bound to possess useful information, and might prove handy in a fight.

Carter nodded. "Let's go."

They packed their meager belongings and headed down the corridor, skirting the Ghahanjhin border throughout most of that day. Around supper-time they opened a four-panel door and entered the sparkling luminance of the Looking Glass Marches, the mile-wide buffer surrounding that country, a mirror-filled maze serving as a line of defense. Carter intended to cut through the marches to reach the western Aylyrium border. Although he could see no one, he knew they were being watched by men armed with short bows and blow-guns.

"I should lead from here," he told Bartholomew. "My inner maps allow me to traverse the maze."

"Now, now, Master Anderson. Storyteller is old, as you have said. I know the way. Just follow me and you won't have to stop to consult those maps of yours."

So saying, he set out across the passages, striding as surely as a man walking down a country lane, unperturbed by the deceptions created by the endless mirrors and clear panes of glass.

"How can you be so certain of your steps?" Carter asked.

Storyteller glanced over his shoulder and flapped his patchwork coat like a bird. "Oh, there is nothing to this. I have *flown* through these parts. I think of the house as my own."

"I have always thought of it as *its* own."

"That's right. You've got it just so. But I am right, too."

From his name and reputation, Carter expected his companion to be always telling wonderful tales, but the opposite proved true; Jonathan Bartholomew exuded a deep joy, a splendor of spirit manifested not in stories, which he told only for a reason, but in the tone and flow of his words, in the ivory bastions of his bright smile, in his dark face and glistening brown eyes.

They passed through the Looking Glass Marches without seeing another soul, and entered the warm, buttermilk halls of Aylyrium. The security of the border resting on Ghahanjhin's clandestine shoulders, the men did not encounter any sentries, and were soon strolling over tessellated Holdstock carpet, replete with shimmering silk borders from the Early Aylyrium era. Argent banners streamed from the high ceiling. The glass doorknobs held brass butterflies with outstretched wings.

Aylyrium was an old civilization, where the first chamber-states were said to have arisen. Many of the classic philosophers—Wainamoinen, Vergilius, Oromanes—had made their homes in Aylyrium; John Whitbourn's revolutionary *Humanity Considered as a Counterpane* had been written near the site of ancient Arkover, where the learned still gathered in the hallowed halls of the Disputatium to discuss their speculations and theories.

The deeper into Aylyrium the travelers went, the grander grew the corridors, until they walked along an elegant concourse. Windows lined both sides of the paneled passage, which was four stories tall and framed in Aquitanitan cherubesques. Tiny palmettes, interspersed with daises, were etched around the edge of every lintel. Shops appeared, selling cloth, books, chocolate from Querny, and exotic furniture from Far Wing. The travelers passed through courtyards open to the sky, with tall oaks and mulberry trees rising between green paving stones and trumpet vines flowing up stone towers; the air hung sweet with the fragrance of lilacs.

"I love coming here," Carter said. "Such fine architecture. So many artists and artisans."

"It reminds me of the cities outside the house," Bartholomew said, "only cleaner."

"You have traveled beyond Evenmere?"

"No, but I have seen glimpses from afar. The entrance to Evenmere hasn't always been where it is now. At times, it has stood near, or even within, cities."

Carter frowned. "I didn't know that. I lived in the outer world for fourteen years. It always seemed alien to me. Too many endless reaches. Vast plains; desert wastes. I prefer a world that is all house."

"There is great beauty in the outside world: canyons and rainbows, sunrise on sprawling plains, hawks in flight, lions passing through the veldt. The world, both inside and outside of Evenmere, is good, unless people make it otherwise."

"It's hard to think so, with my son in peril. I have faced dangers to the house before, and more than once despaired of making it through. Yet we prevailed in the end; and I have learned things are not always as dark as they seem. But this threat to Jason . . . I wish I knew what to do."

"It's nearly noon," Bartholomew said, as they passed beside an outdoor cafe. "The best thing to do is to have lunch."

The travelers seated themselves in fluted chairs at a bronze table. A waiter dressed in velvet breeches, a jabot, and a long matching coat took the men's orders, and they were soon feasting on Aylyrium apples and a delicate stew of freshwater fish. To

Carter's own surprise, under Jonathan's quiet gaze, he found himself relating his encounter with Doctor Armilus.

Carter finished, adding, "Armilus was able to reach my son
in the dream dimension when Jason was outside the Inner Chambers, but failed to gain entrance last night, so my boy should be
safe. Still, I can't be certain. You strike me as very wise. What
would you counsel? What more can I do?"

"I would suggest you eat your stew," Jonathan said. "It is
quite good."

Carter lifted his eyebrows. "Have you no other advice?"

"Oh, no," Jonathan replied. "No, no. Storyteller does not
advise. Storyteller tells stories."

That night they lodged at an inn with arched portals, walls
painted to simulate emerald, dun, and red marble; and intricate,
polychromic ceilings embossed with windmills, entwined maple
leaves, and children at play. A West Highland Terrier named
Wallace greeted every guest at the door.

The dining hall was divided into small rooms, and that
evening Jonathan went about his work, telling tales beside a half-
moon hearth. Within the hour, the inn's patrons had deserted the
other chambers to flock around him. They sat in wooden chairs and
low couches before him, faces upturned, enthralled as children before the spell of his deep, melodious voice. Sometimes he sang,
sonorous and unaccompanied, sometimes he chanted. The fire
crackled its warm approbation; the shadows sank comfortably into
the corners.

Jonathan's tales were not cozy fables, but stories filled with
cold beauty and deep sorrows. His words went to the heart, pierc-
ing first one member of the audience and then another, as if each
tale was intended for a specific person. Whenever the blow struck
home, it showed in the eyes of the listener. The faces of some grew
radiant; others took on a haunted expression. One woman fled the
room in tears. A burly man, with two long scars running down his
face and neck, bowed his head and blubbered. And still Jonathan
continued, stroking with slender fingers the terrier that had crept
into his lap.

Carter noticed one other thing about Storyteller's stories: each in some small way suggested the importance of either being responsible to others, or of serving those in command of the social and political order of Evenmere. As the minstrel had said, he reinforced the rule of the house.

The hour drew close to nine, when Carter intended to return to his room, but he found himself so comfortable in the overstuffed chair, which was just the right distance from the fire; and he felt so safe listening to Jonathan, he decided to remain. He muttered the Word Which Masters Dreams, making the room quiver only slightly, and so enthralled were Storyteller's listeners they did not even notice.

Lord Anderson found himself once more in the Gray Edge outside the Inner Chambers. He unlocked the Green Door and made his way down the hall.

In Jason's room he discovered the lamp sitting on the dresser; his son had yet to go to bed. He sat in a chair to wait, and soon caught a flicker out of the corner of one eye, and the lamp stood on the night stand.

After making his rounds throughout the Inner Chambers, he returned to the chair in Jason's room and used the Word Which Brings Aid. Moments later, the butler came tramping up the stair.

"You rang, sir?"

Carter smiled. "I never ring."

"No," Mr. Hope said, "you only summon me from a sound sleep."

"Not technically, since you're still in one. I need to know if you've learned anything about Jonathan Bartholomew. He and I are traveling together."

Hope sat on the bed. "You wouldn't believe the number of references I've found. And that's only as far back as the fifteenth century."

"He is as old as he claims?"

"I suspect he is old as moist earth. I asked Enoch about him. He grinned and called him a grand fellow. He said you could never mistake him for an imposter because no one can do what Jonathan can."

"After this evening, I know what he means," Lord Anderson said. "I can't describe the way he can tell a tale. Cuts you like a cleaver."

"He has been discreetly involved in the affairs of the house for generations," Mr. Hope said, "always far behind the scenes. The reason I missed references to him before is because he is called by dozens of names: Storyteller, Minstrel, Vagabond, Spinner. It took hours of cross-referencing to discover it. I wouldn't have found it at all, except his true name, Jonathan T. Bartholomew, crops up occasionally." Hope gave a wry smile. "He is certainly a mystery. I think he is trustworthy within limits, but take warning: he usually has his own agenda, one that may contradict yours. The records suggest he was generally welcomed by previous Masters, but had conflicts with some."

"I'll keep it in mind. I trust Enoch's judgment and my own instincts. If you find anything else about him, let me know."

The two friends kept the vigil together that night without seeing any sign of Doctor Armilus.

As for Jonathan T. Bartholomew, as the evening waned the timbre of his tales grew soft as thistledown, the stories stirring hearts with memories of rocking chairs and quiet hearths, of peace within a happy home, of mothers' croonings and fathers' laughter, of being carried drowsy to bed to sleep long beneath warm covers. He sang a final song, and without speaking a word the listeners drifted to their rooms to fall into dreamless slumber.

When Jonathan and Lord Anderson were alone with the dog and the dying fire, the minstrel lifted Carter as easily as a man might a child, and carried him upstairs to his room.

Aylyrium

Carter woke the next morning, still in his clothes, but with his boots and hat lying neatly by his bedside. He felt less refreshed than on the morning before, rather thin, as if the nightly treks were gradually wearing him away. This came as a surprise, especially since this had been only his second night in the dream dimension. Clearly he was mistaken about there being no consequences to repeated visits there, and he wondered, with a grim dread, how long he could keep it up. He rose, bathed, and went downstairs to find Jonathan sitting before the hearth as if he had never left. Yet the minstrel looked bright and fresh.

"Good morning," Jonathan said.

"Good morning. Do you ever sleep?"

"Kitten naps, here and there."

"Thank you for taking care of me last night. I hated to leave the party."

"The night went well?"

"Very."

They breakfasted on biscuits, eggs, bacon, and oranges. As they dined, the other wayfarers began drifting into the chamber. The woman who had left weeping the night before came shyly to Jonathan; with wisps of tears in her eyes she bent to hug his slender neck. "Thank you," she said. "Thank you."

"That's all right." He patted her back with his long, delicate hands. "That's all right. No need to say more."

Others entered and gave Jonathan jolly waves, conspiratorial winks, and warm handshakes. Coins began to stack up on the table: copper, silver, and even gold. One man presented the minstrel with a leather bag, but Storyteller handed it back without looking inside.

"You have given too much," he said softly. "And you will need every bit of it for the thing you must do."

The man looked confused, then a brilliant smile lit his features. He clasped Jonathan's hand as if to wring it off, and immediately left the inn.

The burly man came last. With his head down like a scolded child, he placed a locket on the table. "I've carried this in anger, m'lord," he said. "And I'm going now to set things right with my brother."

"The woman in the locket forgave you long ago," Jonathan said.

When they were gone, Carter and Storyteller sat eating in silence. Finally Lord Anderson said, "I am humbled. I have my position and my power; I am given a grand residence in the Inner Chambers. Now I see I have been but the protector of the physical world, while you do the great work of the spirit."

"Ah, the big fish eat the little ones," Storyteller replied. "But sometimes they just eye one another, nose to nose, in respect. There is plenty of room in the ocean."

The professors of Aylyrium reside within seventy ivory towers, carved from the tusks of long-extinct mammoths. Their chambers overlook the rooftops of the great university. In the mornings, the professors pour down in long, thin lines, wrapped in robes of gold, silver, imperial purple, or royal blue, their tassels tapping against their mortar boards, their stern and ancient faces sagging from the weight of the vast knowledge within their venerated brains.

They make their way over frayed carpet down the seventy stairs converging into the Great Stair, a wide expanse descending into the muscular Gothicism of Tabard Hall. The east wall is paned glass, so the morning sun pours in, meeting the professorial stream.

Trumpets blare as the first scholar places his revered, scuffed shoe on the stone floor; the echoes swirl down the cloistered ways until every college is alerted. From there, the preceptors disburse, each to his own place, and the work of the university begins.

Carter and Jonathan sat watching the procession from over-stuffed chairs in the midst of Tabard Hall—the sunlight on the colorful robes, the statuesque faces of the professors. It had taken two days, from the time they left the inn, to reach the university.

Lord Anderson studied their heavy brows and wizened countenances. "My wife, Sarah, says people's ears and noses continue to grow throughout their lives, nature's joke to make the elderly look wise and funny as gnomes."

"I must be an exception," Jonathan said, "or by now I would have a weather-vane for a nose and ears flapping in the wind."

With the day begun, the travelers approached a potbellied man in a gray robe and silver sash, standing beside the Great Stair. Upon introducing themselves, they were led up the stair a short distance and ushered into a side door leading through a labyrinth of corridors finally ending in a tidy chamber with an equally tidy man seated at a desk, scribbling with a quill pen.

"Secretary Bipwhine," the escort said. "This is Lord Anderson and Mr. Bartholomew."

The secretary rose, removed his spectacles, and gave the pair an appraising stare. Apparently satisfied, he bowed and said. "We did not expect you until Tuesday, Lord Anderson, but it is good you have come. Chancellor Tremolo has been anxious to meet with you."

"My plans were unexpectedly changed, and there was no opportunity to send a messenger," Carter replied. He had originally intended to talk to the chancellor about bringing the telegraph through the university.

Bipwhine disappeared behind a door, and a lanky man robed in black soon appeared, eyes glazed with the beginnings of cataracts. The crown of his head was bald, with wisps of gray hair straining from behind his ears.

"Lord Anderson! So good of you to come," the chancellor said. "So good. Come in. Bipwhine, we must have tea! And *this* is Storyteller! A bit of a celebrity, if the tales are true."

The men shook hands, and Tremolo led them into a fastidious office, nearly bare of decoration, save for a large Lippenhost vase in one corner, a wooden wall plaque stating: *Our Goal is Education*, and a host of framed degrees behind the chancellor's chair. The desk was large and mostly empty.

"Never mind the mess," Tremolo said, though there was none. "I was in committee meetings all day yesterday and haven't had a chance to straighten my office. You cannot imagine! So many *interesting* thoughts in education, so much *variety*! We are changing the world, gentlemen. In a hundred years, the teaching discipline will be irrevocably different. It *boggles* the mind to think of it. We are looking now at the Inverse Logic method of instruction; I have all my professors using it. Once properly applied, the student leaves the classroom retaining *everything* the instructor says. This is far superior to the Randall approach we were using two years ago."

The tea arrived and Chancellor Tremolo paused to take a sip before launching into a detailed explanation of educational theory. Lord Anderson made a polite comment or two, but as they were utterly ignored, soon dropped into calm nods, recognizing the chancellor as one who had held power so long he no longer listened to anyone but himself. Five minutes into the monologue Carter began to grow impatient, but before he could speak, Jonathan interrupted.

"Do you like to fish, Chancellor?"

"I . . ." Tremolo halted, taken aback. "Well, that is—"

"Do you like the scent of the air beside the Fable River, the light of sunrise, the soft peeping of the water fowl, the worm on the hook? Do you like the slow drawing back for the first cast, arm locked in placed, the quick release, the line snaking out? Wading into the water, its coolness rushing round your knees? The drifting of the line, the swaying of the trees, the motion of the river? The first nibble, sweet as a girl's kiss, and suddenly taut? Do you like to fish?"

Chancellor Tremolo's expression abruptly melted. His eyes gained intensity. "I *love* to fish," he said, a soft smile creeping over his face. "I don't get to go as I once did, of course. The responsibilities of the university, you know."

For a few minutes they talked of worms and hooks and

lures, and Carter saw that Tremolo cared little for educational theories after all. With the chancellor a human being once more, Jonathan said, "Master Anderson has come to ask about the College of Poets."

The chancellor gave a sigh, as if wading back to shore after a long, happy day. Carter could almost see him putting away his tackle box.

"Lord Anderson, normally I would not discuss this particular subject. You must understand that what I tell you is strictly confidential. But you being the Master, it may fall under your jurisdiction."

Tremolo's voice grew conspiratorial. "It seems to have started with Doctor Armilus, who was dean of Poets' College until we learned of his anarchist activities. Not just one of those intellectuals espousing anarchist doctrine, either—universities are a sanctuary for every kind of theory—he was the real thing, connected to a bombing at Nianar that killed seven school children."

"I know of him," Carter said.

"From what I understand, he was far behind the scenes. He was arrested but escaped custody while awaiting trial. But he was only the first to leave. Professor Shoemate, the chair at Poets' College, was the next to go. A brilliant woman, very likeable, easy to work with; she took a leave of absence and never returned. Shortly thereafter, the other professors began acting peculiar."

The chancellor's voice dropped even lower. "There are rumors that they began visiting other parts of the house, spreading some sort of—I don't know what to call it—poetry doctrine. I have been investigating; we have even formed a committee, but it may be a moot point, as every one of the professors of the Poetry College has vanished."

Carter raised his eyebrows. "How many?"

"Twelve. They quit teaching classes. Just stopped. Their families are frantic. And recently, Professor Hector from the music department, a friend of Professor Shoemate, has also disappeared. He was last seen Thursday night entering the library reading room where the College of Poets used to have their monthly meetings. There have since been rumors of strange occurrences there. Students are claiming the Poetry College is haunted; it's gotten so bad they refuse to enter the halls. We had the police investigate. They found nothing at the college itself, but have witnessed odd lights nearly every night in the upper stories of the library which vanish before the officers can reach them."

"I shall go to the Poetry College at once," Carter said. "Perhaps I can find something the police missed. I want to see the library reading room as well."

"Anything you can do would be wonderful," the chancellor said. "The College of Poets is locked up, but I will alert the officers to allow you entrance. And I can inform the police to stay away from the library this evening to give you free rein. Would you like an escort to the college?"

"I prefer to go alone. Directions will be sufficient."

"My secretary will see to it. Thank you so much for your aid, Lord Anderson, Mr. Bartholomew. I must admit, I feel helpless. The professors' families are heartbroken. When this is over, I may take a long vacation, do a bit of fishing, try to forget the whole business."

"That is a good thought," Jonathan said.

"And to think it started with poor Professor Shoemate," the chancellor continued, walking the two men to the door. "I wonder what became of her?"

After obtaining directions from Bipwhine, Carter glanced back toward the chancellor's office. Tremolo was leaning back in his chair, casting an invisible line toward his trash receptacle.

As they made their way down the Great Stair, Jonathan said, "The journey to the College of Poets is a task for the Master. There are three people I promised to visit when next I came this way, and one for certain has a broken heart."

"Very well. Don't expect me for supper. I'll eat on the way to the library."

Jonathan departed and Carter made his way through passages bordered by everything from heavy Gothic gargoyles to dainty primrose wallpaper and carved miniatures. The University of Aylyrium had grown into its spaces one room and one college at a time, resulting in a riotous collection of offices, lecture halls, and laboratories, the architecture varying from chamber to chamber.

After an hour's march, he reached a rotunda on the main floor, where he approached an officer in a scarlet uniform stationed beside leather-bound doors with *College of Poets* carved in flowing script upon the lintel. Surveying the room, he saw other doors all around, each labeled with the names of various schools, including the controversial Shea College of Paraphysics.

"You must be Master Anderson," the officer said. "I have orders to let you into Poetry College, though I wouldn't go in there myself for the world. It's become a wicked place, no doubt about it."

Carter grimaced, wondering if people enjoyed saying that sort of thing when he *did* have to enter. But as the officer unfastened the lock and threw open the doors, revealing a long, ascending stair, Lord Anderson realized the man was correct. Something was definitely wrong, something that sent a chill through him.

He licked his lips, not wanting to cross the threshold. He could sense the shifting of the Balance, feel the dark hand of Chaos controlling the rooms above. The stairwell appeared to waver beneath the single gas jet, as if this portion of the house were no longer quite substantial.

He looked at the officer, who goggled in fear at the long flight.

"It's gone ghostly!" the man exclaimed.

Carter drew his Lightning Sword, startling the man. Golden light streamed off the serrated blade, and where its luminance touched the steps, the stairway seemed more solid.

Lord Anderson strode to the bottom of the steps, his boots clumping on the worn, wooden floor. Shivers ran along his neck as he grasped the bannister rail. He half-expected it to be insubstantial; it was iron cold instead, a biting frost that made him flinch from its touch. When he placed a foot upon the steps, he could feel the chill through his boots.

He climbed to a level even with the single gas jet. Though the light cast a half circle on everything below, beyond this point the illumination failed, as if unable to penetrate the darkness.

In seeming defiance, his Lightning Sword glowed brighter, filling the stair with its soft light. He glanced back at the officer, who stared up at him with frightened eyes. "I'll be just outside if you need anything," the man gasped, quickly shutting the door behind him.

"I am certain you will," Carter muttered scornfully, though he could scarcely blame the fellow.

He made his way up the stair, ascending several flights before stepping into a common room apparently scorched by fire. The walls and carpets were blackened, the hanging documents consumed. Several portraits hung on the wall, their faces burned away to empty, staring ovals. The couches, chairs, and end tables remained intact but seared at the edges.

He stepped through a doorway, mindful of the power of the Poetry Man he had faced in Ghahanjhin. He wished Jonathan had accompanied him. As Master, he had traveled many times alone and did not fear the solitude of empty passages, yet here he was afraid. He sensed chaotic forces all around, permeating the very walls.

He passed through benighted rooms, the light from his sword casting shadows about him. The mysterious forces grew stronger the deeper he went, and he followed their scent the way a hound tracks a rabbit. The air crackled with static electricity, making the hair on the nape of his neck stand on end; the doorknobs startled him with mild shocks. He found it increasingly difficult to move forward, as if he struggled against a stout wind.

He hesitated at a half-opened door bearing a sign inscribed with the words *Erin Shoemate, Professor of Poetry*. Pushing the door wide with his foot, he stepped inside.

The scorching was worse here. The desk lay in shambles, one of its legs charred away. He made a slow circle of the room, not certain what he was looking for. A few scattered papers lay about, containing snatches of poetry, various names, and cryptic memos.

Bookshelves, ornamented with the carved faces of gargoyles and filled with smoke-damaged volumes, lined the walls behind the desk. Carter frowned. If the books held any clues concerning the professor's disappearance, it would require a day's hunt to discover them. Vowing to have Mr. Hope initiate a thorough search, he turned toward the desk. The top two drawers were empty save for pens, rulers, and paperclips. The bottom one held a number of papers which had escaped the fire, but these proved to be only student essays.

Playing a hunch, he brought a Word of Power to mind.
Talheedin!

The room trembled at the Word of Secret Ways, an alarm-
ing noise in the silence. He glanced around the chamber and was
rewarded by a blue glow surrounding one of the wooden gargoyles
adorning the bookshelf. Feeling along its head, he discovered a
small button. He pressed it. With a click, the gargoyle swung outward, revealing a hidden compartment.

Within the cubbyhole he discovered a thin, half-burned volume he soon identified as Professor Shoemate's diary. Placing the
book in his jacket pocket, he left the room and continued along the
corridor, moving past other offices until he came to a pair of massive doors.

Taking a deep breath, he gripped his sword and wrenched
both doors wide, using so much force they struck the walls. The
noise boomed through the silence.

The light of his Lightning Sword played across the wooden
floorboards of a large assembly hall. As he moved forward, the
blade's illumination revealed a singed tapestry on one wall, a
heavy oak desk, and a herd of scattered chairs. So strong were the
forces of Chaos, so acrid and biting, he fancied he could taste
them.

He made his way around the chamber, keeping close to the
wall. Random books, their pages ripped from their spines,
sprawled across his path. Broken rulers and yellow scraps of paper
lay beneath his tread. He made the full circle of the room, the
floorboards creaking at every step, but found nothing.

As he approached the desk, it seemed to waver in the dim
light, like a specter of long-dead furniture. He placed his hand on
its surface. The wavering ceased; the desk felt solid.

The usual kinds of items were upon it, a quill pen and
bottle of ink, a broken saucer and chipped teacup, a few scorched
papers. He lifted the topmost page, lecture notes written in a small,
neat script on the use of iambic pentameter in medieval Corovia.

A hand touched his arm.

He leapt back with a shout. In the previously empty chair
sat a woman. A strangled gasp escaped his throat.

"Hello, Carter."

His breath hissed between his teeth. Without replying, he

lifted his sword to see her clearly. A tremor of shock ran through his frame. His whole body turned frigid.

"Come and give your mother a kiss," she said sweetly.

"What are you doing in the dark?"

"I have waited here so I could warn you," she said. "Come to me, child. Surely you remember me?"

"I remember," Carter said. She had died when he was five. He could scarcely breathe.

"Then let me hold you in my arms. It has been so long. So many years. Haven't you wanted it?"

"The dead do not arise until the appointed time."

"My love demanded that I do so."

She was exactly as he remembered, the slender dark beauty, the soft voice and warm expression. "What do you want to warn me about?"

She glanced around the assembly hall as if her eyes could penetrate the darkness. "The Poetry Men have tapped into the power of Chaos. They will destroy the foundation of the house by attacking those in charge of the Balance, the members of the Servants' Circle. You must stop them or beauty will vanish from the universe. No more the numbered sequence, no more the rising and setting of the sun. No more the passing of the minutes and hours, the footprints of time. You must prevent it. But first, come into my arms, and I will hold you and tell you how precious and perfect you are, and love you with a mother's everlasting love." She raised her arms, beckoning.

When he mastered himself enough to speak, Carter's words were ashes in his mouth. He had known, of course, it was not really her . . . "Such talk gives you away, Lady Order."

The woman slowly lowered her hands to her side. "A shame. Yet it changes nothing. I can *be* your mother. Serve me. Embrace me. I can give you back your childhood. The innocence. The love. Is that not what mortals long for?"

"If I do as you say, what a prize you would possess! What a ruin you would make of the house with me to drive Chaos back."

"You have been unkind to me!" she cried, her lips pouting. "You misuse me, letting these Poetry Men wield the essence of Chaos. They are making him too strong!"

"Then tell me how to stop them."

Order shook his mother's head, the soft curls rustling in the silence. "They *must* be stopped."

"How are Doctor Armilus and Professor Shoemate involved?"

"I do not know them. They have not touched me."

Carter bowed his head, gathering his strength. "Very well. Depart from this place."

"I have been drawn here, given physical form by the Chaos within these walls."

"And the Master bids you leave. I will set right the Balance so neither you nor Chaos hold the upper hand." Lord Anderson's voice rose to sudden fury. "Go! I command it!"

The woman vanished. Carter raked in his breath, his eyes swarming with tears. "Cruel, cruel Order," he murmured. "Such guileless deceit. How little you understand us." Despite her seeming intelligence, she was not alive in the strictest sense, but a Force with a single nature.

He walked to the center of the assembly hall, and there, where the fields of Chaos were strongest, spoke in a loud voice. "Old Man Chaos, you have dared too much! The Master of Evenmere orders you to release these chambers!"

A deep, booming rose from the four walls, like distant drums. The assembly hall shook, nearly tossing Carter off his feet. An amorphous figure took form, gray and misshapen, its shoulders humped and uneven, one arm shorter than the other, its long, ash-gray face liquid as melting candle wax. The slogging form of Chaos.

"The red rose in the blue-stained glass!" it shouted, eyes glistening. "The agents of entropy! Wild wolves in the garden. Darkness and darkness and bitter longing! Get back! Come forth! The world-tree enters!"

As quickly as it appeared, Chaos sank away, vanishing into the shadows; but even as it went, Carter encountered resistance, as if another will opposed his own.

He suddenly found himself in a different place, hurled there with breathtaking rapidity. He stood in a circular chamber within a tall, crimson tower. A long window revealed rows of battlements beneath a violet sky peppered with blue, unwinking stars. A lamp burned on an ebony desk at the other side of the room, where sat a woman in an upholstered chair. Though Carter judged her to be somewhat younger than he, her hair was silver. She had deep, brooding eyes. Infinite sorrow consumed her features as she sat reading lines of poetry.

She looked up, placidly meeting Carter's gaze. Without a hint of surprise, she asked, "Are you a Seeker?"

"Who are you?"

But she only sighed and returned to her book. "Come and see."

Going to the desk, Carter looked over the woman's shoulder. With a shock he discovered that the lines throbbed with an energy as strong as that of the Words of Power; scanning them shook him to the core. He tore his eyes away only with great difficulty.

"How can you read that so calmly?" he asked.

She glanced up again. "How can I stop?"

Carter abruptly found himself back in the chamber at the College of Poets. Only a few seconds had passed since he banished Chaos, for the room still shuddered from the effects of the creature's departure. Gradually, the supernatural chill vanished from the air. The Lightning Sword dimmed. Carter drew a lantern and flint from his pack as the last rays of the sword died. The lamp flamed high, a sign that the Balance had been restored to the rooms.

Shuddering, he stumbled from the chamber and back down the stair. The exit door was locked, and so greatly was he shaken by what he had seen, it took an effort not to use his sword to shatter the mechanism. Instead, he drew a deep breath, sheathed his blade, and rapped harshly. The officer opened the door at once.

"Did you find anything, sir?"

"Enough," Carter said. "You won't have any more problems with these rooms."

The man raised his eyebrows. "Very good, sir. I will report it to the chancellor. Are you well, sir? You look deathly pale."

But Carter waved the man away and went to sit on a bench beneath the rotunda. Worse even than the shock of seeing his dead mother apparently returned to life, he had never experienced anything like the vision of the woman in the tower. It had been somewhat like entering the dream dimension, yet different as well, somehow more *real*. He could not be certain, but he suspected his physical body had actually been transported there. It was as if power were being siphoned into Chaos; and when he touched that power, it put him in contact with its source. That dreadful book. It had contained fundamental energy much like that of the Cornerstone of Evenmere. It could create and destroy; it might even be able to change reality. What was he up against?

Who was the woman, and what was she doing with the book? Was she somehow the root of the Poetry Men's might? He had to find out. He had been able to restore the College of Poets from its chaotic state with a word, for it had contained but a fragment of that power, but he doubted even he could oppose it directly.

He pulled the diary from his breast pocket, reminded of the question Chancellor Tremolo had asked as he and Jonathan were leaving.

What of Professor Shoemate? Carter thought, running his hand over his mouth and staring down at the diary. *What indeed of Professor Shoemate?*

The Library

U pon leaving the College of Poets, Carter returned to his room to read the professor's journal. The first few pages were irretrievably scorched, while the surviving leaves were written in what he assumed to be a foreign language. This led him to the Linguistics Department, where he spent two hours being passed from professor to professor. Textbooks were consulted, theories propounded, and heads thoughtfully scratched, as the experts eliminated, one by one, various tongues from Thedrian to Old Iphrisian.

Finally, a short, curly-headed philologist named Reuel appeared from the depths of the building, took one glance at the writing, and in a clipped voice declared, "It's not a language, but a letter-for-letter substitution. You just have to puzzle it through." He promptly hobbled away, leaving the other professors nodding their heads and saying it was perfectly obvious. They soon created Carter a key.

Over lunch at the university commons, he set to work translating the diary. Judging by her rapid scrawl, Erin Shoemate had learned the system well enough to write it fluently. Clearly, she was an intelligent woman. By mid-afternoon, he had finished his translation.

With several of the pages ruined by fire, it was difficult to follow some of the professor's often-esoteric references. She wrote of old legends and pseudo-scientific literature—the tales of Lost

Atlantis, the Centric Theories of Bromsky, even quoting Anton Trombone's peculiar, phantasmagorical epic, *Beyond Yonder*, tying them together with a book she seemed to have stumbled on, a "great key" she believed would lead her into "True Poetry."

The next section of her journal was ruined, and when it resumed, she was preparing to seek "the portal of the book." The top half of the next page was scorched beyond recovery, but the remaining section stated she would "go first to the Palace of the Decemvirs in Jossing, and then to the Tower of Astronomy."

Lord Anderson closed the diary. Had Erin Shoemate found what she was seeking?

A quick visit to the chancellor's office soon answered the question. An old photograph of the professors of the College of Poetry revealed a younger version of the woman Carter had seen in his vision, standing in the second row beside Benjamin Armilus.

He grimaced thoughtfully. The fact that the doctor and Professor Shoemate had worked together could not be a coincidence. What was the connection?

As the afternoon waned, he made his way through the paneled corridors to the university library entrance, a lobby with tessellated tile, Ionian pillars tipped in silver, and a three-story marble statue of King Mosiva, the builder of the first library in Evenmere, enrobed and bearing a heavy scroll. His hair flowed backward from his face; his serene eyes looked down.

Carter sat on a bench and studied his inner maps, bringing to mind the passages surrounding the library, learning the way by heart. The complex represented a fascinating challenge, a building in a perpetual state of growth, having expanded over the centuries to seventy separate chambers on ten floors, connected by a series of seemingly endless warrens. The interior was wooden stairs, dark oak beams, and high chandeliers. After an hour of study, Carter rose and made his way past the doorman along the smooth marble tunnel leading to the Stacks.

A few students milled around the front desk, but Lord Anderson soon left them behind. He journeyed between narrow aisles beneath cloistered ceilings of arched stone, his boot-steps heavy on the wooden boards, the musty scent of the volumes hanging in the air. The gas jets hissed in the silence; moths fluttered around the flames; the corners lay hidden in shadow.

As in the College of Poets, he sensed chaotic influences as he ascended to the upper stories, and he wondered if he would see Lady Order again. He passed along gloomy stairs, making his way to the drawing room on the eighth floor.

Within a narrow corridor decorated with hanging tapestries, he spoke the Word of Secret Ways. The room trembled and a blue square of light appeared around a tapestry depicting eagles in flight. Moving the fabric aside, Carter searched until he discovered a slender button embedded in the flowering ornamentation on the wainscot border, which caused a section of the wall to open inward. He drew his lamp from his pack, lit it, and slipped inside.

Cobwebs thick as string covered the corridor. Carter drew his sword and raised his lamp high, searching for spiders large enough to spin such strands. Seeing none, he cut through the webs, which shriveled beneath the power of his blade. Turning sideways to avoid the filaments, he followed the thin passage until it ended at an intersecting corridor. He veered to the right, following his inner maps, and soon came to a spy-hole. Pressing one eye to it, he discovered a room lit with candles. By his pocket watch, the time was twenty past seven. According to the chancellor's secretary, the poetry meetings normally had been held at eight, so he sat cross-legged on the floor to see if anything would occur.

He hated waiting like this. He had spent far too many hours of his life doing so. He particularly hated waiting for something dreadful to happen. The minutes dragged until nearly quarter till, when a soft rustling sounded in the room beyond.

Rising, he saw through the spy-hole a young, wire-haired man, presumably a student, setting out pads and pencils. Eschewing the use of the gas-jets, the man lit additional candles. He moved carelessly about the room, apparently unconcerned that the meeting was neither scheduled nor sanctioned by the university.

One by one, other men and women of various ages drifted into the room, until about twenty of them stood awkwardly around the table. Though they appeared to be strangers, they did not attempt introductions. Several were clearly agitated. Sweat beaded their brows; they kept clasping and unclasping their fists. One muttered over and over, "I just hope it helps."

"Are you certain he's coming?" a thin woman, who could not stop wringing her hands, asked the wire-haired man.

"I am certain," the man replied, "or, if not he, some other representative. He has never broken his word. I would swear to that."

"It's probably poppycock," a middle-aged fellow with spectacles growled, wiping his brow with a handkerchief.

"You will see it isn't," Wire-hair replied. "If you will take a seat, I will serve some tea."

The group complied. With beverages before them, they fell silent, staring into their cups.

When Carter's watch showed precisely eight o'clock, footsteps sounded in the outer corridor, and a Poetry Man dressed in a green robe appeared. A mist rose from his collar, obscuring his head, so only patches of his face could be glimpsed through the haze. One woman gave a shriek at his bizarre appearance, and the rest eyed each other, as if to see who would bolt first.

"Good evening," the poet said. Carter could not tell, either by his looks or his voice, if this was the same one who had tried to kill him. He noticed a chameleon, green as the poet's robe and tiny enough to be mistaken for a brooch, clinging to the man's left breast. "I will begin by asking you how you knew of tonight's gathering."

The group again exchanged hesitant glances.

"Let us not be stilled by fear," the Poetry Man said. "There are bridges to be crossed. Out with it, have your say, if you would find what you have lost."

"I . . ." one man stammered. "A voice in the wind told me of the meeting."

A sigh of relief circled the table. A woman spoke, "A bird in the Commons sang it to me."

"It was the rustling of a cottonwood," a man said.

So it went, one after the other, each glad to unburden himself of his strange vision.

"But what does it mean?" a gray-haired gentleman demanded.

"What is that which troubles you most?" the poet asked. "What is your pain? What deadly stains give your eyes their shadowed, hollow look? Unless you say, it can never be expunged."

"I am . . . a writer," a portly woman said. "There were always days when the muse would not come, but never like this. The words are . . . gone. I can't even remember how to fashion them! I read my past writings and they seem works of genius compared to the drivel I pen now."

"I was—am—a poet," a slender, dark-haired man said. "My volumes have been printed in Aylyrium and Ooz, and sold through fifty countries. But now I am dust dry."

A balding man, near tears, drew a flute from a case at his feet. It glistened dully in the candlelight. "I have entertained thousands," he said. "I have been numbered with the great. I play now and the notes sound shrill. At first I thought it was my ears, until I saw the faces of my audience. I have heard the same in players less-skilled than I. The music is leaving Evenmere."

"My eyes cannot see the colors of the palette," an artist said.

A man in drab brown stood. "I am unlike any of these. I am a scientist. I don't know what I am doing here, but my experiments have begun to fail, and I don't know why."

"Our first scientist," the Poetry Man said. "Yet others will follow, brought by the hollow tune of despair. First the tears of the artists, then of the artisans."

"What can be done?" someone asked.

"I know where your art has gone; I know where your talent lies," the poet said. "Would you dare to seek it out? You must pay a price to find the flames of your delight. Many men have sought it; braver souls than yours have tried. There they met the angels' laughter or the devil's deadly eyes. What say you? It may be more than you can bear."

"I cannot continue like this," the spectacled man said. "To live without heart . . ." He waved his hands helplessly in the air.

"Whatever bargain you propose," the portly woman said, "I will pay the price if I can."

"The price you pay is but your own," the poet said. "I am only a herald, sent to show you the fount of Creativity, for I have stood in the light and would share the flame. Are we agreed? If any fear, let him depart, the door I now disclose is not for the faint of heart."

As one, the desperate company agreed.

"Then behold," the Poetry Man turned his palms upward. "The silver door."

Light fountained coin-shiny from his hands. Carter stepped back from the spy-hole, dazzled by its purity. By the time he recovered enough to look again, a silver portal had risen before the poet, a door adorned only by the magnificent light streaming from behind it.

The Poetry Man strode to the door, turned the knob, and flung the portal wide.

The light was nearly unbearable; heavenly, beautiful, beckoning. Carter gave a cry of surprise, an exclamation echoed by everyone around the table, who clambered to their feet.

"Come," the poet said. "Come and greet Divine Inspiration."

The company asked no questions, but one by one, like moths to fire, shuffled toward the door.

Carter grasped the pommel of his sword until it bit against his flesh. He was neither artist nor poet, yet he too yearned to enter that portal, and for a long second stood paralyzed by his yearning.

Yet he was still the Master, and had faced the Poetry Men's temptation before. "No," he whispered, denying his own impulses. Then, realizing the true peril, he shouted through the wall, "No, wait!"

There was no immediate exit from the secret passage into the room. He sprinted down the corridor, consulting his maps for another way out, which he found in the hall outside the drawing room. Slipping from behind a portrait, he hurried to the door of the chamber. It was locked. He destroyed the mechanism with a single blow of his Lightning Sword, shattering wood and iron.

Silver light bathed the entire room. The last member of the party was stepping over the threshold, while the Poetry Man stood alongside, gesturing with a half-bow and a wave of his left hand.

"Stop!" Carter cried, but if the final victim heard, he did not respond as he slipped through the opening.

"Lord Anderson, a pleasant surprise," the poet said. "Have your eyes seen? Have you come to partake? I have been sent to make Master and servant obsolete, the fleet passing of history. The day of the house is done. Come and be as one with us."

The door beckoned, and Carter realized he could not resist its temptation long. The Poetry Man, face hidden by the mist, gestured toward the portal.

"Do not tarry, my friend. It will not remain open forever."

Carter fought the urge to enter the long silver corridor; he could see the party just ahead, all argent, making its way toward the source of the light. His right foot moved forward, unbidden. In another moment, he would cross the threshold.

Before the last traces of sanity could leave him, he reached deep within himself and saw, far in the darkness, the Word Which Gives Strength. It rose through the blackness; he felt its burning flames, and spoke it in a rush.

Sedhattee!

The room shook so violently the poet had to grip the doorway to keep his balance.

Power rushed through Carter. The appeal of the door diminished to bearable levels. He turned toward the Poetry Man, who retreated.

"My puissance is exhausted with the summoning of the door," the poet said. "I bow before the power of your Words. Yet, will you deny the spark that binds Existence? Do not, I say! Adore our good gift. Enter and embrace it! Only then will you see the strength of heaven's generosity."

But Carter moved rapidly toward his adversary, sword ready. "Release them."

"They are not mine to release or summon back. To retrieve them, you must go where they have gone."

Carter stepped closer, but the poet danced away and fled toward the door. Unable to reach his foe, Lord Anderson drew his pistol and fired, but the man ducked and the bullet missed his head by a fraction, chipping wood from the door frame. The poet vanished through the doorway.

Carter wanted to give chase, but he had to help the others. After momentary hesitation, he took a deep breath and crossed over the silver threshold.

All was argent within; the light permeated everything. Carter seemed to be standing within a boundless void, even the floor beneath him undetectable. The company was far ahead, making its way uncertainly through the brilliance.

He dashed after, thankful for the Word Which Gives Strength. But not even the Word could still his terror of what he might discover in this place. Whatever lay before him, its very presence, seen in its full majesty, would surely destroy him.

He reached the thin, spectacled man at the end of the line. Grasping him by the shoulder, he cried in a loud voice, made louder by the silence. "You must come back! You have been deceived. There is only death here."

The others turned and stared at him, silver as ghosts, and might have been specters for all they heeded him.

"You are wrong," the spectacled man said, brushing his hand aside. "It is life."

Carter watched helplessly as they continued on. Another portal gaped ahead, the source of the silver flame. Lord Anderson summoned the Word of Hope and spoke it into the silver void. If the silver room were an illusion, the Word would banish it.

Rahmurrim!

The whole world seemed to shake; the Word echoed as if across vast distances, and everyone except Carter tumbled to the ground. But when at last the reverberations died, the void remained unchanged, and the members of the company save one rose again and continued toward the portal.

The man who remained stood up and stumbled toward Carter. It was the scientist.

"What am I doing?" he asked. "I don't belong here! Please! I can't face what's in there!" He pointed toward the second portal through which the others were now passing, shouting in joy at what they saw.

Carter grimaced. This was no illusion. Rather, he waded in pools of reality far beyond anything he had ever experienced before. Despair swept over him. He could do no more for the others. He dared not enter the final doorway.

Grasping the scientist's shoulder, Lord Anderson led him back toward the entrance. Before they had gone a dozen paces, they heard the cries of joy behind them change slowly into choked, pathetic screams, going higher and higher until they ended with a whining cry.

"Don't look back!" Carter ordered. Together, they pulled one another to the doorway and stepped over the threshold into the drawing room, where they tumbled to the floor, their strength gone.

The silver light grew even brighter, forcing them to shield their eyes, as if every vestige of grandeur were pouring out of the doorway. The brilliance continued to grow, until Carter could see it from behind his eyelids.

He had to shut the door before the light consumed both of them. Rising, blind, he stumbled to the portal and tried to seize the knob, but each time it slipped, insubstantial, from his grasp.

Carter stepped back, knowing what he had to do, hoping he had the will to accomplish it. He struggled to bring the Word Which Seals to his mind. It rose gradually, reluctantly, but at last came tearing from his throat.

Nargoth!

The luminance vanished, and with it the door. Carter toppled to the floor, panting for breath.

The scientist crawled over to him, then glancing up, cried, "Deliver us!"

Carter looked around. At their places at the table, as if they had never left, sat the members of the company, their skin the color of milk, eyes wide, mouths open in soundless screams, every one of them dead.

Maneuvers

Doctor Benjamin Armilus whistled snatches of song from *The Green Kingdom Suite* as he made his way up the Long Stair, which he had been ascending for three hours through a gloom lit by sporadic lamps.

"I never mind a good climb," he said to the ebony beast at his heels. He had accustomed himself to its molten eyes and shifting form, but as a gentleman, found its pungent odor offensive. He had hoped Lord Anderson had destroyed it, but had discovered the creature standing beside his bed when he awoke from the dream dimension. Swallowing his disappointment, he had thereafter begun treating it as a favored pet.

"A wonderful avocation, climbing," he continued. Notwithstanding his bulk, the doctor was not fat. A proponent of Physical Culture, he trained daily, and his immensity disguised solid muscle. "Man against architecture. Splendid for the thighs." He whistled again.

He seldom traveled alone, yet this particular mission required a certain amount of privacy. His adherents, especially those who might not approve of his plan, did not need to know everything. Besides, the beast made his followers nervous; it tended to drool on them while they slept, like a chef anticipating a bite of soufflé.

The Long Stair led ever upward, its distant lamps like stars. Despite his aching legs, he did not pause to rest. He prided himself on his ability to prevail against long odds, to strive until the victory was won. By sheer willpower, he had never been sick a day of his life, and had overcome his opponents, both inside and outside the Society, by his own dogged persistence.

He glanced at the beast and murmured, "No pun intended."

Currently he was in high spirits, having finally returned to power after the years of exile resulting from his opposition to his predecessor's unimaginative and dangerous plans. One did not change the world overnight. His goals were more realistic. He intended to place an anarchist in the position of Master of Evenmere. Once that was done, other objectives could be met: the members of the Circle of Servants replaced, the ruling class expunged; the house could be fine-tuned. Of course, there were difficulties to be addressed—much had been written in *The Book of Lore* about the High House choosing its Masters—but he was confident he could work out the details.

Nighthammer was the one who had brought the doctor the first hint concerning the existence of the book, during the time when Armilus had been dean of the College of Poets. The blind poet, bearing information learned from Chant, had carried a scroll obtained in the marketplace at Breen, a tome written in the poetic forms common in ancient Histia. His curiosity piqued, Armilus had enlisted the aid of Erin Shoemate, lead professor of Poets' College. Although he knew a smattering of Histian, she had provided a proper translation, revealing the tale of twin volumes, *The Book of Lore* and *The Book of Verse,* the first a book of knowledge and power, the second a volume giving an understanding of poetry. The doctor had naturally been drawn to *The Book of Lore.* Working with Professor Shoemate, he had sought, off and on for the last five years, to find a way to break the seal on the chamber where the book was hidden. To that end, he had pieced together the crumbling parts of a cuneiform tablet from Moomuth Kethorvian, killed an aging professor at Nianar for a bit of yellowed foolscap, and stood one entire night listening to the echoes of velvet bats flitting across the galleries in Reddington Valley, until a single word came echoing across the canyons, sixty seconds before the first light of dawn.

He tightened his lips into a thin line. He had been making good progress. What he had failed to realize was that Erin

Shoemate had been equally obsessed with locating *The Book of Verse*. Obviously, she had succeeded.

The doctor had never wanted to involve Lord Anderson in the acquisition of *The Book of Lore*, but the coming of the poets had forced his hand. Unfortunately, the volume had not been straight-forward. More of a puzzle, really. Armilus had pored over it, seeking to wrest its secrets. Lesser men would have found it a hopeless task, yet in a matter of days he had determined the proper course.

He didn't understand everything, of course. There were still mysteries. He glanced at the ring on his right hand, a band gray as iron, with a black, oval stone at its center. It had come from a pouch sewn into the inside cover of the book. Following the volume's instructions, he had put it on. Since the ebony beast had appeared soon after, he suspected the two were related, a theory he wanted very much to test. He would have already done so except that the ring had melded itself into his skin and could no longer be removed.

He studied it a time, this bit of magic, and shook his head. According to his personal theory, Evenmere had been built ages before by an ancient, advanced civilization, and the seemingly mystical elements of the High House were merely remnants of their superior science, a conclusion he had reached after more than twenty years of first following and ultimately abandoning Ludwig Tieck's *Theory of Ordered Construction through Random Mechanics*. He had determined, despite the author's creditable mathematics, that the prerequisite "electromagnetic medium" could not have assembled the house by driving nails into boards. Besides, no one could quite get past the question of the stone gargoyles.

Every force, Armilus believed, whether used by the Master or the anarchists, arose from the same source. The unbelievable energies displayed by the Poetry Men were surely but another more potent and dangerous branch.

He stopped whistling when he neared the head of the stair. The carved, sliver-figure of a night-capped Man in the Moon stared at Armilus from the balustrades. Above the doctor stretched the seated form of a stained-glass angel, with flaming hair and midnight eyes, a golden sword in his right hand.

"Beautiful work, that." He held a high regard for fine art.

Within his quarters he possessed two original paintings by Opperpebb, a Minasian vase, and a silk kite from Toofrun of High Gable.

He took a doorway to the right. Apart from his quest, he had a secondary reason for coming this way, a bit of business requiring a slight detour. He passed through a winding corridor and down a short run of steps to an austere chamber with threadbare carpet and a bookcase containing the complete works of Saevius Nicanor. Removing one of the volumes, he pressed a secret latch, causing the bookcase to swing aside, revealing a comfortable room furnished in the Victorian manner. A single figure, dressed in a robe, sat upon a low sleigh bed.

"Who's there?" the man asked. "Who is it?"

"Good afternoon, Nighthammer," the doctor said. "It's Armilus."

The blind poet gave the slightest gasp. "Doctor. You frightened me. I . . . I expected no one until supper. This is an honor."

Nighthammer rose and bowed from the waist.

"I was passing through the area and wanted to inquire on your health."

"That . . . that is very good of you," Nighthammer replied, still standing. His nostrils curled, probably catching a whiff of the beast. "I am well. And highly grateful. Grateful you spirited me away, I mean, before the Master came looking. I suppose he would have come, wouldn't he? Even if Chant were against it? He said I wouldn't be arrested."

"The Lamp-lighter? I didn't know you were so close."

"Close? Oh, no." The poet spoke rapidly, his voice trembling. "Not friends by any means. But we have known one another many years. You know how it is in the world of spies. I mean, he was a pleasant enough fellow, but I never . . . I mean, he made me feel a fool. Said he always knew I was an anarchist. Do you think it true? How could he? He isn't one to lie."

"Why do you think I ordered you to reveal your affiliation?" Armilus rumbled. "Since they didn't realize we knew that *they* knew your real identity, your confession made the deception more believable. We've known for years."

Nighthammer drew back, brow furrowed. "You . . . knew? But . . . It—for years? All that time, all my service was in vain?"

"You served the cause. Be content with that."

"But your lordship must know how long I—"

"Do you always address members of the Brotherhood as lords? Have you forgotten we have no inherited rank?"

"I . . ." Nighthammer's face paled. His mouth worked but he said nothing.

"Sit down," Armilus ordered, with a grim smile.

The poet dropped to the bed as if shot.

"No inherited rank," Armilus repeated. "We are all equal, all agents of the Society, working together for our common cause."

Nighthammer contorted his lips, trying to smile. "That's true. We are each part of it—the Great Work."

"And in that work, who knows what service can do the most good?" Armilus asked. "Or what action can give one away? A nod of the head, a momentary glance. Which is why it is so important to keep you hidden from the White Circle Guard. I want them to gain nothing."

"As do I," Nighthammer said. "Not that I know much, of course. Only what I was told to say, and a little about the book and . . . and such."

"Especially about the origins of the book. Because you were there from the beginning, the Comte de Cheslet told you more than he should have, I think. He does that sometimes. A good man, but a bit too academic, too free with information."

"I am sure he was circumspect. I am sure—"

"I am certain he wasn't."

The two sat in silence, the poet a portrait of apprehension, Armilus considering an act of murder. The doctor carried a gun, though he had powerful hands and strangulation would do as well. It was quieter, more peaceful, like drowning a bird as he had once done as a child; one watches it writhe but hears no sound.

Still, conservation of resources was important, and it was a mistake to kill a staunch follower except in the gravest necessity. It cowed the others, leeching away their loyalty. With the party split and the Poetry Men a threat, Armilus could not spare any of his adherents.

The doctor glanced around the room. This was the reason he had come, to see how well the poet was kept and to ensure, either through death or security, that no one would interfere with his plan. A truly excellent plan.

"But a trifle fragile," he said aloud.

"What, Doctor?" Nighthammer asked.

Armilus stood. "Nothing, my friend. Nothing at all. Having satisfied myself of your comfort, I must be on my way."

The man tilted his head uncertainly. "So soon? I should have offered you tea. Would you like some? But of course you're very busy. Thank you for coming. It was too kind."

Armilus reached out and clapped the man on the shoulder. Nighthammer jerked, giving a half-shriek.

"Good day then," Armilus said. "Thank you for your excellent work."

"Yes. Thank you, my . . . thank you."

Armilus left the room. As he stopped to close the bookcase, he studied the poet, wishing he could be certain the man would not be found.

As he stood in indecision, the Black Beast leapt back into the room and sprang at Nighthammer's throat. A surprised scream filled the air.

By the time the doctor reached the bed it was too late. The animal had been efficient. Armilus found he was not, after all, displeased, except by the fact that the creature had apparently reacted to his thoughts.

"The price of ambivalence, I suppose," he said, warily patting the beast on the head. "One should be careful what one wishes for."

As Chant strolled across the Yard carrying his ladder, he paused beside the stone well to admire the evening skyline. The sinking sun pierced the clouds massed on the western horizon, turning them pink and orange and royal blue, lending them the semblance of the faces of gods gazing over the rooftops of Evenmere, their expressions eager and evil and dreadful and good. A sudden shiver ran along his back; he found he had no poem to match their majesty.

His eyes still fixed skyward, he took the worn path leading to the white gate hidden behind the grape arbor. A score of spar-

rows fled from beneath the vines and soared over the eaves. Withdrawing his keys, Chant unlocked the gate and slipped outside the
Yard. Following the cobblestone path that skirted the low wall, he
made his way to the solitary lamppost. Positioning his ladder, he
ascended to perform his duty.

He had just lifted the globe and struck a match, when he
noticed a figure out of the corner of one eye, coming along the low
wall surrounding the Yard. The stranger's garb, orange down to his
hat, cloak, and boots, gave him the appearance of a mountebank.
He squatted to pluck a long-stemmed blade of grass from among
the bricks, and chewed on its end.

"Good evening," Chant said, glancing around uneasily to
see if the fellow had companions. The lamppost stood beyond the
grounds of Evenmere, in the everyday world where colorfully-
dressed men were seldom seen.

"Greetings, Lamp-lighter," the man replied, his voice soft
and pleasant. His nose was crooked, his eyes fanatically bright beneath wire-rimmed spectacles. Wisps of thin smoke rose from under his collar. "I saw you admiring the clouds. Spectacular, aren't
they?" As he spoke, minute sparks flitted off his tongue.

"Remarkably so." With studied care, his eyes fixed on the
newcomer, Chant finished lighting the lamp and descended the ladder, casually placing his left hand close to the pistol in his coat.

"When did you first volunteer for your duties?" the stranger
asked. "When were you first drawn to the fascination of the
flame?"

"You are mistaken," Chant said. "I did not seek my position, but was appointed. *Surprised by joy, impatient as the wind—*"
The Lamp-lighter broke off, for to his astonishment tongues of fire
came from his own mouth, accompanying his verse.

"There now, do you see?" the man said, chuckling. He
reached into his pocket and withdrew a red salamander, which
climbed onto his shoulder. "The flames refute your denial. You
have heard it, the love of fire, the kindled desire for the spark, the
heart of light engulfing the dark."

Chant retreated a pace. "Who are you?"

"Poetry and flame. How alike they are, how bright the fire
of phrases burn. You know, who have seen it within your heart."

"I have seen it," Chant admitted.

"And it has filled you with longing. You, who have lit the suns, playing fast and loose with Promethean fire. Like the gods. Chant, Lamp-lighter, Light-bringer. Yet, though long-lived, you are mortal. Have you sought the eternal? Do you hear its name, whispered by the mumbly-men, drifting down the rainbows, penned within a mother's gentle tears?"

Looking at the stranger's face, Chant saw, instead of eyes, nose, and mouth, flaming stars such as he had but dreamt of. He gave a gasp as every one of his longings rushed upon him: for his departed father and mother; for a lost love who had hanged herself long ago beneath a beam at Totman Chapel; for other, deeper desires that had haunted him throughout his life, unrequited cravings found on lonely nights beside dim flames, yearnings summoned by the soft melody of a viola, or a battle paean sung *a cappella*.

"Who are you?" Chant asked again, and his voice was aflame now, streaming out in burning daggers.

The Poetry Man's words were likewise tipped in blue fire. "My name is unimportant, only my mission matters. I wield energies that formed and molded the world. Leave this architectural panoply, come with me to lands strange beyond desire."

"No," Chant said, shaking his head heavily. "What you offer is too grand." He drew back, blinded by the flame of his own words.

"It is not," the other said. "I have seen the faces of the gods and yet I live."

With a bound, the Poetry Man rushed toward the unlocked gate. Chant reacted instantly, placing himself between the intruder and his goal. They faced one another, scarcely four feet between them. Chant drew his pistol.

The Poetry Man laughed. "Put away your petty toys. Are we boys, to play these childish games? I seek to bring the joy of flame into the chambers of your lord."

"No." Chant backed toward the gate.

The Poetry Man followed. Chant fired. The bullet came flaming from the barrel, a white-hot bolt that incinerated before it reached its target.

The intruder rushed forward, seizing Chant, and beneath his grasp, white heat scorched the Lamp-lighter's arms. Chant pulled free, leapt to the gate and fled inside, drawing it shut behind him.

He secured the lock just before the Poetry Man reached it. The intruder tore at the gate, vainly attempting to pry it open.

"You cannot pass!" Chant cried. "Go back where you came." Though the low wall seemed a barrier even a child could surmount, so long as the gate remained fastened the wards of the house prevented any from entering.

"Oh no, friend! I'll not leave this portal until it is tested in fire."

The flame from the Poetry Man's mouth now flowed continuously. It flickered around the grass, igniting it. The fire ran along the ground with fantastic speed, licking at the low wall and lapping against the gate. Still, the gate did not burn.

The wildfire spread toward the trees surrounding the house. The blaze ran up the first trunk, an ancient oak; the leaves caught all at once; the hoary titan burst into flame. The fire spread from bough to bough.

The coattails of the Poetry Man caught next, the threads burning, yet he stood unmoved. "Come in!" he cried, gesturing wildly like a man standing in the waves of a sea. "Come in! It's fine."

Chant retreated, hurrying from the arbor so he could see over the low wall. The whole woodland beyond the house was going up in a huge conflagration. The Poetry Man blazed, but stood laughing, unharmed.

Chant drew close to the wall. The fire was so hot it melted the lamppost, which bent over to kiss the scorched earth, but no heat crossed the barrier.

The storm raged on, and at its center, where the poet stood, a white gash appeared, as if the flame were hot enough to scorch Existence itself, peeling it back like a wrinkling picture on canvas.

The intruder screamed, a combination of ecstasy and terror, as the white heat blotted out his form, leaving the gash hanging suspended a foot off the ground, a blank hole into emptiness.

Chant stood gaping as the fire spread around the house, nursing burned arms that he, who had been given mastery over fire, had thought no flame could scorch. If the poet had reached the Yard, he would have surely destroyed the Inner Chambers.

Doctor Armilus, rehearsing phrases from a pocket-book on the Histian language to make use of the time, passed over wooden floorboards through a wide corridor like a vast banquet hall. Stepping through a double-doorway, he found himself in a courtyard beneath a midnight sky. A group of towers stretched above him, the stars of the Milky Way hanging like trinkets over them. The half-moon washed the flagstones in white.

After some searching, he found the proper door. Though he prided himself on his ability to pick a lock, he knew that nothing save the single gold key he carried, a duplicate of the one used by Enoch the Windkeep, could gain entrance. Its theft had cost the lives of two of the three anarchists who had removed it from a chalcedony box in the chambers of the Locksmith of Loft. The beast beside the doctor whined softly as he inserted the key. The lock opened with a soft click and Armilus smiled in grim satisfaction.

He made his way up a sweeping stair. The creature bounded behind him, hissing softly like grease on a hot pan, taking the steps two at a time. Armilus searched the rooms, one after another, until he came to the chamber of the Eternity Clock, whose enormous face looked out from one wall. The room itself appeared utterly mundane; a bed stood beside the clock; sparse decorations hung on the wall; a few chairs lay about.

"Lovely," he said. "Simply lovely."

The hands of the clock were set at three seconds after 11:50, but the second hand did not appear to move. From his reading of *The Book of Lore*, he knew this to be an illusion; the hands did progress, but too slowly to be seen. The book claimed the clock was the mechanism that controlled time.

He stroked the hands, speculating with vast delight on the paradox that might occur if he moved the time backward the barest fraction. He applied light pressure against the second hand, but it remained steadfast even as the book had foretold, beyond the power of mortals to budge. He wished he could spend a few hours experimenting with it.

"But," he observed wryly to the beast, "I fear I lack the time."

He drew a prismatic vial from his black bag, held it carefully beneath the second hand, and unstoppered it.

A sucking arose from within the bottle, barely audible at first, but growing in intensity, until its resonance forced him to clutch the container with both hands. Even then, his entire bulk shook from the vibrations. He planted his feet wide, struggling to hold the vial in place. The suction grew; he felt the skin of his jowls being pulled downward. The force became nearly unbearable; the second hand trembled. He bent his strength of will toward keeping the container in position.

Just when he thought he could bear no more, a flash of golden light passed from the second hand into the vial. With a click that seemed to shake the entire house, the clock moved forward one second.

Armilus stoppered the container and the vacuum ceased. Triumph flushed his heavy face. Eyes shining, he retrieved his bowler hat, which had tumbled to the floor during the struggle. As he looked at the vial, however, glistening golden with the captured time, his expression grew somber. Whatever the true nature of the Eternity Clock, he had just stolen a fragment from it. If, as some said, it marked the amount of time remaining until the end of the universe, millions of people might never have time to be born.

"Yet one must break eggs," he muttered to the beast. He gave a rueful smile, feeling suddenly like a god.

Summoning and dealing with the police in the aftermath of the murders in the library had made Lord Anderson late entering the dream dimension, but he was soon hurrying through the gray mist of the Long Corridor beside the Green Door leading into the Inner Chambers. As he passed down the men's corridor and the butler's corridor from the back of the house to the transverse corridor, he glanced out the narrow window alongside the door leading into the Yard, halted in disbelief, and rushed into the twilight to face the charred countryside and the white gash hanging surreal in the evening light beside the melted lamppost. A half-sob escaped him. He drew a deep breath and slumped onto a bench beside the well, an empty throbbing in his chest. The charring continued to the horizon, leaving the few standing trees in scarecrow ruin.

When he spoke the Word Which Brings Aid, he expected Mr. Hope to appear, but after several moments, the back door opened and Sarah stepped out, dressed in blue silk.

"Carter?"

He rushed forward and hugged her fiercely, speaking in a hoarse whisper, "I am glad it was you. Very glad. Are you and Jason all right?"

"We are both fine, except for worrying about you. We have heard strange reports."

"I've had a dreadful time of it. And now, seeing this . . . Father and I used to ride our horses through that wood. I was afraid something had happened to you. It would be more than I could bear."

She held him close, stroking the back of his hair with her hand. "I know. We're sick at heart. How little significance we give to place until it is gone." She glanced down at her garments. "This isn't what I was wearing. I don't even own a dress like this."

"It has to do with your self-image in the dream-world."

Sarah spread the skirt to study the material. "It's rather fetching. Perhaps I'll have one made."

Carter released her and sat down on the bench beside the well. "Tell me the whole story."

Sarah did so, ending with, "Chant is as disconcerted as I've ever seen him. Captain Nunth brought a contingent of the Fireman of Ooz, but the flames were spent by the time they arrived. Mr. Hope sent riders at dawn, who reported the devastation ends four miles down the road. Nunth was baffled both by the speed with which it consumed the trees, and the way it died instead of contin-uing through the forest, as if it worked with purpose. The poet could not penetrate into the Inner Chambers, but at least three of his fellows have been sighted within the house, often accompanied by anarchists; they melt away before our troops arrive." She glanced at the twisted lamppost and said bleakly, "No humor in-tended. If they unleash such flames inside Evenmere . . ."

She took his hand. "Tell me what has been happening to you."

When he had finished, she said, "Oh, Carter, how horrible! Seeing your mother like that!"

"Lady Order said the poets would strike at the Circle of Servants," Carter said. "I wonder how she knew?"

"Chant," Sarah said, placing her hand over her mouth.

"He was clearly the target. You must have Major Glis dispatch men to accompany both him and Enoch on their rounds. We must also station guards at once at Shadow Hall, the Tower of Astronomy, the Quadrangle of Angles, all the rest of the Circle. And tell Mr. Hope to send men to make a thorough search of the College of Poets. Where are Chant and Enoch now?"

"Chant left for Keedin this morning, and Enoch has gone to wind the Hundred Years Clock."

"The Clock! I forgot about it. Of all the times for him to be so far away."

"I know, but Mr. Hope has pored over the records; there isn't any question of Enoch not going. Disaster will follow unless the clock is wound."

"Enoch told us as much already," Carter said, suddenly overwhelmed. "A fine use of Hope's time when he should be seeking information on the poets."

Sarah's eyes flashed. "Don't get irritable with me, love. I sharpen my tongue each night with a file. You haven't a prayer."

A bolt of anger ran through Lord Anderson, but it vanished when she gave him a smile.

"Oh, bother!" he cried. "It isn't you I'm frustrated with. Nor William. I'm sure you're as worn as I."

"Worn but not filed down."

"It's just . . . my course is clear; and it isn't what I want. I have to find Erin Shoemate and *The Book of Verse*. I believe she is the key to the poets' might. Her diary said she journeyed first to Jossing, then to the Tower of Astronomy. With Jossing in ruins, I must seek the Grand Astronomer, to see if he knows where she went. But I want to be here with my son."

She laid her palm against his face. "There is no help for it. And we even lack verse to comfort us. When last I went to my books, I found the lines dissonant. When I tried to play the flute the tones were garbled and hideous. Chant is the same. He suspects the poetry is being siphoned away and used as raw power."

"Poetry as a weapon? It sounds ludicrous. And yet . . . He paused, considering. "Lady Order said the poets were tapping into

Chaos, but I think that is only her perception, based on the results of their actions being so chaotic. The power I have witnessed is fundamental, elemental force, not unlike the Words of Power or the energy of the Cornerstone."

"Words have strength," Sarah said. "Civilization is built upon them. Chant spoke of facing what he called Immortal Fire, the word *fire* given physical form, the essence of flame."

"Whatever it is, it is too terrible to be controlled." Carter repressed a shudder. "I'll speak to Jonathan of this. Being a master bard, he may have some insight."

"You seem to trust this Storyteller," she said. "We have all heard of him; but how do you know he is who he says? It seems suspicious, his attaching himself to you at this time."

"His first appearance probably saved my life."

"A ruse perhaps, to set you off your guard."

"Have you been spending too much time with Chant? His cynicism is rubbing off."

Sarah blushed. "Is it? Or is it just the constant intrigues of the house? If I suspect conspiracies, it is because there is always one going on at some level or other. You would not believe what the upstairs maid did yesterday to undercut the hall boy."

For the first time that evening, Carter laughed. "I wish that were the worst of our troubles."

"You find it amusing; I threatened to send her to debtors' prison. Told her Major Glis would escort her personally. I haven't time for such nonsense."

"We haven't any debtors' prisons."

"She doesn't know that. It's in all the romances."

"You always cheer me," he said, kissing her cheek and rising. "You needn't worry about Storyteller, or I am no judge of men. I should look at that gash."

"Must you? It frightens me."

"You'd best stay in the Yard."

He passed beneath the grape arbor and unlocked the white gate. The grass up to the fence line was black ash that powdered on his boots as he approached the mysterious gap. The white void hung in the air, a two-dimensional hole in the world, obscuring the sky behind it. He walked around it. It appeared exactly the same from the back. He shivered.

"Can you give me a tree branch?"

Sarah found one lying on the ground and handed it over the low wall. He used it to prod the opening. The part of the limb that crossed into the gash disappeared, but returned whole when Carter withdrew it. He pitched it into the blankness and it vanished without a sound. He disregarded the impulse to thrust in his face.

He realized just how exhausted his day's battle had left him when he tried to summon the Word Which Seals. It came only with the greatest effort, but finally appeared in his mind, floating in darkness, the letters aflame. When he spoke it, it echoed over the distant hills. The air quivered expectantly; the rent began to close, the blankness shrinking upon itself. Within moments, all trace was gone, leaving only scorched earth and the warped lamppost.

"Much better," he said, staggering from his effort. "I seem to be using the Word Which Seals too much lately, as if the universe were springing leaks."

He and Sarah made the rounds of the house together that night. When at last the lamp drifted from the dresser to the night stand, Carter held his wife in a long farewell.

"I wish I had known I could reach you through dream during our early years," he said. "There were so many nights when I longed to see your face."

"Much of your experience as Master has been trial and error. It seems a chancy way to run the universe."

"We live a chancy existence."

"A burden shared is a burden halved," Sarah said. "A scientific fact, like osmosis and steam engines."

They kissed and Carter ordered their awakening.

Lord Anderson awoke back in his room in Aylyrium. He groaned, ran his hands over his eyes, and rose to bathe and dress. Trudging wearily down to breakfast, he threw himself into a chair across from Storyteller, who sat eating strips of an orange.

"You have had a bad time of it," Jonathan said, in a voice that was not a question. "Is your Lamp-lighter all right?"

Carter gaped. "How could you possibly know about that?"

"The walls of Evenmere have ears, Master Anderson."

Carter studied his companion, wondering just how far his abilities went. He wished he knew more about the man. When the minstrel gave no further explanation, Lord Anderson said, "On top of everything else, I am beginning to feel—I don't know. Not exactly weary. Thin. Stretched. My mind seems fogged. In my previous experiences, I always woke refreshed from the dream world. But the last few days . . . I don't know how much longer I can continue these nightly excursions. Some sort of cumulative effect, I suppose."

As they ate, Carter related all that had occurred.

"We have too many mysteries," Jonathan said, frowning down at his plate. "I have never heard of the tower where you saw Professor Shoemate, just as I had never heard of this *Book of Lore* you discovered."

"You can hardly be blamed for that. Evenmere is too large for anyone to know everything about it."

"You misunderstand me." The minstrel's brow was unusually furrowed. "Storyteller has been in this house for centuries. Over the ages, I have learned many things, some small, some great. The tower I might have overlooked, though it seems strange not to have even heard the rumor of it, but this book is too important to have escaped my notice. There are many in Evenmere who know me. I will put out the word and see if we can learn more about the book and tower."

"Good. Have you noticed any change in your own abilities, as far as the draining away of poetry, writing, and music?"

"I have not. Perhaps my talents are so small there is little to lose." He laughed, then grew grim. "Each of these things you mention, even music, stems from the love of story. Everything grows from it. It is the root that raises us above the animals. The dog and the cat tell no tales; they do not sit before the fire and speak of the old days. If these poets grow strong enough, I too may fail. I should like to continue on with you."

Carter brightened. "I would be greatly pleased. You will save me the dreariness of traveling alone. But I need to leave at once."

"My bags are always packed, Master Anderson, for I carry their contents on my own two shoulders."

The companions were soon trudging down a red corridor leading away from the university. They journeyed that day through Aylyrium, and at Jonathan's suggestion stopped for the evening at Brown Study, a series of chambers entered through a plain, four-panel door, filled with leather chairs, oak beams, and fireplaces with massive inglenooks. Most of the rooms were deserted, but a servant soon appeared, a thin fellow with a thatch of gray hair sticking almost straight up, dressed in a red coatee with white trim, epaulets, and a double row of brass buttons down the front.

"Steward Moonslack at your service," the man declared, giving a half bow. "Welcome to Brown Study. If you like, my wife can prepare your dinner."

"Thank you," Carter said. "That would be most agreeable. The generosity of Brown Study is legendary."

"It is due to the beneficence of Father Brown," Moonslack replied in a bored monotone, as if reading the lines. "These chambers were deeded to his family seven centuries ago by a house-grant from the Aylyrium Polenuein Council. A bit of a traveler, he was known for his kindness, and dying without heir, set aside a trust to ensure sojourners should always be well treated, as is only good and proper."

"Yet you do not truly think so," Jonathan said.

Moonslack's long face contracted in surprise. "I said nothing of the sort, sir."

"No, you did not."

Moonslack shrugged and rubbed his hand over his chin in what Carter soon realized was an habitual gesture, as if he searched for a missing goatee. "It ain't always worked out the way the father thought it would. He was smart enough to make sure no one remains more than two days, but we get a lot of unsavory characters, ne'er-do-wells rather than gentlemen like yourselves." He gave Storyteller's patchwork coat a look of obvious disfavor.

"Then you are a fortunate man," Jonathan said, "for perhaps you have entertained angels unaware."

"Them stories sound good to children, but my wife and I ain't seen no angels hereabouts. And don't believe people are grateful. They take plenty and give little."

The man halted, perhaps wondering if he had said too much. "But that ain't your concern nor mine, gentlemen. Dinner will be served in the upstairs drawing room at six o'clock sharp. If you will follow me, I'll show the way."

The drawing room, like the rest of Brown Study, was furnished with the sort of careless bachelor comfort that made Carter wish he liked smoking a pipe. The meal, a simple fare of stewed rabbit served on a small table in one corner, was overdone and under-seasoned, but neither of the travelers complained to their dour host.

As Moonslack poured the after-dinner coffee, Jonathan said, "If you and your wife would like, I would repay your kindness with a tale or two. I have a small gift that way."

"We usually go to bed early," Moonslack said.

"As you wish. Should you change your mind, I will be right here."

As soon as Moonslack exited, Lord Anderson said, "Your offer is more than he deserves. What a sour fellow! If his master were living, he would be dismissed from service. Have you ever been here before? He obviously doesn't know you."

"Father Brown was still alive the last time I came, almost twenty years ago."

Storyteller took a sip of coffee from a cracked china teacup and began to sing a low, melodious tune, so somber and sweet, with such beauty and power that the whole chamber seemed to bend forward to listen, the walls resonating with his deepest tones. Carter sat entranced. After a time, as if in answer, Moonslack returned, followed by a heavy woman with tattered hair and haunted eyes. They sat together on a low couch across from the travelers.

When Jonathan finished, the woman said, "That was just lovely."

The minstrel gave a bow of his head, and Moonslack said, "This is m'wife, Rosemary."

"A pleasure," Jonathan grinned. "Let me see if I can draw a story or two from my hat."

He actually told three tales. The first concerned a cat born with only three legs. The other kittens made sport of it. The kitten did not become a hero in the end, as Carter expected, but died instead, slain by a badger, and despite the other kittens' guilt at their treatment of it, only the mother cat mourned for long.

The second story was of a man who had but a single daughter, who ran away. The father waited, looking out the window, year after year for her return, but she never came back.

Finally, Jonathan said, "There was once a young man whose father was very rich and who drank too much and was cruel beyond measure to his son. And there was another lad about the same age, who was taunted by his classmates, who called him slow and dim-witted. But his parents loved him with all their hearts, and though poor, tried to give him the best they had.

"One day, when the poor boy was fourteen, he met the rich man's son, who saw the lad as a target for the cruelty his father had taught him. The poor boy didn't know about brutality, for he had never seen it, and he went trusting with the rich boy. When the rich boy, who was taller and stronger, threw the poor child onto the ground and would have beaten him, the lad resisted. But the rich boy did not know the depth of the anger within him. He killed the weaker boy and left his body for the wolves of the Upper Stairs."

To Carter, the tales seemed strangely disjointed, yet when he glanced at the couple, he saw Moonslack glowering, his face stricken, and Rosemary silently weeping, her hands over her eyes.

"That's a damned fool tale," Moonslack said, lurching to his feet. "I thought you a minstrel."

"When the child died," Jonathan continued, "you were working. You couldn't have been there."

Sheer hatred shone from the man's eyes. But abruptly, beneath Jonathan's calm gaze, his features crumbled. "I should have been!" he cried. "I should have known!" He dropped, weeping, back onto the couch. "My David was innocent, and he beat him to death like an animal!"

"Moonslack," the woman said, lifting her hands to her husband. He fell into her arms; they clutched one another, desperately weeping.

"If your son were here in this room," Storyteller told the woman, "he would tell you that he forgave you long ago for the argument you had the day he left, for he loved you very much. You have longed for justice against the one who killed him, thinking he escaped. It isn't so. David's murderer has faced injustice his entire life. It follows like a wolf, rending his heart. If you would be healed, you must forgive both yourself and him."

"Oh, that is a hard saying!" Rosemary cried.

"Only because you can't see the pain within your son's killer, so deep he doesn't even know it exists."

For several long moments, the couple wept, then clutching one another, rose to go. But the woman turned back at the door, rushed to Jonathan, and kissed his hand, whispering, "In all this time he ain't once cried."

When they were gone, Carter wiped his own eyes with the back of his coat sleeve. Finding his voice, he said hoarsely, "You came here specifically for this."

"It is the work of the Storyteller, who sees into the heart."

"You have shamed me," Carter said. "When I met Moonslack I judged him rude, uncivil. How hastily I dismissed him."

"Sometimes my stories are intended for more than one hearer."

"Will they recover?"

"Perhaps they will, if they take my words to heart. If not . . ." Jonathan lifted his hands in a shrug. "It is not my task to *make* anyone do anything, Master Anderson. But if they do, Moonslack will become the good steward he once was, and this place will return to the refuge it was intended to be, instead of a home for bitterness. Those who stay here will be touched by Moonslack's spirit, and will carry its goodness into every corner of Evenmere. A small healing, spread through many rooms, it will serve the house and the Balance."

But when Carter entered the land of slumber that night, he could not take his mind from Moonslack, who had not been with his son when the child needed him. The murder was not his fault, yet the boy had still died.

Was Storyteller trying to warn him about Jason? And how many more nights could he continue entering the dream world before his strength was gone? Something, he knew, would have to give.

The Astronomy Tower

Within the attic of Jormungand, Jonathan paused to sip water from a flask. The dinosaur shifted his weight uneasily on the creaking boards.

"You have a way with words," Jormungand said. "You tell a pretty tale, but you are a liar. I am the Last Dinosaur, who sees the comings and goings of the house. I observe the human mites in their petty struggles; in all of Evenmere, only I possess the gift of far-seeing. Yet, by your own admission you told Anderson that you knew of the poet's assault on the Lamp-lighter. Impossible!"

"I saw it because I was there."

"Oh ho! So now you're a ball, bouncing from Aylyrium to the Inner Chambers and back in a single night. You do Father Christmas proud."

"Storyteller never lies."

Jormungand studied the dark, unwavering face. "Even if your tale is true, you relate nothing new. I thought you would be amusing. Why, even Anderson is more entertaining! It's nearly lunchtime, the most important meal of the day, and if you can't sing a song or serve up a bawdy story, I will devour you. Sautéed, I think. I prefer mine well-done."

The dinosaur's fetid breath blew against Storyteller's face, but Jonathan looked straight into those ancient, bloodshot eyes. "There you sit, your great big self and your hungry ol' eyes, facing an old man who has walked the halls of this house since before you were imprisoned. You were made to be as you are, all appetite and no regret. If I am to die in this attic, that will be as it will be; but I think you should listen to the rest of my story."

Jormungand moved his massive head nearer and sniffed Storyteller, displaying jagged teeth and red gums. Saliva dripped from his jaws to the floor. "Why should I?"

"Because you are curious, and that isn't like you. Not like you at all. Curiosity is not one of your traits; it isn't lizardy, one might say. Yet here you are, curious as a kitten with a ball of string. The reason why is because the story isn't finished but is still unfolding, and even you don't know how it will end. And you wonder how Storyteller knows so much of it."

"I have watched you for ages, rambling here and there, but there is more to you than I suspected," the dinosaur rumbled. "Who are you? What do you want from me? Why must you tell me this tale? What do you get out of it?"

Jonathan grinned. "You have asked more than three questions. According to your own rules, I have the right to eat *you*. But never mind. Never mind. I tell you this tale because storytelling is part of ritual, and this is the time and place for that, here in his attic on this particular day. The tale must be told, because that too is part of the unfinished story, and everything will be made clear in the end. Storyteller sees to the heart, and though you have already witnessed the circumstances unfold, you haven't understood Lord Anderson's fear for his son, or Doctor Armilus' callousness, or the mad desires of the poets."

"What do I care for the braying of sheep?" Jormungand asked. "You think your little stories matter? I tell you what touches the human heart—pain scores the mortal soul; fear gives meaning to dull lives; death ends all in futility. I am the Great Hero, the lone voice crying from my prison, giving the world the One Great Truth, that existence is futile and without plan. Your stories accomplish *nothing*! Lift the human spirit today and it is trampled into the muck tomorrow. Flesh and bone give way to earth, and all the past is forgotten."

Jormungand blew hot flames into the depths of the attic, lighting its recesses for miles. The heat of the blast drew beads of sweat from Jonathan's brow.

But Storyteller gave a brave smile. "That's right, old lizard, you have your place, and it is a grand one, an attic kingdom filled with the despair of the whole world. But like many of those who spend all their time alone, you make too much of it."

"My *place*?" Jormungand roared, sending the boards shaking. "My place? There *is* no place but mine. *I* am the quintessential Entity. I am what is important. What are you? An artist! A poet! A wandering tramp!"

"That's right. That's right. But words, if they are true and strong, if they speak to the soul, have power to survive the ages."

Jormungand growled, clearly disliking the course of the conversation. He, who usually cowed his visitors through fear or death, was unused to debate. "Human souls! Caterpillar hearts! And you speak of humanity's tiny span of existence as *ages*? That's the kind of humor I like. Go on with your story and be done with it. I was in a bad mood when you arrived, and you've done nothing but annoy me. I doubt you will survive the evening."

"Maybe I won't," Jonathan replied, staring at the dinosaur with his strange, dark eyes. "Curiosity isn't one of your traits; but murder, now, that surely is. Where were we? Ah, yes, we return to Master Anderson, in his journey to North Lowing . . ."

The lantern flame danced. Jormungand's eyes flashed. The dust lay thick on the attic floor.

By noon of the next day Carter and Jonathan Bartholomew entered Tucks Hall, a wide chamber stretching mile after mile across the border between Aylyrium and North Lowing. A marble channel, half a mile wide, ran down its center, the great Fable River flowing from the Sidereal Sea. Hand-stamped tin tile adorned the ceiling, and square shafts, ducts sealed in winter, allowed light and rain to enter. Multicolored mosaic floor tile depicted the history of the river—battles fought, children born along its banks, treaties signed beside its slow, serene waters. Squat trees with ivory bark and lime-pale leaves rose in ordered rows from patches of bare earth, forming umbrella canopies. White ivy lined the banks. Pale frogs, small as a little finger, squatted beneath the twining branches. Occasionally members of the Guild of Dusters and Burnishers, dressed in their dark blue uniforms and caps, scrubbed their way past.

The travelers journeyed down the bank until long after noon, when they reached an ornate bridge too narrow for two to walk abreast, with iron railings sculpted into tiny leaves of ivy. They crossed above the whispering waters to the center of the stream, where the bridge widened to accommodate a guard station.

A sentry appeared, wearing the traditional *heeki* of North Lowing, a white undertunic wrapped in black strips of cloth that lent him the appearance of a mummy, with a chain-mail jerkin over all. His beard was trimmed and oiled to a point; a side-arm hung from his waist. He looked over the travelers with eyes dipped in suspicion.

"Who wishes to enter North Lowing?"

"The Master of the house," Carter said, "and Jonathan Bartholomew, its minstrel."

The guard's eyes widened slightly, but he gave Carter's Lightning Sword and Tawny Mantle a careful scrutiny, and required Lord Anderson to show his Ring of Office before saying, "Very well, my lords. Pray pass, but mind the laws of the land, which are posted along the way."

Jonathan reached into his ragged jacket and produced a slender book with a vellum binding. "Here, my friend. This is for you."

"What is it?" The man lifted his nostrils slightly, as if Storyteller were offering poison or a bribe.

"Why, it is a book, a tiny thing read in an hour," Jonathan said. "I bought it for you in Keedin two months ago."

The man took the book with a disbelieving stare. "For me?" he said gruffly. "You don't even know me."

"That's true, Nimikos," Storyteller said, and the two departed, leaving the man standing in the middle of the bridge staring after them, holding the book as if it were a dead fish.

Carter gave his companion a questioning glance.

"It will heal his heart," the minstrel explained.

"I rather wish I had your job."

Jonathan grinned and began to whistle.

The northern half of North Lowing is called the Golden Steppes, an indoor wilderness with some of the largest chambers in Evenmere. Golden oaks, yellow and sultry in the half-light, grow beneath the ceiling shafts; the wood floors curve to form hills and canyons. Deer, hares, raccoons, even bears and wolves, make their dens in false caves or on ground left open to the earth.

With each step the travelers took, the character of the land seemed to change, so that one moment they passed paneled friezes with ethereal flowers, and bay windows inlaid with leaded glass, and the next, gazed up from deep shadows at tall obelisks forming black mesas. They stopped for the night in an alcove of oak paneling, with carved bronze warriors from mythic Gost inset in the wood.

Following a supper warmed beside the small hearth, Carter, anxious to reach the Inner Chambers before Jason's bedtime, climbed into his bedroll on the polished boards and slipped into dream. He spent a lonely vigil guarding the empty halls until midnight, when he used the Word Which Brings Aid to summon Sarah. The two of them passed the rest of the night talking beside Jason's bed. When she remarked how tired he looked, Carter did not admit how utterly worn he felt, or how he feared being unable to continue his nightly watch.

He woke the next morning tattered and chilled and feverish, scarcely able to focus his thoughts, and he and Jonathan were on the road an hour before his mind cleared enough for coherent conversation. He feared he might become lost if he continued his treks into the land of slumber, unable to wake from the world of dream, leaving his body a husk and Evenmere without a Master.

No sooner was he feeling better, than a passing burnisher gave the travelers more bad news. North Lowing was astir with the news of the death of the Smith of Welkin Well, another of the Circle of Servants, slain by a Poetry Man while traveling through Fiffing. His apprentice had taken over his duties, but Carter had known the Smith, and the loss of his wisdom and experience was a terrible blow. Lady Order had clearly been correct: the poets were targeting the Servants' Circle, seeking to undermine the whole foundation of the house. But for what purpose? To replace it with some system of their own? Or did they believe that doing so would somehow help them spread their strange doctrine?

Mid-morning brought them to The Desolation. When Carter had first returned from exile, the anarchists had opened the Door of Endless Dark, releasing the Black River, which had seeped into North Lowing, cutting a wide swathe through several miles of the house. Carter had sealed the Darkness Door and the Black River had dissipated, leaving nothing but a smooth channel.

"Are you all right, Master Anderson?" Jonathan asked.

Carter laughed bitterly. "I hate coming here. This is just one more result of my stealing the Master Keys. The enormity of what I did, out of envy and petulance . . ."

"You were not the first to fight in a war without knowing you were a soldier."

"Small comfort, that."

"To be sure, but the battle is always too grand for either the infantryman or the great general to completely comprehend. You think because the anarchists used such a small thing as your jealousy, the consequences should not have been so terrible. But there is no small jealousy, no tiny envy. The world turns on acts of nature and acts of the heart. Thousands can die in an earthquake; thousands can perish from the actions of one person. Nothing is small. Your enemies have been called renegades, anarchists, Architectural Reformers, The Society for the Greater Good, the Extremists, the Fundamentalists—a hundred other names, but always the same danger—for every person, in his own way, is both anarchist and agent of the law. Every Master, in some fashion, has faced attacks upon the Balance. Rooms have changed, changing worlds, and still the Masters struggle on. The battle is ceaseless, the true enemy, Entropy, irresistible. Sooner or later, it will prevail."

"You make it sound hopeless."

"It is not, Master Anderson. It is full of hope. It is hope itself, for each minute of existence carved out of nothingness is a triumph for life. This house, its great walls and golden halls, will someday fall, and the last Master with it, but the buildings of the heart, for good or ill, will remain."

"I don't understand."

"That's right," Storyteller replied, "nor can any of us, for we dwell in this house, this fragile home, and it is all we see."

At the count of three, the eight men in dark suits and black hats lifted the ebony casket and placed it in the back of a narrow hearse designed to navigate the halls of Evenmere, a carriage drawn by four pairs of black bicycles. Two women in mourning dress drew dark veils over their faces, clutching their handkerchiefs but shedding no tears.

"Now remember," Heit Nizzle, the Comte de Cheslet, said smoothly, as one of his followers opened the carriage door to usher him and the women inside, "widows weep, but funeral directors keep a tight smile on their faces, either in defiance of the eternal darkness, or in exultation of a lucrative business arrangement. Let us proceed."

The men took their positions on the bicycles, and at the command of the Lead Stroker, began pedaling steadily down the opulent corridors of Ooz, a country of tall steeples, carved putto figures, trompe l'oeil, wide ceiling frescoes and broad, circular naves. The shutters were crimson with small carvings of pelicans at their borders.

"Most excellent," Nizzle said, addressing his remark to the Contessa Angelina du Maurier immediately to his right. "We had best settle in. The journey will be long."

The contessa, a striking woman, tall and regal, blonde-haired and green-eyed, currently served as his assistant. She was the most ambitious person he had ever met. He suspected he would eventually have to kill her.

She gave a smile anyone but Nizzle would have thought genuine. Her voice, surprisingly low for a woman, had great appeal. "The accommodations are excellent as always, Count. A very comfortable coach. But how shall we while away the time? Cecilia has brought cards. Perhaps a bit of whist? Or you could tell more about what we are attempting."

Nizzle glanced at their other companion, a ten-year-old girl who was clearly terrified of her chaperones. He had not wanted to bring her, but Armilus had insisted the disguise would be incomplete without a child. How the doctor loved his theatrical touches! Usually he was right, of course—the man was as brilliant as he was merciless for the Cause, but it was a bit wearing at times.

Nizzle returned du Maurier's smile. "I fear these are not matters to be discussed before the young one. Anyway, the doctor's orders were explicit. I am to disclose nothing until we reach our destination."

Angelina put on a pretty pout. "Not even a hint?"

"Ah, but wouldn't that take the pleasure from our arrival? You must leave me my little surprises. Whist will make the time pass quickly."

Actually, he despised cards, but the more the contessa knew, the more dangerous she could become. For some reason, Armilus trusted her. Perhaps he knew of some secret crime she had committed.

The funeral party soon left Ooz behind. They followed the Long Corridor most of the day before reaching double doors leading into the northern portions of Nianar. Heit Nizzle grew anxious; Prince Clive kept a strict watch along his borders. Here was the first test of the anarchists' disguises.

"Look sad, ladies," he ordered. "Especially you, Cecilia. Remember, you have just lost your father."

Three soldiers dressed in blue armor met the carriage.

"Papers, please," the sergeant in command ordered the Lead Stroker, who produced forged documents.

A young soldier with crisp, intelligent eyes opened the carriage door on Nizzle's side.

"Your papers?"

Nizzle took a set of folded sheets from inside his breast pocket. "All three are here, along with the burial permit."

The soldier examined the documents. "And you are Louis Castaigne, traveling from Ooz?"

"Yes," Nizzle replied. "My brother spent much time in Nianar as a boy. He always wanted to be buried in the Quavering."

The soldier eyed him carefully. "Is that where he usually stayed?"

"No, in Lowlight District, but they visited the Quavering often."

"With which family did he stay?"

"The Barrie household."

"I grew up in Lowlight," the soldier said. "I don't recall this family."

"He died without heir many years ago. He would have been old when you were a boy."

"Your face looks familiar," the sentry said to the contessa.

"Have we met before?"

"I do not think so, sir."

"Perhaps if you would lift the veil," the soldier suggested.

"That will be enough, Private," a voice commanded from the opposite side of the carriage. Nizzle turned to see the sergeant, his hand protectively covering Cecilia's where it lay on the coach rail. The girl had tears in her eyes. "The Barrie name is an old and respected one, though your generation has forgotten it. We will let these people pass."

"Yes, sir," the soldier replied, handing the count back his papers and stepping away from the hearse.

The sergeant, still patting the girl's hand, gave her a sad smile. "I am sorry for the inconvenience. And I am sorry about your father."

"Thank you, sir," Cecilia said, her voice a gasp.

"You are very kind," Angelina said, touching the sergeant's hand with her gloved fingers.

The doors to Nianar opened; the coach passed in.

Once they were out of earshot, Nizzle gave an exhalation of relief. "As usual, the doctor was right. That man recognized you. Only the girl saved us. An excellent performance, young lady. The tears looked real."

Cecilia wiped her cheeks. "I was being pinched."

The contessa smiled sweetly, dabbing away her own tears, which were entirely feigned. "I will buy you some sweets to make up for my necessary cruelty."

Nianar is a country of cupboards and wardrobes, with Rococo carvings, vast arcades, and pleasant fauns grinning down from the ceilings. It is ruled by its prince, acting under the direction of a democratic body called the Lion Council.

Heit Nizzle unfolded a map from his pocket and studied it. Leaning from the carriage, he called directions to the Lead Stroker. They soon turned away from the main halls, moving toward narrower passages. Finally, when the carriage could go no farther, Nizzle ordered it abandoned.

The men unloaded the casket. Nizzle led down carpeted halls, followed by the pallbearers, with Cecilia and the contessa behind. They were soon met by an old man bearing workman's clothes and a pick-axe.

"Mr. Castaigne?" he asked.

"You must be Mr. Rebeck," Nizzle said.

"Just so. Have you the proper papers from the Legatees of Deucalion?"

This was the password, created by Armilus, to ensure the men's identities. Nizzle replied with the proper form, "Quite legal, attested by no less than Doctor Coppinger himself."

The two shook hands.

"So sorry to hear of your loss," Rebeck said, smiling.

Nizzle, remaining in character, gave a stiff nod of his head. "Yes, well, he journeys to a better place."

The caretaker led the party down a side-corridor to a stone door scarcely wide enough to accommodate the casket. Passing through the portal, the company found itself facing a sprawling cemetery in an outdoor quadrangle two miles square. Evenmere rose four stories high on every side, gray-brick walls without windows or balconies. Tall rowans, lonely sentinels, shaded the gravestones. The sun shone gold from a cloudless sky. A raven pecked its way along the grass.

"This way, please," Mr. Rebeck said. "No other interments are scheduled for today. You won't be disturbed."

A mausoleum stood in the center of the grounds, splotches of moss greening its white stone. A grave lay open beside it. Rebeck led the mourners into it. Before they had even crossed the threshold, he had lit a lantern. Shutting the door behind them, he led to the back of the structure, where he twisted a stone angel, causing a section of the wall to open outward, revealing a descending stairway.

More lanterns were lit and the company passed down the stair. Rebeck, still standing in the mausoleum, called down to them.

"I'll keep watch from the cemetery grounds. Send word if I can be of assistance."

Nizzle offered no reply. The anarchists passed down several flights. Carved gargoyles and gibbelins stared at them from the newel posts. They reached a corridor at the bottom of the steps. The air smelled of the dusty dead; mold blackened the plaster walls. The contessa drew close to Nizzle's side.

"How does Lord Anderson bear traveling through such

dank passages?" she asked, her nose curled in disgust. "If I were he, I would have the walls painted and decorated, adorned with bronze sculptures by Boris Yvain and oils by Vielle. One could always dispose of the workers afterward to maintain secrecy. Perhaps I would spare the decorator. Losing one is always a disaster."

"Such a statement is hardly a proper attitude for a member of the Brotherhood," Nizzle replied. "It discourages loyalty."

She smiled sweetly. "It was but a jest, from a member of the Brother *and* Sisterhood. How did you learn of the hidden door?"

"Armilus, of course."

"From the book he stole? I would like to have a glimpse of it; wouldn't you?"

Nizzle did not reply, having no wish to admit what the contessa, who never asked an innocent question, really wanted to know: how far the doctor had trusted him with the information in *The Book of Lore*.

They wound through the passage, bearing their burden, until they reached an empty room with a yellow door at its far end.

"Contessa, you and Cecilia will remain here until we return," Nizzle ordered.

"The girl should stay, of course," Angelina replied, "but I must come."

"It is dangerous and no place for a woman."

"Doctor Armilus didn't think so, or he wouldn't have sent me."

"Doctor Armilus sent you only because he required a widow in mourning."

"My instructions are otherwise." Her eyes were all innocence.

Nizzle sighed. The contessa was undoubtedly lying, yet he had no way to confirm that until he spoke with the doctor again. If she were telling the truth, and he denied her, he would be lowered in Armilus' esteem, while the contessa would be raised; if she were practicing deceit, the doctor would admire her assertiveness. As she had doubtless reasoned, it would be better for him not to mention the incident at all.

"Each of us must follow orders," he said smoothly. "After you, my lady."

He let the rest of the company proceed him through the yellow door, then turned back to the girl. Taking her by the hand, he gave her his pocket watch, saying gently, "You will wait here until six o'clock this evening. If by that time we haven't returned, we are probably dead. You shall go back to the cemetery and present yourself to Mr. Rebeck. He will see you are fed and escorted home. Repeat back what I just said."

When Cecilia had complied, Nizzle gave her an encouraging smile and turned to follow the others, leaving her alone with his watch and a lantern. He found his followers clustered together on a high balcony. Along one wall, narrow stone steps lined with cracks led downward into absolute darkness.

"Where are we?" the contessa asked, her voice a whisper.

"The Great Understair," Nizzle replied, just as softly. "Ratcliffe, you are the point scout, followed by those carrying the casket. The rest in single file behind it. Keep sharp; keep quiet. Try not to disturb anything. We are several hundred feet in the air; if you go over the side you will not survive. When we reach the bottom, touch nothing without my permission."

The anarchists eyed the black void to their right, their faces pale. Nizzle took some satisfaction in seeing a momentary hint of fear in the contessa's glance.

"There is still time to turn back, my lady," he said, adopting an attitude of concern. "Your dress will make the going more dangerous."

She mastered herself instantly, with a coolness he could not help but admire and despise. "Women are used to the difficulties of our apparel. It gives us the poise men lack. Perhaps you would walk to my right, to lend an arm?"

He glanced at the open gulf and gave an innocent smile, thinking how simple it would be to ease a man over the edge. "Perhaps not."

"Then let me take the rear, so someone heavier than I won't stumble and drag me down."

"Very good." Nizzle stepped forward, taking a position behind the casket.

Ratcliffe moved forward, lantern held high. With the need to maintain appearances gone, only four anarchists carried the casket, the two men to the outside forced to walk perilously close to the edge.

The descent made Nizzle's calves ache; the time passed dreadfully slow. He wished he had not given his watch to the girl.

When they finally reached the bottom, they found themselves in a long corridor ending at a single blue door. As they approached, the door rattled, as if buffeted by strong winds. Standing before it, Heit Nizzle spoke a peculiar phrase, given him by Armilus from *The Book of Lore*.

"That should remove the ward of protection surrounding it," the count said. "But be certain, on peril of your life, not to touch the knob."

The count motioned to his followers, and Mr. Ratcliffe lifted the coffin lid and retrieved quantities of dynamite from within. At Nizzle's command, the anarchists, mouse-careful, placed the explosives along the door hinges and withdrew, trailing a long fuse behind them. The fuse was lit; it burned hissing down the corridor. The contessa placed dainty fingers in her ears.

The explosion rocked the walls. When the smoke cleared, the door swung wide on the surviving bottom hinge.

"Hurry along," Nizzle ordered.

They stepped onto an open plain, a chamber of vast proportions beneath a gargantuan brass dome, lit by an overhead light as bright as the sun. It took time for their eyes to adjust to the sheer sweep of the countryside, which stretched mile upon mile before them.

"Where are we?" the contessa asked. "Why is it so disorienting?"

"Normally, because of the curvature of the earth, the horizon is only about three miles away," Nizzle explained. "We are seeing much farther now. This is the Quadrangle of Angles, the foundation of Evenmere's existence. The three dimensions of our universe emanate from the Cornerstone of the house, and are made manifest in the Quadrangle. Be careful as you walk. Distances can fluctuate and we need to stay together."

Despite his own warning, the count gasped as took a single step, for he seemed to travel miles. Glancing back, he spied his followers behind him on the distant horizon. One by one they moved forward, their legs stretching toward Nizzle, the bottoms of their boots appearing unnaturally large. Then they were beside him, gaping in astonishment. Only the contessa laughed when she reached him.

"You find this amusing?" Nizzle asked.

"I find it an adventure, but dislike having my figure thrown out of proportion. Where are we going?"

"To find a bit of space. Together now, let us take a step forward."

Thus they made their way through the strange country, one step at a time, all trying to aim the same direction. Even so, they sometimes found themselves miles apart, and had to be constantly regrouping.

Abruptly the effect ceased and their strides became more uniform, so that every step covered about a mile, making the landscape steadily rise before them.

"We have passed through the Wavering Zone," Nizzle said. "Be alert."

Beneath the bronze arch of the sky, they walked through green fields with clusters of grapes tall as a man, and trees small as a finger or so gigantic their height was lost in the sky. Nothing was proportionally correct. At any moment, they might find what they had thought a mountain to be an ant-hill, or a hillock a towering peak. Nizzle's head began to ache.

From a muddy pool, an enormous figure rose before them, an animal so dark that at first Nizzle thought it the Black Beast that accompanied Doctor Armilus. Yet, this was not the darkness of form, but the blackness of the Void. Within that emptiness glowed oceans of distant stars. A pair of red suns formed the creature's eyes. Its lion's body, ebony and wavering stars, stretched long and lean across the fields to the horizon.

"What have we here?" the creature said, its eyes glittering down upon them, its voice distinctly female.

"We have come to bargain for a bit of space." Nizzle said.

"I hope you brought a good container," the creature said.

"A box of iron," Nizzle replied, "lined with equations, incantations, and feathers from phoenix wings."

"Speaking of boxing." The Empty Beast gave a careless flip of her paw, sending seven of the anarchists sprawling. The blow missed the contessa, while Nizzle, a fencing master, ducked gracefully beneath it.

The Empty Beast pounced on one of the anarchists, holding the shrieking fellow between her claws. She opened her mouth, revealing black fangs silhouetted against pulsing quasars.

"I have a moment of time!" Nizzle shouted, waving a vial taken from his pocket.

The Empty Beast paused. "Hmm? Say what?"

"If you will put my colleague down, I said I have a vial of time."

"Time, you said? I like time. I like to run my paws through it. I like to feel its softness against my skin. You have the time, you say? I have the place. A little time, a little space, there's so much I can do, so much I can create, given time. Could you, perhaps, spare me some time, then?" The creature's voice exuded feline eagerness.

"It is possible we might reach some arrangement."

"Where did you find the time?" the Empty Beast asked.

"It was taken from the Eternity Clock."

The Empty Beast released her victim. "There aren't many seconds left, that you should siphon one off. It's difficult for space to spread without time, and my existence depends upon it."

"We took only a single second."

"Only one?" she said. "One time is never enough. I wish I had all the time in the world."

"I cannot promise you that," Nizzle said smoothly, "but if you help us find a bit of space, a morsel of dimension, you can have half the time."

"Only half? I prefer the full time."

"Alas, that is impossible. I only brought half. The rest of the time was needed for other things. Part time or nothing."

She gave a kitten snarl. "Very well, I will help you, but it will be dangerous. I can't protect you from everything. Come along."

They followed the Empty Beast, mile by mile, across the Quadrangle of Angles.

"Now what sort of space are you looking for?" the creature purred. "There are many different kinds, more dimensions than you can imagine. Some say there are eleven, some twenty-seven, and some say millions. Others claim there are but three, not counting time, of course, which is the sauce on the soufflé. We are always short of time, but have every dimension here, the Baron of Angles not scrupling to forebear working with imaginary numbers."

"Three will be sufficient," Nizzle said.

"I know just the thing."

She led them to a city, sometimes towering, sometimes quite small, made of inches and cubits and meters and miles, flaring here and there into grand dimensions. They had some trouble passing through the gate, which sometimes became too narrow, but at last they walked the streets. Fine grains of gray dust covered the avenues.

"You can pick up a bit of space here," the Empty Beast said.

"Where?" asked the contessa.

"See the dust? That's the three-dimensional material. It's so common, it's left lying around."

At Nizzle's order, Ratcliffe produced the iron box, which was small enough to fit into a man's hand. Nizzle opened the lid and withdrew a silver spoon.

"My time first, if you please," the Empty Beast said.

Nizzle removed a vial from his pocket, and spilled its contents onto a pocket handkerchief. The musky odor of time rose into the air. "Take your time."

The Empty Beast clutched the handkerchief between her paws, purred in pleasure, and rolled over on her back, the cloth draped over her nose, her eyes an ecstatic blue.

"I can do so much with this," she said.

Nizzle knelt in the street and shoveled a few grains of Dimension into the iron box. Instantly, a loud cry filled the land. Shadowy forms wheeled overhead.

"You may want to run," the Empty Beast purred.

"We had an agreement," Nizzle cried.

"I let you in," the creature said, "but the Baron of Angles will punish to the full measure any who attempt to remove a single grain of dimension. He is coming now, and you do not want to meet him."

"Back to the door!" Nizzle shouted. Clutching the box, he sped away, not waiting for his minions.

The city gate loomed before them. Nizzle increased his

pace. As he crossed the threshold, he glanced back. To his surprise, the contessa was right behind him, sprinting like an athlete. All his followers, except for one, passed through the portal, but the gate shrank as the last reached it, and he struck his head against the lintel and tumbled to the ground. Before he could revive, a shadow from above covered him.

Nizzle ducked low and ran faster, the man's screams echoing at his back. Another shadow passed over his own form. Daring an upward glance he saw a creature like a great bat flapping above him, its talons extended. He drew his pistol and fired. The monster gave an grating scream and crashed to the ground.

Ratcliffe, being younger and stronger, passed Nizzle, but was snatched up and carried into the sky.

Somewhere to Nizzle's left a distant gong sounded, and a face in a far mountain range turned to glare with accusing eyes. It lifted itself up, the boulders forming a body and limbs, the Baron of Angles coming to protect his kingdom. Clouds roiled overhead; shafts of lightning split the sky.

They reached the Wavering Zone. Because of the varying distances brought by every footfall, Nizzle lost track of his fellows. Fortunately, being able to surmount miles at a time worked to his advantage. He saw the door ahead, framed within a dark blue wall, and had nearly reached it when another shadow crossed his own. Sharp talons tore at his back; he fell face-first to the earth, attempted to rise, and was knocked down again.

A shot rang out; an animal shriek came from above. He looked up to see one of the bats spiraling away, blood coursing from its head. As he bounded to his feet, he saw the contessa standing at the doorway, a small pistol drawn.

He glanced back once more. The Baron was almost upon him, a gray form towering into the sky, his hand reaching down, mile after mile, seeking the iron box.

Nizzle ran. When he was still several feet away, the shadow of giant fingers darkened the sky above him. He leapt, stretching his form almost vertical, and crashed over the threshold.

Without stopping, he rolled to his feet and sped after the contessa, who had already begun her retreat. He caught up with her, and together they rushed along the corridor and up the stairs, not pausing until they stood once more in the room occupied by young Cecilia. They leaned against the walls, breathless, their sides aching.

"I said . . . it . . . would be dangerous," Nizzle panted.

"But you didn't say . . . it would be . . . undignified," the contessa replied. She laughed, her eyes brimming with excitement.

Though they waited over an hour, none of the anarchists who had accompanied them appeared. Only later, when they were once more traveling through the corridors of Nianar, did Nizzle ask Angelina du Maurier why she had fired the shots to save his life.

"Why, Heit Nizzle, you surprise me. Are we not comrades, all serving the Great Cause?"

He grimaced, suspecting it had more to do with the fact that he had been carrying the iron box.

"I wonder," she said, almost to herself, "what it would be like to be the wife of the Baron of Angles?"

Twilight descended in North Lowing, the sunlight abandoning the ceiling shafts one by one, turning the rooms to gray, sending the birds to their roosts.

Carter and Storyteller had left The Desolation behind several hours before, and now approached a granite wall at the end of the chamber. The Dally bridge, also of stone, straddled the Fable where three branchings passed from the wall through a trio of archways, the river a rushing tumble where the waters conjoined. A single lamp burned on this side of the bridge.

"Do you see anyone?" Carter asked, peering through the gloom. "There should be a company of the White Circle Guard. The Dally is strategically important. Armies passing from Loft have to come this way, and any Poetry Men journeying east might cross here."

"There is only one person on the bridge," Jonathan said. "Someone with a good heart."

"I can't make anyone out. You must have excellent vision."

"I do not see with my eyes, Master Anderson. I feel her."

"Her?"

True enough, when they had drawn closer, Carter sighted the slender figure of a woman. The post-lamps at the bridge's corners were unlit, but a lantern hung from a rail-post beside her, making her golden hair glisten.

"Lizbeth?" Carter called. "Is that you?"

The woman seized the lantern and hurried to hug Carter's neck. "I have waited half the evening!" she said. "When I saw two where I expected only one, I wasn't sure it was you. I wanted to hide, but there was no place."

"What are you doing out here alone? You should have an escort. This is unsupportable!"

"Terrible things have happened in the last two days," she replied. "I will tell you as we go. Who is this dark fellow?"

"Jonathan T. Bartholomew, at your service." The minstrel bowed low, dignified despite his tattered garb.

"Are you a trustworthy person?" she asked.

"Oh yes, lady," Jonathan replied, grinning in delight.

"You must forgive her," Carter said. "This is my brother's wife, Lizbeth. She can be quite direct."

Lizbeth's blush was visible even in the lamplight. "Have I offended? I am sorry. I spent my childhood imprisoned by the anarchists. Etiquette sometimes escapes me."

"No, no," Jonathan said. "Your question shows a woman without even a glimmer of guile. It is charming."

"Not always," Lizbeth replied.

They crossed the bridge, their steps resounding on the stones, the stream singing in the dimness below. Carter glanced at his sister-in-law. She was more beautiful than ever: high cheekbones, a pert nose, eyes of the palest blue. The years of living with Duskin had been good for her, and in many ways she had adapted to her new life. Yet her expression remained haunted by her years of imprisonment. Adjusting to the role of a consul's wife had been difficult for her. Sarah had taught her much, and Duskin had been patient, but there would always be a uniqueness about Lizbeth that was both her curse and charm.

"Tell me what has happened," Carter said. "Is Duskin well?"

"I don't know. I am frightened for him. We heard reports of the Poetry Men over a month ago, but did not realize how dangerous they were. When Marshal Inkling followed your orders and sent a battalion of the North Lowing Guard to protect the Tower of

Astronomy, Duskin went with them. You know how he hates to miss out on that sort of excitement. But a company holding Lookfar Passage was wiped out this morning by uncanny energies. We had word you were traveling this way, and there was no one I trusted to send, so I came to await your arrival."

"Does Duskin know where you are?"

"No one does. I thought if I told anyone they would try to stop me."

"Oh, Lizbeth," Carter groaned. "The whole household must be in an uproar. If Duskin knew he would be furious."

Tears sprang to her eyes. "Would he? I thought it the most expeditious course."

Carter had momentarily forgotten how volatile his sister-in-law could be. To stave off an outburst, he forced a smile and laid a comforting hand on her shoulder. "It was very brave, and the news is vital. I'm glad you came, but you must learn to trust those around you. There were plenty of men who could have met us with the message."

Her brow furrowed. "I will try to remember. Sometimes it is easier to do what must be done than to leave it to others."

Carter consulted his inner maps. A force planning to attack the Astronomy Tower might well come through Lookfar Passage. If that were the case, he needed to get to the tower before them, though he would have preferred to escort Lizbeth back to the safety of Lowing Hall first.

They passed over the bridge and through an arched passage, leaving the canyons of North Lowing behind for gray stone corridors with carved gargoyles and dog-faced ghouls peering from the ceiling, statuary given grim aspect in the shadowy glow of Lizbeth's lantern.

"This passage is called Disquieting," Lizbeth said. "There is not a gas-jet anywhere down its length. It serves as a defensible corridor between the bridge and the capitol. The statuary is intended to discourage intruders."

"I have traveled it many times," Jonathan said, "and know the stories told of it, of ghosts and dreads and splotchy deaths. That's right. But none of them are true. The darkness is warm and comfortable as an old mitten. An adventurous darkness. I like it very much."

"Do you?" Lizbeth asked, clearly delighted. "So do I. I love its solitude, its stone steps, even its gargoyles, who look more like monkeys than monsters to me. I was alone for so long, it isn't easy always having so much company, so I come here when the press of people overwhelms me. I often make up stories as I journey along. By your name, you must understand that. Will you tell us a chronicle to pass the time?"

"I never recite stories for entertainment; I only tell them to cheer the human heart, and have none for you."

Lizbeth frowned. "Truly? You think me cheerless then, or too cheerful? Mostly I am worried about my husband. But what an odd gentleman you are! I would have thought you could tell a tale at a finger's snap."

"Have you read *Robinson Crusoe*?"

Lizbeth beamed. "I love that book! When I returned from my captivity, having owned only a single copy of *Wuthering Heights* to read, I visited a library and sat for an hour, astonished to remember so many books could exist. I've heard that *Robinson Crusoe* is about a real man who, after being rescued, grew shy and reclusive."

"The book comforts you," Jonathan said.

"Like him, I was forged by my years of imposed isolation. The silence is like a holy temple to me, for I found happiness there even in despair."

"Yet it was so lonely." Jonathan watched her with his dark, quiet eyes. "That's right. A terrible loneliness, thick as thorns."

"There is both pleasure and pain in being alone," Lizbeth said. "One can find oneself within it."

"And it is a place of retreat," Jonathan said. "Fearing for your husband, you wish you could go there again."

Lizbeth gave him a wary glance.

"None of that, now," he said. "There is nothing to be ashamed of. More than once Mister Crusoe must have longed to return to his little island. You have great inner strength, Lizbeth Powell Anderson. You have passed through the fire and flowed out pure gold. Your courage will always overcome your longing to hide."

Tears came to the corners of Lizbeth's eyes. "How do you know so much about me?"

"I am Storyteller, who sees to the heart."

"I have learned," Lizbeth said, with great earnestness. "I have learned not to talk to myself when others are present, as I used to do in the solitude. I have learned not to quote *Wuthering Heights* as I once did, for though I know it by heart and it often springs to mind, it is not a book one should live by. But it's hard not to want the old refuge sometimes."

"That is why I haven't a story for you."

"Because of the darkness within me?"

"Oh no, child. Because there is so much light. You are blinding as the sun, so bright I can scarcely look at you."

"High praise indeed, considering its source," Carter said, not a little astonished. "I have always thought well of you; apparently not nearly as much as you deserve."

"Isn't that the way with everyone we love?" Jonathan asked. "But you should watch her. That's right. This one could teach you worlds and worlds."

"I am so glad you've come," Lizbeth said, taking both their arms. "Very glad."

They soon left Disquieting and passed through corridors leading to a spiraling stone stair, the beginning of the Tower of Astronomy, its ascending gas jets forming distant constellations in the heights. Carter led the way, sighing at the prospect of an arduous and monotonous climb. At first the tedium of the journey was broken by intersecting passages, but these soon ceased, leaving only the endless steps, a lack of breath, and aching calves and thighs.

"I have never been this way before," Carter said. "When I learned of the Circle of Servants, I invited its members to the Inner Chambers. Some came, but the Grand Astronomer sent his regrets. I planned to visit him another time when I was on my way to Loft, but he sent word that it wasn't convenient. Mr. Hope was incensed, claiming he had insulted my authority, but Duskin assures me the astronomer is merely eccentric."

"Arrogant is more like it," Lizbeth said. "I care neither for him, nor for his demeaning attitude toward my husband. But his wife is nice."

They reached another intersecting corridor, running away from the spiral stair like a spoke from a wheel. Down its length,

Lord Anderson spied a wide aperture open to the night.

"Let's take a look," he said, moving toward the embrasure.

They found themselves on a balustrade, looking not at a blue sky but into the black reaches of space. Two towers stood in the darkness; and around them hung the stars.

They were every color, including those hues for which mortals have no name. Their size varied from that of a child's ball to seething orbs large as an assembly hall, suspended around the towers like inset gems. Stars also hung below the balustrade on which the companions stood, as if the Earth had vanished, leaving only the towers and the celestial lights.

Carter glanced above and below him at the walls of their own tower. Its base was lost in the darkness, its pinnacle a dim shadow miles above them. Stone walkways passed from this, the Central Tower, to the two visible towers.

"Duskin told me of this," Lord Anderson said. "They really are stars?"

"They are," Jonathan replied. "Stars hang from each of the Nine Towers, like jewels at a fine lady's throat. The sun neither rises nor sets upon them."

"Of all the stories of Evenmere, even Mr. Hope was skeptical of this one," Carter replied. "Stars are vast, gaseous clouds, millions of miles in circumference, burning in the vacuum of space."

"That's right, Master Anderson," Jonathan said. "That's right. And they are also fairy lights hung on the Astronomy Towers."

"Representations?"

"Both representations and realities."

Carter found another embrasure farther down the corridor, where he could see another tower. Looking at the stars flaming at its top, thick with the pulse of eternity, burning as they had done throughout the eons, left him hopeful and lonely and joyous and filled with his own insignificance, as stars often do. The part of him that was the Master felt their mysterious relationship to the Balance. If time had allowed, he could have studied them for hours, seeking to comprehend that connection, but he tore himself away, comforted and discomfited.

"Let's get to the top and see the rest," he said.

They ascended another long hour, occasionally stopping to visit other portals with stars hanging in empty space, some seeming less than an arm's length away, others draped around the surrounding towers like Christmas candles. Toward the end of their journey the suns lay thick as a mantle, the sparkling pearls of the Milky Way shimmering in a net across the highest spires.

At last the travelers reached two North Lowing Guards armed with short swords and pistols, the first of a squad stationed in pairs every hundred steps along the stair. One of these recognized Lizbeth, making it unnecessary for Carter to display his Ring of Office, and they were passed on until they came to an oak door standing wide, with a gun crew at its threshold manning a shrapnel cannon pointing down the stair.

They entered a circular chamber draped in floral rugs, with Morris tapestries of peacocks on acanthus backgrounds covering brick walls. A fireplace curved along one side, surrounded by desks, end tables, and fat chairs with threadbare arms. A young boy dressed in a hooded gray robe approached at once.

"This way, please," the lad said, without other words of introduction. He led them up a stair into a chamber large enough to hold a thousand people, though far fewer were currently present. Along with several men and women dressed in the same gray robes as their guide, there was a company of soldiers from North Lowing, garbed in their *heekis*, and a company of the White Circle Guard.

"This is the Main Observation Hall," their guide said. "Please make yourselves comfortable."

"Thank you," Lizbeth said, but the boy had already turned back toward the chamber below.

"A warm reception," Carter said.

Rows of machinery, all levers and gauges, spouts and valves, lined the curvature of the walls. Various types of viewing devices, from telescopes to stereo-optic lenses, ranged along the sides of the domed ceiling, pointing out into the darkness. The robed workers moved from telescope to telescope, preoccupied with their duties, while the soldiers, used to the long periods of waiting that comprise the military life, sat or lay upon the floor, playing cards, sleeping, or reading. The room was dimly lit, undoubtedly to facilitate stellar observation, and it took Carter a moment to spy his brother. Duskin sat cross-legged in a stuffed chair, distractedly biting his lip, his usually immaculate frock coat wrinkled, his blond hair unkempt. He looked worn beyond hope, this brother who was always so carefree.

Lord Anderson hurried to him, calling his name.

Duskin looked up, brightened, and rose to clasp his sibling. "Carter! I'm so relieved to see you! We're in a bit of a stew."

"So Lizbeth said."

Perplexity filled Duskin's features as he caught sight of his wife. "Lizbeth! She shouldn't be here. It's too dangerous."

Lizbeth rushed into her husband's arms and burst into tears. "I was so worried about you!"

Duskin looked at his brother in helpless embarrassment.

"She helped us find our way," Carter said, eliciting a grateful glance from Lizbeth.

"I'm sorry," Duskin told her. "I thought you knew I was here."

Lizbeth stepped back, wiping her eyes. "I don't mean to make a scene, but after the news from Lookfar, I didn't know what might have happened."

"You've heard, then?"

Jonathan, trailing behind Lord Anderson, said, "News travels fast through this old house."

"This is Jonathan Bartholomew," Carter said, "sometimes called Storyteller. He's been an enormous aid."

"*The* Storyteller?" Duskin's eyes widened. "I've always wanted to meet you."

"And here I am," Jonathan said, extending his hand.

"I'll show Jonathan the telescopes while you two make plans," Lizbeth said.

"I would be honored," the minstrel replied, though Carter suspected he had seen the Towers before.

"I don't like her being here," Duskin said. "How in the world did she—"

"You don't want to know. There's nothing to be done for it now."

Duskin rolled his eyes. "I'm sure she has an explanation. After we married I thought we would make a place for ourselves, but the adjustment has been hard. She doesn't always fit in with the other women; she's too direct and too beautiful; you know how emotional she can be."

He shrugged. "Don't misunderstand. I love her desperately, but she sometimes misunderstands things in the oddest way."

"She spent a long time alone."

"I know. And look at her now." He pointed to where she was guiding Jonathan toward the lens of a great telescope. "There she is, the face of an angel, charming your friend so you and I can have a minute alone. I tell you, Carter, sometimes I could worship her and sometimes I would like to strangle her with my bare hands."

Carter grinned. "Then you have found true love. No doubt she feels the same."

Duskin started to say something, then closed his mouth and grinned. "I suppose she does. I'm not always the best husband."

He glanced around the room, his eyes growing bleak. "I have no business going on about my personal affairs. A company is dead, and we don't even know our enemy."

"Tell me the situation."

"As soon as we received Marshal Inkling's message, we brought additional soldiers to the Tower from Lowing Hall, even though the small force already here could hold off an army coming up those steps; it's the only way in, you know. I'm glad we did, especially after the destruction of the company at Lookfar—Captain Hadden and eighty men. Apparently two Poetry Men appeared and enchanted the soldiers with some kind of siren song. The handful who survived managed to resist it and escape. The victims were found scattered through the passage, their expressions filled with horror. Our scouts report the poets are approaching the Tower, leading a large group of anarchists. I'm sick about it, Carter. When you appointed me to help in the reorganization of North Lowing, I didn't dream something like this could happen."

Duskin ran his hands over his eyes. "I may not be cut out for this. I was actually beginning to enjoy it, too. King Edgemont is a jewel of a fellow, just too old to do the work. With both his sons dead, the monarchy in North Lowing is finished, anyway. But he is finally starting to trust me enough to give over some real authority. We've rebuilt Tharken Pass. It's painted in seventeen colors, as in ancient times. Captain Hadden and I had dinner there three nights ago, when the sun was just falling into twilight and everything absolutely glowed. He regaled me with the best after-dinner stories. What will I say to his wife?"

Duskin turned his head, struggling to master himself. His mouth twisted; tears touched the corners of his eyes. Carter clasped his shoulder.

"It wasn't your fault. You weren't his commander."

Duskin looked into his brother's eyes. "No, but I was the one who convinced the king to send them."

"You couldn't have predicted it," Lord Anderson said softly. "We never know where the hammer may fall."

They fell silent, until Duskin squared his shoulders and cleared his throat. "Yes, well, life is never easy, is it? Have you met the Grand Astronomer yet?"

Carter glanced around. He had already noticed a tall man in a white robe and skull cap, who carried himself with authority. "No. I'm surprised he hasn't introduced himself already. Surely he noticed our arrival."

Duskin gave a wry grin. "Make no mistake; he won't come to you. He's a proud one. Come along."

Duskin led Carter to the Grand Astronomer, a slender man apparently in his early fifties, with a long, austere face, Greek nose, and imperious eyes.

"Astronomer Phra," Duskin said, "may I present Carter Anderson, Master of Evenmere? Carter, this is Edwin Phra, the Grand Astronomer."

The astronomer gave a low, sweeping bow that made his silk robes whisper. "Lord Anderson." His voice was deep and formal. "We should repair to my upper chambers. The conversation of such as we is not a matter for common ears."

Phra led Lord Anderson to a spiral staircase at the far side of the hall, which took them to a paneled room with a single portal through which a long telescope peered. There were two more doors, one closed, the other standing half-open to the room beyond, revealing spartan living quarters. The chamber being without chairs, both men stood.

"I am glad to finally meet you," Phra said coldly, one eye arched. "For almost a decade you have served as Master, yet you have only now, at a time of crisis, come to call. The week your father occupied your position, he appeared at once."

Carter raised his own eyebrows in surprise, both at the man's presumption and his apparent age. Clearly he was older than he seemed, perhaps even as long-lived as Chant. "The significance and even the existence of your office eluded me at first. As you doubtless recall, I invited you to the Inner Chambers as soon as I knew to do so."

Phra's dark eyes lit with perplexity. "This is the Tower of Astronomy, the most important structure in Evenmere. You tell me you were unaware of its magnitude?"

"References to the Servants' Circle are scarce," Carter replied.

"Your butler should have informed you."

"He found nothing to indicate the relationship."

"You should replace him. He is clearly incompetent."

Carter tried to keep his voice level. "It would have been helpful if you, or any of the other members of the Circle, had appeared at the Inner Chambers to advise me of your positions. Or at least sent word. And I did try to call upon you, but you refused to see me."

Phra again gave Lord Anderson that expression of half-puzzlement, half-contempt. "The Masters have been coming to me for generations. I cannot be wandering the house when the stars must be watched. The system is too delicate, and I am often too busy to receive guests. You should have persevered. Look through that glass."

Taken aback by the sudden command, Carter grudgingly stepped across to the telescope. He adjusted the eye-piece, bringing an orange star with six circling planets into focus.

"What am I seeing?"

"That is the Lotinius system, once a double star with twice as many planets. There are two modes of organization in place in Evenmere: the structure of the house affects the overall patterns of the stars, and I keep those patterns in balance. Three hundred years ago, a group called the Philanthropists leveled a portion of Eastwing with fire, causing a shift in the universe. This was one of the results: six planets and a sun gone. I did what I could. As soon as I sensed the fluctuations, I tried to compensate with the astrolabical levers, but the damage was too extensive. One of the satellites was inhabited by a crude form of animal life. Stars die naturally as part of the process of existence, but none should perish before their time. As you can see, mine is the greatest responsibility in Evenmere; I cannot waste my time with other concerns."

Seeing no need to argue the point, Carter asked. "May I see the mechanisms you use?"

"Of course."

Phra led through the previously closed door, which opened onto a narrow stair. They ascended to a larger chamber obviously positioned directly above the dome in the room below, for telescopes passed through the floor and beyond to the ceiling, making the room a mechanical jumble. At its center lay a glass dome with the star field replicated in three-dimensional splendor within. Levers, buttons, and valves surrounded the dome, covered with mysterious labels such as *Foumal Ht.*

"From this room," Phra said, "I regulate the course of the stars."

"All of it, from this chamber?"

"There are other controls on the spans crossing the towers, but this is the central mechanism."

"And the Poetry Men are coming here. What will happen if they reach this room?"

"We must not allow it," Phra said. "We *will* not. They must not tamper with the stars."

"They would do worse than tamper. They are fanatics with unbelievable power, who may intend on destroying the towers."

"No one is that mad."

"They are."

Phra stood silent, his face growing pale. "If that were to happen, order would be lost. Gravity shifts, stellar explosions, suns blowing across the universe like fireworks, Existence itself losing cohesion. Everything would go."

The blood left Carter's face. Words failed him.

The two returned to the Main Observation Hall below. Some message must have reached the soldiers, for they were awake now, sitting in silence beside the mechanisms along the walls, guns ready. Jonathan passed among them, giving them encouragement.

"So that is the minstrel," Phra said. "I have heard of him for generations."

"Let me introduce you."

"Don't bother," Phra replied. "He is obviously nothing more than a vagabond. He and his little stories may have some small place in the Balance, but he certainly does not hold the cosmic importance of you and I. Besides, I am not one for idle conversation. I will retire to my chambers to await the assault with my wife, Blodwen."

"Lizbeth told me you were married."

"You sound surprised."

"Some of the other long-lived, such as Enoch and Chant, have chosen to remain single."

"It is understandable. Our wives age and die, while we do not; but I have learned to adapt, and have had several companions throughout my life. My assistants will prepare a bed for you in our guest quarters."

"That won't be necessary. I will wait with the men. A room for Lizbeth would be appreciated."

"My people will see to it." Phra gave a nodding bow and retraced his steps up the spiral stair.

Carter joined Duskin and Lizbeth, who were sitting on a pair of low stools.

"Have a pleasant chat?" Duskin asked.

"I have never met anyone more aloof."

"It's the danger of having the word 'Grand' in your title," Duskin said. "It makes you realize how humble Enoch is, who has lived centuries longer."

Carter laughed. "Ah, but Enoch is merely in charge of Time. As Phra pointed out, he is master of the most important thing in Evenmere."

"And where would Phra be, without Chant to keep the stars lit?" Lizbeth asked.

"Still, I understand the astronomer's intensity," Lord Anderson admitted. "Who knows how I would feel if I were Master for hundreds of years? Makes you understand why we should be replaced now and then."

Carter withdrew his pocket-watch and raised his eyebrows in concern, for it was after ten o'clock. "Duskin, I must enter the dream dimension to guard Jason."

"We need you here. Our scouts say the Poetry Men are less than a mile from the base of the Tower. An assault may come at any moment."

"We could wake you, if necessary," Lizbeth said.

"That is impossible," Carter said. "By its nature, once I am within the dream, I have to wake myself."

He stood in a sudden agony of indecision. "I will have to pass back and forth between waking and sleeping. It's the only way."

Carter laid out his bedroll in a quiet nook between the spiral stair and the wall. Lying on his back, he spoke the Word Which Masters Dreams. The room trembled only slightly, and he was soon walking the Inner Chambers once more.

Chastising himself for his tardiness, he hurried to his son's room. The position of the lamp indicated that Jason was asleep. For all Carter knew, Armilus could have already found his way into the dream. Why had he wasted time speaking to the overblown astronomer? What kind of father was he, to forget his son?

Cursing the paradoxes of the sleeping world, he momentarily paced the floor, then spoke the Word Which Brings Aid, hoping to summon Sarah or Mr. Hope. To his surprise, Jason himself came drifting down the corridor, dressed in blue pajamas and looking puzzled.

"Hello, Papa," the boy said, as if Carter had never been away.

"Hello, Son." Carter scooped the lad into his arms, hugging him tightly. "I love you so much. You know that, don't you?"

"I love you too, Papa. Where is Momma?"

"Oh, this is just a dream you're having and she isn't in it."

"Oh." The boy's brow furrowed thoughtfully.

"Let's put you in your bed, and you can tell me about your day."

Once Jason was tucked in, Carter sat by his bedside. Dread welled within him as he thought of deserting his son to return to the Tower of Astronomy.

"We had bread pudding after dinner," Jason said, "and Mr. Hope played ball with me."

"You like Mr. Hope, don't you?"

"Yes. He's funny."

"Funny old Mr. Hope."

Lord Anderson!

Carter leapt to his feet. The voice came from down the hall.

Carter debated leaving Jason in his bed, but picked him up instead.

"Who is that?" Jason asked.

"Hush." Carter went to the door and glanced around its corner. The hallway lay in the twilight cast by a single gas-jet burning at either end, and a heavy figure waited there, his face half-illuminated. Behind him stood the beast Lord Anderson thought he had killed, or another exactly like it.

"Nothing rash, sir," Doctor Armilus said. "No Words of Power, no Lightning Sword. I mean no harm; I want only to parley."

Keeping close to the doorway, Carter turned sideways, putting himself between his son and any weapon the doctor might be carrying.

"I would like to approach, but won't get too close," Armilus said. "Are you agreeable? A temporary truce?"

"Come ahead." Lord Anderson wanted to set Jason down, to send him back to his room, but feared doing so, lest this be some trick. Carter drew his pistol from beneath his jacket.

"Far enough," he said, when the doctor had come within a dozen paces.

Armilus halted. A contest of wills seemed to occur, each man waiting for the other to speak first.

It was Armilus who broke the silence. "As you can see, Lord Anderson, I have finally penetrated into the Inner Chambers. It was difficult, even with the help of *The Book of Lore*."

"What do you want?"

"To demonstrate my capabilities. Your son, as you must realize, is not safe; but let us not lose sight of my goals, of which the child plays no part. He is only a pawn, a means of controlling you. I am actually fond of children and would rather not waste my energies threatening young Jason." Armilus curled his lip in distaste. "A black strategy really, rather beneath any of us. I have a proposal."

"I won't relinquish my responsibilities."

"So you have said. You are an honorable man, Lord Anderson, as was your father before you. A shame that such as we are not allies, but . . ." Armilus gave his massive shoulders an almost imperceptible shrug. "Still, for both our sakes, some understanding must be reached. The Poetry Men will soon assault the Tower of Astronomy. If they destroy it as they did Jossing, the consequences are unimaginable."

Armilus paused. Carter remained silent, wondering how the doctor knew of the invasion.

"A truce, Lord Anderson. A truce and I vow to never again attempt to steal or harm your son. Not only that, but my men will do what we can to protect the Tower of Astronomy and the rest of the Circle of Servants. In return, you will not actively work against my party so long as the Poetry Men are a threat, unless you see that we are directly endangering the house."

"Everything you do endangers the house."

Armilus gave the barest smile. "You of all men know better. This is not some childish play, utter good against complete evil. We are both men of principle. I ask only for some leeway. I am rebuilding the party; let me do so. Between us, we will end the threat of these poets."

In utter weariness of mind and soul, Carter glanced down at Jason, not daring to admit how badly Armilus' presence in the Inner Chambers unnerved him. Even now he needed to return to the Tower of Astronomy, but could not leave his son. Nor could he continue this draining nightly vigil much longer. He thought of the attack on Chant and the burning of the forest, the death of the Smith of Welkin Well, the annihilation of the company at Lookfar Passage. Everywhere, Evenmere was besieged. He had thought to divide his energies between protecting Jason and saving the house; he should have realized he could never do both.

"A truce," he finally said. "For tonight, and until the Poetry Men are defeated. But if I see that your actions imperil Evenmere, I will oppose you. And I will be the judge to decide if you cross that line."

The doctor gave no hint of emotion. "No arbitration? Very well. This is not a time for pride. The stakes are too high. I will trust to your honor. We have an agreement."

"How can I trust a murderer?"

"Yes, I have murdered," the doctor replied, his mouth

turned down in a scowl. "I have murdered for the greater good. I have become hardened to murder for the Great Cause. But I do serve a cause; I am not merely a fanatic. The Poetry Men are insane; they will kill us all unless we stop them. So you have the word of the Supreme Anarchist not to harm your son on this or any other night. Jason is free. Good evening, Lord Anderson."

Armilus touched his hand to the brim of his bowler and vanished, leaving Carter trembling in rage and despair.

"Who was that, Papa?"

"A very bad man. If you ever see him when you are alone, you must run as fast as you can and hide in the deepest corners of the house. Do you understand?"

"Yes."

"Now let's get you back to bed."

Carter tucked Jason under the covers. "Sweet dreams, child. Now return from here to a dreamless sleep."

Jason slowly faded away, leaving Carter heartsick and alone. He had done that which he had never thought to do. He had made a deal with the devil himself; and the consequences of that action might bring ruin to all of Existence.

Battle for the Tower

Carter brought himself out of the dream dimension, waking in the Main Observation Hall to find Phra shaking him by the shoulder. "You must rise, Lord Anderson. Our foes are nearly upon us."

Carter stood at once, unreasonably irritated at the astronomer. "What do the men report?"

"Nothing as yet," Phra said, "but they soon will. I perceive our enemies approaching, burning with an energy akin to that of stars. I have never felt anything like it before, except from the heavens. Can you sense them?"

Carter paused, opening himself to the house. "There is a slight shifting of the Balance, but nothing more. The impressions you are receiving must be related to your particular talents."

All around the chamber, the soldiers were already on their feet, readying their weapons, mostly pistols since battles in Evenmere usually involved fighting at close quarters. Duskin was speaking to Lieutenant Sedger, the officer in charge of the White Circle Guard, a warrior Lord Anderson had known for years. Carter gave a wave to the two men, and Duskin broke away and strode to his brother's side.

"Sir!" a man called to Duskin from the chamber entrance. "Captain DuLac sends word that a company is climbing the stair."

"We'll be right there." Duskin turned a pale face to Carter.

"DuLac is a good officer. He will have a fine career if we live until morning. Are you ready?"

Lord Anderson drew his pistol and Lightning Sword. "Yes. Is Lizbeth safe?"

"As safe as any of us can be. She's with Phra's wife in the upper chambers."

Together the brothers hurried to the downstairs chamber. The captain and thirty of the soldiers from North Lowing stood crowded into the small room. A heavy table had been placed against the double doorway to form a low barricade.

Carter strode to the opening and stood beside the shrapnel cannon, looking down the long stair curving away to the left, from whence came echoes of scattered gunfire. The attackers must have encountered the first of the pairs of North Lowing soldiers. As per their orders, the sentries would fall back to the barricade.

Being the only route to the upper chambers, the stair made for a defensible position; the enemy would be limited by an ascent only wide enough to accommodate four men walking abreast. However, without any windows overlooking the stair, the defenders could fire only from the doorway. DuLac's men would have to rotate their positions to allow time to reload. If the assailants managed to reach the barricade, the fighting would be close. Because of the lack of space, most of the soldiers remained upstairs in the Main Observation Hall, ready to serve as reinforcements.

The first pair of sentries came hurrying up the steps and scrambled over the blockade, their boots thumping against its oak surface.

"You may want to step back, Lord Anderson," Captain DuLac said. He was broad-shouldered, with a round face and keen eyes. Beads of sweat glistened on his forehead.

"The shrapnel-gunner and I will meet the initial assault," Carter said. "Have your men ready."

"Very well, sir."

More of the sentries passed over the barricade. Finally one of them shouted, "We're the last. The others didn't make it."

Carter felt the cold fear that always crept into his stomach right before deadly action. He drew a deep breath and blew it out again. The gunfire had ceased. He heard pistol hammers being cocked behind him, sharp and succinct in the silence.

From around the curve of the stair fifty yards below came a shout, followed by the noise of running men: the jangling of equipment, the thrumming of boots on stone. The first assailants, dressed in anarchist gray, appeared.

"Wait for it," DuLac ordered. "Wait for it."

Carter strained to see the poet he assumed would be leading the company. At last, behind the first two lines of soldiers, he glimpsed a green robe adorned with a flaming sun.

He raised a Word of Power into his mind, drawing it into his throat just as the artilleryman lit the fuse of the shrapnel cannon. The weapon discharged, deafening in such close quarters, sending smoke roiling to the ceiling. The anarchists screamed as shot and shrapnel tore through their lines, parting them like ninepins, leaving the Poetry Woman revealed, passing unharmed through the wounded and dying ranks.

Carter released the Word Which Manifests.

Falan!

A golden wave swirled toward the poetess. She lifted her arms as if to deflect the blow, but was cast, along with her men, far down the stair.

Face flushed, Captain DuLac cried, "First line, fooorward!"

Lord Anderson stepped back to make room for the ten stern-faced soldiers who crowded around the doorway, five kneeling, their weapons braced on the top of the barricade, five standing behind these, pistols aimed.

The enemy recovered quickly and bullets streamed up the stair, sending one man reeling and felling the artilleryman, who crumpled against the shrapnel cannon. Another soldier hurriedly took his place.

"Hold your position!" DuLac ordered. "To your mark. Take aim! Fire!"

In the midst of the cacophony, pain stabbed through the center of Carter's head, a tearing that could only come from a drastic shift in the Balance. So closely aligned to the relationship between Chaos and Order was he that he gasped in agony, as if wounded. He fell to one knee and Duskin sprang to his side.

"Are you hit?"

Several soldiers massed protectively around him, weapons ready. It took a moment before he could breathe enough to respond. "Something is happening in the chambers above. I must go there."

"I'll go with you," Duskin said.

"No. Remain here and help DuLac hold. I'll send word if I need you."

Rushing alone up the stair, Carter swore in astonishment at the seemingly limitless power of his opponents, for the Main Observation Hall was bathed in a radiance emanating from a poet emerging from a newly-created corridor on the opposite wall. Face glowing with a brilliance too bright to look upon, the Poetry Man spoke in a clear, high voice, audible even above the din.

I am light!
Put off these bonds of mortal man,
Give way to grace, the way of gods;
Enraptured, never fear again
That you will lie beneath the sod.

I am light!
The starlight answers shining dim,
The favored moon reflects the glow;
Take hold the splintered diadem
Embrace the endless, radiant flow.

Flashes careened from the poet's tongue with every word, lambent whirls of energy, whipping the air like a scourge.

While the defenders stood frozen in wonder and surprise, scores of anarchists poured from the new passage, firing as they came. Bullets whizzed by Carter's head, echoing off the stone steps and walls. Soldiers reeled under the onslaught. A North Lowing man directly in front of Lord Anderson dropped to his knees, blood rilling down his chest.

"Get down!" Lieutenant Sedger shouted.

The men threw themselves on the ground, Carter with them.

"It *is* starlight!" Phra cried, not far from Carter's side. The astronomer stood upright, ignoring the shells passing all around, his expression suffused in rapture. "True starlight brought to earth!"

Carter had already witnessed one group of men entranced by the power of the poets. Leaping back to his feet, he gave the astronomer a rough slap on the face and pulled him to the floor. Somewhere in the back of his mind, even in the midst of the danger, he thought that if anyone deserved a hard rap, it was Phra.

The astronomer's eyes refocused. He raised a hand to stroke his cheek and glared at Lord Anderson. "What are you doing?"

"If you give in to temptation, they will snare you. I need your help. They nearly defeated me once before."

Carter spoke the Word Which Gives Strength.

Sedhattee!

The room shook, and he immediately felt invigorated. Perhaps because the astronomer also served the Balance, the Word seemed to bolster him too, for his eyes lit with grim determination.

"For the Nine Towers!" Phra cried, his voice booming through the chamber. His words summoned a white shield, sword, and armor, and an ivory helm for his brow, all cast from starlight. Raising himself to his full height, he no longer appeared a pompous aristocrat, but a Greek warrior, tall and lean, his dark eyes flashing with the reflected rays of his pearl blade. It seemed to blind the anarchists, for their firing nearly ceased.

"To me!" Lieutenant Sedger shouted, making use of the momentary advantage. "Form lines to this side!"

In answer the Poetry Man cupped his hands, creating a beam of rising crystal-blue lambency that solidified into a clear staff. Seeing this, the anarchists quickly recovered, and the defenders hurried to their commander beneath a storm of fire, men dying on every side, a terrible slaughter. But as soon as the path between Lord Anderson and the enemy was clear, Carter unleashed the Word Which Manifests.

Falan!

The rippling bolt of power flung the approaching ranks of anarchists off their feet, but the Poetry Man raised his staff and the wave parted before him. The effort seemed to weaken him, however, for he momentarily slumped against the wall. Creating the corridor must have drained much of his energy.

Carter's action bought the defenders precious moments to regroup, and the North Lowing soldiers, led by a company of the

White Circle Guard, quickly formed ranks along the wall opposite their opponents. Although the revolvers used in Evenmere are capable of cutting a six-inch hole in a man, the armor of the White Circle Guard could withstand a discharge at close range, so those men were placed in the front lines.

Carter grimaced. It was the best that could be done, but it put them with their backs to the stair leading down to the chamber held by DuLac. If the captain failed, the defenders would be caught between their enemies.

Clouds of smoke rose as the defenders returned fire. Men fell on every side. Carter saw Storyteller on the ground, writhing and clutching at his head, but dared not pause to give him aid.

Lord Anderson turned to Phra. "We have to stop the poet."

Dustin crouched close enough to the shrapnel cannon to feel the heat rising from it, a position he had assumed when one of the soldiers at the barricade fell. He was not afraid, but filled with the old thrill that used to envelope him during a gnawling hunt.

Then there was only time for combat, as the enemy charged up the steps, firing wildly.

The shrapnel cannon erupted, tossing steel shards down the stair, sending men shrieking and clutching their faces and chests. Still the enemy advanced, their eyes blazing with a fanaticism far different than the intellectual demeanor displayed in former battles. One nearly reached the doorway before a half-dozen bullets sent him spinning back down like a ghastly, bloody top, and the illusion that this was no more than the slaying of gnawlings deserted Duskin entirely.

He glanced at the captain, who was impassively urging the gunners to speed, and Duskin saw that here was courage indeed. For his part he kept calm, taking careful aim and firing with an almost mechanical precision, yet driven by the desperation that Lizbeth would be left unprotected, should the company fall.

The next round from the cannon drove the anarchists back, giving the defenders a brief respite to reload. Duskin had just refilled his pistol chamber when the stair abruptly began to tremble with a quaking that quickly grew in intensity.

The poet, who had vanished beyond the defenders' line of sight after the initial advance, strode up the steps, her face shrouded in a green mist.

"Starlight, star bright," she called, chanting the words over and over in a sing-song voice. "The first star, the first star, the first star."

Power rolled before her, an emerald light of stars and suns and stars and stellar mass and stars and starlight and stardust and star-shine and stars. Always stars. A sun-hot wave rolled along with the radiance, a licking fire, and where it touched the steps they seemed to waver, as if in a heat mirage. Sweat broke across Duskin's brow; he could feel the scorching breath of the inferno.

"Back!" the captain cried. "We can't stand against that!"

They retreated from the barrier just before it erupted into flames. In an instant it was consumed, melting the shrapnel cannon into slag, leaving the doorway open. Despite the fear of being burned alive, DuLac kept order, forcing the men to make a tidy re-treat under covering fire. They crossed the small chamber and backed their way up the stair. Duskin and DuLac, the last out, glanced back to see the rolling energy filling the room.

The poetess appeared at the doorway, her followers by her side. Bullets tore at the stair, forcing Duskin to dance backward. The captain, two steps above him, gave a cry, reached for his head, and collapsed into Duskin's arms.

"DuLac!" Duskin gasped. He dragged the captain to the top of the stair, into the arms of his men, but the officer was already dead.

In despair, Duskin glanced around the chamber and saw the anarchists pouring in through the newly formed passageway. The battle had degenerated into fighting at close quarters. The other an-archists would soon be up the stair. For the first time he considered the possibility of defeat. Fear gripped him as he thought of Liz-beth.

He spied his brother and Edwin Phra battling the Poetry Man. The poet was clearly on the defensive, and his features seemed insubstantial, as if the use of his power was consuming him. Carter struck with his Lightning Sword, breaking the poet's staff. The creature fell to his knees, and Phra came in for the kill. A shout erupted from Duskin's lips. Here was vengeance for the captain's death.

With their foe vanquished, the pair turned toward the anarchists. Seeing Carter's demeanor and Phra's flashing starlight sword, Duskin stood mesmerized by the awful power of the Master and the Grand Astronomer. Dreadful and irresistible as ancient gods, moving together behind Phra's shield, carving swathes through the enemy forces at every turn, they cowered the anarchists wherever they went.

A rush of heat arose behind Duskin, reminding him of his own position. Glancing back, he saw the Poetry Woman ascending the steps, the stone melting beneath her feet. He pointed his pistol at her breast and fired, and though his aim was true, the bullet veered away, striking the anarchist directly behind her, who tumbled to the ground, clawing at his shoulder. Duskin retreated, crying his brother's name.

A blast of fire and Duskin's shout caused Carter to turn toward the new threat. The poetess had just reached the top of the stair, but Lieutenant Sedger was already dividing his company, sending some of his men to battle this second front.

Lord Anderson tapped Phra on the shoulder. "Only we can deal with her."

The Grand Astronomer nodded. Phra's shield had increased in size until it was large enough to protect both men, and they moved together, making a backwards retreat from the anarchists' line. Once safely to the rear, they turned to meet the poetess.

Immediately they encountered resistance, an invisible force emanating from their opponent, pressing against Phra's shield. As one they advanced, but seemed to move in slow motion, as if slogging through high water. Sweat beaded their brows. Carter's legs began to ache.

"Lord Anderson, Astronomer Phra!" the Poetry Woman cried above the din. "Why do you struggle against what is beautiful and true? Why do you fight against the stars themselves?" Bullets ricocheted around the poetess, but none touched her.

Neither Lord Anderson nor the astronomer replied. Carter suspected they might be fighting a losing battle. Scores of anarchists were hurrying up the stair, fanning out in an arc. More anarchists were still exiting from the new corridor. In a few moments the defenders would be hopelessly surrounded.

Although the force against which Carter and Phra struggled had the feel of a physical barrier, it sapped the soul as well. How Carter wanted to surrender to the call of the stars, to stand forever beneath the evening sky, lost in their wonder, hushed by their vastness! The joy of his long life used as a snare against him, the astronomer faced an even more terrible trial. Carter heard Phra sobbing even as they struggled.

Though bereft of their commander, at the urging of their sergeant and Duskin, DuLac's men had joined with the second front sent by Lieutenant Sedger, and now formed lines behind Carter and Phra, reinforcing them as they plunged into the anarchists' ranks. Lord Anderson knew he and the astronomer must be taking the brunt of the poetess's attack, else the soldiers could never have stood against it. Glancing from behind the shield, he saw the woman less than ten yards away, her face lost in green mist. So close, yet every step an agony. His heart hammered; his lungs rattled like a bellows. His legs felt afire.

He had to do something before it was too late. He sought the Words of Power. In such a crisis, the necessary Word often came drifting up without being specifically summoned, as if the Words themselves knew what was needed, but this time none did. He finally decided on the Word Which Seals, hoping to close off the source of the poetess's power. The Word came only with concentration, and it was hard, keeping his mind focused on both it and the struggle to move forward. He finally drew it to him, lifted it to his throat, and sent it through the air.

Nargoth!

The room shook. Carter gasped and clutched his temple as a searing agony stabbed into his forehead. Momentarily, he could neither breathe nor see. When the world swam again into focus, he saw the Word had failed, and the failure brought him to his knees.

"That which is opened by starlight is not so easily contained!" the poetess cried. "Why do you fight me? Give in. Give in."

Phra seized Carter's arm, steadying him until he could regain his feet.

A noise, louder than the battle, thundered out of the stair-well. Some disturbance had arisen *behind* the advancing anarchists. Carter did not have time to see more, as bullets fell thick around the company, forcing him to press close to the shield.

Inch by inch they drew within a foot of the poetess, who stood implacable. Carter saw her with minute clarity: the green robe, the stitches of the sun sewn upon it; the green mist covering most of her face, leaving glimpses of hair or cheek or eye. A tiny lizard pendant, the same green as her garment, stared out with black, unwinking eyes from her collar. She held her hands up, palm outward, trembling as if she could scarcely contain the power.

Carter stepped from behind Phra's shield and struck with his Lightning Sword. An emerald, rectangular barrier appeared in the air between him and his adversary, blocking the stroke. Phra attacked from the other side, and the barrier parried again.

"I am not so easily taken," she exulted. "I am the spring, and you, the fading winter. Yield to the glories of the new season."

Carter drew back his arm and delivered a thunderous blow against the barrier. The noise of it reverberated through the chamber. Lightning licked its surface, but it held.

"Lady Hantish!" one of the anarchists shouted. "We are attacked from below."

Carter thrust against the barrier again, his sword's energies crackling across its surface. A tiny fissure appeared in one corner.

"Phra, we must strike together," Lord Anderson said.

The astronomer nodded.

The two men lifted their blades. Bullets sliced the air around Carter's head as he made his play.

They struck as one, starlight and lightning pouring from their swords. The barrier broke into shards, leaving the poetess clasping her empty hands. The mist around her face withdrew, revealing eyes filled with a tormented fever.

"Fools!" she cried, her voice a puzzled agony. "I could have given you the stars!"

They struck again, both together, cutting her down.

With the Black Beast at his back, Doctor Armilus crawled

on hands and knees along a dusty passage angling ever upward, so narrow he struggled at times to squeeze his great frame through. He brushed aside thick cobwebs woven by black widow spiders.

An abominable end that would be, he considered, *The Supreme Anarchist slain by half a thimble's worth of poison, body never found, carcass left to rot in a secret passage. Where's the drama in that? Glad I thought to bring my gloves.*

He thumped a spider from the center of her web, brushed aside the filaments, and crushed her with the butt of his pistol. *The Book of Lore* had revealed secret passages so old, even the Masters had forgotten them. In all likelihood, this particular way had never before been used. It would allow the doctor to bypass the stair leading into the Central Astronomy Tower, and take him past the Main Observation Hall into the upper chambers.

Like much of what Armilus did, this was a gamble. Lord Anderson could sense that there were secret corridors in the Tower, and might have used the Word of Secret Ways to reveal them so he could set sentries to keep watch. If so, and if the guards were not too numerous, Armilus would try to eliminate them. He hoped it would not come to gunplay, however. So lacking in finesse.

He came to a spyhole. Peering through it, he saw an empty corridor. A latch opened a hidden door in the paneling, and he rolled nimbly to his feet, gun at the ready. The Black Beast came to the opening, sniffed the air, and hopped down. The pair proceeded along the passage, which intersected a hallway. Down the length of this passage, Armilus heard the distant sounds of combat.

He paused, momentarily confused. According to his infallible memory of the maps he had studied, there should not be a corridor at this point. It took him only an instant to realize, with a shock, that this was one created by the poets.

He studied it. Both the walls and ceiling were carved oak, with scarab beetles, lizards, snatches of poetry, and runes throughout. Lambent light from tall braziers fell golden upon the boards, making the entire lane shimmer like a heat-mirage.

He frowned, and as had become his habit, addressed the beast. "Magnificent! This took enormous power. Our opponents are immeasurably strong."

Fortunately, none of the poet's people were at this end of the passage, else it might have ruined his plan. As it was, he wondered how it would affect the counter-attack Heit Nizzle was currently leading. A company of the doctor's followers should already be engaging the rear guard of the poetry forces charging up the Central Tower stair. Neither Armilus, nor Lord Anderson for that matter, could have anticipated the poets creating a second front.

Armilus grimaced. He would have preferred to lead the attack himself, especially considering that Nizzle, having traveled all night to bring the doctor the iron box of Dimension, was exhausted. But Armilus could depend on the man; the devils that drove the count would never allow him to do less than his best. Besides, the business at hand required a certain boldness, a bit of flair. He couldn't be everywhere at once.

The beast growled, and Armilus shook his head to clear it. He must hurry if his plans were to go well. It had been a risky business from the start, menacing Lord Anderson's son, draining the man's resources when he desperately needed to stop the Poetry Men. The fanatics were the dangerous variable, one the doctor had underestimated at the beginning, even as he had used their threat to obtain *The Book of Lore*. But shifts in power between factions always suggested opportunities for advancement, and if Armilus could succeed in his plan, he would be able to nullify both the Master and the poets. Even if he failed, his truce with Anderson could not but help the anarchist cause. Flexibility was so important in such circumstances.

Despite the echoing gunshots and the cries of the wounded and dying, he strode past the poets' corridor with almost casual calm, until he stood before a large painting of nymphs frolicking in a wood. Depressing the bottom corners of the gilt frame caused it to pop open, revealing another secret passage. With the beast at his heels, he slipped inside and closed the door behind him, walling himself into absolute darkness.

After a bit of fumbling he struck a match, revealing a small chamber with a wooden ladder leading upward. As he began his ascent, the beast followed by transforming its paws into hands. Armilus mentally added this previously unknown talent to his list of facts concerning the creature.

The match burned his fingers before he was halfway up the rungs, causing him to growl and fling it away, but having already spied a circular trapdoor overhead, he did not light another. It lifted with the turn of a handle. He had to contort his frame to force his bulk through the narrow opening into the upper room where Carter and Phra had looked at the stars.

After giving a cursory glance at the glass dome with the three-dimensional star field, he withdrew from his jacket pocket a small magnifying mirror, the iron box from the Quadrangle of Angles, and a silk handkerchief adroitly removed through the charms of the Contessa du Maurier from the vaults of a minor prince of Moomuth Kethorvian. After studying the room, he recognized the required mechanism, a telescope of unusual design, with four sets of eye-pieces. He scanned his memory for the list of operating instructions from *The Book of Lore*, and after several moments of meticulous fiddling, found the star he sought, a blue sun in Arcturus. Using the mirror, he reflected the starlight from the lens onto the silk handkerchief. Where the image touched the cloth, it glowed the same color as the star. For precisely two minutes, as judged by his pocket-watch, he allowed the rays to fall upon the silk. He placed the handkerchief within the iron box of Dimension, realigned the telescope to its former settings, and hastily returned the mirror and box to his pocket.

The beast gave a low growl. Turning, he discovered two women at the doorway. One he assumed to be the astronomer's wife; the other—Lizbeth Anderson—he had seen years ago.

"Who are you?" the taller woman demanded. "What are you doing here?"

"Ah," Armilus said, touching his hand to his bowler. "You must be Blodwen Phra."

"I am."

"Allow me to present my card," the doctor reached into his pocket and produced his pistol. "It is not my inclination to kill women; however, in this particular case, unless I am permitted to leave, I must make an exception."

Blodwen stepped between the doctor and Lizbeth. "Pass then. Whatever you have done, my husband will ensure you answer for it."

Armilus gave a slight bow while the animal at his feet growled. "No, beast," the doctor ordered. "These are too lovely to be slain, and it makes no difference whether Lord Anderson knows I was here. We have a pact."

The hound whined in its longing to destroy, and with some satisfaction Armilus noted the fear the creature brought to the women's eyes—its dreadful darkness, its horribly intelligent gaze, its musky scent filling the room. They would have a story to tell, at least.

Gun raised, Armilus led the animal past the women toward the trap door. The beast growled again, as if in prelude to an attack.

"No!" Armilus cried, so violently both Lizbeth and Blodwen jumped. "I said *no*! You cannot have these! It fits no plan of mine."

The creature slunk to the doctor's feet. He opened the trap door and ordered it down.

"Adieu, good ladies," he said.

"How did you know of that door?" Blodwen asked.

Armilus gave a slight smile. "Wonderful, the things you can learn by reading. Good evening."

He exited, pulling the door closed behind him, hurrying down the rungs in case the women found a weapon to use against him.

When he stepped out of the secret panel, back into the corridor, the sounds of battle had died away, leaving only the noise of the wounded and of soldiers crying orders. Not wishing to be seen without his followers to support him, he ignored the corridor created by the poets and followed the secret passage to the small room below the Main Observation Hall, where he found Nizzle, haggard and triumphant, giving orders to another anarchist.

"Doctor!" Nizzle cried, in high exultation. "You have arrived. Excellent! We caught them between our forces and Lord Anderson's, exactly as you planned. Both poets were slain. The Radicals did not surrender as logical men would have done, but fought to the very last, shouting snatches of poetry and incoherent slogans. It was a magnificent slaughter. We are preparing to depart to avoid any difficulties with the White Circle Guard, who may lack the proper degree of gratitude."

"Wait. There is someone upstairs I want to see. Come along."

"Is this wise?" Heit Nizzle asked, following behind. At his gesture a handful of anarchists joined them.

Upon reaching the chamber above, Armilus called across

the room. "Ah, there. Master Anderson!"

"Doctor," Nizzle protested. "The Master himself! We—"

Armilus raised his hand for silence. "Be calm. Keep your place."

Lord Anderson turned and approached the anarchists. Immediately, several members of the White Circle Guard took positions around him. The doctor strolled leisurely toward him, halting only when they were ten paces apart.

"What do you want?" the Master asked.

Armilus gave his slight smile. "I trust your casualties were low?"

"Much lower than they might have been."

"We have been allies this day, Lord Anderson," Armilus said, "exactly as I told you. Seeing you standing there, I cannot help but admire how imposing you look—tall, dignified—so different from the young man who returned from exile when I was but a junior member of the Council."

"If you are looking for thanks, you will receive none."

"Hah!" the doctor boomed. "Exactly right. We both understand our own motives. I'm simply making an observation. It seems to me that the anarchists have shaped you. We haven't meant to, but we have taken you through the fire and produced fine work. Exactly the opposite of our intentions."

"I trust I have done the same for you."

"Touchè. Worthy adversaries have that effect."

"Do you have a point?"

"Only this. I did what I promised. Through it, we both achieved victory. It is worth the sacrifice. Remember that. We can be friends for a time."

"We are never friends," Anderson said.

Duskin appeared beside the Master, pistol raised, but Lord Anderson pushed his wrist gently down.

"Carter," Duskin said, "do you know who he is? This is our chance!"

"This is not the time."

"But—"

"*No!*" Lord Anderson said, lips taut.

Armilus gave a tight, satisfied smile.

"Remove yourself from the Tower of Astronomy," the Master ordered the doctor. "You have free passage. If any of your men remain by the turning of the hour, they will be shot on sight."

The doctor placed his hand on his stomach and gave a half-bow. "As you wish." He turned to his followers. "Heit Nizzle, assemble the men. Let us be off."

The anarchists formed loose ranks and departed, Nizzle hurrying them along with many a backward glance. Armilus followed slowly behind, the Black Beast at his side.

He had enjoyed that small exchange. Besides reinforcing Anderson's promise, addressing the Master with familiarity had raised the doctor's prestige before his followers. It had also placed a shade of suspicion on Anderson himself in the eyes of *his* minions. One never knew when a slight detail like that could pay off.

The doctor whistled off-key, then addressed the beast. "A good day, overall. A very good day, though I think I must soon find a way to kill one of these Poetry Men."

"That . . . could . . . be . . . done," the beast replied.

Armilus, eyes wide in amazement, hand suddenly trembling, took a full minute before responding.

As soon as the anarchists had departed, Carter turned away and nearly walked into Storyteller.

"Master Anderson." The minstrel looked unusually grim.

"I saw you go down during the fight," Carter said. "Are you injured?"

"Not by any bullet. Like yourself, I am tuned to the Balance. The appearance of the new corridor ran through me like hot coals, but I am spry as a pup now."

Carter studied the man's face. A shadow of pain behind his eyes suggested Jonathan was not as well as he pretended.

"It struck me hard as well," Carter said. "I suppose being aware of the Balance for so many centuries—"

"That's right, Master Anderson, but there are always troubles. Right now I am troubled by what the Supreme Anarchist meant by his peacock gloating."

"We have a temporary truce," Carter admitted.

"What kind of truce?"

Carter told what had happened in the country of dream, and for the first time saw Jonathan's face fill with anger. The minstrel clutched his forehead with one hand.

"You don't know what you have done, Master Anderson. You don't know what you have done. You may have sacrificed Evenmere."

"I had no choice. My son—"

"There is always a choice," Jonathan said. "Always. You have given them more power than you can imagine. Not just Armilus, but the forces of Chaos."

Lizbeth rushed up just then. "Carter, during the battle a man came to the chamber above, followed by some sort of animal. We think he must have stolen something, but we don't know what."

Storyteller sat on the floor, weeping and moaning from behind his hands.

Shadow Valley

For the remainder of the night Lord Anderson, Duskin, Lizbeth, and—at Carter's insistence—Jonathan Bartholomew slept in the guest quarters of the Grand Astronomer, while the soldiers kept watch below. Lord Anderson did not fully trust Armilus' promise to leave Jason alone, but that night he had no choice; using the Words of Power had drained him completely. For the first time, he realized the ramifications of their pact. The doctor knew Carter would keep his word, while Carter had no such assurance.

Despite his anxiety, he soon dropped into a deep, dreamless sleep. He awoke much later, and finding it still dark outside, fumbled for his pocket watch, which read 12:02. Two towers, adorned with burning stars, stood outside his window, and at first he thought it must be midnight, until he remembered that daylight never came to the Tower of Astronomy, and he had retired after the witching hour. With astonishment, he realized he must have slept till noon.

He sat up in bed and the sudden movement sent a jabbing pain along his shoulder. He slowly rotated his arm, working out the soreness, then rose and dressed by starlight. Stepping from his room, he encountered Edwin Phra approaching along the corridor.

"Ah, Master Anderson, I was just coming to find you. Lunch is about to be served, if you would care to join the company."

"Certainly," Carter said. "Is Jonathan there?"

"I assume he is downstairs. A presumptuous fellow. Tried to tell me some odd tale over breakfast, as if I had time for that sort of thing."

"His stories can be instructive. I would like him to lunch with us."

Phra raised his eyebrows. "If you insist, though it seems a strange breach of protocol."

"I do insist." Rankled by the astronomer's arrogance, Carter spoke more sharply than he intended, but if Phra noticed he gave no sign.

Carter followed the astronomer to a small chamber overlooking the star towers. Duskin and Lizbeth were already there, seated around an oak table with a woman wearing a green silk dress with wide pagoda sleeves.

"I must leave you in the capable hands of my spouse, for I have to be about my duties," the Grand Astronomer said. "Blodwen, this is Lord Carter Anderson. Lord Anderson, my wife, Blodwen Phra."

"A pleasure to meet you." Blodwen's soft voice possessed a slow, eternal quality, as if the timeless heavens outside the window had seeped into her soul. She was tall, with deep brown eyes, hands fine as sewn silk, and a smile so small as to be merely an upturn of her lips.

"The pleasure is mine," Carter said, giving a slight bow.

Jonathan soon joined them. After the minstrel's rebuke the night before, Carter expected to meet a cold reception, but Storyteller gave him a warm greeting and a subdued smile. He sat down heavily and glanced around. "You must forgive me today. I am a bit under the weather. My head feels like someone punched a hole through it. But don't you worry. I will be just fine. I have good bones."

Over a lunch of braised goose, Lady Blodwen told the names of the stars hanging on the towers, and where they stood in the heavens, and how many planets revolved around each one; and showed her locket, with miniatures of her son and daughter within, who were grown and married and living in Aylyrium. She gave off a quiet assuredness, a serenity of spirit warm as a candle-glow, a stark contrast to her husband's coldness.

"Don't you find it wearing, living always in the night?" Lizbeth asked, staring out at the stars. "Do you ever long for blue sky?"

"Oh, yes," Blodwen said. "The stars are like the ocean, too vast and terrible to contemplate for long. It does make one lonely. When it becomes too much, I visit my mother in the Downs of Gen."

"How long have you and the astronomer been married?" Duskin asked.

"Eighteen years this spring."

"Does it bother you, his having had so many other wives?" Lizbeth asked.

Carter groaned inwardly at his sister-in-law's impertinence, and Duskin lowered his eyes to the table, but Blodwen patted Lizbeth's hand and said, "The Grand Astronomer has the admirable trait of loving his current wife best. He may seem aloof, but he bears a great responsibility and needs a touch the stars cannot give. Whatever he remembers, Edwin never mentions his five previous marriages."

"But you will grow old, and he will not," Lizbeth persisted, causing Duskin to look so uncomfortable Carter had to suppress a grin. "It seems hard."

Blodwen glanced down at the table, her serenity untouched. "It is both a joy and sorrow. Yes, my beauty will wane, while his will not, yet he is steadfast, and when I am an old woman, he will care for me and tend me if I grow ill, and love me still, perhaps in the way a son loves his mother, or a father his daughter who cannot care for herself. Have you read Yeats? *But one man loved the pilgrim soul in you, And loved the sorrow of your changing face.* Edwin loves the pilgrim soul within me. What more could any woman want?"

"That's beautiful," Lizbeth said. "Do you love my pilgrim soul, Duskin?"

That, at least, brought a smile to Duskin's face. "It describes you well, my dear. You are certainly mercurial in nature."

"Lord Anderson, Lizbeth tells me you know the man who stole into our rooms last night," Blodwen said. "My husband discovered that a bit of light was siphoned off a star in the Arcturus system. The intruder tried to erase the signs of the theft, but the machinery is far more sophisticated than any but the Grand Astronomer can conceive. Edwin cannot think of any use to be made of the captured starlight."

"Tell me the entire story again," Carter said. "Any detail might be important."

Together, the women related the facts of their encounter, leaving Carter with a sick feeling in his stomach. He should have thought to guard the secret ways.

"So helping us stop the Poetry Men was just a ruse," Duskin said.

"No," Carter replied, "Armilus wants the poets thwarted, but it must delight him to earn our gratitude while stealing from us. Imagine the man's cheek, confronting me for his own amusement after the battle, gambling I hadn't already been told of his theft."

"Whatever his reasons," Lady Blodwen said, "he was kind enough to spare us."

"Armilus has killed before," Carter replied. "I would not willingly cast myself upon his tender mercies. But perhaps you recently met one of his associates? My original reason for coming was to uncover the whereabouts of a woman named Erin Shoemate, who holds the key to the source of the poets' power."

"Professor Shoemate connected with the doctor?" Blodwen said. "That seems an odd pairing."

"In what way?" Carter asked.

"In every way. Erin Shoemate spent three days with us, and I have never met a more delightful woman. She is the soul of honesty, if I am any judge. Surely you cannot suggest she is an anarchist!"

"More of a dreamer, actually."

"That would fit her exactly," Blodwen said. "She was wholly concerned with art and literature, and was seeking an ancient book, one she thought would lead her to what she called True Poetry. She read me some of her own poems, which were quite good."

"Why did she come here?" Jonathan asked. "Did she think you had this book?"

"No. She had just spent several weeks of research in the Palace of the Decemvirs, looking for clues to the location of a portal called, in ancient times, the Eye Gate, which she believed would lead to the volume she was seeking. In the records there, she found a single reference, written by a Minasian explorer who claimed to have visited the gate. In his account he listed the exact date of his discovery and the precise time of moonrise on that particular evening. She came to us to discover the region of Evenmere in which the moon was visible at the horizon at that time, somewhere south of East Wing and north of the old Iphrisian Dominion."

"That account must have been written hundreds of years ago," Carter said. "Were you able to supply the information?"

"Our records are quite precise. In fact, I can send a servant to fetch a copy of what we gave her."

Lady Blodwen gave instructions, and before the meal was done, a messenger returned with a yellow envelope. Opening it, Carter found a drawing of the moon at three-quarters, and a map of Evenmere indicating a fifty-mile strip to the east.

"It is a large area to search," Blodwen said, "but based on the explorer's account, Professor Shoemate believed the Queen of Shadow Hall possessed additional information on the Eye Gate's location. She intended to visit Shadow Valley, to see if its monarch could help narrow the search."

Lord Anderson frowned and glanced at Jonathan. "Another of the Circle of Servants. From the reports I would prefer never to set foot in Shadow Valley, but I see no other choice. We should be off immediately."

"That will take you close to Lowing Hall," Duskin said. "Our scouts report no further signs of any poets, and I need to return home to report to King Edgemont. Lieutenant Sedger will remain in charge here. We could accompany you part of the way."

"I doubt the poets will soon strike the Tower of Astronomy again," Lord Anderson said. "They took a bad beating, and Phra is stronger for having resisted their temptation." He withdrew his pocket watch and glanced at Lizbeth. "Can you be ready to go by two?"

Lizbeth smiled. "Don't ask me. You've forgotten I came without luggage."

"Then I will ask Duskin. Brother, can you have your wardrobe ready?"

"I can manage. I need only confer with the lieutenant."

"Two it is, then," Carter said.

Jonathan Bartholomew made his way up the circular stair of the Sixth Tower. As he advanced, the stars outside the embrasures grew nearer. A third of the way up, he stepped into a circular room filled with machinery. Choosing one of six doors, he crossed onto a stone bridge linking the Sixth and Seventh Towers. Above and below him hung the cold stars, their slow rotations making the bridge seem to sway. The other towers were visible, rising majestically into the night. The heights did not frighten him; he had trod this way before.

Edwin Phra stood at the very edge of the span, looking down, apparently lost in contemplation until the echoes of Jonathan's boots roused him. He raised his head and gave the minstrel a cold glance, but remained silent.

"Do you like looking at the stars, Grand Astronomer?"

"They are a source of infinite wonder." His voice was clipped and cold.

"That's right. That's right. You stand here, basking in the humming of the suns, looking at the light of other days, listening to the music of the spheres."

"If you've come to tell me some foolish story, you can spare your voice. I have lived hundreds of years and have heard them all."

"So instead you stand here, thinking of your childhood friend, wondering if you could have done anything to save him."

Phra took an unconscious step away from the void. "How do you . . .? How dare you address me concerning that!"

"You have no time for my stories, so I must speak plainly. That's right. You have lived a long time, but you are a babe dandled at the knee compared to the lifetime of the Storyteller. He came long ago, when Evenmere dressed itself in columns older than the ruins of Minasia. He was at the bedside when the first Grand Astronomer died at an age little more than your own. He played ball with the seven-year-old boy who was your predecessor. And he will remind you that you reign in this starry kingdom because you were chosen to do so, and if your pride grows too great, another will take your place."

Phra lifted an eyebrow, but his expression remained otherwise unchanged. "I do not subscribe to the superstition that Evenmere chooses its servants. Is this all you came to tell me?"

Jonathan gave his large smile. "That was for free, so you could tuck it in your pocket and rub it between your forefinger and thumb. You are a man who makes much of respect, so affronting your dignity is the best way to get your attention. Did you know that a second of time was stolen from the Eternity Clock?"

Phra's eyes widened slightly. "That could affect the stars."

"It could affect everything. It *will* affect everything. It was surely Doctor Armilus. I have connections throughout the house, and he is being watched whenever he can be found. But now Lord Anderson has made a truce with him."

"The man is slipshod. It is a wonder he ever reached so high a rank."

"That is a question for another time, but the ramifications are great. He has taken a step toward the side of Chaos. As a result, it may happen that he is removed and replaced by a new Master."

"Removed by whom?" Phra snorted. "You?"

Storyteller ignored the question. "If this happens, his successor will be young and lacking in experience. He will need guidance."

Phra looked down at the void, as if trying to see something within it. "I am kept quite occupied, but in our present crisis, if a new Master appeared I could be ready to . . . assist him. I could send a message to the other members of the Circle of Servants, urging them to do the same. They would listen to me."

"That is a good thought. The word of the Grand Astronomer would carry considerable weight."

"It is all I can promise."

Jonathan nodded his head and the two men stood looking out into the darkness.

Finally, Storyteller spoke again. "Your friend—"

"Don't patronize me with some homily that it wasn't my fault, or that he is in a better place."

"I will say nothing of the sort, not knowing his fate. It *was* your fault, and his father's fault, and his own fault. But you were young and did not know how your words would affect him; and the mask of pride you wear will not protect you until you forgive yourself." [1]

With that, Jonathan turned and strode away, his patchwork coat streaming behind him.

Immediately after lunch, Lord Anderson repaired to a warm bath in preparation for travel. The company assembled in the Main Observation Hall, including at Lieutenant Sedger's insistence a half-dozen of the North Lowing Guard to escort Lizbeth and Duskin back to Lowing Hall. Blodwen expressed her regrets that the Grand Astronomer's duties prevented him from seeing them off, so they passed without ceremony down the winding stair. From there they journeyed east along the steppes.

When they were within an hour of Lowing Hall, where Duskin and Lizbeth kept their residence, they were forced to part company since Carter and Jonathan would be traveling farther east.

"I regret we can't come with you," Duskin replied, "but we'll do what we can here."

Carter gave his brother a hug, and in so doing, found himself unexpectedly emotional, as if he were deserting him. Blinking back tears, he embraced Lizbeth, then he and Jonathan set off again across the steppes.

At five o'clock that afternoon they passed out of North Lowing and entered the winding corridors of the Uffolloff Heights, a portion of the house built across a range of small mountains. They journeyed an hour along the corridors called the Toes, a wavering north-south passage lying at the mountains' feet, and soon began their ascent, along corridors angling from side to side to avoid becoming too steep. Where sharp inclines were unavoidable, stairs had been built. Blue molding with crenelated borders covered the walls; Prussian-blue carpet sheathed the floors; Nottingham lace adorned the windows. Hundreds of portraits of the founders and heroes of the Heights peered through the gloom, their eyes yellowed with age.

---

[1] To find out more about Phra's story, read *The Star Watch* for free at
www.james-stoddard.com/Starwatch

The gradual slope of the passages, after the earlier descent from the Astronomy Tower, left the travelers aching. They spent the night in one of the quaint Victorian drawing rooms scattered along the corridor. Wanstead sofas served as beds, and the fireplace box had plenty of wood for a cheery blaze.

They dined on bread and cheese. Distrusting Armilus, Carter wanted to check on Jason, but had a little time before he must go. When they had sat in silence awhile before the flickering fire, Lord Anderson sighed.

"What is the young Master thinking?" Jonathan asked.

"Mostly that I don't feel that young anymore." He smiled. "Actually, I was thinking that if not for Armilus and the Poetry Men, this would be a grand adventure. I am forever fascinated by the winding halls of Evenmere, the endless corridors, the uncountable stairs. One would think I would weary of it, but I never do. It's like tramping in a forest, where every turn brings a new vista: here a gnarled cabinet hoary as a man, there a weathered statue faded by the sun, a stream, a rock formation grinning like a ghost—that is Evenmere. As if I were on a treasure hunt."

"I am sure the house appreciates your appreciation," Jonathan said.

Carter laughed. "Enoch puts it the same way, talking about it as if it were alive. It does feel like that sometimes. He says it wasn't always Victorian architecture, but has changed over the ages. Are you old enough to remember that?"

"A house old as time *would* change. Think of what it has seen. So many wonderful lives, so many exquisite souls. No one should be surprised if it takes on a life of its own. Or was alive from the beginning. There is a very old story about Evenmere, you know. It tells how, when the house first came into existence, it stood in a great silence, in a universe without planets or suns or any other thing, filled with nothing but diffused light passing through gray mist. No ground existed beneath the mansion, only that mist in every direction. Evenmere did not know who had built it; it did not know to even ask the question. It dwelt, the only dwelling in that emptiness, for an unknown length of time.

"One day, the clocks scattered through the mansion started ticking, so Evenmere knew Time had begun its great race. Outside, the rain began to fall. The house felt the earth form beneath it, pebble by pebble, until its foundations stood on solid ground. The rain made ponds and lakes and mighty oceans in the low places, and the waters came pouring over its verandas, passing through its doorways, cutting channels within the house, streaming down what would become the Fable River.

"In the place we now call the Tower of Astronomy, lights appeared as clouds of gas. They coalesced, becoming glowing stars. The mists cleared. Evenmere stood upon a world, on a plain covered in waving grass, the buttery light of the sun overhead.

"With the waters came life. Fish appeared in Evenmere's rivers. Animals rose along the bank. And one day, long after, a boat slipped down the Fable. Within it, dressed in gray and gold and green and scarlet, were the First Ones, men and women young and beautiful as the sunlight shining in Evenmere's eaves. The High House watched with interest these new people inhabiting its halls, but though it understood their tongues, it had no way to speak to them. Nonetheless, working subtly, it showed them how to work the mechanisms of the house. They learned that doing so enabled them to keep the universe in order, and that became the mission of their lives.

"With everything running well, Evenmere rejoiced to be alive, listening to its ticking clocks, watching the burning stars surrounding the Astronomy Towers, hearing the ghosts play in the Room of Horrors, observing the shadows creep from the Valley of Shadow. Other people drifted in through its doors.

"But as is the way with people everywhere, as more folks entered its portals things became complicated. Some opposed those who ran the mechanisms of the house. This confused Evenmere. And so, again working in silence, it created the position of Head Servant, to coordinate the work of the other servants. Eventually, those who followed that servant came to call him the Master.

"Since that time, the house has struggled to keep the Balance against those who would undermine it."

As if in answer to Jonathan's tale, the floorboards, settling for the night, gave a comforting creak.

"A lovely story, though flawed," Carter said. "If the house couldn't speak, it could never reveal what it saw in the beginning. But imagine the things it would tell us if it could. These old boards . . ." He glanced at the pictures on the wall of landscapes and wide-eyed children. "The first question I would ask is why so much of it is empty. Why so many unoccupied chambers?"

Jonathan took a sip of tea from his tin cup. "That is a good question. My answer is if the house is nearly infinite, it is too enormous to be filled."

Carter laughed. "*Nearly infinite*; there's an impossible turn of phrase. You are probably more widely traveled than anyone. Do you really think it endless?"

"Not endless, but very large. The universe itself has an end, Master Anderson, and what lies beyond it, who can say? Perhaps other universes. Perhaps universe after universe sitting on long shelves like blue marbles. But if Evenmere represents the universe, why should it not be mostly empty of life, as is the universe itself? Think of the distances between the stars. Living creatures make up but a small part. So too the house. But do not think, because the distances are great and men small, that size is relevant. No! A great whale is many times larger than a human, yet humanity rules the world. So too the size of the universe humbles us, as when we stare out of the Tower of Astronomy at the hanging stars. But the human spirit, when grounded in compassion, can be large as Leviathan."

"Yet many are mean-spirited," Carter said, "and life plays cruel tricks that sometimes leave us bitter."

"Children have the greatest souls, if they are raised with love, for they have faith in the wonder and mystery of the world. Adults must remember that and find it anew. Eventually, all secrets are revealed."

Carter chuckled. "It seems to me many things in my life remain hidden, and Evenmere has a million secrets. Are you still angry with me for making a truce with Armilus?"

Jonathan was silent for so long Carter grew uncomfortable. "Anger is for a single moment, Master Anderson. It hasn't any good use thereafter. I am worried, but what is done is done. We must concentrate on finding Professor Shoemate and learning the source of the Poetry Men's power. Finding it, we must somehow put an end to it. It is a desperate course, requiring all our strength and mind."

At the appointed hour, Carter walked once more in the land of slumber. The Word Which Brings Aid summoned Mr. Hope, and Carter grimaced, for he had hoped for Sarah, who would have been more understanding of his agreement with Armilus.

After Carter related the news and told of the battle, Mr. Hope sat down in the rocking chair in Jason's room, lips pursed, his round face a mask, and did not speak for so long Carter finally burst out, "Well, say it and get it over with!"

"Sorry," Hope said. "It's a lot to absorb. Messengers reached us this evening about the fight, but the details were lacking."

"Are you appalled?"

Hope raised his eyebrows. "Appalled? No. Your actions were justified. Concerned."

"Jonathan said the same thing. What are you thinking?"

"Too many thoughts at once. Given your weariness, your need to protect Jason, and the threat to the Astronomy Tower, you did what you thought best; but one can be logical, correct even, and still take the wrong path. You have bound yourself to a nebulous promise not to interfere with the anarchists unless they present a danger to the house. More concrete terms would have been better."

"Do you believe he will honor our bargain?"

Hope's brow unfurrowed. "I actually think he may. I have been researching Doctor Benjamin Armilus, who has proven to be a fascinating character. His mother died when he was fourteen, killed by a thief in their home. His father became interested in the anarchy party shortly thereafter, but never officially joined. He *did* become distant, traveling for business, so Armilus was often left alone, and soon fell in with his father's anarchist connections. He continued the association throughout his university career, rising rapidly in rank within the party, and has served on the Anarchist Council for over ten years, despite briefly falling out of favor. During much of that time, he worked first as a professor, then as dean of the College of Poets, surreptitiously using his position to recruit students to the cause. A voracious reader, possessed of a

photographic memory, he may have one of the finest minds in
Evenmere. He is fluent in Latin, Gostian, and Old Aylyrium, and
conversant in six other languages. He values personal loyalty, even
beyond loyalty to his party. He has a high sense of drama; he loves
the grand gesture, as evidenced by his confronting you after the
battle. He also loves little inside jokes, even at perilous cost—
Chant pointed out that the doctor's pseudonyms, Mr. Simular and
L'Marius, are anagrams for Armilus. As the clown, he even
stressed the spelling of Simular with a *u* to Jason, and used the
name L'Marius despite the possibility that you might have known
the real bosun's name."

"Beyond audacious," Carter said, "perhaps pathological."

"Indeed, but more germane to your question, Armilus is, in
his way, an honorable man, with a convoluted code of conduct. I'm
not saying he wouldn't break his promise, but he would do so only
if absolutely necessary. My guess is that since he has the truce he
wanted, he will dismiss Jason from his mind."

"That's some relief, assuming you are correct."

"Right. But . . ." Hope hesitated.

"What?"

"I don't know how to say this."

"You're a lawyer, Will. You always know how to say it."

Hope smiled. "Actually, I'm a butler. Very well. It doesn't
do any good to have advisors unless they are frank. You may have,
with the best of intentions, broken a fundamental law of the
house."

"You are the second person tonight to speak of the house as
if it were alive."

"Perhaps not the house itself, but the principles behind the
house. I have been doing a lot of reading. The Master must answer
to a higher calling, even if it means sacrificing those around him."

"Are you saying I should have forfeited my son?"

Hope winced. "No. I mean, I don't see how you could; but
the Master has obligations beyond those of ordinary men."

"And what should I have done?" Carter demanded. "Let
him have Jason? Let myself grow so weary I became lost in
dream? Where would Evenmere be then?"

"I'm not condemning you. I'm warning you that there may
be consequences. The house demands much."

"The house demands too much!" Lord Anderson turned and paced back and forth across the room, then sat on the bed and ran a hand through his hair.

"I'm sorry," he finally said, his voice low in defeat. "You're right, of course. I suppose that's what makes me so angry. I've been trying not to think about it. I've seen it every way but the way it really is."

He looked Hope in the eyes. "I have betrayed Evenmere."

"You did what you thought best."

"I allowed my love for my son to take precedence over my duty. I didn't have to keep watch over him every night. I could have remained at my task, protecting the manor. If the Poetry Men succeed, Jason may die anyway. It's as if I've stolen the Master Keys all over again."

"I didn't tell you this to make you feel guilty," Hope said. "I want you to be prepared, in case there are repercussions."

"Of what sort?"

"I don't know. There are principles concerning the Balance that are beyond my understanding, perhaps beyond *anyone's* understanding. Because you weren't willing to sacrifice Jason, something else may happen. I know that's vague, but you need to watch for it, try to be ready."

"Something involving my boy?"

"It's not some cosmic scale, weighing one action against another. It's rather that events have been tipped toward the side of Chaos. Anything you can do to shore up the cause of Order might be useful."

Carter frowned. "You don't understand what you're asking. Whatever I do to affect Chaos or Order can have unpredictable— even disastrous—effects. I wouldn't know how to go about it."

"Then all I can advise is to watch for whatever opportunity comes your way."

Carter grimaced, despair gripping his heart.

Following Carter and Jonathan's departure, Duskin, Lizbeth, and the soldiers soon reached Lowing Hall, a sprawling set of apartments overlooking a channel of the Fable. Terraced steppes of white marble surrounded the house, so that looking out from the upper stories was like gazing over glacial plains.

Duskin went at once to confer with King Edgemont, leaving Lizbeth on her own for a few hours. After several days of being surrounded by people, she invariably welcomed her time alone. Eschewing any assistance from the maid, she ran her own bath, and after luxuriating in its warmth, dressed and went to the sleepy library nestled in the southern portion of the house. Despite its small size, the shelves were carefully stocked, and she was soon lying on a floral fainting couch, immersed in the flowing prose of Yodner's *Paradoxicon*.

The room was warm, and the author's slow images of velvet curtains against sand and sea gradually lulled Lizbeth, until she could scarcely stay awake. She had just finished the section where the whole sky rolls up at twilight, revealing the Swain Rider, when her eyelids grew too heavy to keep open.

It seemed she had remained so for only a few seconds before a scraping rumble caused her to start. At first, she thought she must still be asleep and dreaming, for the bookshelf at the end of the couch had swung outward, revealing the maw of a lightless passage.

She sat up, completely alert the moment her feet touched the floor. Rising, she examined the bookcase and discovered a hidden latch and hinges. Impulsive by nature, she took a lit lamp from a table, and holding it aloft, stepped into the benighted passage.

The walls were of cedar, and their fragrance filled the air. She stood at the top of a stair leading down into darkness. Without hesitation, she descended the wooden steps, which creaked beneath her weight. She, who had traveled so many such passages, did not think of danger or entrapment, but went like a hound enthralled in the hunt, her eyes shining with the prospect of adventure.

The stair quickly ended, opening onto a passageway blocked at one end by a wall. She glanced back only once at the rectangle of light from the library before proceeding down the hall. The passage took several turns, and intersected another hallway with a large plumbing pipe running along the ceiling. She hesitated, uncertain which direction to go, before choosing the left.

After journeying another hundred yards and encountering two more intersections, she decided to turn back. Such a labyrinth should be reported to the officials; if they did not already know of it, it represented a weakness in the palace defenses.

Walking back, she was surprised to discover that the original intersection was much closer than she remembered. Having a keen sense of distances, she took the turn to the right with slight perplexity. It seemed incorrect. Had there been four intersections instead of three? She shook her head, certain there were not. Nonetheless, she backtracked to the last junction and looked to the right.

The continuation of the plumbing pipe in that direction told her she had not come that way, so she must have been correct the first time. She undertook her previous course again, but with the nagging feeling she was traveling wrong. Yet when the passage took several turns, as it had done on the way there, she grew more assured.

As she continued, she became aware of a slight sloping of the hallway, taking her gradually deeper. Odd she hadn't noticed it before. She bit her lower lip and hurried along.

When a half-hour passed without her reaching the stair, she halted. Still, thinking she must have miscalculated the time spent, she went twenty minutes more before admitting she had missed the way.

There was nothing to do for it but turn around. She passed once more through the series of turnings, but when she reached a straight way again, she found the floor sloping again, as if she were traveling the same direction as before. Worse, her sense of direction, which was quite good, told her she *was* doing so.

Two hours later, lost in Evenmere in a manner she had never been before, she paused, remembering Carter's stories of traveling through the dream dimension. Was *she* in a dream? Did she only think she had awakened in the little library? She shuffled her feet. Everything felt quite real, but it was said the land of slumber was not as an ordinary dream.

If she were dreaming, or even if she weren't, was she being directed somewhere? If so, by whom and for what purpose?

"The only way to find out," she whispered, as she used to whisper to herself during her imprisonment, "is to go and see."

As if in answer, the glow of a single gas-jet rose fifty yards down the corridor. She blew out her own light to save its oil and set out with purpose.

Three days later, hungry, foot-sore, her only sustenance water found in underground taps, she came to a blank wall lit by another lamp. In her stupor, she nearly walked right into it, then stood dumbly staring, as if trying to decide from whence it came.

Rousing herself from her lethargy, she pulled a lever on the wall. A panel rolled back. She stepped into the library in the Inner Chambers.

A figure, sitting in a chair among the stacks, glanced up and gave a gasp. It was Sarah.

"Lizbeth, where in all of Evenmere did you come from?"

"Is it real, or is it a dream?" Lizbeth asked, stumbling into her sister's arms.

When Carter awoke in the drawing room, he found the fire stoked and Jonathan sitting in a chair, eyes half-closed as if having never slept. Lord Anderson did not disturb the minstrel's contemplations, but lay looking from behind his eyelashes at the wall covered with paintings and portraits, thinking he might manage another hour's slumber before they had to leave. He soon gave this up, however. Hope's warning had left him too anxious to sleep.

The travelers set off after breakfast. Throughout the morning they toiled up the Heights, over scarlet stairs and along sloping corridors lined with amber tiles. Around noon they reached level ground and a pair of double doors manned by a gray-haired gentleman in a gray kilt, with an enormous black felt cap descending down his back like a shawl. A dove was painted on his forehead; an emerald hung at his throat.

"Welcome to Loft, good sirs," he said, in a clipped accent. "Please state the nature of your business and your intended length of stay."

"I am Carter Anderson, Master of Evenmere, and this is the bard, Storyteller. We intend to pass beyond Loft into Shadow Valley."

The man raised his eyebrows. "It seems the stuff of legends

has appeared at my door. Very nice, but not very scientific. Do you have a real reason for entering Loft?"

"The reasons are as I stated," Carter said. "I realize Loft is not part of the White Circle—"

"Nor ever shall be," the man replied. "This poppycock about the Master controlling the mechanisms that run the universe! Sheer nonsense. As bad as the anarchists. The problem is the initial hypothesis, that the house was originally built by anyone. How droll! How unimaginative."

"And was it not?" Carter asked.

"Current theory demonstrates that Evenmere arose from cross-circular magnetic vortices—patterns created from sequenced non-patterns."

Jonathan glanced around the hall. "To me, a doorknob looks like someone made it."

"Only because we are within the environment where a doorknob is recognized as a doorknob. You see, because we are *within* the house, it seems wholly natural to us, as if it were planned, but actually it is a chaotic event—a happenstance occurrence. Thus, anything done by the Master or anyone else in Evenmere could not possibly affect the physical universe outside the house. The mathematical equations show it quite clearly."

"You seem over-qualified to be a doorman," Carter said.

"Actually, I am a professor at the Loftian Physical Sciences Institute. However, in Loft, we subscribe to the belief that all are truly equal, and for one month of the year every citizen toils at a task of which he is unfamiliar."

"I think you make a passable gatekeeper," Jonathan said, "but what of the man who took your place?"

"He is a cabinet-maker by profession. I must admit his lectures concerning the nature of the universe are weighted toward the shaping of wood and the chemical properties of certain glues, yet this too can be invaluable to the student and proves the importance of educational variety."

"Although this is vastly instructional, we need to press on," Carter said. "May we pass?"

"As soon as you state your true reason for entering Loft and the length of your stay. I have a form to fill out."

"We are bakers wishing to see the Great Kitchens of Loft,"

Carter replied. "We should be here less than a week."

"Is that the truth?" the man asked.

"As surely as you are a doorkeeper."

The professor furrowed his brow, but scribbled the information down on a piece of paper and unlocked the double doors.

"You know," the professor said, as if reluctant to see them depart, "we live in exciting times. At the rate scientific thought is progressing, within the next twenty years we should reach a full understanding of the entire cosmos."

"I can scarcely wait," Carter said.

As the professor shut the door behind him, Jonathan said, "Aristotle of Chalcidice said the same thing."

"You knew Aristotle?"

"He found his way into the house one day. He had some good ideas, but was humbled in a debate with Usandra of Querny, a woman with a honey tongue and brilliant mind. Some good came of it. He studied under her for two years and was less prideful when he took her teachings back to Greece."

The companions traveled that day through pleasant corridors paneled in golden oak and blue floral carpet. Like High Gable, much of Loft lay in the upper reaches of the house, above a maze of twisting passages named the Lower Bogs. In summer, the Loftians opened the hall transoms and outside windows, allowing cool breezes to waft through the corridors. Its people were easygoing and unsuspicious. Travelers filled the passages, and for a time the companions fell in with a boisterous troupe of musicians journeying to a concert at Geist Hall, who sang and played flutes and stringed *bayayals* as they went. Being still in the mountains, Carter and Storyteller passed over sky bridges connecting portions of the house, paneled corridors with great oval windows looking miles down on deep valleys with cottages scattered along their slopes and goats and sheep roaming the mountainsides.

The Loftians were enormously fond of every kind of headgear, and besides the cowl worn by the doorman, adorned themselves with spiraling caps, towering turbans, splayed pith-helmets, and drooping wide-brimmed hats that hid the wearers' faces, so they looked like strolling frowns. The hats were dyed brilliant colors, and it was like walking through a fair. Golden paneling shone beneath the light of chandeliers; the sweet outdoor scent filled the halls. Loft seemed a place where people could sit and read and think and talk and concoct whatever ridiculous thoughts they wished, and believe them unopposed all their lives. It was, in short, leaning toward decadence, and rumors had reached the Inner Chambers that its treasuries were destitute.

Despite the urgency of his mission, Carter, having seldom been this far east, took some pleasure in the journey. Before learning of the Poetry men, it had been his original plan to bring Jason and Sarah to an inn beside the Sidereal Sea, where water spouts formed in rainbow hues.

Four days they traveled through Loft. From the day Jossing was attacked, Carter had not been near an entrance to the attic, but toward evening they approached one, and he informed Jonathan he would take the opportunity to see if Jormungand could tell him Professor Shoemate's location.

"Dare you trust that old dragon?" Storyteller asked.

"I not only don't trust him," Carter said, "I dread facing him. It's always dangerous. But he is required to answer any three questions the Master asks, and I must make the try."

But when they reached the place where the stair was supposed to be, it was not there, and when Carter rechecked his inner maps, it was as though it had never been. Neither did he sense secret passages anywhere in the vicinity.

"Impossible!" Carter said. "I mentally traced my way here two nights ago."

"Perhaps you were mistaken."

Carter shook his head. "No, this is the spot. Evenmere has changed, but I sense no chaotic force at work. This wasn't caused by the poets."

There was nothing to do but go on, but later that night, remembering Mr. Hope's warning, Carter worried that the lost passage was some ramification of his pact with Armilus, and decided to seek the attic through the world of dream. He had never attempted to do so before. Would Jormungand have more power over him within the dream dimension? It seemed unlikely, and yet . . .

Not a little uneasy, he lay down and spoke the Word Which Masters Dreams. Immediately he found himself walking down the passage to the attic. This time, the stair he had sought was there. He ascended the creaking steps, which ended at a door. Opening it, he was met by an impenetrable mist. He lit his lantern, but its light illuminated nothing; even the floorboards were invisible, as if the attic did not exist in the dream world. He dared not walk into the fog, lest he lose his way and perhaps never awaken; so he stood and called Jormungand's name. No echoes returned; no answer came. The eerie loneliness of the place chilled him. When he could bear it no more, he returned to the waking world, thoughtful and uneasy, wondering if something had happened to the reptile, some new danger of which he was unaware.

They departed Loft the next day, past another doorkeeper who usually worked as a dentist. As he and Jonathan strode away, Lord Anderson could not help but wonder who was handling the man's patients.

The golden hallways of Loft gave way to gray stone. There were no more windows, and the sparse gas-jets cast long shadows, leaving the ceilings and corners lost in a gloom astir with vague movements, as if darker forms brooded within them. Lord Anderson's eyes darted from side to side in vain attempts to catch sight of them; he kept expecting something to step out of the murk. A shiver ran up the small of his back.

"No need to be anxious," Jonathan said, the whites of his eyes scarcely visible in the dimness. "They are only shadows leaving Shadow Valley. They pass down this corridor, little patches of darkness tickling the walls as they go out into the world. There, they will be a child's shadow dancing on the lawn, the darting shadow of a bird in flight, or the cool shade of trees on hot summer days."

Carter gave an uneasy laugh. "One would think shadows but an absence of light."

"That's right. That's right. And they are also fragments of darkness escaping Shadow Valley. It is a wonderful world, Master Anderson."

"Frankly, it doesn't always seem so cheery. I've been thinking darker thoughts. Is it coincidental that the poets attacked both the Palace of the Decemvirs and the Tower of Astronomy, the first two destinations of Professor Shoemate's quest?"

Jonathan frowned. "I hadn't considered it. Why would they do so?"

"Perhaps to obscure her trail and prevent anyone from following her. If that's true, we can expect them to appear here too."

"Dark thoughts indeed, Master Anderson, but worth considering. Best we hurry along."

Within the hour the travelers reached the entrance to Shadow Valley, an enormous, vaulted door cast in solid onyx. Members of the White Circle Guard, sent by Marshall Inkling, kept a wary vigil. Out of the keyhole, shadows slithered one by one, assuming various shapes as they dropped to the floor and made their way along the dark corridor. In the gloom they resembled serpents.

After speaking to the soldiers a moment, Carter drew his Master Keys. According to Mr. Hope's research, there were only two keys to Shadow Valley, one owned by the Master, the other by the Queen of Shadow Hall. No one else ever went there, or ever wanted to.

He waited until another shadow slithered out the keyhole before inserting a gray skeleton key. The mechanism turned with a loud echoing clang. He withdrew the key and stood back.

The door slowly creaked open, as if pushed by a strong wind. Around its edges hordes of shadows streamed out, scampering happy as rabbits into the halls of Evenmere. As the door drew wide, the tide of onrushing shades diminished to a trickle, and the travelers could see deep darkness within, with dim lights like distant constellations, whose soft glow revealed high ebony halls of wood and stone set in vast reaches both above and below the door. Only the pattering of the fleeing shadows broke the silence.

Carter turned to Jonathan. "Few Masters come here willingly. One who did a century ago never returned to the Inner Chambers. In light of the danger, there's no reason for you to risk your life."

"I am not afraid, Master Anderson. I have passed through this country before and met its queen. I want to see the old girl again."

"You accompanied one of the Masters?"

"I came alone, to see what could be seen."

"You continue to amaze me. According to our records, none save the Masters have ever been allowed into Shadow Valley. If I had known, I would have asked you more about Queen Moethus."

"It took a bit of convincing to get through the gates," Storyteller said. "As for Queen Moethus, she is centuries older than Astronomer Phra and many times more proud."

Carter raised his eyebrows. "I find that hard to imagine."

Jonathan laughed. "You just be your respectful self and maybe she will tell us what we want to know."

The minstrel lit the lantern from his pack and held it aloft. Lord Anderson led the way onto bare, black floorboards shining dully in the lamplight, along a broad walkway with a gulf of immeasurable depth on either side.

The shadow country was both insubstantial and fluid, as if the whole land were in constant motion. The distant lights shone blue. The high ceiling shifted like clouds, creating figures of gargoyles, children's faces, horses, dragons—myriads of ebony forms, darkness within darkness.

"What a country!" Carter exclaimed. "I can scarcely keep my balance."

"There are places more awful than this," Jonathan said. "As one moves farther from the Inner Chambers, the lands grow ever stranger, but there is also great beauty, lovely as leaves and laughter."

The companions traveled several miles along the black gallery above the abyss of Shadow Valley. Because Carter often had to close his eyes or shift his focus to keep from stumbling, he failed to see the two shadow guards stationed before an ebony portal until he and Jonathan were nearly upon them. Their voices wavered, as if they spoke from a great distance, but the black tips of their lances, prodding against the men's chests, were quite solid. Their heads were round as globes, and their cloaks hung behind them in tatters. They wore black breastplates. Their features, hidden in their dark faces, looked blank.

"Who enters the halls of Queen Moethus?" one of the guards asked.

"The Master and Jonathan Bartholomew," Carter replied.

"You are not the Master who came here last," the guard replied. "Show the sign of your office, that we may know you."

Carter lifted his right hand, revealing the ring with seven stones cut in seven concentric circles, representing the Seven Words of Power.

"It is as has been described," the sentry said. "Do you wear the Tawny Mantle?"

Carter allowed the Mantle to drop from his shoulders, covering him from neck to heels, so that he became one with the shadows.

The guard laughed. "This is a token of might? I see you plainly."

"Then you have eyes others do not."

"Do you possess the sword of the Master?"

Carter slipped his Lightning Sword an inch from its scabbard, and its golden light shone brilliant amid the darkness. The shadows screamed in terror, and the whole country cringed before the illumination. Carter resheathed his blade, and the guard cried, "No more, for you are surely the Master of Evenmere."

The sentries lowered their lances and allowed the travelers to pass. Far beyond the portal stood the shadow of a man eight feet tall and impossibly thin, who bowed at the waist. As with the guards, his eyes were invisible. His nose was long and sharp, and a semblance of a top hat sat on his head.

"Welcome," he said in a spectral voice. "Welcome to the Master and the Runemaker. Welcome to Shadow Hall."

"How do you know us?" Carter asked, since the guards had not announced them.

"When one shadow learns a thing, every other knows it," the shade said. "That is why it is best not to plot in the shadows. This way, this way!"

Turning, he strode off, moving in utter silence, yet raising his feet as if stamping with every step.

The shadow-walls of the corridor gleamed like polished wood, while shadow cats pressed themselves against the travelers' ankles and shadow birds and shadow butterflies fluttered about their heads. The inhabitants of Shadow Valley were known to be capricious, and Carter kept his hand close to his sword. As they proceeded, their guide gradually divided, until there were two of him walking in step. These, in turn, divided again and again, until a squadron of identical marching shadows filled the passage. They broke their eerie silence by humming in a minor key, every voice the same. The tune echoed across the shadow halls and down into the shadow chambers; and came reverberating back in long waves.

After several minutes the shadow guides said over their shoulders, "There used to be words, but the words have been stolen, and now we cannot sing our shadow songs properly."

"That is partly why we came," Carter said.

"Oh, we know a little of that," the guides said.

"What do you mean?" Carter asked.

"That is not for these shadows to say, but only the shadow of the queen herself. Come along!" And the echoes returned, *Come along . . . Come along . . .*

Carter gave Jonathan a wary glance. "You may wish you had taken my advice and stayed behind."

"We will do what we can. It is all we can ever do."

For a long hour, the companions trod past the shifting forms of Shadow Valley. Gargoyle faces bubbled and churned on the ceiling; shadows poked arms and hands and feet and legs, claws and wings and babies' tongues out of the walls, beckoning, gesturing, warning, raising fists and flapping appendages. It seemed to Carter that every shadow of his past drifted by. He saw the shadows of his mother and father. The shadows of the men he had killed passed one by one down the hallway, and their number appalled him. He saw the shadows of his regrets, of all he should have done, of the times he could have been more loving to his wife or spent more time with his son; the shadows of Duskin and Lizbeth and Sarah and Jason, Chant and Enoch and William Hope, and even his own shadow, for in these halls he and Jonathan's shadows loomed large, and Carter's shadow met itself and the two walked arm in arm together for a time.

He also saw shadows of happiness, of times spent playing as a child, of courting Sarah, of the birth of their son. The whole corridor was filled with the shadows of his past, the shadows of his present, and even the shadows of what might yet be, so that he saw great joy and terrible suffering and shadows of sacrifice beyond what any man could bear. With a jolt of fear, he saw the shadow of Doctor Armilus walking hand in hand with Jason. He witnessed vast battles and the shadows of death circling, so that he had to bat them away like flies. Looming high above, he saw the shadow of Jormungand, looking down with shadow teeth, swinging his shadow tail, and the Tigers of Naleewuath, and a hundred other things, so that when the companions finally came to the chamber of the Queen of Shadows, Carter felt a hundred years old.

But Jonathan only gave a long chuckle. "Now there were

many stories in *that*, and I have found a thousand tales to tell."

They were ushered into a hall so vast and dark its walls were invisible in the gloom. Their shadow guide seemed to collapse in upon his many selves, until only a single form remained.

Blue torches stood in shadow sconces. A noise like a distant howling wind whistled overhead. A wavering throng, barely discernible, crowded around the black walls of the chamber. The travelers were led before a vast throne, where sat the shade of a woman, tall and lithe, the outline of her dark tresses falling to her shoulders. Another shadow stood behind to her left.

"My queen," the guide said with a bow, "I present Carter Anderson, Master of Evenmere, and the minstrel, Runemaker."

Carter gave a slight bow with his head, a carefully considered courtesy. As Master, he bowed to none, but he needed to be solicitous without losing his status as an equal. Jonathan, however, neither bowed nor gave any other sign.

The queen made an imperious gesture with her hand. Her voice was ghost-thin. "So the old Master, Gembeard, is dead."

Carter thought quickly. "Master Gembeard died two hundred years ago, Your Majesty."

The queen gave a laugh, soft as the breath of a child. "So long? Time swirls quickly in the outer world, and the Masters seldom visit us."

"After I became Master," Carter said, "in accordance with the ancient custom, an invitation to visit the Inner Chambers was slid beneath the door to Shadow Valley."

The queen sat back in her throne and turned her head to the figure standing beside it. He whispered in her ear.

"We recall your invitation," she said, "and according to the convention, we declined. We do not leave our shadow realm. You would not wish to gaze upon us in the Bright World. We would be too terrible to see. But you, Runemaker, have visited us before. You amused us then."

"I am glad, Your Majesty."

"It is memorable because we are seldom amused. We desire to hear more of your tales, which were concerned with subjects foreign to our thoughts and often difficult to understand. That must be postponed until later, however, for now we are troubled. Tell us, Master Anderson, why you have come."

"For two reasons, Your Majesty. The house is imperiled by enemies who call themselves Poetry Men, agents of Chaos and Entropy possessing great and terrible power. They have targeted the Servants' Circle, assaulting both my Lamp-lighter and the Tower of Astronomy. The entire High House is endangered."

If what Carter said surprised the queen, she gave no indication. She sat silent for several moments, while the strange, distant wind howled overhead.

"The Circle of Servants," she finally said, giving her soft laugh. "We are said to be members of that circle. Perhaps we do not wholly agree with everything they stand for. The Tower of Astronomy—all that light. As long as there have been shadows we have been queen. We too have studied the Balance; we sense the shifting of light and darkness. Each day we send our subjects, our soldiers of dark, out to fill the world with shadow, and yet the world is never filled. Why is this, Master Anderson?"

"The world is shadow and light, Your Majesty. How can there be shadows without light, or light that casts no shadow? The two, as you know, depend upon one another."

"You cannot say *what* we know. What is the second reason for your presence at Shadow Hall?"

"We are seeking a woman named Erin Shoemate, who may have recently been here."

"Tell them nothing, Your Majesty!" a voice cried from out of the darkness.

Every eye turned toward a form that stepped from among the ranks of sycophants, a hooded figure swathed in black robes with a dark sash covering the lower half of his face. His eyes were fevered; sweat beaded his pale brow. A dim, blue light arose between his folded hands, emanating from a black diamond, large as his fist.

Carter's hand went to his sword, though he did not draw it.

Immediately the palace guards surrounded the figure, their spear tips close to his heart.

"Hear me, Queen Moethus," the man entreated, in a voice as ephemeral as the ruler's own. "Do not tell them what they wish to know. Have we not spoken of the Greater Road? Are these not sacred things? Remember the wonders I bring."

"Beware, Your Majesty," Lord Anderson said. "I don't

know how he slipped past our sentries, but he is one of the Poetry Men."

"Silence!" the advisor standing beside the throne commanded. "Silence before the queen!"

The whole assembly fell motionless.

"Those who come to Shadow Hall," she said, "are the guests of Shadow Hall. Since we received the poet, we have had many interesting talks. But he will not tell us how we shall behave. We will do what we choose."

"My apologies, Your Majesty," the Poetry Man said, lowering his head.

"You are pardoned. We recall this Shoemate. She knew of the Old Times and did not fear us. She had courage. She was looking for a place in the desert of Opo known as the Eye Gate."

"If I may ask, Your Majesty," Carter said, "were you able to answer her question?"

"We did."

"I would very much like to know what you told her."

"That does not much interest us." The queen turned her head toward the poet. "It is as you told us; they speak the same of light and darkness as did the Masters before them."

"They do not comprehend," the Poetry Man said, "but I have come to bring you truth: you need not send your shadows to be withered by the burning sun; their might should not be wasted thus, murdered by the daystar kiss. I say be done with luminance, embrace the night and know True Shadow cast without the dread refulgence."

Carter hesitated, uncertain how to counter his enemy.

"Your Majesty, if I might?" Jonathan asked.

"We will hear what Runemaker says."

"Long ago, a seer came to the king, saying: 'Because you have misused your authority and oppressed your people, you will die in seven days.' When the seer departed, the king, fearing death, ordered his blacksmiths to build an iron box large as a room. On the eve of the sixth day, he entered the box, after which it was sealed with pitch. Then the king thought to himself: 'Within this box, I am safe. No enemy, nor weapon, nor any disease can reach me. When the seventh day is past, I will leave the box and so escape my fate.' But the box was sealed too tight, and when the air was expended the king died."

The queen was silent a time. "So, if we believe what the Poetry Man says and accept his offer of True Shadow, we will, shall we say, seal our fate?"

"Light is needed for shadows, no matter what this man says. You and your country will be destroyed. Where will the world be then, without shadows to define it?"

"That is what truly concerns them," the poet said. "Where would *they* be without both shadow and light? When we are done, the universe will become a place of Absolutes. Shadow and light, good and evil, such dualisms are illusion." He held high the black diamond. "The gift is here in Incarnate Form. You need only accept it. Imagine the shadows forever dancing across the world, shadow separate from light, darkness swirling in ecstasy. Think of it, my queen, take what I would give!"

"Don't listen to him," Carter said. "He is himself deceived."

"Three days the poet has spoken to us," the queen said, "and we would heed his words, for we can feel the power he controls. It calls to us. The shadows saw the approach of a Master, so we waited to see what you would say, but you only repeat the same sad story. It is time the world was made new, with we sole ruler of Shadowland. You may pass through our kingdom, but you will not interfere in this, for we accept what the poet would give us."

The Poetry Man stepped forward to hand her the diamond. As the queen reached for it, Carter drew his Lightning Sword. Beneath that golden light, the land of shadow shrieked with one vast echoing scream, the shadows fleeing backward. But one of those was the queen clutching the jewel to her breast.

"Too late!" the poet cried. "Too late! Once more, divine avatars walk the worlds. Oh, glory, glory!"

And far away, the queen shouted. "See, it comes! How beautiful it is!"

A darkness, greater and more vast than that which had been before, fell upon the chamber, overwhelming the rays of Carter's sword until it cast but a slender light. One by one the blue lamps went out. Gigantic forms moved in the swirling ebony overhead, Shadow Incarnate come to earth. The stress of their regard beat upon Carter, so terrible that if they fell fully upon him, he knew he would become no more than a shade. Through the blackness, he heard the queen give an ecstatic shriek.

"It's too late to help," Jonathan Bartholomew said, his voice level. "The old queen, who never faltered before, has failed Evenmere. We must escape. Follow me and keep the light of your blade close."

A pair of shadow guards tried to block the men's path, but gave way before the sword's glow. The companions hurried down the length of the long chamber in the opposite direction from which they had come. It was so dark, Carter wondered how Jonathan could even tell where he was going.

Storyteller came to an abrupt halt just as Lord Anderson sensed an upheaval in the Balance. Jonathan reached down, feeling along the floor.

"What are you doing?" Carter demanded.

"It's just right . . . here," Jonathan said, and on the last word, he pulled with both hands and a section of the floor came up, revealing a long stair. Without hesitation, the minstrel hopped onto the first step and hurried down, calling over his shoulder, "It's the short way out."

Carter followed behind, wondering how anyone, even knowing it was there, could have located the passage in so much darkness.

They made a nightmare run down the stair. Carter fixed his eyes on his feet, concentrating on keeping his balance on the narrow steps, the dim light of his blade revealing cracked, ebony walls of stone on either side.

At the bottom, they reached a chamber of unknown size. Not even pausing to consider his way, Jonathan led into the empty darkness.

Carter gasped, feeling the Balance straining ever farther to the side of Chaos, even as the shadows hardened before them, as if they were pushing their way through deep water. The Lightning Sword became their only hope, for it cut easily through the shadows. Carter took the lead, thrusting his blade before him to sever the material darkness.

"Keep going, straight ahead," Jonathan ordered. "The east door is close by, but Shadow Valley is collapsing on itself."

Carter glanced upward and suppressed a cry of surprise.

The shadows were indeed contracting; the hitherto hidden ceiling had descended enough to be seen by the sword light. The cries of the shadows, which had continued even after the men plunged down the stair, changed from joy to a deep groaning, a deafening cacophony, as if all of Shadow Valley were in agony, and the queen's voice loudest of any.

"Lord Anderson!" she wailed, her voice resonating through her whole country. "What have we done? What comes cannot be borne. Save us!"

Carter halted. With great difficulty, he blocked out the stridency and searched for a Word of Power that might help. But no Word drifted before his mind's eye; he could find nothing to halt the onslaught.

"I can't stop it!" he shouted.

"My beautiful Shadow Valley!" the queen cried. "My beautiful valley!" Her voice trailed away into the uproar.

Carter pressed forward. The way grew increasingly dense, forcing him to hack and slash with his blade, as if he were cutting through thick jungle. The noise was unbelievable—the cries of humans, the shriek of horses, the whine of dogs, the squawks of birds—the sound of Shadow Valley being murdered, so loud he wanted to huddle in a ball and clutch his ears. He thought he must go deaf. He felt the weight of the whole shadow world pressing against his shoulders, bowing the men's backs with the load. Small talons began clutching at the companions' feet from behind, slowing them even more.

The glow of the sword dulled the farther the men went, until it was little more than a firefly light in a gargantuan darkness.

"The door is right before us," Jonathan said, "but our time is nearly up. Spare none of your might."

Jonathan's voice, calm in the face of death, inspired Lord Anderson to redouble his efforts. He cut with renewed haste, shearing through the coalescing shadows, giving his strength to the task. His arms ached; his breath came in gasps.

The darkness was right above them, pushing their heads down against their hunched shoulders, forcing them to crouch. Carter tried to slash harder, but his limbs were giving out; he was slowing down and could do nothing about it. His lungs burned. He had neither the will nor the time to use the Word Which Gives

Strength. They weren't going to make it.

I'm going to die in a close place, he thought, with rising panic, *just as I've always feared.*

And then he saw, scarcely ten yards away, a soft glow peeking beneath the threshold of a door.

The sight of it was enough. He pushed through his fear and got his second wind. He had a system for cutting through the shadows now, and he worked with precision, slashing in a V to right and left, and thrusting through the gash with his boots.

Despite the nearness of the door, their progress was slow. The ceiling continued to descend. Unable to even crouch, the men dropped to their knees. It made using the sword even more difficult. Carter hacked frantically from side to side.

The roof pressed against their backs. Being the taller of the two, Jonathan was forced to crawl on hands and knees.

Only a few more feet. Carter had one hand on the ground. The roof was pressing against his head and back. He dropped lower, crouching on all fours.

His sword struck the door.

"We're through!" he shouted.

"The keys," Jonathan commanded. "Unlock the door."

Carter struck it instead, putting his remaining strength into the blow, trying to break it with the power of the sword.

It held.

He struck again.

It withstood the blow.

"The keys, Master Anderson!" Storyteller said. "Quickly now."

With fumbling hands, Carter grasped his brass key ring. The light from his sword had failed, but he held the ring close to the threshold, using the illumination from beneath the door. The ceiling forced him to drop to his elbows. He could not find the key.

He fumbled through the ring again, trying to keep calm, knowing he was about to die. Several of the keys looked similar; in the uncertain light it was difficult to tell.

He concentrated, pushing aside the fear of impending destruction. Every key gave off its own unique and subtle emanation. He closed his eyes, as he held each of the possibilities in turn. There was time for only one try.

He took the one he thought correct, doubting his decision as he made it. With trembling hands, he fitted it into the lock. The door had shrunk with the ceiling, else he would not have been able to open it. The lock resisted. With a moan, he twisted harder.

It turned with a loud click. Carter flung the door wide. Warm light pierced the darkness.

He scrambled through the opening and turned to help his friend. Jonathan Bartholomew poked his head out, his body flat against the ground. The chamber was closing; there was scarcely room for the man's back. He squeezed his shoulders through the opening.

"I'm stuck," Storyteller said.

"No!" Carter shouted. He looked directly into Jonathan's dark eyes, still calm but with the beginnings of despair, as the entire weight of Shadow Valley pressed upon him.

With a sobbing cry, Carter seized Storyteller under the arms and pulled with every vestige of his might.

The minstrel's back and waist came out. His thighs; his calves. His foot was caught! He gave a cry of pain.

Then he was free.

Jonathan was out. Carter gave a rasping shout of triumph as the opening collapsed with a crash.

A roar like the screaming of the whole universe filled the chamber. Carter clapped his hands over his ears. An explosion came and he saw no more.

The Winking

Enoch, accompanied by a squad of the White Circle Guard, stood on a high balcony looking down at a vast quadrangle near the border of the Land of Twelve. They had crossed through Nianar and over the Terraces, and spent the last three days winding their way through Corovia.

"What does the lieutenant think?" Enoch asked his companion.

Wulf Cumby scratched his chin, while the fourteen members of his squad looked on. Despite his rank, he was no more than thirty, with a long face, blond hair, and pale, intelligent eyes. "According to my maps, after we descend, the only way out is over the Ounceling Bridge. Not only will we be vulnerable to an attack from above, we could find ourselves hemmed in between here and the crossing."

Enoch sighed and shrugged. "Are you right? You must be, but I wanted to travel farther this evening."

"If the Windkeep knows a way to reach the Land of Twelve without crossing the bridge, we could continue on," Cumby suggested.

"The Windkeep does not," Enoch said. "Or rather, I know seven ways to get to the Hundred Years Clock, but it would take at least sixteen extra hours. I came this way because of the bridge, but if we can't reach it before evening, we should wait until tomorrow."

He pulled out his pocket watch, consulted it, and shrugged. "Already, I should have been at the clock. I would have been, if not for these violent poets. We have time, but we must cross the Ounceling no later than sundown tomorrow."

"Then I would like to encamp here, if it meets the Windkeep's approval."

Enoch grimaced. "That's the trouble with getting old. You live long enough, everybody wants your approval. What, you think I'll turn to a mummy if I don't get what I want?"

"No sir, not at all. But if the Windkeep—"

"Call me Enoch."

"If Enoch wants to—" the lieutenant's face turned scarlet. "I mean, if you have a preference—"

"You know what I want to know? Why they call you Wulf. It's a good strong name, but I wonder, did your mother give it to you?"

"My real name is Steven. My men started calling me Wulf after the Battle of Middlecourt. I was attacked by a gnawling in the shape of a wolf. I lost my gun, but managed to kill it with a broken pen-knife."

Enoch laughed. "A pen-knife? We should call you Lion."

"I was lucky."

"Not lucky. I know luck. Luck is finding a shekel somebody dropped. Killing a gnawling with a pen-knife—that's meant to be. Do you mind if I smoke?"

"No, sir."

Enoch produced a red clay pipe and tapped it against the railing. The soft scent of tobacco filled the air. "I know about luck. Especially with military men. I remember Corporal Rollory at the Battle of Pennywash. What did he know about strategy? Him and his hundred men, caught between two thousand. Vance, I told him, you should climb through the Upper Rafters and see where you come down. He could have ended up anywhere, but he landed right at his enemies' backs. That's more than luck."

"You knew Field Marshal Rollory?"

"He was like you, hardly old enough to shave, but look what happened. I'm glad he took my advice."

"In school, they said he drew his soldiers together and outlined the whole plan."

Enoch waved his hand dismissively. "He didn't even know where he was! But he had spunk. Sometimes that's all you've got. Spunky Vance, I called him after that. He named his son after me. I thought that was nice."

That evening, as had become the custom during the journey, Enoch told stories at the evening meal. The squad sat in a circle on the wide balcony while the old Hebrew spoke of Rollory, and the Rout of Soffuth, and how Alexander the Great once entered Evenmere. But none of the soldiers knew who Alexander was.

"You should read more about the outer world," Enoch said. "A lot goes on there."

"I always thought the Outside was just a myth," one soldier said.

"So did I," Cumby said, "until I went with Major Glis to the Inner Chambers and stood at the Front Door."

"What did you see?" the soldier asked.

Cumby shrugged. "It was like a gigantic courtyard, with lots of trees in the distance, and a statue and green lawn up close. A road led down around a hill. You couldn't see any more of the house. Evenmere ended right there."

"Were you scared, Lieutenant?"

Wulf gave a smile that Enoch had seen in men who would someday be great leaders. "Not scared. I grew up at Innman Tor, and there's a lot of sky there too, but it *was* disturbing."

"A whole country outside the house," the first soldier said, "the end of Evenmere."

The warriors fell silent, awed by the thought.

Enoch took a puff from his clay pipe. "Not the end. The outside world is inside Evenmere, too."

"How is that possible?" Wulf asked.

Enoch shrugged. "How should I know? How do they put those little ships into bottles?"

"They blow the glass around the ship," the lieutenant said.

"Evenmere is like that," Enoch said, "except it's both the ship and the bottle."

Seeing their puzzled looks, he shrugged again. "A good thing I wasn't brought here to be a teacher. I was never good at explaining. You should read about Alexander sometime. I met him on the Long Stair once. A handsome boy. He reminded me of Rollory.

I thought to myself, *so this is the great commander*. He didn't die like the stories tell us; he's still around somewhere, lost in the house. But there were greater warriors when I was a lad in Aram. Nimrod—I should tell you about him. Now *he* was a mighty hunter."

Early the next morning, the squad descended a long, slender stair. They passed along the quadrangle most of that day, and by evening came to the Ounceling Bridge, which spanned a channel filled not with water, but with a flowing rainbow of glistening colors.

"What is it?" the lieutenant asked.

"It's called the Stream of Time," Enoch replied. "You swim in it, you come out either older or younger, depending on which direction you go."

"Don't people flock to it by the thousands?"

"They would, if there was any certainty to it, but you never know what will happen. You stay too long, you might get lost in it and never have existed at all. If you do make it ashore, it will be a different time; maybe a thousand years away, everyone you knew long perished, or all your friends unborn. It's dangerous—being sucked down by eddies, or slipping into a still pool, trapped there for eternity while time passes you by. Only a fool would dare the Stream of Time. Sometimes someone near death makes the try. Not one has ever been seen again, at least not in this age. In all my years, I never met anybody who claimed to have done it. Time is tricky. You stick your finger in, it's like getting too close to the fire."

"How do you know so much if no one has ever come through it?" a soldier asked.

"Time and I, we have an understanding."

They watched the passing of the Stream of Time. A sweetness like twilight on summer days resided in its soft murmuring, but the swift movement of the strange waters soon made the soldiers melancholy.

"Are you really as old as they say?" Wulf asked.

"I've lived a long time."

Wulf Cumby, who was both a soldier and a bit of a poet, kept his eyes on the Stream of Time. "Most people would love to do what you've done, seeing the generations pass, living through so much history. It's an amazing gift."

Enoch raised his hands in a shrug. "What do they know, who haven't lived it? I look at this stream and see my life as a shaft of sunlight, spent in a minute. Is that a bad thing? Not for me. No one wants to leave familiar places, but my wife, my children, and my grandchildren have already gone through death's door. I miss them. I like seeing the swiftness of the water. I like knowing it will soon carry me away to lands too strange to imagine."

"Some would say there isn't any price too great to live so long."

Enoch sighed. "Is my long life a price, when you just called it a gift? Maybe it's both. But you're right; I have been gifted beyond hope. I should be glad. I am glad. I have a clock to wind. We should hurry before time passes us by."

They left the bridge and trekked out of the quadrangle into a corridor lined with blue-velvet wallpaper. Before they had gone a hundred paces, a scout hurried back to report at least forty anarchists approaching, led by what appeared to be a Poetry Woman.

Cumby ground his boot heel against the floor. "If we hurry, we can catch them in a cross-fire. Or we can retreat, try to work our way around them."

"No," Enoch said. "From what I hear, these poets can't be stopped by bullets, and it would take too long to avoid them. We have to reach the Hundred Years Clock. We should return to the bridge."

Cumby nodded. "The far bank is a defensible position, but I don't see—"

"It's me they're after," Enoch said. "They know if they keep me from winding the clock, it will go badly for Evenmere. But that bridge; I told you I came this way on purpose. They don't know what I can do on that bridge. They don't know anything. We should hurry."

The squad made their way back to the bridge and crossed to the other side, where the lieutenant organized the men around the structure, using its stonework and the trees along the banks for protection. But Enoch paced across the bridge, removing his greatcoat to reveal glistening chain mail. From a silver scabbard covered with runes and inlaid with topaz and lapis lazuli, he drew a two-handed sword adorned with ivory and pearls. His eyes shone brilliant as he grasped the blade, and with his Assyrian curls and fierce, ancient face, he suddenly seemed much more than a kindly old clock-winder.

Wulf Cumby hurried to the Windkeep. "Enoch, you need to take cover."

"I need to be here."

"I'm under orders to safeguard you."

"You think you can protect me? You can't. This poet, I feel her coming. She's meant for me. Don't worry; she wants me, she can come get me. I'll give her more me than she knows how to handle. Keep your men under cover. Don't fire unless they fire first."

"We'll lose the advantage."

"Against her kind of power, there isn't any advantage." Enoch clasped Cumby by the shoulder. "Don't fear, lad, just do as I say."

As the lieutenant returned to his men, he heard Enoch mutter, "Do I know what I'm talking about? I hope so. If not, Carter will have to hire somebody new. Let's see what an old man can do."

He moved to the center of the arching bridge, an easy target standing at its highest point. He glanced from side to side and raised his sword, its point glistening as it caught the light. Striding to the side of the structure, he dipped the blade into the Stream of Time. The prismatic colors ran up and down the weapon's length, and when he lifted it, it radiated such intense hues as could scarcely be borne by the unshielded eye. Streams of light cascaded around him, starlight-glistenings washing over his armor, washing over the lines of his ancient face.

With a grim smile, he turned toward the anarchists pouring out of the corridor which the squad had just abandoned. As they entered the quadrangle, the enemy fanned out, not yet firing, undoubtedly hesitant to cross the hundred yards of open ground between them and the ensconced White Circle Guard.

Light streaming from her face, the poetess appeared, thronged by her gray-clad followers, her flowing, high-collared robe the same golden hue as her upswept hair.

"Keeper of Time!" she cried. "I have found you at last." Her voice rang in exultation, as if he should be glad at being discovered. "Come to me, Hebrew from the dawn of the age. Let us speak of matters beyond mortal understanding."

"I'll wait right here," Enoch shouted back. "You want me, you come over here."

She spoke to a subordinate, words that did not carry to the men on the bridge. He seemed to be arguing with her, but at last she raised her hand and he stepped back and bowed in compliance. With a smile, she approached the bridge, seeming to glide rather than walk. Without pausing at the foot of the span, she flowed up the arching stone until she stood within ten feet of the Windkeep.

"Time, time, time," she said, "and you the keeper of it." Her face blazed; she seemed suddenly taller, a goddess; immortal, immovable. "But I can show you the eternal. I can show you ecstasy. Do you hear the calling, Enoch? Do you hear the summons?"

The soldiers at the bridge stood in silence, awed by the lady's power. Wulf Cumby abruptly found himself unconsciously stepping toward her, and held himself in check only with an effort.

"If I were you, I wouldn't stay here," Enoch said. "I have a clock to wind."

"Forget the clocks, mere measurements of the ephemeral. Embrace the reality! Feel the wonder, the wonder beyond wonder of timelessness—no more the guardian of the passing moments, no more enthralled by the terrorizing seconds, the murdering minutes, the debilitating hours. Life eternal, lived outside the temporal. Never knowing death; never knowing decay. Life! Life as it was meant! Life!"

Overcome by her majesty, the soldiers dropped their weapons and hid their faces. Cumby felt himself moving forward again, his hand reaching toward her.

Enoch shrugged. "You know my story? You know who I am?"

"I know all about you. I have seen your soul. I have——"

"You think you know me? You want to tempt me? I've seen the face of God. You, you're just a person. I gave you your chance."

The poetess looked full into Enoch's eyes. Seeing the calm

assurance there, she hesitated. Slowly, fear entered her gaze.

The Windkeep stepped forward. His sword, swirling with the colors of the Stream of Time, swept in a smooth arc. The poetess raised her hands to create a shimmering shield, but the blade passed right through it and continued through her body. It did not cut her, but her form collapsed in on itself, withering to the shape of a bent crone. Horror filled her features; a scream slipped from her open mouth, only to abruptly end. Then she was gone, whirling away in a cloud of dust.

An anguished cry rose from the anarchists' ranks. Their second-in-command, seeing their leader destroyed, raised his pistol and fired. A dozen others followed suit, sending a volley of shots at the Windkeep.

All the days of his life, Wulf Cumby never forgot the sight of Enoch on the Ounceling Bridge. As the Windkeep raised his sword again, its arcane energies swirling around it, something happened to Time itself upon the span. Cumby heard the discharge of the anarchists' weapons, saw the smoke rising from the barrels, but as the bullets reached the bridge, they slowed, hanging nearly suspended in the air. The Windkeep moved his sword in a wide arc, knocking the pellets down as they came. He stepped to the side to avoid others, his image blurring with the speed of his movements.

When the last bullet had been rendered useless, he called back to Cumby. "Hold your fire, lad. I will deal with these." His brown eyes blazed, a warrior from ancient days, terrible in his wrath.

Wulf Cumby hesitated. Every instinct urged him to attack before the anarchists drew too close, yet the command in the Hebrew's voice restrained him.

"Hold your positions!" Cumby bawled to his followers.

The anarchists charged, discharging their pistols, their weaponry turned on the lone figure on the bridge. Dozens of shells hurtled toward Enoch. Again he moved with supernatural celerity, to the right, to the left, dancing with slight movements, avoiding the volleys, blocking some with his sword.

The anarchists came on, swarming over the bridge, but as they stepped into that strange zone of Time, their movements slowed. Despite Enoch's advantage, the sheer number of adversaries confronting the Windkeep made Cumby gasp in fear for him.

Enoch moved with a grace that belied his frame, weaving in and out, parrying pistol-bayonets aside, never once using the edge of his blade as he had against the poetess, but striking with fist or sword hilt, so the anarchists fell stunned yet alive. Some he thrust over the embankment into the Stream of Time, where they vanished into the haze of the current.

As the foremost anarchists crumpled to the ground, leaving a brief respite, Enoch flicked his sword, hurling the rainbow colors that glistened along its edge. Wherever the cascades of brilliance enveloped the anarchists, the men vanished without a trace.

Enoch strode forward, brandishing his blade, exiling his enemies into nothingness. A few more shots rang out, but he either avoided them or batted them down with careless disregard. His face shone in the many-hued light; he went about his work with the meticulous attention he gave to winding his clocks.

The anarchists had poured onto the bridge; now they vainly sought to flee. The Windkeep moved through them, around them, ahead of them, a blur compared to their crawling movements. When the few survivors discovered him waiting at the far end of the structure, they threw down their weapons and fell to their knees, sobbing in fear and despair.

So overawed were Cumby's men, not a one had fired a shot.

Enoch raised his hand, and the rainbow colors deserted his sword, leaving it a dull gray. Both the anarchists and the Windkeep returned to their normal speeds, as Time resumed its former course.

"Lieutenant Cumby," Enoch called, "I believe these gentlemen want you to accept their surrender."

As if in a dream, Cumby stepped forward, trying not to show fear as he walked onto the bridge and ordered the sergeant to take command of the prisoners.

Cumby turned to Enoch. "If I hadn't seen it myself . . ." He fell speechless.

For the first time since the battle had begun, Enoch smiled, the grin of a young boy. "Did I know for certain it would work? No. But I hoped."

"How did you do it? Where did you send them?"

Enoch shrugged. "Some to the past, some to the future; none of them to be seen again by anyone alive today. I am the

Keeper of Time, Wulf. Time isn't mine to command, but on this bridge, with Time around me, there are things I can do. They shouldn't have tried to face me here."

The lieutenant frowned. "Isn't sending them into the past dangerous? Couldn't they change the present?"

"Who knows? Not me. But I never kill unless I have to. Every person has a path to walk. Who am I to cut their journey short? Even the blackest of hearts has a chance to reform. Let this be a lesson to them. Maybe some will learn something and start new lives wherever they end up. That isn't in my hands."

"And the Poetry Woman?"

"Gone, but I won't regret her death. She was already dead. There was no returning from what she had become."

"I don't understand."

Enoch studied Cumby closely. The lieutenant suddenly felt like a child beneath that kind scrutiny. "Like I told you, I'm not good at explaining things. You live long enough, it comes to you. Believe me."

"How old were you before it 'came to you'?"

Enoch gazed along the span of the bridge. "Three hundred? Eighteen hundred? Who remembers? I should have kept a diary. I'm not much for writing things down."

At Cumby's orders, the sergeant, accompanied by five soldiers, set off to escort the twelve remaining anarchists east into Corovia, while the rest of the company continued with Enoch to wind the Hundred Years Clock.

Unlike Enoch, Lieutenant Wulf Cumby did keep a diary, and in later years, in his memoirs, he wrote: *So we went with the Windkeep of Evenmere, the Keeper of Time, the Immortal Hebrew who claimed to have once walked with God, the Wise Man who could not explain his wisdom because we were too young to understand. We journeyed to the Land of Twelve, where he wound the Hundred Years Clock, and never again, during the remainder of our travels, did I suffer the delusion that we were protecting him.*

Carter woke with the dull roaring of the destruction of Shadow Valley still echoing in his ears. The polished floor beneath him reflected his disheveled features. Shards of fallen ceiling plaster lay all around. For a brief while, he could not remember where he was. Gradually he came to himself and sat up. Jonathan lay on the floor, clutching his stomach, his knees raised to his chest, his face twisted in agony.

Carter crawled over to him. "Are you all right?"

The minstrel moaned, but did not answer.

"Jonathan?"

Storyteller waved a hand, bidding Lord Anderson wait. It was several moments before he recovered enough to speak. When he did, his voice came soft and strained, and Carter, partially deafened, understood him only by reading his lips.

"I'm all right. That's right." Jonathan took a gasping breath. He had his hands over his eyes. "Don't worry about old Storyteller, Master Anderson. He's a flinty one. Sturdy as an old tree, he is."

"Are you wounded? I don't see any signs."

"Wounded to the heart. A hole scooped right out of me."

Lord Anderson put his hands to his temples, which had begun an incessant throbbing. He gradually became aware of how horribly the Balance had changed. The entire universe had shifted, teetering toward Chaos. Feeling sick and abruptly faint, he covered his eyes with his hands.

After several minutes, he recovered himself enough to glance around. They were in a small, empty antechamber, upheld by eight Ionian pillars, with sky-blue walls and sunlight shining through oval windows with lace curtains. After the dark of Shadow Valley, the room seemed extraordinarily bright. The door they had come through had resumed its usual height. A matching door stood on the opposite wall.

"It felt like there was an explosion," he said.

"Shadow Valley is gone," Jonathan replied. "This door here . . ." From his prone position, he pointed in the direction they had come, "this door is the one we entered from Loft, the one that opened *into* Shadow Valley. The valley is gone, winked out of existence. The house has come together and closed the gap."

"Gone?" Carter repeated numbly. "What are the consequences?"

"We know at least one. Look around, Master Anderson.

Look around. Look behind you. The sun shines through the window, but we have no shadows."

From the time Carter awoke, the room had seemed oddly wrong. Now he understood why. Without shadows, it appeared flat, two-dimensional.

He crawled to his feet and drew the lace curtains. Beyond the glass stood a narrow courtyard, with a tall oak at its center. He could not tell the time of day, for no shadows lay beneath the tree, nor could he easily judge size or distance without the contrast of darkness and light.

"Is the whole world like this?"

"Oh, it got everything," Jonathan said. "Evenmere is wounded. *Everything* is wounded."

Carter sat down and moaned, his back against a wall. "Can it be repaired?"

"Heaven knows, Master Anderson. Heaven knows. Queen Moethus has betrayed her stewardship. I watched her; I saw her pride; I knew she had become arrogant, but she had served well and I thought it would be all right. I *thought* it would be all right. I should have done something."

"Are *you* all right?" Carter asked.

Jonathan looked directly at his companion. His eyes were wild, unfocused. "I am not all right. I will not be all right, Master Anderson. I may never be right again."

"There was nothing you could have done. The Poetry Man deceived her."

"Storyteller sees to the heart. I *should* have known. The wound to the worlds is deep."

Carter fell silent, unable to even begin to fathom the ramifications of the loss. Lord Anderson was the Master, the guardian of reality, and if Existence had changed, it was not the minstrel's responsibility, but his own.

Carter raised his head, sensing a familiar presence. He rose and threw open the far door. Despite his certainty of what he would find, he was unprepared as Lady Order seized his coat collar with both hands and lifted him into the air. She held him suspended, her eyes twin fires, one half of her symmetrical face marred by a melting disfigurement not unlike the ruined features of Old Man Chaos.

"Traitor!" She shook him like a dog shakes a rat. "See what

your treaty has done to me! My beautiful face! Why do you betray me?"

Before Carter could reassert his authority, Storyteller's voice boomed out. "Unhand him!"

She turned. Jonathan had risen to his feet. She dropped Carter, who landed hard, but stayed upright. "You!" she cried. "Are you against me as well?"

"We have all been injured," Jonathan said.

"You must *do* something," she insisted. "You are the Master, and *you* are—"

"Begone, Lady," Storyteller said. "You don't do us any good. Return to your place."

She fell silent. Without a backward glance, she turned and walked down the corridor.

Carter watched her go in amazement. "You banished her with a word. I thought only I could do that."

"Sometimes the forces of the house listen to me, if I say it just right."

"What did she mean? Was she referring to my truce with Armilus?"

Jonathan blew a ragged breath. "It does nobody any good to talk about that, Master Anderson."

Carter continued staring at his companion, until at last Jonathan raised his hands in a shrug. "You made a truce with the anarchists. Now, anybody can make a truce with anybody else and that's well and good. But not the Master. You aren't just a person. You *represent*. Yes sir, you *represent*. In a way, you *are* Evenmere. In a way. When you, the Guardian of the Balance, made your agreement with the doctor, it nudged the universe toward Chaos. Among other things, it caused *rifts* in reality that allowed the Poetry Man to reach and influence Moethus. When she fell, the Balance was tilted even more. It's like falling dominoes, Master Anderson, one bit of Chaos leading to another."

"Then I've committed an act of treason," Carter said miserably.

"Now don't you go listening to Lady Order. She's not even alive. We have been struck to the heart today, but it was the queen who failed, a victim to greed. Moethus held fast for many generations, but she let a tiny creeping voice enter her, and over time it filled her with jealousy of the very light that gave her shadows life. When the Poetry Man came, he flamed that spite. All things flow from the spirit, Master Anderson. Governments are made up of their people. So long as they are men and women of character, the nation stands. The battle was lost in the queen's heart; the rest is only the result."

Carter kept silent.

"You don't let your face look that way, Master Anderson," Storyteller said. "We've got no time to be discouraged. You have made your mistakes, it's true, but we have a job to do. We have to find Erin Shoemate, and we have to do it soon. Our time is short, indeed."

"But the queen never told us the location of the Eye Gate."

"No, but we know she told Professor Shoemate, who went looking for it in the desert of Opo."

"Opo is a large country, and we don't know what we're looking for."

Jonathan Bartholomew nodded. "That's right. That's right. I have been through Opo many times, but have never heard of the Eye Gate. All we can do is search."

They left the chamber and trudged along a marble corridor. Lord Anderson glanced down to where his shadow should have danced before him. Seeing nothing, he wanted to weep.

With Shadow Valley gone, the desert of Opo lay directly to the southeast. Within an hour's time, the travelers passed through a tattered velvet curtain, where the corridor made a radical change from marble to rococo.

"The Opo begins here," Jonathan said. "Are you familiar with it?"

"I've skirted its borders before and have studied the chronicles concerning it. I know it's deserted because of tainted water."

"Once it was a great kingdom," Storyteller said. "The people were tall and blond, powerful men and amazon women who traded throughout the house, taking their fierce boats to every shore of the Sidereal Sea and far down the Fable River. I sat many an evening with Prince Tawfaw upon the Grand Terraces to watch the sunset. When the water was poisoned years later by the anar-chists, thousands died before the cause was known, including King Aduadel and his court. In later years, people came to call it *the* Opo, the way we say *the desert* or *the wilderness*. Only thieves and vagabonds inhabit it now, thus the expression: *as evil as the Opo*."

"The desolation of so large a region must have swung the Balance far toward Chaos," Carter said. "The records say the Master at the time did nothing to correct it, that it corrected itself. I don't understand how that is possible. It makes me question my own efforts to regulate the Balance."

"I knew that Master," Jonathan said. "He was very old and had learned when to act and when to refrain from acting. You are still young, Master Anderson. There is always more to learn."

"I suppose that's true. Sometimes I wonder if I will ever understand the High House."

Storyteller laughed for the first time that day. "Why, no, Master Anderson, you will not, and that is a fact, no more than those outside the house really understand their world. It is too com-plicated. When you think you have it puzzled out, you see it from another angle, and there it is, completely different."

They trudged through the hodge-podge of architectural styles of the tattered chambers of the Opo, past moth-eaten drap-eries, stained carpets, and faded tapestries.

"I sense Chaos here," Carter said. "Not surprising. It cer-tainly looks chaotic. I suppose the architecture was different when it was inhabited."

"That's right. It has changed, becoming terrible and wild."

The gas jets did not function anywhere in that country, and the travelers went mostly in corridors illuminated by the light from skylights and narrow windows. The lack of shadows actually made it easier to see. Fearing his supply of fuel might fail, Carter used his lantern only when necessary. Jonathan, who possessed night vision scarcely less keen than a cat's, was enormously helpful, leading them through the darkest ways.

They camped that evening in a third-story chamber. Once it must have been beautiful, with a beamed ceiling, polished floor-boards, and a glistening chandelier, but like the rest of the Opo, it had fallen into ruin. Mice had gnawed the tablecloths and furniture legs; water had stained the ceiling; someone had cut a jagged piece from the carpet.

The house was warming with the spring, but they lit a fire in the arched fireplace for the comfort of its light. Lacking firewood, they fed the flames with a broken rosewood side-table. They opened the high windows on the south wall, and soon had a soft breeze, scented with honeysuckle, swirling through the room to ease the odor of decay.

The fire burned sterile, casting no shadows, leaving Carter with an aching regret at the mystery that had gone out of the world. He wondered if he would ever sit in happy melancholy again, or whether all that was bittersweet had departed the house with the shades. Jonathan was weary and taciturn, and they ate a cold meal and took to their bedrolls, where Carter fell into a troubled sleep.

That night, he dreamed of fleeing through Shadow Valley as it winked out, but in the dream he did not escape, and the darkness ground him into the floor. Just before he vanished completely, he found himself falling down a well. The water loomed before him, but he woke before he struck it, covered in sweat.

Three times he had the same nightmare, and after the last one he rose to find the morning sun peeping through the windows into a stark and shadowless world. To his surprise, Jonathan was asleep; he had begun to believe the man never required slumber.

That day the two men journeyed through the ruin of Opo, past tattered banners hanging in empty halls, broken furniture in dusty rooms, and rusting iron in moldering wood. Children's toys lay shattered on the hearths. The loss of the shadows, which changed everything in a hundred small ways, intensified each detail of the desolation.

It was a difficult journey. The loss of the shadows left Carter uneasy, and worse, he could sense, like a stuttering nervousness running through his body, other forces further affecting the Balance. Perhaps Jonathan sensed it as well, for he walked as one scarcely knowing where he went, eyes unseeing, sometimes stumbling against a wall or table, occasionally muttering to himself. They spoke little that day, and Carter longed to be back in the Inner Chambers, surrounded by the comfort of his friends.

They stopped for the night in an antechamber beside a long corridor. Like everything in this part of the house, the room smelled of mice and mold. The companions ate in silence, and

Lord Anderson threw himself into his bedroll, too drained to summon the strength to enter the dream dimension, though he needed to confer with Mr. Hope.

Long past midnight, Lord Anderson was awakened by Jonathan's soft calling. He was instantly alert. The fire had died in the hearth; the room lay dark, and Carter saw his companion as a darker darkness within it. His hand gripped Carter's shoulder.

"Master Anderson, I have received word of a clue that may help us. I must journey swift as a crow, but will return as soon as I can."

"You're leaving me? What sort of clue? Who brought it to you?"

"Never mind about that. It will either be useful or not. I must be off."

"But where are you going, and how will you find me again?"

"Two days' journey, less if all goes well. You search the Opo as we planned, and I will seek you out."

The pressure left Lord Anderson's shoulder. "Jonathan?" he called, but heard only the sound of receding footfalls.

Carter stood and lit a lantern, bringing its soft light to the room, but the minstrel had already gone. Lord Anderson hurried into the long corridor beyond the chamber, only to find it empty. He stood gaping. The man must have gone at a dead sprint to disappear so rapidly.

Seeing there was nothing to be done, the Master returned to the antechamber, where he built up the fire and threw himself back on his blankets. He fell asleep feeling lonely and deserted, wondering if there were more to Jonathan's leaving. Perhaps he had found Carter's role in Shadow Valley's loss unforgivable.

Even apart from his friend's sudden disappearance, the next day's journey was distressing. In distant parts of the house, he heard peculiar animal cries, as if fabulous beasts wandered Evenmere. The eyes of portraits seemed to follow him. The walls and floorboards creaked incessantly, the whole house in an agony of travail. Chaos was winning and he did not know how to stop its advance.

Earlier, he and Jonathan had decided to travel south toward the ancient Opoian capitol, hoping that whatever they were seeking might lie there. But as Carter went, he grew increasingly discouraged by the sheer size of the country and the hopelessness of his quest. He needed more information.

By noon he was passing through winding corridors angling gradually downward. These soon led to Beam Forest, a series of chambers covered with miles of pillars painted the color of tree bark, supporting a ceiling filled with carved acanthus leaves dyed pale green, their hue mirrored by green floor tile on a brown background. Olive lacework descended in fans from the pillars, giving an illusion of branches. Standing beside one of the myriad brownstone archways and looking across the pillared chambers was like gazing over a forest in mountain heights, cracks spidering the bricks, spiders spinning webs between the counterfeit greenery, the splash of water gurgling through channels along the slopes. Fountains and sculptures lay scattered among the boles. Skylights, their glass etched with foliage, spread patchwork squares of sunlight on the floors, and would have cast leaf-shadows had shadows still existed. Carter, swearing he could almost smell the humus, half expected the forest to gradually become real.

Incongruities filled Beam Forest, for the people of the nearby country of Iphris had made it a memorial to those who had died before their time. Children were frequently represented, and keepsakes hung from the boles and lined the archways: beads, silver spoons, thimbles, wooden soldiers, porcelain dolls, stuffed bears, hair bows, and combs. Tiny portraits of youngsters gazed across the woodland. Carter found the pictures of boys the same age as Jason oppressive. For all its beauty, the silence of Beam Forest was the uneasy quiet of the graveyard.

He had read of the forest, but had never journeyed there. Several historic battles had been fought within its boundaries, and it was reputed to be haunted, a legend reinforced by the Dowagers of Beam, full-sized portraits, hoary to the point of hideous caricature, whose frames hung suspended from the boles. Despite their name, they were not all images of women. Folklore made various claims about them: that they had sold their souls for immortality, or were murderers and suicides, or trolls who had lived in the forest before humankind. They had been there for hundreds of years, and though they wore normal Victorian garb, their garments were said to change from century to century.

Carter encountered the first Dowager after passing through an archway. It stood less than a foot away, its eyes level with his own. He gave a shout of surprise, leapt back, and had his pistol half-drawn before realizing his mistake.

He stared at it, breathing sharply, chuckling nervously at his error, but beneath that grim gaze he found nothing amusing. The subject was incredibly lifelike, the portrait of a woman dressed in gray. She had silver hair, a hawk nose, black pinpoints for eyes, and black, bushy eyebrows. Her whole face was a map of wrinkles. Carter stepped back again, unnerved by the illusion that she was about to move. He found it incomprehensible that any artist had wished to capture such repellant features.

"If I stand here long enough," he murmured at last, "I shall imagine she *has* moved. I must go, old girl." Despite his attempt at levity, he wished he had never broken the silence.

Though he had always loved the moments of quiet and the desolate places of Evenmere, he grew increasingly uncomfortable. The Dowagers became more numerous, so that one was always visible wherever he walked, its eyes invariably on his own, as if the subject had shifted position to see him. Again and again he came unawares upon the portraits, lurking behind pillars or beyond archways, leering at him, giving their evil, conspiratorial grins. By the time he cast himself into an overstuffed chair for his dinner, he was all nerves.

He produced a bag of salted beef from his pack and unstoppered his flask, determined to enjoy his meal. *At least when I'm sitting still, I can't run into one of the vile things. I'm perfectly safe here.* But he did not feel safe. He tried to resist the urge to look over his shoulder, knowing what he would see. He told himself it was foolish; he could not possibly sense the lifeless eyes of a Dowager burning on his shoulder, but it wasn't any good. When he could no longer bear it, he turned, glancing instinctively to his left.

With a start, he found, at the very place he had expected to do so, a Dowager peering at him from between the boles fifty yards away.

He repressed an urge to move to a position beyond the

creature's gaze, fearing if he did so he would be unable to travel the forest without giving in to panic. Reminding himself that this was but a creation of oil and pigment, he finished his meal without looking at it again. But he found himself anxiously tearing at the jerky, gobbling his food to be quickly done. He wondered if the Dowagers had originally been painted to frighten away invaders. If so, the artists had done their work too well.

Finishing his meal, he hurried his provisions back into his pack and rose to leave. He dared another glance at the portrait and his blood turned to ice. For the barest instant, he tried to convince himself that his imagination had made the figure seem to move, that the dim illumination through the skylights had tricked his eyes. But even as he thought it, the ancient gentleman clutched the picture frame with a gnarled hand and gradually and painfully stepped out of the portrait, using his knobbed cane to steady himself.

Carter's courage momentarily failed; he stood frozen with horror as the creature, thin as a banister rail, its skin corpse-pale beneath the brim of its top-hat, turned its head from side to side, inspecting the forest. Lord Anderson dared not move as those eyes passed over him, though he knew he could scarcely be overlooked. Fastening his gaze upon the Master, the Dowager raised its cane in salute and headed in his direction, its movements slow and stiff in the manner of someone approaching an old friend at a train station.

Carter struggled to understand the situation. Retreat seemed his best course, and he strode quickly away.

The man followed after, shouting something unrecognizable. Carter did not run as he was tempted, but kept a rigorous pace. Each time he glanced back, he saw the Dowager falling farther behind, futilely waving his cane, an incongruous caricature, like a stork in gentleman's garb.

An archway lay ahead. He passed through it, his back pressed against the right-hand side of the stone passage, and peered carefully out. There was nothing to his left, but a portrait hung to the right, its side turned toward him so he could not see its occupant.

Carter stepped to the left, keeping his distance. The frame wavered slightly, as if stirred by a wind, and as it turned toward him, he saw it was empty.

A hand clutched his left shoulder.

He gave a shout, spun, and struck the Dowager a heavy blow to the face. The creature, a bent crone, went down. Despite his terror, he stood momentarily bewildered at having hit an old woman. Such misgivings vanished, however, as with a snarl and an expression of utter hatred she shrugged off the blow and started to rise.

With his sword, he slashed her across the midriff. The blade cut her in two, as if she were only canvas. Her upper body tumbled to the ground, leaving the lower portion still standing. She did not bleed, but was filled with a white, plaster material. The severed portion lay with its hands braced on the ground. Without a suggestion of pain, the Dowager turned her evil head to glare and hiss at him. She crawled toward him, dragging herself along. He backed away, hurrying deeper into the forest.

Through his fear, he tried to think. He had to get out of the forest no later than nightfall; the thought of meeting the Dowagers by lamplight sent shudders along his spine. With an effort of will, he forced himself to pause long enough to consult his inner maps. It was difficult to concentrate on finding a new path while watching for danger, but he finally discovered a nearby stair leading to a series of attic spaces.

A noise like rustling paper arose behind him. He whirled. An old man bore down on him, wielding a sword stick. Carter stepped to the left and parried with his Lightning Sword, rending his enemy's weapon. The creature advanced and Carter stabbed him in the chest. The Dowager walked right up the blade, heedless of any discomfort. They stood face-to-face, and the Dowager gave an animal growl, revealing pointed fangs. Carter jerked his sword to the left, sawing through the creature. Like the woman, he did not bleed, but tipped over, overbalanced by the cleft portion of his body.

Carter hurried away. The attic stair was two hours away; the thought of meeting a company of the Dowagers spurred him to a trot, though he dared not risk exhaustion by running too fast. For a half-hour, he traveled unmolested, easily outpacing the Dowagers he sighted in the distance.

Finding it difficult to keep his direction amid the maze of boles, he had slowed to a vigorous walk once more, when he spied a figure moving to his left. Carter hid behind one of the wider columns, and peered around it. This was not a Dowager, but a man dressed in anarchist gray, carrying a pistol. Keeping out of sight until the stranger passed, he drew his Tawny Mantle around him and continued on his way, more wary than ever, but hoping by his unexpected turn to the west to outwit his trackers.

This fancy was dashed moments later when a bullet ricocheted off a column close to his head. He crouched, trying to pinpoint from whence the volley had come.

"What is it?" a voice called.

"I saw an indistinct shape over this way," another replied. "He must be wearing his cloak."

By their words, Carter knew the anarchists were searching specifically for him. This confirmed his suspicion that it was the poets who had somehow given the portraits life.

The lack of shadow somewhat mitigated the effects of the Tawny Mantle, which—even with its chameleon properties—could not completely hide him from any who knew to look. Feeling completely exposed, he slipped away and found shelter under the protection of an archway. From his vantage point, he searched the downward slope of the forest, until he saw at least one figure creeping from bole to bole. The anarchist raised his hand, as if signaling to others; Carter guessed he would soon be surrounded. He sheathed his sword and drew his pistol.

Under the camouflage of the mantle, whose colors became those of the leaf-patterned carpet, he crawled away. For nearly twenty minutes, he traveled in this fashion through the forest.

When he thought he had gone far enough, he rose, only to turn and discover an anarchist passing from behind a bole thirty feet away. The man glanced toward him, his gun wavering, his sight confused by the mantle. Carter fired, dropping him with a single shot.

Lord Anderson broke into a run, while someone shouted behind him, "Over here! Hoffman is down."

"Can you see the Master?"

"I don't—I'm uncertain."

Carter dashed madly through the forest, hurdling the channeled streams, depending on his mantle to obscure him.

A barrage of fire erupted to his right and he flung himself to the ground. He counted at least six anarchists and assumed there were more. Several of the Dowagers, bearing canes and sword-sticks, were also moving toward him.

He concentrated, seeking a Word of Power. Behind the darkness of his closed lids, the Word Which Manifests rose, though it did not blaze brightly, but smoldered like wet coals, as if mirroring his exhaustion. By an act of will, he bent his thoughts upon the Word until it brightened. He raised it to his lips, feeling it burn his throat.

Falan!

The forest shook. A golden wave of power spread before him. When it touched the Dowagers, they crumbled into bits, dissipating and drifting to the ground like papier-mâché. Those anarchists unprotected by the columns were thrown back, and one of the pillars itself swayed and toppled, bringing a portion of the roof down on the anarchists' heads.

Carter bolted. His foes were calling both behind him and to his right, but their voices grew increasingly distant. He ran until his breath came in gasps, forcing him to slow to a walk.

Having gained a temporary respite, he kept low and continued on.

For well over an hour, he saw no further signs of pursuit. He was nearing the stair to the attic spaces, passing through an archway into a clearing with a stone altar at its center. He moved cautiously around the edge of the circle, staying near the columns.

"Greetings, Lord Anderson."

He turned and fired twice at a figure dressed in an olive robe. Though his aim was true, the bullets missed their target, ricocheting off the floor to either side.

"A poor reception," the woman said. Her hair was cinnamon blonde, her eyes bright green; she was tall and slender, not yet thirty, and unlike her counterparts', her face remained unobscured. "Is it your custom to shoot women on sight?"

Her robe had a question mark embossed on it; her voice held the strange, stirring quality characteristic of the poets. An aura of power surrounded her of tree and root and growing things. A yellow-spotted lizard curled around her throat like a necklace. Taking careful aim, Carter fired again. The shot went wide, and Lord Anderson backed from the clearing.

"Do not fear me!" she cried. "I am Fecundity, bringing the world to fruition like a goddess of old. Observe."

She touched one of the support columns and it flowered, becoming a true tree, its branches and leaves opening, reaching toward the sky. "The Dowagers I animated, my minions to watch for you, carved from the trees that became their canvases, the vegetation that formed their pigments. I can give you this power. You can become as we are."

Carter used the Word Which Manifests again.

Falan!

The wave of force blew the leaves from the tree and sent the Poetry Woman to her knees.

Lord Anderson had nearly been bested by one of her fellows; he and Phra combined had scarcely defeated another. Fearing the cost of failure, he dared not press his advantage, but fled once more, running at full speed, his boots slapping against the floor, down a sloping course ending several minutes later at a forty-foot bridge spanning the tall, concrete banks of a rushing stream.

The Poetry Woman stood beside the bridge, having somehow anticipated his course. Hearing the shouts of the anarchists behind him, he glanced over his shoulder. They were approaching in a wide arc, the way men drive animals in a hunt. He was trapped.

"Perhaps you are right," he said to the poetess, in order to buy time. "Perhaps I should surrender."

She smiled, her eyes ecstatic. "Do you begin to understand? Do you hear the wild calling?"

In truth, he did; he felt the throbbing of the earth and the calling of life, seeking to draw him. As he approached her, the center of its passion, the impulse grew stronger. Each of the poets tapped into a different fundamental archetype: fire, earth, water, growing things. Could that be a weakness as well as a strength? A memory of childhood fairy tales came to his mind, of woodland sprites who drew power from the earth and could not cross water or leave their own country.

Without hesitation, he acted on the impulse, drawing closer to the flowing stream, moving slightly to the woman's right, aiming toward the bridge.

She stepped to her left, keeping herself between him and the span. As he concentrated, seeking another word, he wished he had used the Word Which Gives Strength, for he was nearly done in. As if in slow motion, the Word Which Manifests struggled to lift itself through the darkness.

"Try no deception, lest I grow harsh," she warned.

Part of him wanted to give himself to the cold power of this woman. Its beckoning had grown stronger, a feeling similar to lust, but purer, almost holy. He thought of Jason and brought the Word to his throat.

The lizard around the woman's neck hissed as Carter spoke. *Falan*!

The force of the Word, that would normally spread out in a great wave, blazed forth against the Poetry Woman, throwing her from her feet. She stumbled backward, nearly toppling into the water, but caught herself at the bridge railing and tumbled onto its wooden surface.

Before she fell, Carter was already sprinting toward her. Separated from the leaf carpets of Beam Forest, her glory had vanished; she seemed only an ordinary woman. He grasped her by the collar. The lizard tried to bite him, but he slapped it away, and it fled, peering and hissing at him from behind the safety of her neck.

"How did you know?" she cried.

Without answering, he cast her over the railing. She shrieked as she fell twenty feet to the stream, but he did not pause to watch her descent. Seeing their leader deposed, the anarchists began firing, and bullets whizzed around Carter's head as he bolted across the bridge. A bronze door stood open before him. He rushed through and shut it behind him, but there was no way to secure it.

He fled through a rustic corridor of bare boards leading to a stair. As he ascended, he heard the noise of pursuing feet below.

He had been lucky at the bridge in realizing the poets were tied to the avatars they summoned.

He passed the first landing, which opened onto a long hallway. Three levels remained above him, but when he came to the next one, he left the stair and hurried along a corridor, pausing only to light his lantern before passing into a deep gloom. Multiple branchings led from the passage, and if he could occasionally double back on his path to confuse his bootprints on the dust-laden floor, his enemies would be hard pressed to follow. He consulted his maps, and was soon traveling down passages scarcely wide enough for one person, past small, half-finished rooms without doors, the slats and wall studs still visible in their interiors. The ceiling sloped downward from a height of ten feet in the corridor to less than five at the far corners of the rooms.

The attic was hot, its silence oppressive. Though he was certain he had left the Dowagers behind, he kept expecting to turn a corner or peer into a doorway and find their infernal, staring eyes upon him. His own footfalls disquieted him, making him wary of every step; his apprehension grew as he passed rooms with cow skulls hanging from the ceilings and animal bones scattered across the floor, as if the remnants of ghastly rites. Because his lantern cast no shadows, everything lay stark, bare, unnaturally flat.

The heat seeped into him, leaving him sweating and weary. He intended to travel through the night to ensure his escape, but by midnight he was stumbling on his feet and had to rest, if only for an hour.

He tried to find some place of concealment beneath a stairway or in a nook, but the corridors and bare rooms stretched on and on. He did not relish the idea of being trapped within one of the chambers, nor of lying down in the narrow hall. At last he found a place where the corridor widened to form an antechamber. He threw his bedroll into the darkest corner and lay down, the odor of dust heavy in his nostrils. He longed to enter the land of dream, to check with Mr. Hope and make certain Jason was well, but dared not do so while the anarchists sought him. Feeling miserably vulnerable, he doused his lantern and tried to sleep.

Over the years, he had adopted a certain attitude whenever he found himself in a deserted, often benighted way. Knowing he had done all he could, he released the troubles of the day, mentally picturing laying them into hands larger than his own.

Yet his sleep was disturbed, for he dreamed he walked the Transverse Corridor in the Inner Chambers. The hallway was dark and growing darker, and he knew something horrible was coming, something he couldn't see in the gloom. Something of Chaos. Growing nearer . . . nearer . . .

He woke with a start to find a Poetry Man standing over him, holding a candle in his left hand, his right hand upraised, palm open, glowing with a light of its own.

Lord Anderson rolled to the side as the poet unleashed a

lightning bolt from his outstretched hand. Where it struck, the boards exploded, sending wood shards spearing across the room. Carter dove into the narrower portion of the corridor, and turned, speaking the Word Which Seals. He did not hear his own voice; the thunder had deafened him, but a golden sheen rose to cover the portal between him and his foe.

The poet stepped to the sealed doorway, holding his candle aloft, shading his eyes as if the light's reflection off the barrier kept him from seeing through it. Without knowing how the man was connected to his lightning avatar, Carter doubted he could defeat him as he had the woman at the bridge. He fled, guided by the Poetry Man's candlelight.

Thunder boomed in the passages behind him as the poet released his might against the seal. The lightning flashes illuminated Carter's way until he reached a turn fifty yards farther down. Though he had lost his bedroll, he had slept with his backpack slung over one arm, and still held it and the lantern strapped to it. Halting only long enough to light the lamp, he scurried down the passage. He doubted if even the poet's power could destroy what the Word Which Seals had created—that corridor would be blocked until Carter chose to open it—but eventually his foe would seek another path. By then, Lord Anderson intended to be far away.

Yet as he fled, he kept expecting to see another of his enemies approaching through the darkness. In this way he passed a hapless hour, until he began to sense, as the Master can, hidden passages nearby. He spoke the Word of Secret Ways and began searching for the familiar blue glow.

At first this proved fruitless, until he passed a bare chamber and saw a faint rectangular illumination on the low, slanting ceiling. A quick search of the room revealed a knob hidden behind a support joint that released the trapdoor. The ceiling was high enough to require him to stand on tiptoe to throw the door back. He would have to jump up and catch the sides of the opening to pull himself through.

On his first attempt, he discovered he could not enter the hatch while wearing his backpack, which had the lantern tied to it. He was forced to release his hold, douse the lantern and then, working in absolute darkness, throw his gear in first and follow after. When he raised himself through the aperture, he banged his skull against the roof. Despite the shock, he maintained his hold, and keeping low, pulled himself through the opening.

"Why am I always hitting my head?" he snarled, his whole world a blanket of pain.

When he had recovered and relit his lantern, he found himself in an oaken shaft only high enough for going on all fours. He groaned, but shut the trapdoor and crept on hands and knees for several hundred feet before resting on his forearms to catch his breath.

A moment later, he heard the creak of the trapdoor opening. A dim light appeared down the shaft. He did not think he had the strength to summon the Word Which Seals again. Before him, the tunnel veered to the right, and he made a crawling dash toward the turning, expecting at any second to hear the release of a lightning bolt.

None came; perhaps the poet had exhausted his strength. As he reached the corner, Carter drew his revolver. The passage was too narrow for him to turn around, so he leaned back and fired twice without aiming. The bullets whined down the shaft, but there came no answering cry of pain. Undoubtedly, the poet was as impervious to gunfire as his comrades.

A mad race ensued, Carter scurrying away, the Poetry Man following, neither speaking, their lamps the only light in that elongated darkness. The tunnel branched in several places, and Carter kept his maps close to his thoughts to trace his way. How could he elude his opponent when his every motion left marks in the dust?

For a half hour they rushed through the tunnels, until at last Carter came to the blue glow of another secret way. He found the latch and slid aside a panel opening onto the bare desolation of the attic. Leaping down, he closed the door behind him and fled at top speed, eager for a chance of escape. He passed down a passage, turned right at an intersection, left at another, and slid to a halt before a new secret way. Sweat broke across his brow as he fumbled to find the unlocking mechanism, but at last he discovered a wooden button hidden among the slats. An entire portion of the wall swung up, opening into a dingy passage. Carter stepped inside, grateful to find it was not another tunnel. He closed the door and hurried down it.

For a while, the corridor doubled back the way he had

come. He passed spy-holes every hundred yards, with elegant, wooden chin rests. With his lantern shrouded, Carter gazed through each in turn, and soon saw the poet shuffling along the passage, holding the candle low to perceive footprints. Lord Anderson would have given much to learn if an unexpected assault could harm the creature, but had no way to reach him through the wall.

For another hour he followed the secret passage, taking intersections when they presented themselves, veering always to the south and east.

He sat on the floor to rest and study his maps, and in so doing, felt the full weight of his exhaustion. He could not concentrate; the maps kept slipping from his mind. After a time he sighed, and with grim resolution, summoned the Word Which Gives Strength, the only Word that makes the Master stronger after its use. Inwardly he groaned, knowing it would take a terrible toll when its effects wore off, yet he had no choice. As soon as he spoke it, he felt renewed; his mind cleared; his situation seemed less hopeless. He gulped water from his canteen and returned to the maps.

From his current location, the secret corridor forked in three directions, one leading up a stair to a higher level. With some consternation, he saw another passage intersecting this one, that could have allowed him to reach his current position much more quickly. He shrugged. The mistake was already made. Rising, he headed toward the stair, which he reached in twenty minutes.

The steps creaked as he ascended, and he kept his sword ready, but did not meet any enemies at the top. He followed another interminable passage, unique in having occasional slits in the floor, allowing glimpses of the corridor below. As he neared one such opening, he detected a gleam of light below. Mantling his own lantern and sheathing his blade, he knelt and peered through the gap.

His foe must have made up time by taking the passage Lord Anderson had missed. Clearly, the poet knew almost as much about the secret ways as any Master, and was tracking Carter with the skill of a bloodhound. Perhaps he could sense Lord Anderson's power. Whatever the source of his ability, Carter could have wept at the sight of him. No doubt he would soon find a way into this passage as well.

He hurried through the gloom, wondering if his enemy ever required sleep. As soon as possible, he left the secret way. He had traveled far enough east to bypass Beam Forest, and now left the high attic, descending the rickety steps of a circular stair. A wide hallway lay at the bottom, and he continued until dawn toward the Sidereal Sea, taking a winding course intended to confuse his pursuer.

By the time the morning sun warmed the panes of Evenmere, the Word Which Gives Strength had worn off, leaving him stumbling on his feet.

He came to a set of double doors opening into a large study. According to his maps, the door at the far side of the room led to the ruins of the Opoian capitol. He strode toward it.

"The chase is done," the voice of the poet said behind him.

Without turning, Carter bolted for the far door. A blast passed overhead, striking the door, shattering it to pieces. The impact hurled Lord Anderson off his feet. Blinded by the flash, he rolled onto his stomach and tried to rise, but his legs gave way beneath him.

"You were beaten by no less a foe than exhaustion," the Poetry Man said, "while I remain fresh, filled with power. Too late to submit; you should have surrendered when you could."

Carter could feel his enemy's energies, hot on his face. Still unable to see clearly, he spoke the Word Which Manifests, though it came ragged from his throat. He felt it leave him in a splattering wave that caused his enemy to yelp in pain.

Carter crawled to his knees. His eyes began to clear; the Word had thrown the poet against the far wall, but he was already trying to rise.

He had no more strength for running. He pulled his pistol and fired, but the bullets veered from his foe, riddling the wood panels with holes. Recovering his Lightning Sword from where it lay on the floor, Carter made a desperate charge, only to be cut off by a sheet of lightning descending between him and his target, a sizzling curtain of voltage he dared not cross.

"I will use . . . whatever means necessary to stop you," the Poetry Man cried, half panting. "Whatever power. Even if I perish, it will be wonderful beyond words. That is why you cannot win! It is too glorious."

Fingers of electricity crackled up and down the chamber, pushing Carter against a corner. He was trapped, done for. The poet had beaten him.

He did the last thing he could, drawing deep within himself to summon the strength to speak the Word Which Brings Aid.

Elahkammor!

Beneath the hissing, electric cacophony, the Word's effect could not be heard. No one could possibly come in time. Even if they did, they could not challenge the poet's might.

The Poetry Man stood, arms above his head, a vortex of lightning coruscating between his palms.

"Don't you realize you've tapped energies we were never meant to control?" Carter cried, trying to stall, shouting to make himself heard above the storm.

"The apples of the gods!" his foe replied. "The Promethean fire. You have a parochial attitude for a child of the modern age. Man was meant to command all things."

Carter sought a way to get beneath the surrounding current. "Not until he learns to control himself!"

With a mad, skeletal grin, the Poetry Man stepped forward, bringing the lightnings closer. Lord Anderson retreated until his back was against the wall. In desperation, he struck at the flashing curtain with his Lightning Sword. Current flowed back through his blade into his arm, wrenching a scream from his lips. He slammed against the wall and slumped to the ground. His sword hung, trapped, within the electric field. His whole body felt numb. He could no longer rise; he could no longer resist. He could not even lift his hand to protect himself. He thought he might be dying.

The poet stepped through the curtain, his body so enmeshed with the force flowing through him that he appeared as rolling lightning in human shape. Looming over Carter, he reached his hand toward his victim's head.

Something cold abruptly washed over Carter. He thought it must be his blood. The poet stiffened and shrieked. Carter spied a figure at the doorway, spraying a steady stream from a fire hose onto the poet, who disintegrated with a dreadful crackling, like all the world's lightning going out at once. The stench of burnt flesh filled the air.

Whether from the effect of the water, or because of the

poet's passing, Carter found he had enough strength to move. He turned toward the doorway just as Doctor Armilus stepped into the light, his black familiar padding behind him. The anarchist twisted shut the valve on the hose, cutting off the flow from a line connected to one of the many outlets used by the Firemen of Ooz to fight house fires. He carried a pistol, but kept it aimed away from Lord Anderson.

"I am owed for this one," Armilus said, with a grimacing smile.

Carter glanced at his Lightning Sword, lying several feet away. He could never draw his gun in time.

"Why?" he asked.

The doctor raised his eyebrows. "Not from any sense of compassion. I had been searching for a Poetry Man because I wanted to see if I could kill one. I was told the use of an opposing element might do the trick. I am gratified at my success. No doubt you feel the same."

Carter climbed to his feet, his entire body trembling with weakness. The beast growled.

"None of that!" Armilus commanded the hound. "You and I, Lord Anderson, are the only ones standing between the poets and the destruction of the house, so regardless what my strange ally wishes, I need you alive. I *am* a man of honor, and we have a truce. Even my own defeat is preferable to the victory of these lunatics."

"Then your time would be better spent discarding your plans and aiding me."

"Perhaps," Armilus said, "but there is opportunity whenever power shifts. I am still discovering new uses for the knowledge I took from *The Book of Lore*, things even the Masters feared to accomplish."

"Do you understand what your actions could do to the Balance?"

Armilus waved his hand in dismissal. "If I succeed there will be a new Balance. You and the Masters before you—think of what you could have done if you'd had the spine. Makes the blood pump."

"If you believe that, you're as mad as the poets."

"No harm in enjoying one's work. I'm afraid I must be going. Just remember what I did for you this day."

Armilus passed into the darkness, the Black Beast behind him. No longer able to keep his wits, Carter swooned.

"Why didn't you kill him?" the beast hissed, when they were out of earshot.

"I gave my word," the doctor replied wearily. "If you wanted Anderson dead, you should have waited a few moments instead of ripping us from our place and transporting us here. The poet would have done the job for you."

Armilus grimaced. He had always prided himself on his ability to bear up under physical pain, but had never felt anything so terrible as that instantaneous journey—he had actually thought it was killing him. That would have put a pretty end to his plans.

"I was not the one who brought us."

Armilus turned and studied the beast's hideous face. "What do you mean?"

"Anderson summoned us with the Word Which Brings Aid."

"He can transport people as he likes?"

"The Word searches for someone close at hand. If none are found, it fails. Because you are linked to *The Book of Lore*, it was able to reach you through the dream dimension." The beast chuckled, a dry coughing noise. "One of the drawbacks of reading the book."

Armilus glanced down at the black-stoned ring welded to his finger. "There are more of those than I first imagined. I don't like it one bit. On occasion the anarchists have been able to move physical objects through dreams. It takes time and incredible energy. Lord Anderson did it effortlessly, making me less than his pawn. How could the Word know I would help him? That almost suggests a controlling intellect."

"Of that, I know nothing."

"Besides," Armilus grumbled, "if you wanted to kill him, why didn't you? I doubt I could have stopped you."

The beast growled. "I do not understand what you mean, Doctor. Did you not summon me when you opened *The Book of Lore*? Did I not tell you how to destroy the poet? Am I not yours to command?"

So long as I am useful, Armilus thought. "As usual, you avoid answering the question. I don't know *what* you are, or what you represent. Chaos, maybe. Entropy itself, perhaps. Why won't you tell me?"

The beast chuckled again. "I am the Thing of the Book. That is all I know."

"Hardly. You lie for pleasure. I wish I had something as grand as the Words of Power, instead of a smelly, dangerous dog. Let's find a place to sit. I need to think."

"Of course you do," the beast replied, its voice thick with irony.

Does it know everything? Armilus wondered. In truth, he was going to faint unless he sat down. And the beast was beginning to terrify him. He could feel its will pressing against his mind, maybe reading his thoughts, perhaps even trying to control them. He had to learn what it was and how to command it before it was too late, or his plans would end in disaster.

Carter woke soon after the doctor departed, knowing he should leave before more enemies appeared, but despite his intentions, his weariness kept him from rising. After a momentary struggle, he drew his Tawny Mantle over himself and fell into a dreamless sleep.

The last rays of sunset shone through the windows at the far end of the room before he shouted and flung his eyes wide, deeply startled. The chamber lay empty, an ordinary drawing room save for the wet, charred carpet and the bullet-holes in the wall; but something was terribly wrong. Something in the Balance had just changed, something important and dreadful, but he could not pinpoint it.

He ate enough from his dwindling supplies to give himself some strength. Despite sleeping through the day, he was still mentally and physically exhausted, but he had to enter the dream world and confer with Mr. Hope to find out what had happened.

The Word Which Masters Dreams came with difficulty, rolling into his mind like a heavy stone, shedding nearly no light.

He spoke it with an effort and passed into the land of slumber, where he found himself standing in the gray mist of the Long Corridor, facing the Green Door. He fumbled with the Master Keys, found the malachite key on the bronze ring, and unlocked the door.

It opened onto moonlight. Carter faced the front of the house, looking out toward the driveway and the statue of the monk. The Inner Chambers was gone, winked out of existence, leaving only bare earth where it had been.

The Long Way Down

Three days had passed since Jonathan T. Bartholomew parted company with Master Anderson, and he had yet to reach his destination. When the winking of the Inner Chambers occurred, the shifting Balance had struck him as a physical agony, leaving him writhing and feverish, too incapacitated to travel for the better portion of a day. Better now, he was still unable to journey at his accustomed pace. Yet, when he wished, he could march at a tremendous speed, and his capacity to go without rest bordered on the superhuman, so that even in his impaired state, he was already in Aylyrium.

His trek took him far north of the university, close to the border of Ooz, in an area of catacombed chambers where vagabonds and outlaws were known to hide. Few gas-jets burned along the gloom-shrouded corridors, which even the lack of shadows failed to make more definite; but as in so many of the halls throughout the centuries, Jonathan had walked here before, and he moved with assurance, not bothering to light his lamp.

He entered a large, windowless chamber, empty now, though the scent of lilac and candle wax suggested recent occupation. He moved through the darkness to the far wall. Raising his hands to his chin, he closed his eyes. A grumble of pain escaped his lips as the wall abruptly opened, a narrow aperture just wide enough to allow passage into the next room.

He stepped through. The chamber was well lit and in good

order, with comfortable furnishings and a bottle of wine and loaf of bread on a linen tablecloth. Scarcely glancing around, Jonathan removed a heavy portrait of a silver-haired octogenarian from its place, disclosing a large wall-safe. He studied it, and with a smile of satisfaction, dialed the combination.

From within, he withdrew *The Book of Lore* and set it on the table. Pulling a hunk of bread from the loaf, he took a bite and chewed it thoughtfully as he opened the volume. His eyes passed quickly over the pages, darkening occasionally as he read. After only a moment he looked up, forgetting to chew.

"I've found it! And Lord Anderson doesn't know. I'll have to hurry to gain the advantage."

He shut the book and abruptly stiffened.

"I have a gun and will use it," a feminine voice behind him said.

Jonathan turned to face a beautiful woman holding a small pistol.

With a nodding bow, the minstrel said, "Contessa du Maurier? A pleasure."

The contessa lifted an eyebrow in surprise. "And you are?"

"Jonathan T. Bartholomew, traveling singer and teller of tales."

"How did you unlock that safe?"

"I am Storyteller, who sees to the heart, not just of people, but of other things, too. And you, once an urchin in Dumon with a drunken father and a cowed mother, don't want to shoot me."

Her blue eyes sharpened. "Threatening to slander my reputation will get you nowhere. I won't allow you to leave with that book."

"That's right. It will stay." He lifted the volume to return it to its place.

"No," she ordered. "Leave it on the table."

"You have great ambition, Countessa," he said, ignoring her words and putting *The Book of Lore* back in the safe. "But it wouldn't be good for you to read this book. As like as not, it would kill you." He shut the safe and locked it. "A lovely lady such as yourself—why, that would be a shame."

Without glancing her way, he moved back toward the opening through which he had come.

"Stop!" the contessa cried. "You will remain here until I summon my associates."

"You don't want me to do that, ma'am," Jonathan called over his shoulder. "You have too many secrets, and Storyteller knows every one of them."

He stepped through the opening, which closed with a hissing sound, leaving du Maurier gaping.

Jonathan hurried away, having already dismissed her from his mind.

I've got to hurry, he thought. *Or everything I've worked for will come to ruin.*

Carter made his way along a winding stair in the upper stories of the Opo, scarcely able to put one foot before the other, his heart dead within him. The Inner Chambers was gone, and with it Sarah and Jason and William Hope, all of them vanished—possibly annihilated—but if alive, perhaps forever unreachable.

It was exactly as Jonathan had said; he had compromised his honor for nothing, and by so doing changed the Balance and brought disaster. He had been a traitor his whole life; he would probably die a traitor.

He had only one prospect: a handwritten note penned in Mr. Hope's neat hand, found lying at the entrance to Evenmere, as if he had left it outside the door in the final moment before his dissolution. Because Lord Anderson had been in the dream world when he read it, he was unable to retrieve it, but it contained only six words: *Palace of Opo. Eye Gate below.*

Lord Anderson and the butler had last spoken just before the disaster at Shadow Valley, so Mr. Hope could not have known Carter was journeying through the Opo. Apparently, Hope's research had uncovered Professor Shoemate's route.

Although he was already in the region of the ancient Opoian capitol, there was no one in that deserted country to give directions to the palace. He spent an hour tracing his way through his maps without knowing exactly what he was looking for, until he found a white edifice adorned with ancient, carved emblems, standing alone along a wide corridor.

Throughout the day Carter traveled toward it, trying not to speculate on the fates of his loved ones. At eight o'clock that evening, within a mile of the building, he found his way blocked by an impenetrable wall of debris created by a collapse of the corridor. After consulting his maps again, he backtracked for an hour, descended a stair, and continued toward his goal, only to find his path again barred by rubble. He suspected the poets were intentionally obstructing his path.

Four o'clock in the morning found him desperately seeking another route, hurrying though a carpeted corridor silent save for the whispering of an occasional gas-jet, his lantern lit to fill in the spaces of darkness between the sparse flames. His strength had flagged at midnight, forcing him to use the Word Which Gives Strength. Under its influence, he could go several more hours, but he dreaded how he would feel when its effect faded.

His frustration had grown through the early morning hours. His maps were nearly useless; every path he tried met defeat. He found walls where none should be, stairs intended to ascend turning downward, hallways doubling on themselves. Evenmere shifted around him, causing havoc with his sense of the Balance. Despite his best efforts, he was siphoned always east, ever farther from his objective. The changes increased, doorways sealing themselves behind him, making retreat impossible.

At last, weary beyond hope, certain he was being led to his destruction, he threw himself onto a low couch in a dreary side-chamber and fell into a bleak sleep.

When the Winking came, Lizbeth and Sarah were in Mr. Hope's office in the gentleman's chamber, while Jason played beneath the billiards table. William sat behind his desk, studying a book. He murmured, almost to himself, "I think I have something."

"About the professor?" Sarah asked.

"Not precisely. Did I tell you about the message Enoch sent yesterday?"

"Not a word." Sarah turned to her sister. "Did he mention it to you?"

Lizbeth sat on the sofa, arms folded, looking down as if listening.

"Lizbeth?"

She raised her eyes, a bit startled. "What? I'm sorry. Were you speaking to me?"

Sarah repeated her question and Lizbeth shook her head. "This is the first I've heard of it."

"Sloppy of me," Mr. Hope said, rubbing his eyes. "None of us have slept much since the shadows vanished . . ." His voice trailed off, his gaze shifting across the stark, shadowless room. Carter had last been seen by the White Circle Guard just before he and Jonathan entered Shadow Valley.

Sarah patted his arm. "He is made of stern materials. I refuse to believe he has come to harm." But her voice quavered as she spoke. "Now what about Enoch?"

"When he went to wind the Hundred Years Clock, he verified what he had already sensed: someone has snatched a second of time from Existence."

Sarah raised her eyebrows. "I doubt it will be missed."

Hope laughed wearily. "Enoch thinks otherwise, but it reminded me of the starlight Doctor Armilus took from the Tower of Astronomy, a similarly abstract artifact. Assuming it was he who stole the time, I asked myself what he wanted it for. Nothing came to mind, until I received this book from one of my agents." He held up the worn leather volume he had been perusing. "I've had my people scouring the Mere for information about the Eye Gate and *The Book of Verse*."

"You know they call your emissaries Hope's Minions now?" Sarah asked. "The rumor is you have an army of them traveling throughout the house, performing various arcane duties."

Mr. Hope frowned. "I fancy the name, though they're hardly an army. Closer to a battalion, really. At any rate, hidden within these pages is a reference dating back seven hundred years to the destruction of ancient Opo. *The Eye Gate stands blind, with none now left to watch.* A single note, but it sent my minions, as you call them, seeking anything concerning Opo. An unusual description on an ancient vase led to a scroll in the Aylyrium Museum of Antiquities. According to it, the Gate of the Staring Eye was located beneath the Opoian palace, and was a portal leading to a world of elemental energies—Time and Dimension,

Shadow and Light, Water and Fire, Earth and Air. The kinds of power the Poetry Men wield."

"And a connection with the items Armilus stole," Sarah said.

"Perhaps, though a tenuous one. Even if we are correct, the Opo covers miles, and we haven't yet discovered where the ancient palace lay. I wish Carter would contact me. Shadow Valley was near Opo; maybe he can find out something on his end. I need to warn him as well; the scroll suggests dark danger to anyone entering the Eye Gate."

Throughout the conversation, Lizbeth had remained silent, listening with only half an ear, troubled by a vague unease, as if some peril were rising toward them. Now she gave a sudden start.

"Something's wrong!" she blurted, causing her friends to turn to her in surprise. "Something is coming!"

"What do you mean?" Mr. Hope asked.

"I don't . . ." She struggled to put her feeling into words. "It's like when I was imprisoned in the False House, when the rooms would unexpectedly change. It's the same sensation."

Seeing Lizbeth's urgency, Sarah rushed to Jason's side and lifted him in her arms. "What must we do?"

"We need to leave the Inner Chambers. We should—oh, there's no time!"

Leaping to her feet, Lizbeth fumbled across Mr. Hope's desk and grabbed the paper where he had written the words *Palace of Opo* and *Eye Gate below*. Tearing away the rest of his scribblings, she rushed to the open window and threw the scrap out. Scarcely had it left her hand when the Winking occurred.

The three friends gave an involuntary cry. Lizbeth felt herself being torn to pieces. *Just like the paper*, she thought. A darkness swept in from every side, enveloping her, destroying the room. She lost consciousness.

Her first waking thought was surprise at being alive; she felt certain she had perished. She must have been thrown across the room, for she was lying with her head against a leg of the billiards table. It felt solid when she touched it, as if it had never been destroyed.

"Yet it has," she murmured, not really understanding what she meant. "We all have."

The room lay dark, the only illumination a twilight glow through the windows. Mr. Hope had collapsed at his desk; Sarah was pulling herself to her feet and Jason sat on the floor beside her, looking about with wide eyes. Lizbeth rushed to the side of the woman who had been both mother and sister to her, and helped her and the boy to a chair.

"What happened, Momma?" Jason asked.

"It's all right," Sarah soothed, stroking his hair while Lizbeth checked on Mr. Hope.

The butler was soon roused, and together the three of them stepped to the window, Sarah fiercely gripping her son's hand. Nothing lay outside save a vast, impenetrable mist, an unending gray without flower, grass, tree, or even visible earth.

"You felt it before it happened," Mr. Hope said. "What was it?"

"Some sort of change," Lizbeth said, "like a great wave pouring over the Inner Chambers. I can't be more specific."

"Is the rest of the house safe?" Sarah asked.

"I think so, but we are somewhere else. I thought at first we were dead, but I don't believe it now."

"Let's rule that out," Sarah said. "If we were, I think we would feel either better or worse."

The doors burst open and the servants poured in, seeking explanations and instructions. Momentary bedlam followed. For once, Mr. Hope seemed nonplussed, but Sarah, quick-witted as ever, took charge with astonishing aplomb.

"We're in a bit of a pickle, all at sea," she told them, "but not sinking in the brine, at least not yet. Charles, I want you to post sentries at the exits. No one is to go out. We may send an exploratory party later. Meredith, I need a list of everyone who is in the Inner Chambers. For the rest of you, your instructions are to continue your work, while we try to straighten this out."

"But what's happened, m'lady?" one of the serving girls asked, her eyes filled with terror.

"Why, only a little thing, child," Sarah said. "You've gone out for strolls, haven't you?"

"Yes, ma'am."

"The Inner Chambers has done the same thing, taken a bit of a holiday. She's a good girl, though, just like you, and won't have gone far. We'll see where she's wandered to and get her back home before dark. Now let's be about our business."

After the servants left, taking Jason with them, Sarah sat down in a chair and put her hands to her face, though she did not weep. "Do I have any idea what I'm talking about, William?"

"None whatsoever," the butler said, gazing into the gray mist, "but you spoke with authority and that is more than I could manage. Thank you."

"What do we do now?" Sarah asked.

"Lizbeth," Mr. Hope said, "do you have any idea where we are?"

Lizbeth closed her eyes, remembering how she used to feel during her captivity, when the anarchists had given her the power to change rooms of the house simply by willing it. She did not like to think of those times, but they were always a part of her, and she understood what the transformations were like.

Now she listened for those changes, trying to comprehend what had occurred. What had the Inner Chambers *felt* like before the shift? How was it different now? Gradually, an impression came to her.

"We are farther down," she said at last, opening her eyes.

"What do you mean, dear one?" Sarah asked.

"I don't know exactly. Somewhere deeper. Not in the earth; I don't mean that. Deeper. Like we've stepped *inside*."

"Inside where?" Mr. Hope asked.

"Can't you feel it?" Lizbeth asked. "As I sit here, I can sense it—perhaps because we *are* farther down."

"I don't feel anything," Sarah said.

Lizbeth rose to her feet and paced the room, too excited to sit still. "Oh! I never expected to possess anything like the power of the Cornerstone again! But I should have known an object of such might would leave a residue! It's not everything, of course. I can't transform the halls of Evenmere as I could the False House, but I can sense . . ." She halted in the middle of the room. She felt the Inner Chambers about her, the wood and stone, the arches and doorways; she felt the rooms and passageways; she perceived a remnant of expended energy, the cause of the Winking.

She turned to Sarah and Hope and found them staring uncertainly at her. "Don't look at me that way," she said. "I haven't lost my mind. The Poetry Men must have sent us here, the same way they took Shadow Valley. It's the only explanation. The energy used is the same kind of elemental force Carter and Chant both described, perhaps the same as the Cornerstone itself. We've been brought to a place on the same level—or dimension—I don't know what the proper word is—as that Power."

"If that's true, what can we do?" Mr. Hope asked. "Is there a way back?"

"I don't know," Lizbeth said, "but there is a way out of the Inner Chambers."

"I assume you don't mean by the front door," Mr. Hope said, glancing at the misty vacancy beyond the window.

Lizbeth closed her eyes again. "I can sense it, but I can't pinpoint it. As if it were hidden."

"A secret passage?" Sarah suggested.

"Perhaps," Lizbeth said. "It seems . . ." She waved her hands slowly before her, palms down. "Underneath."

"Many of the passages of Evenmere are hidden," Hope said, "but even if we find it, where would it lead? Why should it provide a way of escape?"

"It just does," Lizbeth said. "I've no other explanation."

Eying her sister in concern, Sarah started to speak, but fell silent.

"If it is a secret passage, it might take weeks to find it," Mr. Hope said. "Without the Word of Secret Ways, we would have to go over the entire Inner Chambers an inch at a time."

"We could find the Word in the Book of Forgotten Things," Lizbeth said.

"Oh, child, we can't use that," Sarah said.

"*I* could," Lizbeth said.

"Absolutely not," Sarah said. "We don't know if anyone except the Master can control the Words of Power. It's too dangerous to try."

"Yet they might answer to her," Mr. Hope said. Seeing Sarah's ferocious look, he raised his hand in defense. "Hear me out. Lizbeth has wielded similar power before. She even knew we were about to be spirited away. And here's another thing—she came to us through secret passages, as if someone or something contrived to send her. As if the house itself—"

"Sheer conjecture," Sarah said. "It could just as easily have been the poets, for reasons of their own."

"Regardless," Lizbeth said, "I *am* here. I think I should read the book."

"I reluctantly agree," Mr. Hope said, "but the room is kept locked, and only Carter has a key."

"I was there two days ago," Lizbeth said.

"Impossible," Sarah said. "Carter is relentless about keeping it secured."

"It is unlocked," Lizbeth insisted. "I was looking through the library and tried the door out of curiosity. I'd never been before. The stained-glass angel in the skylight is beautiful; I wondered why you'd never shown it to me."

"We wanted to be certain we could trust you first."

"Very funny."

"Actually, I didn't realize you had never seen it," Sarah said. "Carter treats the room with the reverence of a church. How could it be unlocked?"

"Whatever the case, Lizbeth's path literally lies open before her," William said. "I think we should let her do it."

"I don't like it one bit," Sarah said, staring helplessly at the two of them. "We're deciding this too fast. Is there no other way?"

"I think I should trust my instincts," Lizbeth said. "Through the Cornerstone, I was once attuned to the type of power in this place. I should go where it leads me."

Sarah bit her lip, her eyes bleak. "Very well. We certainly can't remain in this gray limbo forever."

Leaving Mr. Hope's office, they descended the stair to the transverse corridor and made their way to the tall doors of the library, whose edges were covered with scores of seraphs and hippogriffs. Turning the jade knob, the three passed into the library, over the russet cattails and olive frond carpet, past the couches to the narrow door to their left, which Mr. Hope hurriedly opened.

"Lizbeth was right," he said.

"You didn't believe me?"

"Certainly we did," Sarah said, "but you of all people

should know there are times when reality in Evenmere grows tenuous."

The room was windowless, with gold fleur-de-lis on blue carpet, seven buttercup lights already burning in the brass candelabra, and a magnificent stained-glass skylight, red, blue, and gold, depicting an angel with long, golden hair flowing to his shoulders, presenting a heavy book to a man.

Mr. Hope walked quickly to the kidney-shaped desk and withdrew a small skeleton key from its top drawer, which he used to unlock a bookcase lined with blue-leaded glass. The butler drew the large volume from the bookcase, handling it as gingerly as if it were an anarchist's bomb. He set it reverently on the desk, his face grave. "Lizbeth, this book is highly dangerous. You must turn to page seven. I would discourage you from looking at any other page; the consequences can be quite disturbing. Words may appear; we have no way of knowing which ones. According to Carter, the book, or something beyond the book, knows what you are seeking. If we're fortunate, the worst that will happen is that no words will appear. If not—well, I don't know what might occur. Take a seat."

"Can I sit beside her?" Sarah asked. "No, never mind; I know the answer. Some trials must be faced alone."

"You and I should by no means look at the pages," Mr. Hope said. "It's not meant for us."

"Really, William, there's no need to make this a temptation through denial."

"The temptation is real enough, believe me. More than once I've been grateful Carter keeps the door locked."

"You surprise me," Sarah said.

"Some are inclined to drink too much and some aren't," the lawyer said, "but a book that can show us our very souls is a universal temptation."

Lizbeth sat down, her eyes fixed on the volume. Her companions took seats across from the desk.

"There is great power here," Lizbeth said, "like a flame."

She moved her hand reluctantly toward the cover. Upon contact with it, she felt a jolt that made her gasp. "No wonder Carter reveres it. It's so bright. So pure."

She fell silent, her impressions turning inward.

Mr. Hope took Sarah's arm. "Look away."

Lizbeth glanced up and caught Sarah's gaze. Sarah was not an emotional woman, but Lizbeth knew her well enough to recognize her concern. How Lizbeth loved her! Sarah dropped her eyes to the floor.

Opening the book the barest fraction, Lizbeth counted the pages and spread the volume. At first the page was blank, but as she continued to look, a single word appeared in letters of gold. It drew her whole concentration, as if it were the entire world. She said it softly. *Talheedin.* The letters burst into flame but were not consumed; the heat of the burning warmed her face. She spoke it again and felt it sinking into her, becoming part of her. She had thought memorizing it would take an effort; she found it un-forgettable.

The characters went cold, and she suddenly felt weary. The Word was within her, but had taken its toll.

"I have it," she said, "but there is only one. How do I know if it is the Word of Secret Ways? Should I wait to see if others appear?"

Sarah gave an exhalation of relief. Mr. Hope moped his brow with his handkerchief.

"No others will appear at this time," the butler said.

"I want to see one of the other pages."

"Lizbeth, no," Sarah said.

But Mr. Hope placed his hand on Sarah's arm. "I think it should be allowed. As long as it is only one. The book has ac-cepted her. You will be shown a forgotten memory, Lizbeth, which may or may not be pleasant. To my knowledge, Carter has ven-tured to look only three times. Still, it can sometimes be useful. Simply turn to the next page."

Lizbeth glanced up. Sarah, always so calm, was wringing her hands.

Lizbeth bit her lip and returned to the book. In her life, she had seen terrible deeds and suffered many torments; she dreaded revisiting them. Her fingers trembled as she turned the page.

Once more, she saw nothing at first, until a picture grad-ually formed. It was not, as she had feared, of the time of her cap-tivity. She was at Innman Tor again, with Count Aegis, Sarah's father, who had adopted Lizbeth when she was ten. It surprised her how young he looked. His old-fashioned spectacles, so familiar at the time, seemed quaint and funny.

They were sitting in the drawing room of the Little Palace, reading together, but the book had been set aside because it had made Lizbeth contemplative.

"But why did my daddy leave me?" her younger self asked.

Count Aegis looked kindly upon her, and she could tell he was weighing his words carefully. "You must understand, Lizbeth, that your father didn't mean to desert you. I say this, even though I do not know him. Sometimes people become lost—in vice, or a cause, or an affair of the heart, or a thousand other things of the world. He paid a terrible price for his allegiance to the anarchists, losing you. It was nothing you did; you were too little to have done anything."

Lizbeth glanced down at her hands, thinking that through. Finally, she looked up, and with utter and complete confidence said, "You would never leave me like that."

Their gazes met and tears suddenly rose in the count's eyes. His voice rasped slightly, "No, child, I would not."

The vision faded, leaving a blank page. Lizbeth sat in the chair in the small chamber, the mosaic angel looking down upon her. She had indeed forgotten that conversation. Shortly thereafter, she had been abducted and imprisoned for six years. She wondered if their discussion had weighed upon the count during her absence. Though he hadn't abandoned her, it had felt to her as if he had. She wondered if she had gotten over it, or if it still seemed that way, down deep.

She shut the book.

"Are you all right?" Sarah asked.

Lizbeth smiled. "I'm fine." But she did not tell what she had seen. "Where should I speak the Word?"

"Anywhere," Mr. Hope said. "It should affect the entire Inner Chambers. But not in here. Let's at least go out to the transverse corridor."

Lacking a key, they left the door unlocked and entered the corridor.

"You must summon the Word," the lawyer said. "Bring it to your mind, visualizing it with as much clarity as you can. Only speak it when you have it firmly in your thoughts."

Sarah and Mr. Hope stepped back, and Lizbeth closed her eyes. Having a strong imagination, producing an image of the Word was easy, but she gasped as it rose before her. Unlike her other fancies, there was an *otherness* about this; the Word of Power was something she borrowed rather than owned. It burned in her mind, a flame so hot she felt it upon her forehead. It grew before her, until it towered above her, no longer merely a Word, but a structure with doors and windows like a house.

It was not so much that she spoke it; she simply could not contain it. It rushed from her throat, a hot wind streaking into the world. The room shook from its release.

She opened her eyes. Mr. Hope and Sarah gazed expectantly at her. She shrugged. "Is it done?"

"It is," Mr. Hope said. "Somewhat easily, it seems. You have a talent for it."

"No," Lizbeth said. "It isn't like that. One doesn't have a knack, like being good at mathematics. It's more like being carried piggy-back. All one can do is hold on."

"You must look for a faint blue light," Sarah said, "probably against a wall. You're the only one who can find it. Carter always described it as clearly visible."

The three of them walked down the transverse corridor and climbed the stairs to the second floor, Lizbeth seeking any hint of a glow as they worked their way through the bedrooms. In Carter and Sarah's room, she spied a blue line surrounding the fireplace, but that was the passage to Jormungand's attic. Two other secret doors were found upstairs, but in both cases, Mr. Hope knew where they led.

As the threesome moved downstairs, Lizbeth paused. "Perhaps we're going about this wrong. I have an intuition that we should be looking for a way *down*. Where are the lowest rooms?"

"They would be part of the heating system," Mr. Hope said. "Most of it is underground, though there are several outbuildings." He snapped his fingers. "There is a small room. I've never been myself, but I believe it is off the kitchen court."

They hurried through the dining room and servery, into the men's corridor, surprising a hall boy resting against one wall, who scrambled to his feet as they passed. Turning into the house-keeper's corridor, they entered the kitchen court. They had to ask a scullery maid the location of the room, and she brought them to a narrow door leading to an equally narrow stair with another exit at its bottom.

"With all the endless passages of Evenmere, we really should occasionally look in our own kitchen," Sarah said. "Who knows what we might find?"

Mr. Hope led through the door at the bottom of the stair into a red-brick chamber filled with an elongated boiler. A single wall-jet provided a dim light.

"Not much here," he said.

Lizbeth stepped around the side of the boiler and halted. A dim blue glow emanated from one section of the wall. She pointed out its location and the three crowded around it. Sarah knelt and felt along the clay wall. Under the pressure of her hand, one brick tilted sideways, activating a mechanism that pushed a portion of the wall aside, revealing a dark, stooping passage. Just inside, a heavy, black spider hung in her web, opening and closing her mandibles.

"This is the one," Lizbeth said. "At least, it feels right."

Mr. Hope grimaced. "It may have stood unused for centuries."

Sarah stared into the narrow way. "We must organize a reconnaissance party to find out where it leads."

"We haven't anyone to organize," the butler said. "None of the servants will enter there. Jessep and the stable hands might have been willing, but they remained with the rest of the house. I shouldn't care to go myself, though I will, rather than be named a coward."

"But you can't," Sarah said. "You serve best by study. We can't afford to lose you. I shall be the one to make the journey."

"Certainly not by yourself," Mr. Hope said. "Carter would never forgive me."

Lizbeth laughed, causing her companions to turn.

"What's amusing, dear?" Sarah asked.

"The two of you. The answer is right before your eyes. I fear neither darkness nor narrow passages, for I lived in them many years, and the Master of the house must often travel alone."

"Lizbeth! You presume too much."

"I presume nothing. The house has given me a Word of

Power, which it reserves for its Masters."

"But the house has only one Master," Sarah protested. "Carter—"

Lizbeth laid her hands on her sister's arms. "Don't *you* presume too much. Carter is fine, I'm sure. This isn't the choosing of a new heir, but the appointing of a task."

"Someone must accompany you."

"They would only get in my way."

"Child—"

"I haven't been a child for many years. In fact, I had to grow up rather quickly."

Sarah looked helplessly at Mr. Hope, who rubbed his palms nervously.

"There is a logic to Evenmere," he said, "though we may not always understand it. Some *are* appointed. This may be Lizbeth's time."

Tears welled in Sarah's eyes. "I will never forgive myself if anything happens to you."

"It isn't my fondest wish, either," Lizbeth said, trying to look somber, but scarcely able to contain her excitement. Despite the danger, it promised a grand adventure, as when she used to escape into her fancies during her imprisonment. "I'm going to change into riding pants. A dress will be too cumbersome."

A lantern was brought, a pack prepared. When everything was ready and Lizbeth returned, Mr. Hope handed her a pistol. "Do you know how to use this?"

"Duskin taught me. I'm actually a fair shot."

"Runs in the family," Sarah said. "You will be careful, and if you find nothing, you must promise to immediately return."

"I promise," Lizbeth said, hugging her.

Sarah returned her hug fiercely. "Duskin would be beside himself if he knew I was letting you go. Men are like that, you know."

"We won't tell him, then."

They parted. Lizbeth threw the pack over her back, held the lantern before her, and stepped into the passage. It smelled of dust and age. The walls were unfinished; the bare boards showed skeletal. Beyond the boundary of her lantern's light, the passage stretched into darkness.

When she had gone less than twenty paces, she heard Sarah burst into tears, and for the first time the reality of her situation struck her. She had seldom heard her sister cry.

Upon awakening, Carter was herded for four hours, the walls moving to block his every attempt to escape. Hallways closed behind him; doors disappeared. His only choice was to move forward or remain where he was. As he journeyed up and down stairs, along deserted corridors, through empty chambers— driven ever farther from where the ancient palace lay—his anxiety grew.

He turned a corner and found himself at a dead-end. Looking back, he saw the far end of the passage behind him blocked. He was trapped.

A deep rumbling came from the depths of the house. He clutched the hilt of his sword. A vast tearing noise arose, shaking the corridor. The wall before him parted, extending the halls to either side. Within moments, a finished opening stood where none had been before, framing a descending flight of stair.

He studied the portal. If this were a trap, it was an elaborate one. There was no help for it. He gave an involuntary shiver and started his descent.

The stair stretched into the distance, going ever downward without a landing to break the monotony. Gas jets lit his way, his footfalls and the sputtering flames the only sound.

After three hours, he reached a metal door at the bottom. Consulting his maps, he realized he had been led back to his original destination, descending in a straight line that had brought him hundreds of feet below the ancient palace.

"Perhaps I'm being helped, after all," he said, his excitement rising.

Drawing his Lightning Sword, he grasped the knob and opened the door. Complete darkness met him. He lit his lantern and raised it high, trying in vain to see beyond the doorway. He summoned his maps, but nothing about this area came to mind, as if he were no longer in Evenmere.

After a slight hesitation, he stepped over the threshold. A

loud boom sounded and his light went out. Even his sword refused to shine. Startled, he stepped back through the portal. His blade glowed once more.

He took a deep breath, drawing up his courage. Waiting outside the doorway was useless, and the longer he hesitated, the more frightened he would become. He entered again and stood listening in the blackness. The sound of running water grew gradually louder, until he felt its cold grip splashing around his feet. He reached from side to side, trying to discover his surroundings. When he lifted his arms, he encountered a jagged ceiling six inches above his head. He shuddered, seized by his old childhood fears of darkness, drowning, and closed places.

A dim glow rose a few yards away. He moved toward it, then froze in horror. The light emanated from the face of a figure dressed in the uniform of an English bobby. The face, lacking eyes, ears, or mouth, was completely blank.

He gave a shout of terror, every part of him screaming to flee back through the portal. Something made him stand his ground, however, something he could not have identified in that terrible moment, the same anger and determination that had made him face his fear by stepping into dark rooms as a child. Bellowing his horror and anger, he drew his pistol and fired.

Lizbeth followed the passage for more than a mile before she realized it had for some time been gradually sloping downward. The hollow echoes of her footsteps on the bare boards did not frighten her; it was as if she had stepped back in time to walk once more the empty halls of her captivity. At first she felt quite at home with the cobwebs and dust, the solitude and silence; but as time passed, she grew morose at how much of her life had been wasted, how much of human companionship she had missed during the long years of her imprisonment.

She tried to imagine what kind of person she would be if she had spent her whole childhood at Innman Tor. Spoiled, she supposed. Less shy, more comfortable around people. Not so much a dreamer.

But then, she thought, *I wouldn't be me. Perhaps Duskin*

wouldn't love me. Perhaps I would be married to a railroad engineer at the Tor. We would have seven children, and I would dream my whole life of visiting far countries. I would never see the Inner Chambers—no that's not true, because Carter would have taken me—but I would never know the politics of the house or the comings and goings of the White Circle Guard. We would entertain my husband's rough friends, and sometimes he would drink too much and beat me, so the end of my life would be as its real beginning, for I would be a captive in a house with only my tormentor and my dreams of a better life. And perhaps there would be but one book there and it would be Wuthering Heights.

Lizbeth spoke aloud. "*I took hold of Linton's hands, and tried to pull him away, but he shrieked so shockingly that I dared not proceed.*" She shuddered and halted. "I mustn't do this. I mustn't talk to myself and quote from that dreadful, wonderful volume. I mustn't live there."

The oppressive darkness, the shining sanctuary of the circle of her lamplight, suddenly frightened her, as if she really *had* returned to the past. Tears filled her eyes; she stood paralyzed, expecting to hear the voices of her captors.

I am in Evenmere, she thought, forcing herself not to speak aloud. *I am in Evenmere and the past is dead. I am on a mission and must be brave. I will not quote The Book; I am not Catherine Linton; she is a fiction while I am real. I am really real.*

Crying softly, she hurried down the hall.

How long she walked that passage, she did not know. Certainly, more than an hour. She wished she had brought a pocketwatch. The corridor began curving downward in a spiral so steep she had to brace her hands against the walls to keep from tumbling. She recalled the poetry of Earnest Mithell: *Dark circles going down and down, With ever-darkness looking on, And in the eerie wastes I find, The blackest fears of inner mind.*

"Cheery thought, that," she murmured, before realizing this was the first poetry she had been able to recall in days. Chant had said the Poetry Men were draining rhyme away, but down here it was hers again. She wondered exactly where she was. In sudden delight, she recited:

A little frock
A little coat,
A summer's day
A little boat,
A tiny ship
A slender sea,
And all the dreams
I meant to be

This was Mithell too, but in his younger, lighter days. As she ran through the lines, delighting in their cadence, she realized a tiny bit of herself had been stolen when verse was taken from the world, a part she, who wasn't a poet, had not missed until now. It was both a small theft and an atrocity, like filching a dozen shafts of sunlight from the world, leaving a score of dust motes unilluminated. It was nothing and it was everything.

She halted, struck by an epiphany. "It's greed. They speak of high ideals and noble purpose, but it's wanting too much and spoiling it for everyone. They have to be stopped."

She continued her descent, filled with new determination, and came at last to the bottom, where stood an arched stone portal. Despite the lack of wind, Lizbeth's lantern went out as she stepped through the doorway, plunging her into utter darkness. She turned to feel behind her. The archway lay open at her back, but she refused to retreat. She tried to relight her lantern, but the matches failed to ignite.

It never hurts to grope, she thought. *I have played games in the dark before.*

Her hands extended, she stepped forward and immediately met an obstruction. Drawing back, she reached again, experimentally tapping the object, which gave off a hollow metal sound. At first she thought it a wall, but as she worked her way along its surface, she found it was a metal barrel. A foul odor exuded from it.

She turned, suddenly aware of a glow to her left. A light had arisen, illuminating little more than the ground, which was deeply rutted as if by broad wagon-wheels.

"Did you really think you could escape?" a man called out of the gloom.

She gasped, truly afraid for the first time, for she recognized the voice as one she had hoped never to hear again.

She could make out a wooden structure—the corner of a fence line. The glow emanated from behind it. A figure stepped out of a gate and stood silhouetted by the light.

"I have come to take you back," her former captor said. "You will be returned to your prison where you belong."

"No," Lizbeth whispered, so overwhelmed by fear she could not even scream. She felt a child again, small and helpless, wanting only to flee back to the arched doorway, back down the corridors to the Inner Chambers.

He stepped toward her, hands outstretched.

If Sarah and William Hope had not entrusted this mission to her, she would have run. She could fail herself, but she could never bear to fail them. She dropped her lantern and drew the pistol. Holding it with both hands, she aimed and fired.

In the silence, it went off like a cannon, the recoil sending her arms up, making her involuntarily close her eyes. When she opened them again her tormentor was gone, and a steady light, emanating from around a corner, bathed the area. She blinked in surprise and turned a circle, seeking her adversary, thinking she must have missed, but he was nowhere to be seen.

Glancing up, she discovered stars. Despite having been deep underground, she was now outside. No moon hung in the sky, but there was a vague illumination overhead. She was standing in an alley with wooden fences on both sides, the tops of trees visible beyond them, and grass growing everywhere except in the wagon-ruts. To her left lay darkness. She started toward the light.

Past the fence corner, the alley stretched long before her. The illumination came from a tall lamppost. She stood breathing heavily within the comforting circle of light, recovering from her shock. The man who had imprisoned her was long dead. That could only have been a phantom.

Something was different about this alley, and it took her a short while to realize what it was. There were shadows again. She waved her hand and watched her shade do the same. She laughed, and the laugh gave her the courage to go on.

Barrels filled with garbage stood against the fence on either side of the alley. She peered over one of the fences at the houses, plain structures of wood and brick. The windows were dark; a dead silence lay over all. The neighborhood looked deserted. Keeping her pistol close, she proceeded along the lane, leaving the light farther and farther behind.

"Hello, Lizbeth," a voice said.

She leapt to the side, her pistol aimed. A face looked over the fence.

"Who are you?" she demanded.

"Now let's not shoot anyone, young lady. I'm a friend, here to help. Come on in through the gate."

He vanished behind the fence and a gate was flung wide. A porch light burned at the stranger's back, leaving his face in shadow.

"Come along," he said, in an unfamiliar accent.

Without waiting for an answer, he turned toward the house. She followed, staying a safe distance behind. They passed over the threshold and through a narrow hallway into a small drawing room. By the light of two lamps on end-tables, she saw he was dressed in some sort of uniform: dark blue trousers and a sky-blue shirt with a circular shoulder patch displaying the words *Post Office Dept.* above a horse and rider, with an unfamiliar word below. He was well past sixty, with thin strands of hair atop his balding head.

"Who are you?" she demanded again.

"Andrew Carter," he said. "I'm the postman."

"Andrew Carter?" she repeated.

"I know what you're thinking: Carter Anderson, Andrew Carter. Funny coincidence, huh? You can call me Andy. Would you like some tea? They say everyone in Evenmere is crazy about it. I drink coffee myself."

"If we're not in Evenmere, where are we?"

"You should sit down. I'll bring the tea."

She took a seat on the green couch. As Mr. Carter bent down to hand her the teacup, she touched his sleeve.

"What material is this? It's so soft and thin."

"A polyester blend, I suppose. One lump or two?"

"One, please."

Clutching a coffee mug, Mr. Carter took a seat in a floral chair across from the couch. "We've got a few minutes, so I'll try to explain some things before you have to go. You already know that Evenmere is the mechanism that runs the universe, but it isn't the whole machine. More like the tip of the iceberg. That alley out there is a kind of crossroads, full of possibilities. You call it the Eye Gate. It can lead to the most incredible places and times. It's led you down a level, a little deeper into reality."

"So you're saying that this," she waved her hand to indicate the drawing room, "is somehow more real than where I live?"

He grimaced. "*Real* isn't the right word. But you're deeper in, closer to the center."

"How many levels are there?"

"Seven, a thousand, an infinite number—I really couldn't say. You'll never actually reach the center, of course. No one can. But before the night is over, you'll have to go even farther down. You're at the outskirts of the Deep Machine, you see, the mechanism behind Evenmere—the machine behind the machine. I know that comes as a surprise. It's a natural mistake—everybody makes it, thinking whatever level they're on is the fundamental one."

"It makes us rather small, doesn't it?" Lizbeth asked. "I mean, Carter is lord of Evenmere, and it's the last rung."

"Next to the last, but that's looking at it wrong. Every position is important. We each have our part to play."

"You make it sound as if it were a story, like a novel."

"Well, it is a kind of story," Mr. Carter said, "though I'm no literary man myself. A wonderful story and a terrible one, full of high drama and heavy with suspense. There's no point in having a story without drama, is there?"

Lizbeth took a sip of tea to cover her confusion. "Who are you and how do you know all this? Are you in charge of this level?"

Mr. Carter smiled. "I'm just the neighborhood postman. You can learn a lot delivering the mail. I lend a helping hand here and there. There are servants and servants and servants, you know. We're all about service."

"I see," Lizbeth said, though she really didn't understand at all. "When I first entered the alley, I met . . . someone from the past who I know to be dead. Was that real?"

"The alley entrance is guarded and the guardian takes many forms. Time is fluid there. What you saw was from your past, not the present. You were very brave." He smiled reassuringly.

Mr. Carter glanced at his watch, which was tied to a leather band on his wrist. "I wish we could talk longer, but I think you better finish your tea. Lord Anderson may need your help right about now."

Lizbeth set her teacup down with a jar. "Where is he? Why didn't you tell me sooner?"

The postman smiled again. "I thought you needed a minute before you went on. It's pretty scary, entering the alley, and there's a lot of danger ahead of you. Carter made it past the guardian and was here just before you came. If I had known when you would arrive, I would have made him wait, but it can't be helped. Oh, I almost forgot."

He walked over to a narrow bookcase and withdrew a volume. "You better take this. I think it might help."

He held a leather copy of *Wuthering Heights*.

She recoiled from it. "Why that? I never intend to read it again. Besides, I have most of it memorized."

"I don't know why, but you best take it."

She reluctantly put it in her pack.

He crossed the room and opened a door. Nothing but darkness could be seen within. The loud throbbing of engines, previously unheard, rose from its vacancy.

"Carter is in there," the man said. "I can't go myself. You have to find him."

She studied his face. He seemed kind, but she was terrible at judging appearances. She had been tricked before and it had led to years of imprisonment.

He gave her a smile. "This isn't easy for you, but sometimes it's all a nod, a wink, and a leap into the dark. This is one of those times."

She hesitated. "Why is it necessary for me to do this? If the Poetry Men are interfering with this Deep Machine, don't you have bobbies or constables, someone who can stop them?"

"That's a good question, and I'm afraid I don't know the answer. I think it's because the trouble started on your level. In a way, that makes it a little outside our jurisdiction. Not that we won't help if we can. Then again, there are rules to be followed. I know it's a heavy burden, but the fate of your plane of existence depends on you and Carter. Finding Erin Shoemate is the key, I believe."

"Do we have any chance? Can we stop the poets?"

"Again, I don't know, but you have to try. You were chosen for this place and this hour, to succeed or fail. But only you can decide to take the plunge."

Lizbeth nodded her head. She was not one to hesitate forever. She drew a deep breath, raised herself to her full height, and stepped over the threshold.

The light from the room vanished, plummeting her into a darkness lit only by distant, winking flames. The hammering engines were louder; the whole room resonated with the low throbbing. Judging by the heavy echoes, she was in a vast chamber. As her eyes gradually adjusted, she could make out the silhouettes of equipment—tanks and cylinders, great valves, pipes snaking here and there before vanishing in the overhead gloom. The floor was concrete patched with oil-stains. The air smelled of steam, gas, and sulphur. Glancing up, she saw lights overhead, distant as stars and equally as dim.

What now? she wondered, as she stepped forward, pistol ready. There was no clear lane through the mechanical jungle, so she set off at random, making her way through the dimness past rows of equipment adorned with tiny blue gas flames. Fearing to draw attention to herself, she left her lantern unlit.

The noise of the machinery frightened her. *The engines of the earth*, she thought.

After several minutes' travel she paused, realizing she might search such a maze for hours without finding Carter. If she could climb one of the machines, she might get an idea of which way to go.

She picked a relatively quiescent mass, a rectangular block thirty feet tall, consisting of wires, wheels, belts, and levers, whose only motion was a slowly rotating cam-shaft and a flickering gas-jet attached to its side. The thought of climbing it made her uneasy. Without knowing its purpose, she could not guess if it might suddenly come on, crushing her between its moving parts.

She picked what she thought a safe path and ascended. Climbing was easy with so many protrusions, though she had to be careful not to cut herself. Halfway up, she grasped a pipe covered in grease. She wiped it off against the side of the hulk, but it left her fingers slippery.

She saw, by the light of the sparse gas-jets, the concrete floor below, farther down than she expected. She vowed to avoid looking that way again.

At last she crawled onto the top, which was not smooth as she had hoped, but replete with pipes and gauges. An iron dome covered part of its surface. Holding onto the curve of the dome with one hand, she surveyed the cavern. Her altitude seemed to have gained her nothing. It was like looking over the rooftops of Evenmere, a sea of structures without end, lights dotting the ragged hulks.

She turned a slow circle and saw, far in the distance, more lights outlining a long thoroughfare extending out of sight. Much of the noise emanated from that direction. She pursed her lips. The avenue might mean something or it might not; she could find herself going the wrong way. But every other direction looked uniformly gloomy. She had to hope that Carter, repeating her climb, had sought the lighted way.

With a deep breath, she turned to go. She had taken her first step downward, when two apertures fluttered open in the dome, revealing a pair of enormous eyes.

In her attempt to get back and away, she lost her grip and tumbled, scraping her legs and shoulders against the protruding pipes. She caught herself halfway down, a jarring stop. Before she had time to recover, a tremendous cacophony rose. The whole structure twisted and shook, as if coming apart.

She jumped to the ground, landing hard and falling to her knees, but regained her feet and sprinted to the shelter of another mass of machinery. From behind a cylindrical tank she turned to see her former perch unfolding, raising itself upward. Its long, tapering snout and head extended like a turtle from its shell; it stretched itself on four, clawed legs, a horrid, living contraption. Its eyes were golden lights, with a row of smaller, red ones outlining its jaws. Its mouth opened and closed in huffing breaths. Steam rose from the top of its head. Iron teeth glistened in its angular mouth.

It turned from side to side to the screech of metal on metal. Lizbeth pressed close against the tank, but in vain. With a barking *chuff*, the Horrid Contraption moved toward her.

She bolted even as it leapt, and heard its iron paws slam to the floor where she had been. Avoiding a straight path, she wove her way through the machinery, a perilous course in the gloom. Protrusions on every side forced her to dodge and duck. She dared not look behind her, but could hear the Contraption clanking in pursuit.

Other hulks began to stir, stretching lazily, awakened by the noise. On every side she saw lifting heads, opening eyes. A metal paw shot out to grasp her. She darted to one side, avoided it, and ran on.

At last she scurried through a wide opening into a maze of heavy concrete walls. She threw herself behind one of a series of small stone structures, gasping for breath, her side aching.

She had nearly recovered when she heard the rattling of the Contraption echoing through the gloom. She crouched lower. A scuttling, like mice on loose boards, reverberated around the walls, accompanied by the wheezing breath of the monster sniffing its way along. Her first impulse was to flee, but she kept her place.

With practiced silence, she crept along behind the stone structures, all the while picturing metallic teeth reaching between them to snatch her. The snuffling drew closer.

She moved into a peculiar shuffle, pivoting on her hands and swinging her legs forward, then turning a circle and repeating the maneuver, which allowed her to stay low to the ground while covering a greater distance than going on hands and knees. Having perfected this technique during her imprisonment, she could take two such turns and crawl eight paces before turning again, thus preventing herself from growing dizzy.

But Duskin would laugh to see me do it, she thought.

In this way, she drew ahead of the noise of her pursuer, who had slowed to scent her trail. When openings appeared in the rows of structures to her right, she took a path at an angle from the Contraption. This soon brought her to a long line of cylindrical steel tanks, laid on their sides on concrete bases, leaving a gap between the ground and the curve of their steel sides—too narrow a squeeze for the Contraption, though the spaces between each tank left room for the monster's jaws. She rested a few minutes to regain her strength. Growing more calm, she realized she had not eaten for hours, and swallowed a hurried meal of bread and cheese, sitting on the concrete floor beneath the curve of a tank.

Like a mouse, Lizbeth thought. *I could scurry for leagues without it catching me. But is this the way I need to go?*

She hesitated. In her flight, she had lost the direction of the lighted avenue. She needed to look about again. She noticed a ladder, leading twenty feet to the top of the tank. After her last climbing experience, she dreaded using it. She lightly tapped one of the tanks, which gave off a hollow ring.

It doesn't appear to be alive, but neither did the Contraption. And the mechanized beast might see me if I get too high. Where is it, I wonder? Has it given up, or will it follow my trail forever through this wasteland?

When she had remained there about half an hour without hearing her pursuer, she placed her hand on the first rung of the ladder and pulled herself up, ascending in a rush. The steps made a soft ringing under her feet. She looked warily from side to side.

When she reached the top, she discovered that most of the hulks that might have blocked her view were fortunately at her back. The rows of tanks stretched before her, with the avenue of lights beyond. Either by accident or unconscious design, she had run the right way.

She returned to the ground and made her way under the tanks, forced to duck every few feet to slip beneath the lowest portions. Bending and rising made her back ache, and she resigned herself to traveling in a permanent crouch. Whenever she inadvertently struck one of the tanks, it gave off an echoing *zing*.

After over an hour she passed onto open ground. With a grimace, she rose to her full height and stretched her back. A wire-mesh fence stood across her path, a lamp atop every fourth post casting an eerie, twilight glow. Beyond the fence lay more machinery, a desert of mechanization. Following the barricade to a gate, she froze at the sight of a man, standing on her side of the fence staring through the wire, his fingers grasping the mesh. She thought she recognized him at once, but kept her pistol ready.

"Carter," she called softly.

He whirled, his Lightning Sword suddenly in his hand.

"Lizbeth! How in the world did you get here?"

"I don't believe we are in the world at all," she said, springing forward to hug him. "I came from the Inner Chambers."

"The Inner—but they're gone, vanished. Sarah and Jason and Will—"

"I was with them when we were transported."

"They're alive?"

"Quite safe."

He clutched her to his chest and held her for a long moment. A single sob escaped him.

He slowly released her. "Sorry. Didn't mean to get emotional."

"It's all right. Anyone would be." She related what had happened since last they met, and he, in turn, told of his own adventures. After meeting Andy Carter, he had become lost among the machinery and had reached the fence just before she found him.

"Are we going in the right direction?" she asked.

"I don't know. I hope the postman really is on our side. He might have given a little more information. I don't understand why both of us were guided to this place, then left to our own devices. I suppose we have to go forward and trust to good fortune."

Carter raised the sleeved gate latch and they slipped in. A gravel path ran before them, bordered by a pipe fence, with buildings and tanks on every side. Lamps, bright as daylight, shone on overhead towers, creating a world of stark brightness and multiple shadows. Lizbeth wondered what sorcery could make anything glow with such intensity.

As they trudged beneath the cavernous sky, they discussed what Andy Carter had told them of the nature of Existence.

"If this is indeed a deeper reality, it seems terribly chaotic," Lord Anderson said.

After a time, the ceiling began sloping down enough to be visible in the electric lamps; the walls narrowed and emitted a dim glow. The tapering continued until they walked inside a cavern similar to the spiraling interior of a conch shell. The machinery, thickly arrayed on either side, became more sparse, until what remained were tripod light poles, dozens of paces apart, curving downward in an endless line.

"What do you suppose we will find?" she asked.

"I haven't the faintest notion. We are literally out of our waters. Actually, we've left the pond entirely."

"And we are very small fish," Lizbeth said. "It's too vast."

"We have to ignore that and concentrate on finding Erin Shoemate. It's the only way to remain centered."

"Is that how you do it? Completing this task and that, trying not to think of the whole picture?"

"The whole picture is never complete. Evenmere is . . ." Carter waved his hand to indicate the impossibility of it, "substance and shadow, metaphor and solid stone. One is always dealing with the material and the abstract together. The physical aspect we understand, at least most of the time; the immaterial we sometimes comprehend and sometimes only feel. There are always more questions than answers. How can the universe be so organized and so damnably slap-dash? If Enoch misses winding a clock, if Chant fails to light a lamp, if I do the wrong thing . . ."

"And why a dinosaur in the attic?" Lizbeth asked. "I've wondered about that. Or the areas the Servants' Circle oversees— why those particular ones? It's all butterfly wings—so beautiful and colorful; but are the wings for the sake of the beauty, or the beauty for the sake of the wings?"

The road curved always downward, until it seemed to Lizbeth they were surely following the curve of the earth and must soon come out on the far side of the world. Carter's pocket watch had stopped, leaving them to guess how many hours they traveled. They stopped twice to rest and once to eat. At last the cavern narrowed even more, the ceiling descending to little higher than their heads, and they came to a circular opening. Carter drew his Lightning Sword and they crept through.

Steam rose around them, warm but not burning, preventing them from seeing at first. A few paces in, their vision cleared and Lizbeth gasped. They had reached Deep Machine.

The Great Mechanism

Doctor Armilus and the Black Beast descended from the ruins of the ancient palace of Opo along a slanting corridor constructed of smoked glass, so that everywhere the anarchist turned were dark reflections of himself and his companion. The corridor shuddered with his every step, as if suspended by thin supports. The form of the beast had changed; it now resembled a leopard with hands instead of paws. It had grown slightly larger as well.

"How much farther?" he asked.

"Very near, yet an eternity distant," the beast drawled in its hideous, growling tongue.

The doctor winced. It always spoke in half-riddles, covering its thoughts with an air of inscrutability. In showing him the way to Deep Machine, it *was* shortening his quest to ultimate power over Evenmere, but that was small comfort. Armilus wondered when it intended to kill him.

They reached an oak door, incongruous among the smoked glass, opening onto a stone corridor with doors scattered along both sides. Armilus tried the first he came to and found a small, empty chamber.

"Step in there," he ordered.

"Why?" the beast asked.

"If you are truly my servant, do as I say."

The beast growled, but complied. Immediately the doctor

shut the door behind the creature, reached into his inner coat-pocket, and withdrew a packet of dynamite. With careful intent, he retrieved a match, lit the fuse, and held it until it was burned almost to the end. At the last second, he flung the door open, threw the explosives inside, and with a speed defying his size, dove to the floor.

Even with his hands covering his ears, the explosion was deafening. The corridor rocked; stone fell all around. When the concussions died away, he rolled onto his back and sat up. The door had been blown off its hinges; smoke rilled from the chamber. He rose gingerly, his hand on the pistol in his pocket.

A heavy crash sounded inside the room. From out of the smoke and debris, a black figure brushed aside boards and plaster. With labored ease, it stepped into the hallway. Not only had the beast survived, it was now as tall as the doctor's chest.

Armilus released his grip on his pistol. *One must be willing to face realities, no matter how grim. If it decides to kill me, there is no help for it.*

"A primitive trick," the beast said, "using a bomb."

"I am, after all, an anarchist. Why are you now larger?"

The monster gave a convulsive rumble, the eerie equivalent of a laugh. "Violence begets violence, Doctor. I am a bit of violence your violent actions have enlarged. Perhaps now we understand one another better."

Armilus shuddered. "Perhaps."

They made their way down the corridor, the beast at the doctor's heels.

I have confirmed one thing, Armilus thought. *I am this creature's prisoner.*

Hours later, the doctor and his strange companion arrived at a heavy iron door. Armilus reached for the handle.

"Wait," the beast said. "This is the Eye Gate. To cross its threshold is to pass beyond Evenmere."

"To the place of Deep Machine?"

"To a place between places. You will face some type of guardian. I do not know what form it will take. It would be best if it did not see me. I will hide within the ring."

"How do you—" the doctor fell silent and stepped back as the beast began to expand. It billowed upward, turning to black smoke. When its entire form had vaporized, the dark cloud surged forward, pouring itself into the oval stone in the ring on Armilus' finger. As the smoke entered, the ring grew heavier, until the doctor's hand ached from its weight.

Armilus studied it. The beast had appeared within the hour of his taking the ring from the pouch sewn within *The Book of Lore* and putting it on. The creature claimed it made him its master. Was that true, or had it instead been intended for this very time? Why else had the band welded itself to his hand, except to ensure he would always have it with him? Did he dare step through this door, knowing he might not be lord of his own fate? He could find an excuse to retreat, try to buy some time.

He shook his head. He would not back out now. The beast would never allow it. Besides, there was too much to be gained, a universe to win. Great risks must be taken to achieve great rewards. The drama must be played to the end. If it turned out badly, he at least would not be one of those who sat on the sidelines, booing and cheering and smoking cigars. He would be a player; he would carry the ball or lose it in the skirmish. He would make the grand play or fall with a grand stand. That was what life was about.

He chuckled at his own nonsense. Hadn't he dedicated his career to ending what he had just espoused? By reshaping Existence into his own terms, and thereby removing suffering from the world, wasn't he hoping to erase the very struggle he adored?

He laughed again and opened the door. Stepping through into total darkness, he screamed at what he found there, the cry of a small boy facing the thing he most feared. Yet he was a man as well, driven by titanic purpose and will, and he stood up to the waiting monster, rushed at it with his enormous strength, and choked the life from it with his powerful hands.

Afterward, with great weeping gasps, he strode down the alley until he came to a certain gate.

"Here," the voice of the beast spoke from out of the ring. "The portal lies within."

He composed himself, entered the gate, and knocked on the door. A figure in a blue uniform answered.

"Hello, Doctor," Mr. Carter said, his face set and unsmiling.

"Do you know me?" Armilus asked.

"I know of you."

"Then you know what I want."

"Come in, if you must."

The doctor followed the postman down the hallway into the living room.

"I am told this is a reality different from that of Evenmere," Armilus said. "Is that true?"

"It is," Mr. Carter answered.

"Why is it so . . . physical?"

The man raised his eyebrows in surprise. "I had heard you were a clever fellow. It's a good question. Perhaps you were expecting some sort of bodiless spiritual plane? But people *like* bodies, you know. How else can we tell which thoughts are ours and which are someone else's? The body—and physical objects in general—make a solid barrier between a person and the rest of reality."

"You mistake me," Armilus said. "I expected no such spiritual plane, but these ordinary mechanisms cannot be what drive the universe. Alleys and guardians. Doorways into darkness. It's too simple. What is the Deep Machine? Molecular forces, strings of power?"

"Well, that's a little hard to explain, and I'm certainly not the man to ask. I think of the Machine more like a wind-up toy taken out of someone's pocket. One of those gadgets you might find in a clever shop."

"Are you mad?" the doctor demanded.

"No, Benjamin, I'm not, but I am concerned. I don't think you realize what you're getting into."

"I doubt it's any of your business."

The postman shrugged. "My business is helping people. From what I hear, you've taken a lot of chances. You're a man of action. That's commendable. But there comes a time to reassess those actions. Where you're headed right now—it's beyond anything humans can handle. You've seen the power of the poets; you know it's uncontrollable, but you're going to the source of that power, hoping to control it. It's a bad road, Benjamin. Why don't you give it up, go back to Evenmere, and rethink your philosophy? You want to make a difference in the universe? Help a single person that needs it. That's what matters."

Doctor Armilus was tempted to sneer, but was unable to do so beneath the old man's honest directness. It was too much like mocking one's grandfather—especially since his words reflected the doctor's own earlier thoughts.

"I appreciate your concern," Armilus said without rancor, "but I have come this far and must see it through. Can you show me to the portal?"

Mr. Carter sighed and opened the door where Lizbeth had passed. The sound of the engines filled the room.

Armilus gazed skeptically into the blackness. "This is the way?"

"There isn't any other."

"Any words of advice?"

"I've given you all I have, Benjamin. You have to find your own way now."

The doctor nodded and stepped through, into what he would come to call the Place of Machines. He had seen many strange things in Evenmere, but none more peculiar than this. As an anarchist, he had dabbled in both sorcery and science; whether reading Daschett Limbar's *Essays of the Mystic* or Phasho's *Principles of Energy*, he had viewed both as paths to forms of force—if one seemed irrational and the other scientific, that was simply because he did not yet comprehend the underlying propositions. Yet in this region, with its monsters and rows of machinery, what would seem to be a confirmation of his theories struck him as the opposite. The universe was clearly mechanistic, but he had expected to find atomic and cosmic forces driving it, not a realm filled with gears, pistons, and levers.

Dark smoke rose from the ring on his finger, and the beast appeared, an almost human smirk on its face. "We are in, Doctor. Your every ambition is about to be fulfilled."

Carter and Lizbeth stood on a metal deck, the foyer to a

vast mechanism towering into a violet sky speckled with blue stars. So great was its mass, so myriad the machinery upon it, that it took several moments to gain perspective. Every sort of device was represented: levers, buttons, valves, pipes, gauges and tanks, great engines and enormous wheels and pulleys. Shots of steam rose from tall stacks. Vegetation and living organisms served the mechanism as well; flying horses circled it, wolves and dolphins leapt among the pistons, giraffes raised pink tongues to clip the derricked leaves. Lions clattered and klaxons neighed, bluejays tapped and bellows brayed. Part automaton, part forest, part zoo was Deep Machine. In occasional flashes, a vast clock superimposed itself over the entire mass, its face displaying a single scene: a star, a person, a field, a stream.

"What is it all for?" Lizbeth asked.

Carter did not reply. She glanced at him and saw a strange light in his eyes. He pointed. "There, do you see him? When the clock appears. It's Enoch."

Lizbeth gave a cry of surprise, for focusing on any part of the machine allowed its details to bloom before her sight. Carrying a large key, the figure of the Hebrew scurried around the edge of the clock, as if fleeing from the second hand.

"They're all represented," Carter said. "There's the Tower of Astronomy with Phra at its pinnacle juggling the stars. That bright light to the left is Chant lighting the lamps and that pool surrounded by walls of books must be the Mere. There's Jormungand, too."

"I see him! But he's not like the others; he vanishes and reappears."

"It's mirroring our actions." His voice rose in excitement. "If we could understand this, we could fathom so much that happens in the house. Our jobs would be so much easier!"

Lizbeth placed her hand on his shoulder. "But would we be able to comprehend it? It's not here to make things better for us. It just is."

The light in Carter's eyes died. "Just another temptation to make too much of myself. Are you and I shown on it, or are we now out of the picture?"

"We're already standing on it, right here. We can't be in two places at once."

Carter laughed. "Of course! But when we're in Evenmere it must trace our paths through the manor."

"I doubt I am part of it," Lizbeth said. "It seems to show only those directly involved in running the house."

"I think *everything* is part of it. Some cogs are just less noticeable." He shook his head as if to clear it.

"What should we do?" Lizbeth asked.

Carter glanced at the heavens. "I've seen that color of sky before, when I was thrown into the dream dimension. The tower holding Professor Shoemate is up there somewhere. We have to find her."

"There are towers everywhere," Lizbeth said. "How will we know the right one?"

"Not everywhere. Most are in the upper reaches, as one would expect. So first, we ascend."

They crossed the metal deck, their boots clattering on the steel. A black stream ran through a channel at the base of the mechanism.

"The River of Entropy," Carter said. "This must be where it begins. It appears to circle the entire Machine. We must avoid touching its waters at the risk of dissolution."

They found a yellow bridge and crossed over. The din of the animals, the bursts of steam, the flashes of light each time the great clock appeared, affected Lizbeth's equilibrium, forcing her to shield her eyes. They traversed the base of the structure and reached a metal stair. Deep Machine was even stranger up close, and Lizbeth stopped to study its variegated sides, a combination of rock, steel, vegetation, and what appeared and felt like flesh.

"It's alive!" she gasped. "When you look at it, you see farther and farther down—there are minuscule plants and animals— there's a whole city here! Oh, Carter, the entire world literally lies before us."

"All the worlds, more likely."

"What if we brush against it?" Lizbeth asked, "or stub our toe? We could wipe out whole countries."

His eyes widened, but he gave no reply.

Lizbeth examined the stair. "This is safe enough, I think. The walkways were meant to be used, but we might cause dreadful damage if we leave them."

They began their ascent, the metal steps *plinking* beneath their footfalls. The stair angled along, winding across the face of the vast heap. If it had seemed huge before they were on it, it now appeared monumental; Lizbeth felt like an ant climbing a mountain. Regardless how high they went, they seemed no closer to the heights.

What felt like hours passed, and Lizbeth's knees and calves began to ache. They stopped twice to eat and rest, then pressed on until they were stumbling as they went.

"We can't reach the summit in a single go," Carter finally admitted. "We have to get some sleep."

"Sleep where?" Lizbeth asked, bleakly surveying their surroundings. "There's nowhere but the stair. We daren't rest among the crags."

"The stair it is, then. I'll take the first watch."

The steps were narrow and uncomfortable and Lizbeth tried sprawling across them, a less than ladylike position. Her left hip immediately hurt. She shifted, found a better attitude, and closed her eyes. Two minutes later her right shoulder was aching. At last, she sat up and leaned back. The steps pinched her spine, but it was tolerable, and she gradually drifted off.

After ten minutes she woke, needing to shift again.

I have slept in bare rooms on dusty boards, she told herself. *I can sleep here. But I was younger then, and more supple.*

She got little more than a nap, and at last, when she could no longer abide the discomfort, she sat up and took her turn at watch. To her irritation, Lord Anderson pulled himself into a fetal position, and was instantly unconscious.

The man could sleep in a glass jar. Is that a trait the Master learns in his travels? She studied his face in repose. Were his features more lined than when she first met him as a little girl? She supposed so, though she could not recall. He was the uncle she never really had, and a wave of love rushed over her. How happy she had been when he and Sarah had courted. How little she had known of his true work. She wondered if either of them would survive this journey, or if they did, whether they would be able to find their way home.

It's always that, isn't it? Always trying to get home. To get back. To where, I wonder?

But her thoughts were wandering; she was growing silly. If not for her throbbing legs, she would have stood. She removed her boots and massaged her calves.

Odd where one finds oneself. The Astronomy Tower, the Inner Chambers, the Deep Machine that runs the universe. Carter has even been to the world outside Evenmere. I should like to go there sometime and see what it's like. It must be truly fantastic.

When Carter woke, he and Lizbeth ate dried bread and drier meat from their supplies, washed down with a few gulps of water, before continuing on their way.

"Since we have been here, I've lost all sense of the Balance," Carter said.

"Isn't it present here? The Machine looks like a combination of both Order and Chaos."

"It's not the same as in Evenmere, more like something beyond them. I feel as if I've lost my compass on a dark night."

As they approached the heights, they spied tiny yellow lizards scurrying among the bizarre topography, fleeing at the travelers' approach. Distant bird cries pierced the air, though the birds themselves remained hidden. As they made their way around the upper curvature, the angle of the steps leveled off. So enormous was Deep Machine, they appeared to be walking across a broken plain toward a distant horizon. The blue stars shone down from the violet sky, leaving the ether in a perpetual twilight. The magnitude of the Machine made Lizbeth despair of ever finding their goal.

As if in answer, Carter pointed toward a distant, crimson tower. "That one is the same color as the one in my vision."

The stair ended at an earthen path bordered in sunflowers. Tiny cities nestled in the petals, untroubled by the bees and butterflies feasting on the nectar. Lizbeth wondered what it must be like to shelter beneath a butterfly's wings. Or did the people in the cities even know?

They traveled the path for several hours, and then the tower was abruptly before them, red stone against the uncanny sky. Beside the door, at the base of the edifice, stood a sentry dark as shadow, dressed in chain mail, wearing a helmet that revealed cold blue eyes and a deep-red mouth. He stirred at their approach, shifting his heavy axe from hand to hand.

"Stand and be identified. What is your business here? What do you want?"

"Is Professor Erin Shoemate in this tower?" Carter demanded.

The knight glanced up at the edifice. "The professor is here. Three questions you must answer before you may pass."

"I expected something a little less rudimentary." Carter fingered his Lightning Sword.

The sentry smirked. "That's because you're from Down Below. Everyone here knows the more complex things become, the simpler they are."

Unable to make anything of the knight's statement, Lizbeth turned to Carter. By his expression, she guessed he was calculating whether it was better to force his way into the tower, or to attempt to answer the questions. Given the level of power displayed by the poets, he was probably reluctant to match his might against the denizens of this plane of reality. He withdrew his hand from his sword, and she knew he had made his decision.

She turned back to the sentry. "What are the questions?"

The knight held the axe against his chest and recited:

A man is left, a man is right,
One man stands frightened in the night
One man stands scheming in the day
Which man will soon be swept away?

Lord Anderson glanced down. "Can you repeat that?"

"It isn't usually done."

"But it's not against the rules?"

"I suppose not." The sentry gave the riddle again.

"The fact is," Carter said, "my Lamp-lighter is much better at this sort of thing."

"Then you will not enter."

Lizbeth noticed Carter's hand gradually moving back toward his blade. She clasped it, stopping its motion.

"The man who is left," Lizbeth said, "suggests not merely solitude, but because of the tradition associating the left hand with

wrongdoing, and the use of *scheming* of the third line, indicates a
criminal—even a murderer, perhaps. It follows that the man who is
right is an innocent falsely accused by the schemer, waiting
through the night for his execution."

"But what is the answer to the question?"

Lizbeth paused. "The answer is that this is an unjust world,
and unless someone intervenes, the innocent man will soon be
swept away."

"Ha!" the sentry cried. "Well spoken! The idealist would
have said justice always triumphs. The second question: What is
the land beyond the Rainbow Sea?"

Lord Anderson gave an involuntary grimace. "How can
anyone know that?"

"Is that your reply? I ask no question that cannot be answered."

"No." Carter stepped back. "I need to think."

"You have mentioned the Rainbow Sea," Lizbeth said, "but
I know only what you have told me."

Carter's face was hard as stone. "And I know too much of
it." He drew Lizbeth back a few paces and said in a whisper, "If
this sentry is an agent of the poets, can I assume the answer must
be one that would agree with their viewpoint?"

"It seems logical."

Carter paced back and forth in silence, biting his lip. At
last, the knight said, "Your time is up. Either answer or return the
way you came."

"Beyond the Rainbow Sea is the land my father could not
find."

"Lyrical, Lord Anderson!" the sentry said, "and thus, correct! The final question: what am I?"

"That is easy," Lord Anderson stepped forward. "You are a
Poetry Man."

The sentry laughed.

The action that followed occurred almost too quickly for
Lizbeth to see. With one smooth motion, the sentinel swung his
axe toward Carter's head. Simultaneously, Lord Anderson drew his
Lightning Sword, which in this level of Existence had not the
appearance of steel, but of lightning itself. Lizbeth had seldom
seen Carter in his role as warrior, and the speed of his response

astonished her. Thunder boomed as his blade left the scabbard, accompanied by an electric crackle. The weapons met in mid-air and the whole landscape seemed to rock. Lizbeth was lifted from her feet and thrown to the ground.

Half-blinded, half-deafened, she raised her head and looked around. Carter lay sprawled on his back, hands and legs thrown wide, the hilt of his sword still in his hand, its blade broken into three pieces. The Poetry Man was gone, save for a charred scar against the tower wall.

On hands and knees, Lizbeth crawled to Carter, calling his name. She touched his face; his eyes fluttered open.

"Am I dead?" he asked.

Tears of relief sprang to her eyes. "Can you sit up?"

With her help, he raised himself. He looked at his right hand, as if surprised to see it intact. His eyes swept over the fragments of his blade.

"He broke my sword!"

"It's all right, so long as you're alive."

But the look of horror in his eyes said otherwise. "I didn't think anything could do that."

"Can it be mended?"

"I don't know. I—I don't know how."

Lizbeth cautiously picked up one of the shards, which was surprisingly cool. She gathered the three pieces and put them in her pack, then gave Carter some water. Under her ministrations, he gradually recovered, though he kept staring at the useless hilt. Gently, she pried it from his hand and put it with the rest.

"It was my father's before me," he said. "How can we face whatever is up there without it?"

"Your father owned it for a time, but it is not your father, and it isn't you. It is a piece of metal. We will face whatever we face together."

She rose and extended her hands. His eyes focused. He gave her a nod and a shadow of a smile. "Storyteller was right about you."

She flushed at his praise. Together, they opened the tower door and climbed the spiraling steps, their way lit by flaming wall sconces. As they ascended, Carter's eyes took on their old determination; he raised himself to his full height.

The rough-hewn stones were cracked and crumbling. The air smelled dank. They wound their way upward, expecting to encounter an enemy at every step. The torches, trailing above the travelers like distant stars, were too dim to illuminate much beyond a few feet, leaving the heights lost in darkness.

Lizbeth glanced at the floor and noticed what appeared to be a curved piece of wood against the wall. When it moved, she realized it was a gray serpent, four feet long, its red tongue forking in and out.

"I miss my sword already," Carter said.

Through the gloom they passed, the only sound their footsteps on the stair. At last they reached a narrow door. Lizbeth looked down at the torches far below. They had climbed higher than she supposed.

Carter put his hand to the knob. It turned easily, opening onto a circular chamber filled with bric-a-brac, a fainting couch, and a writing desk where a woman sat reading from a book. At the noise of their entrance, she turned and gave them the barest look before returning to the text.

"Professor Erin Shoemate?" Carter asked.

She glanced at them again, her brow furrowed. Her hair was the purest silver Lizbeth had ever seen, like that of the ladies in fairy tales. Her eyes were the palest blue, her skin the lightest white. She looked immeasurably sad.

"You have come back," she murmured, returning her gaze to the book. "I thought you a vision."

"I often feared you were one as well," Lord Anderson said. "Do you know where you are?"

"In Hades, or someplace akin to it. Are you one of my captors?"

"Your rescuers, assuming you wish to be rescued."

"Why would I not? But I cannot go. There is a poem here I'm trying to comprehend." She pointed to the book. "Just when I think I know its meaning, it slips away. Perhaps you can read it and help me."

"I will not, for it is a snare."

"But it is so beautiful. It burns like fire and ice."

"It is burning up the whole world." Carter approached the book. Without looking at the words, he sought to close it, while the professor craned her neck to read around his arms. The volume resisted his strength. He applied more pressure, his face set with the effort, but could not budge it.

Abandoning his attempt, he took the professor's arm. "You must come away."

"If I leave the book, I will surely die."

"You will not die. You will return to living."

Her voice rose in panic. "I shall! They have told me, and it is true. Please don't force me. The words are too strong."

Carter glanced at Lizbeth. "I can try the Word Which Brings Hope, but I doubt it will work. The spell of the book is more than an illusion."

"Wait," Lizbeth said, turning to her pack. "Perhaps one book can substitute for another."

She withdrew *Wuthering Heights*, opened it, and laid it over the professor's volume. Lizbeth stood to Shoemate's right, Carter to her left, watching her reaction. At first, the woman continued reading as if nothing had changed. Gradually, her brow unfurrowed and her eyes cleared. She stared up at Lizbeth with the same intensity she had given the poetry.

"This book—I can read it *here*," she touched the pages, "and I can read it when I look at you. It's inside you. Every word. You've got it inside."

"I do," Lizbeth said, "but it isn't me, really."

"You're right!" Erin cried, as if in epiphany. "This is . . . these are . . . only words! This is . . . I remember this! It is a fiction. A fiction. It has a beginning and an end. It is a tragedy, but the story is complete. Not like the other."

"I would avoid going any further with that thought," a voice said behind them. The three whirled to find a Poetry Man locking the door behind him with a silver key.

This poet was different than the others, taller, his face unhidden, ruggedly handsome, with dark eyes and jet hair. Something in the twist of his mouth reminded Lizbeth of her father.

Falan! Carter cried.

The Word Which Manifests, spoken at such close quarters, had a terrible effect. Lizbeth had seen it used before, but in this deeper reality it was more dreadful; like the Lightning Sword, it emerged as undiluted power. A golden wave shot toward the poet, too swift for the eye to follow. The backlash sent Lizbeth flying onto the fainting couch, knocking the breath from her. As she lay struggling for air, Carter hurried to her side and helped her up.

She glanced at the doorway. The Poetry Man lay stunned or dead and the shattered door hung by a single hinge. Shoemate was gradually regaining her feet. Carter rushed to the professor, guiding her away from the book.

"This way," Carter said. "Lizbeth, help her out."

Taking Professor Shoemate by the arm, Lizbeth led her past the broken doorway to the top of the stair. Behind her, she heard Carter utter the Word Which Seals. As if in response, the whole tower began to quiver, almost undetectably at first, but with growing intensity.

Lord Anderson stepped through the doorway.

"What did you do?" Lizbeth asked.

"I sealed *The Book of Verse*."

"What's happening to the tower?"

"I don't know. Perhaps it is connected to the Poetry Men's power. Let's hurry."

They rushed down the stair, herding the still-bewildered Erin Shoemate along. Plaster dust drifted from the ceiling, shaken loose by the growing vibrations.

"Please, Professor," Lizbeth urged, "you must make haste."

The words had scant effect. Despite their coaxing, Shoemate went as one in a dream, often glancing over her shoulder toward the chamber of the book.

"So the answer to everything isn't in the text?" the professor asked. "But what about the Essence? What about the Primordial Ooze?"

We won't make it, Lizbeth thought. *It would be faster if only we could carry her.*

A third of the way down, heavy chunks of plaster and stone started tumbling about them. A large portion of the ceiling shattered on the steps directly before them.

"Where are we?" the professor abruptly asked, as one coming out of a heavy sleep. "Is this the College of Poets? Why am I here?"

"Our lives are in jeopardy," Lizbeth said. "Please hurry."

The professor looked around at the debris. Finally realizing her danger, she took the stair as fast as she could. The tower was visibly swaying, as if shaken before a monstrous wind.

A serpent rose before them, coiled to strike. The professor shrieked; Lizbeth froze. Carter, trained to action by years of experience, gave the viper a furious kick. It struck at him, catching the heel of his boot as it hurtled over the edge to the long drop below.

"Carter!" Lizbeth shouted.

"I'm unhurt. It couldn't get through my boots."

They hurried on. As they neared the bottom, the palpitations of the structure grew so violent they had to press themselves against the wall to avoid being thrown off the steps. Heavy stones fell around them.

Hurry, hurry, hurry, Lizbeth thought with every step.

They reached the bottom and rushed through the door. The professor would have thrown herself to the ground, but Carter upheld her until they were several yards from the tower. They turned.

The structure was crumbling, tearing itself to pieces. It lurched to the left; it shuddered; it collapsed straight down upon itself. A cloud of dust rose, obscuring it.

"We've won," Lizbeth cried. "We've won."

Carter sat on a rock facing a boulder-strewn field. Beside him, Lizbeth gave Erin Shoemate strips of beef and water from a flask.

"How long have I been here?" the professor asked.

"You vanished from the college six months ago," Carter said. "We know you were traveling during part of it."

"It seems an eternity."

"How have you lived?" Lizbeth asked.

"Lived? Have I lived? Reading that book was like perpetually dying, like following an endless maze. It must be what it feels like to be addicted to opium. I wish I had never seen the Histian scroll. It was what led me to *The Book of Verse*, you know."

"What exactly is the book?" Lord Anderson asked.

"It is Poetry Incarnate, the essence of the beauty of language. I know I shall dream of it the rest of my life. The words were . . . unimaginable."

The professor looked with troubled eyes across the landscape of Deep Machine. "As soon as I began reading, I couldn't stop. I must have become a channel between our world and this one, for the poets soon came to bring me food and to care for me. The first were those I knew from the Poetry College. I would read to them from the book and they would leave changed, bright and beautiful as crystal and roses."

"Mr. Hope said the Opoian Gate was a portal leading to a world of elemental energies," Lizbeth said. "Time and Dimension, Shadow and Light, Water and Fire, Earth and Air. *The Book of Verse* must have infused those energies into the poets."

"I sometimes wondered where they went when they left me," Erin said. "Back to Evenmere, I suppose. Is that how you found me? Through them?"

"Indirectly," Lord Anderson said.

"I wish you hadn't hurt the man in the tower," Erin said. "They are sensitive, peaceful people, seeking beauty and truth."

Lizbeth paled. This gentle woman, clearly ignorant of the destruction the poets had caused, was bound to feel terrible remorse when she learned the facts.

"At least it's over now," Lizbeth said, "and we can go home."

"Is it?" Carter asked. "One thing keeps bothering me. The poets could have stationed a half-dozen of their number to guard the tower and we would never have gotten through. If they were too self-absorbed to maintain their own defense, why were they so calculating in their attacks of the Circle of Servants? Almost as if they were being guided. Until now, I thought Professor Shoemate was directing them."

"Attacks?" the professor said. "What nonsense! Poets don't attack people."

"Anarchists do," Lord Anderson said. "The objects Doctor Armilus sought—bits of starlight, moments of time—what does he want with them? And how does the Black Beast that accompanies him fit in?"

"A beast?" Shoemate asked. "I saw such an animal. But how is Benjamin involved?"

"The doctor is the head of the Society of Anarchists," Carter said. "What do you—"

"Benjamin Armilus?" the professor said. "Impossible! We taught together. He has some anarchist leanings, of course—many of the professors do. And he was wrongfully accused of some crime, but that was nonsense. He can't be the Supreme Anarchist!"

"What do you know of the beast?" Lord Anderson asked.

"Bandits took me prisoner as I was nearing the ruins of Opo. They would have slain me except for the appearance of a creature the size of a mastiff, but more terrible, so black it almost looked faceless. It killed them all; I thought it would murder me, too. Instead, with a sound disturbingly reminiscent of a laugh, it turned on its heels and departed."

Carter and Lizbeth exchanged glances.

"Armilus must have either lied or been deceived when he told me the beast was a product of *The Book of Lore*," Lord Anderson said, his eyes narrowing. "When Professor Shoemate encountered the creature, the book was still sealed in the Mere."

"If Benjamin was looking for *The Book of Lore*, he never told me," Erin replied. "He was interested in the Histian scroll, of course, but I thought it merely intellectual curiosity."

The Master began pacing. "But now we find the beast was involved with both of you. The first time I saw Armilus with the animal, he seemed puzzled by its presence. *Did* the doctor lie about when it appeared to him or . . ."

He abruptly stopped, his faced turning ashen.

"What is it?" Lizbeth asked.

Carter licked his lips. "We have been duped from the beginning. The professor, the poets, every one of us. It has been the beast all along. It used Professor Shoemate to unleash the poets. It is using Doctor Armilus for some other purpose."

"For what purpose?" the professor asked. "What can it want?"

"Perhaps what the anarchists have always wanted," Carter said. "To change the fundamental nature of the universe. But how could it be done?"

Erin Shoemate put her hands to her mouth; her eyes filling with tears. "You've not told me everything. I've caused terrible harm, haven't I?"

"You didn't know," Lizbeth said.

"Oh, but I know now. I begin to understand. *The Book of Verse* taught me many things. There is a cavern called the Cave of Confluence. It is the key to the Laws of Existence in the realms below. Within it, those laws can be changed."

"Are you suggesting that the doctor is coming here?" Lizbeth asked.

"If he isn't here already," Carter said. "And the beast with him. How do we find this cave?"

The professor stood, looked around, and pointed with outstretched arm toward a distant opening in the rocks. "It is there. I saw it in the book. I saw so many things, some too terrible to be borne."

"We must make haste," Lord Anderson ordered. "Everything depends upon it."

Ignorant that Carter and Lizbeth had preceded them, the doctor and the Black Beast had reached Deep Machine several hours before and were steadily angling their way upward, disregarding the stair. The beast had changed again, this time into the semblance of a centaur, its upper body human, its hind parts those of a lizard. Its grinning jackal-head reminded the doctor of statues of an ancient god of death. It reveled in crushing the tiny cities and villages beneath its feet, while Armilus trod carefully behind, disgusted at the senseless destruction. He found useless cruelty intolerable.

"That is our goal up ahead," the beast said.

Thirty feet above them, at the end of a slender path, gaped the entrance to a cave. The sight of it made Armilus shudder. Unearthly, he would have called it, even in this most bizarre of places. It seemed to tremble, like a maw straining to devour its prey. Padding along the narrow path, the creature led the Supreme Anarchist to its threshold.

"Perhaps you should enter first," the doctor suggested.

The creature chuckled. "So little trust in the world."

As it stepped inside, the ebony animal melted into the darkness. Armilus followed, feeling his way among the rough stones, led by the heavy breathing of his guide. A few feet in, his eyes began to adjust; it was brighter than he first thought; a dim orange glow emanated from somewhere before him, reflecting off the black rocks.

When they had traveled twenty yards, the cave abruptly opened into a cavern of vast proportions, as indicated by the long echoes of the doctor's footfalls. The glow lay before them, slightly brighter now, reminiscent of an orange, rising moon. The pair walked through a half-twilight of shapes and shadows along a floor strewn with rough boulders.

They soon reached the source of the glow, an orb hanging without visible support a foot off the ground. Though he betrayed no emotion, the doctor marveled at what he could only describe as a machine. The orb was twenty feet tall and pocked like the moon, but the pocks were fluted channels. Half-animal devices protruded. Momentary vertigo suggested the orb was rotating at a barely perceptible speed.

"Is there a sentry?" Armilus asked.

"The inhabitants of Deep Machine have little interest in coming here," the beast hissed, "and they trust the guardian in the alley to keep those of Evenmere from reaching the orb. Their overconfidence is their undoing."

"Who are *they*?"

"Unimportant. You know what to do."

Armilus withdrew a golden key from his pocket, made from the stolen treasures—the bits of starlight and time and dimension—forged into its present shape under the beast's direction. Coruscating with energy, seeming to grow more or less intangible at any moment, it was the most beautiful object the doctor had ever seen. Holding it almost reverently, he pressed it into the lowest of the fluted channels. He flinched as the orb opened, unfolding itself within the cave, conforming to the rocky surfaces, encompassing everything within.

Sweat broke across his brow, a fear intermingled with triumph. He was within the final mechanism. The possibility of victory was close. But the region where he stood bore little resemblance to any reality he had previously known. There were more dimensions; his eyes could not adjust. The colors, richer than any on earth, beat upon his vision, nearly overpowering him. It was an ecstasy and a terror. He glanced behind him, and the motion of his own head seemed a wonder, as if he turned and saw himself turn, and saw himself seeing himself turn. Yet it was not like that at all.

I am at the Center.

He became aware that he was standing before an abyss, an endless plunge in six dimensions. Between him and the void stood a gossamer web. Or was the abyss beneath him? It was, yet he did not fall. But he *could* fall. That fall would be endless, and he did not understand what prevented it.

He glanced at the beast. Its form had shifted from that of a centaur to a man eight feet tall, black as obsidian, still retaining the head of a jackal.

"Use the key and make yourself Master of Evenmere," the beast ordered. "Make haste! We may soon be discovered."

"A moment," the doctor said. "I must study the thing."

He looked upon the gossamer web that was the engine of Existence. There were uncountable, perhaps infinite filaments, like the strings on a vast harp. Yet as his gaze turned to each, he comprehended their purpose. They were grouped; he had but to isolate the group, and then the individual strand.

This is what we always sought. The ultimate power.

Using the key, he could make the slightest of changes. The very slightest. But he knew the beast would never allow him to do so. It intended to make its own.

"Here," the creature said. "You must place the key here."

Armilus looked at the indicated line, rapidly following it with his eyes, seeing how the universe would be reshaped; and what he saw was a world of war and chaos, eternal battle, desolation, and despair. The worst of all possible realities.

I believe I am about to die, the doctor thought. *Odd how little it moves me; perhaps because it seems as yet academic. Perhaps I will feel more when the suffering begins. Yes, I am certain there will be suffering from this creature who so loves inflicting pain.*

He took a single coin from his pocket and released it. The abyss lying beneath him was real; the object vanished into the endless depths. Why Armilus did not fall, he did not know. He hoped it was not the beast preventing him from doing so.

He dropped heavily to one knee, to be closer to the void, and held the key an inch from it.

"Stay where you are," he ordered, "or the key will be lost."

The monster's black eyes glittered with both hatred and amusement. Armilus could sense it measuring the distance between them. He found his hand gently trembling. "Don't attempt it!" he warned. "You won't reach it in time."

An eon of seconds passed. So volatile was the creature, Armilus half expected it to spring anyway, or cast him into the void in sheer spite.

Finally, it gave a low growl. "You saw something in the web, didn't you? I should have thought of that. But there are more possibilities here than you imagine."

"Who are you? No lies this time."

"An emissary. There are other forces in Evenmere than those you know, always working behind the scenes. Come, we cannot remain at this impasse. Place the key where I told you; do what you came here for."

"Not so quickly. I assume you still require my services, or you would have murdered me and taken the key the minute we entered this chamber. What is it? You can't touch the web, can you?"

The beast growled again. "You are just my kind of man, Doctor. Always thinking. You understand the nature of power. What do you want to be? Master of Evenmere? The position is yours. Lord of the Earth? It can be done. As one of the gods? It can be accomplished."

Armilus drew a heavy breath. He had to take the offensive. This was the time for some solid acting. He relaxed his face and brought out a confident smile. "My friend, a negotiation seems to be in order. If I place the key where you wish, the world will become a nightmare, regardless who rules it. What good is that to me?"

He paused, letting his words sink in. When the beast remained silent, he continued. "You've manipulated us quite masterfully; your strategy has been brilliant!" He raised his voice in warm approval. "You've won my admiration; you've nearly won the game. Let's not throw it away now. If you kill me, the key will be forever lost. Let's reach a compromise that works for both of us."

"Perhaps," the beast said. It began to move its head back and forth in a rhythmic, hypnotic fashion.

"None of that!" Armilus ordered. "An honest negotiation or nothing. I *will* drop the key."

The movement ceased. The beast shifted its feet. "Very well. You want mastery of Evenmere. That can be done by placing the key in a different location."

"And what do you get? Do not attempt to deceive me. The web will show it if you do."

"Unfortunate. I had no way of knowing that until we reached it. If you place it where I say, it will bring Chaos to the ascendency, breaking Lady Order's barbaric symmetry. It is much less than I wanted, but it will have to do. And from your position as Master, you can rule Evenmere as you wish."

Concealing his fear, the doctor kept his expression open and honest. "Show me the place."

The creature pointed. As Armilus scanned the web, trying to keep an eye on both it and his opponent, he saw the monster has spoken more or less truly. This would indeed make him Master of the High House, yet it would also make Chaos incredibly powerful. Could Armilus hold Evenmere against such strength? The doctor had said he could tell if the beast tried to deceive him; now he was uncertain. He needed more time.

He glanced back at his adversary. Behind the creature, he spied a figure striding out of the darkness. Armilus strengthened his grip on the key.

"*Falan!*" Lord Anderson cried, raising his revolver as he spoke the Word.

Armilus dropped as low as his prodigious form allowed to shield himself from the golden wave. Its force pressed the doctor against the web, stealing his breath and sight. When his eyes cleared, he saw the beast had been thrown from its feet. As it struggled to rise, Lord Anderson strode to it and emptied his revolver into its back. It gave a roar of pain; blood dark as tar rilled from its wounds. It quivered as if dying, then rolled over in one smooth motion and sprang at the Master.

Anderson leapt back, agile as a spider, and again unleashed the Word Which Manifests. The beast screamed, a cross between animal and human speech, and fell back to the ground.

The doctor drew his own revolver and fired three shots. One missed, but the other two struck the beast in the head, tearing a huge hole as they exited. The monster collapsed.

The two men froze, waiting to see if the beast would rise again. It dissolved instead, melting into the ground, leaving only a dark stain where it had been. Their eyes met across the residue of their fallen foe.

"It's time we went home, Doctor," Lord Anderson said. "Give me what you have in your hand."

The doctor considered for only a fraction of a second. His immediate instinct was to raise his pistol and fire. Success lay before him, if he could only kill the Master of Evenmere. He believed he had an even chance of squeezing off a round before Carter used a Word of Power. Yet something stayed his hand. Gratitude to his adversary for saving his life? A false sense of loyalty to their truce? Or an intuition?

The doctor rose ponderously to his feet, moving with unnecessary slowness, as if wounded or injured, clutching his pistol and the key. He turned the revolver around as if to hand it over. As Carter reached to take it, Armilus struck him with it, a violent blow to the side of the head. He went down in a heap, blood running along his cheek.

"I am sorry, Lord Anderson," Armilus said. "My work is still unfinished."

A shot rang out. The bullet whizzed over his head.

"Drop your weapon!" a woman's voice called.

The doctor looked around, but could see no one. Apparently Anderson had companions hiding among the boulders. A bad turn of events, but one must follow through, regardless of obstacles.

He turned sideways to make himself a narrower target, a difficult proposition for one of his mass, and pointed his revolver at Lord Anderson's head.

"Unless you are a marksman of significant skill, I doubt you can kill me fast enough to prevent your Master from dying with me. Come out and drop your gun, and he will live."

Seconds passed. *If they are mere followers, they will comply*, the doctor thought. *But if they understand what is at stake, they have no choice but to shoot, even if they love him.*

"Decide now," he ordered, "or I fire."

A hissing voice behind him turned his blood to ice. He

would have preferred being shot.

"Destroy him, Doctor," the beast said. "Let there be death."

A powerful, ebony hand gripped the doctor's own, wrapping itself around the gun, exerting pressure on the trigger. Lord Anderson gave a groan.

At the last instant, Armilus jerked the weapon aside, sending the bullet awry. He expected the beast to pull the weapon back into position, but it did not. Gripping the doctor's other hand, it drew him toward the web.

"We will place the key together, you and I."

From her refuge behind the boulder, Lizbeth gave a muffled cry. She turned to the professor. "Stay here. I must get closer."

"Your bullets will never stop that monster," Shoemate said.

"I'm going to kill the doctor. For some reason, the beast needs him to insert the key."

"It will only try to use someone else."

"Then I have to kill Carter and myself, too," Lizbeth said. "You must run far away so it can't find you."

"Wait!" the professor said, but Lizbeth had already slipped from behind the rocks and was moving closer to get the best shot. Erin Shoemate stepped backwards, retreating, knowing Lizbeth was right. She could be of no assistance if she stayed, might instead bring everything to ruin, yet she could not tear her eyes from the scene.

"If only I could help," she whispered. "If only . . ."

She hesitated. Perhaps she could do something. She had gazed long into *The Book of Verse*. She had seen images beyond understanding. She had touched the Essence of Poetry.

A fool I have been and worse than a fool. That creature used me—used all of us—deceived us, gave us our power. But the power could not have come from it; the force is too beautiful. I feel a fragment still inside me, though the book is sealed and the tower destroyed.

But did she dare use it? She was afraid. The book had been consuming. If she stepped back into that world, it might trap her as it had done before. It might even do more harm.

Lizbeth was still creeping toward the beast.

The professor agonized briefly over her choice. She had to act. She had to be brave, for the sake of her rescuers, by the example of their courage. Put that way, she *could* be brave.

She cupped her hands together, and from their midst rose a single flame, like a dying candle.

"It's all that's left," she said, looking down at the light in wonder. "The last shard I can muster. I have to show it to them. If they see how beautiful it is, they won't want to destroy it."

In that moment, it was not the poetry that controlled her, but she, for the first time in her life, who controlled it. She saw it was her sword and the reason for her making. Here was the flame every poet desired, the star to every wandering barque. To turn away was not only to play the coward, but to relegate herself to the lot of those who never truly live.

It burned azure and golden, purple and emerald. As the flame rose higher, the poetry sang inside her, begging for release, and her months of captivity seemed but the proper end to a perfect verse.

As she raised her eyes from the fire, she heard a shot. Lizbeth stood a few feet from the monster, aiming the pistol with both hands. Armilus was clutching his shoulder. The beast turned, using its body to shield the doctor.

Professor Shoemate stepped from behind the boulders, chanting under her breath:

> *The lines are drawn*
> *The fable's done*
> *The heart and hand and world are one*

The flame rose between her fingertips, haloing outward, and whatever it struck became Poetry.

Professor Shoemate, filled with glory, looked down at herself and beheld, as in an ancient story, a maiden clothed in glowing white. Her hands, ephemeral as a shade's, held not mere flame, but a fire searing bright.

Glancing around her, she saw the world segmented into lined sections vibrating independently, each separate, each part of the whole, a tapestry upon which she and Lord Anderson, Lizbeth, the monster and the massive doctor were stitched. Everything and everyone was changed. The beast towered in dragon shape, as in the tales of old. The doctor, draped in gray and darkness, loomed monumental as a pillar. Lizbeth was transparent in parts, translucent in others, a glass figurine diamond-hard, her long hair rippling behind her, her face angles and lines, beautiful as the moon and the little foxes that roam the fields beneath its glow.

Carter, draped in light, had grown almost too brilliant to bear, yet in his center lay a circle of darkness. The Poetry seemed to revive him, for he raised his head and struggled to his feet.

We are Art now, the professor thought, clapping her hands in delight.

The monster screamed in agony. It turned toward Erin, reached for her with its seeking mouth.

Lizbeth fired again, a shot that sped past the doctor's ear, taking off the tip of it. He clutched his head and—freed from the dragon's grasp—threw himself onto his stomach.

Carter Anderson lurched forward, staggering as he rose. He spoke the Word Which Manifests. It sent not out its golden wave, but Poetry-changed, became a flaming blade in his right hand, the thing he needed most.

"Noooo!" the dragon bellowed. It lurched back and forth, hesitant, looking first at Erin, then at Armilus.

Lord Anderson struck, the fiery sword tearing through armored hide. The leviathan roared its pain and rage, a creature from the long-ago, a tyrant from the edge of time, a fiend from the age of rhyme, violent death and lizard pride, blood and cunning jungle mind. It moved, serpent swift, its head darting in and out, a dance of death.

Miraculously, the Master followed every step, weaving as grass in the wind, avoiding the black lips, the gray teeth. So swiftly did the two struggle, no eye could follow. On and on they danced, Carter striking where he could, his flaming sword the biting gnat, the little dog that brings Behemoth down.

They dropped back, the hero panting but unharmed. Dark blood oozed from the dragon's seven wounds. But these were nothing, its eyes declared. "Scratches," it rumbled, licking its lips.

"Does a dragon ever win in a poem?" Lord Anderson said, giving a grim smile.

The beast roared.

Now that the fighting had slowed, Lizbeth fired her pistol, aiming this time at the creature. Two slugs from the powerful gun went in, blowing a hole in the dragon's side, chipping away scale and bone.

It turned its head, nothing more, a lightning move, and the girl went flying backward and fell among the boulders. The pistol was gone, swallowed in the serpent's maw, and with it the first joints of the third and fourth finger of her left hand. Erin hurried to where she lay, to staunch the blood falling like rose petals to the stones.

The beast extended a bleeding claw. A vortex of darkness formed at the edge of its grasp, a hole in the air. The dragon reached in and pulled Jason Anderson out of the darkness.

Carter froze at the sight of his weeping son caught by the neck, kicking in the serpent's grip.

"Back!" the beast ordered. "Get back or the child dies."

Sheer terror suffused Lord Anderson's face. Erin saw it even from where she stood, followed by other emotions—anger, resignation, determination.

With a bellow, Carter charged the beast, sword drawn high to sever the monster's paw. Too quick, the dragon snatched the boy away. The blade missed its wrist, but struck the beast's side. Seeing the child was useless to it, the dragon snarled, snapped the lad's neck, and cast the corpse aside.

If Lord Anderson fought before, it was nothing compared to now. Given speed by Poetry's naked force, he struck like a whirlwind of fury and vengeance.

Professor Shoemate rushed to Jason's discarded form. But when she touched it, she discovered a soft, spongy material. At first she thought the boy had been transformed; then she realized the truth.

The bullets had wounded the beast; its movements had slowed. Carter cut the dragon's tongue, a cruel blow that sent blood rilling, mixing with the gore from the gun blasts.

It retreated, a sorry sight of dying beast that knows not yet it dies. It tottered; one leg gave way; it fell.

Teeth clenched, Lord Anderson rushed forward to finish the fight.

The dragon dropped its head. Carter raised his sword.

Ere he struck, the monster exploded forth, a sudden move-ment on heavy wings, taking the Master by surprise. Almost the rend-ing jaws caught him; he stepped back just in time. But a scaled claw, large as a board, struck him full in the face, breaking his nose, sending him sprawling.

Erin stood, looking for a weapon, searching for hope where none could be found. Lord Anderson lay still, defeated.

"There are darker poems than you know," the beast smirked, licking its bloody lips and coughing a wretched cough.

A noise behind it caught its ear. It turned. Professor Shoemate followed its gaze.

During the struggle, Doctor Armilus had risen, still holding the key, and made his way to the web. His back turned from the dragon, he was about to insert the instrument into place.

With uncanny speed, the dragon reacted, its long head dart-ing forward, its claws extended to catch the key, moving with a power and grace only Poetry could give it, aiming for the doctor's hand. But Armilus, also given verse's might, secretly watched from the corner of his eye and threw himself down, jerking the key from the creature's path.

The dragon could not halt its momentum. Meeting no re-sistance, it grasped not the key, but the web itself. It roared and roared and roared, the roars of the frustrated, the cheated, the robbed, the ruined, the defeated.

From the midst of the web a Face appeared, and time seemed to cease.

Erin fell to her knees. She had thought she had seen living Poetry. She had never thought to see a Master Poet.

Carter Anderson found himself suddenly conscious, staring into the Face of Eternity.

Lizbeth forgot her wounds, forgot her pain. It was like step-ping out of prison again; it was like being free.

Doctor Benjamin Armilus, Supreme Head of the Anarchist Council, fell backward, wanting to bury his face in his hands, wanting that awful visage to vanish, wanting to never see it again, wanting his eyes forever wide through the eons so he could look only upon it.

A hand, armored in jade, reached out and seized the dragon.

Roaring in fury, the lizard vainly struggled against the irresistible grip. Just before it was snatched away, vanishing into a hole in the air, it changed, revealing its true form—a different sort of reptile, a massive hulk of chaos and power, a dinosaur from the lost ages of time.

"Jormungand," Carter whispered.

The Face was gone and the Poetry with it, leaving four mortals standing before the web.

Carter turned, eyes wild. "Jason! My boy! Where is he?"

Erin Shoemate hurried to his side. "It isn't your son, only a semblance. Your child was never here. It was a last desperate ruse."

Lord Anderson rushed to the body and dropped to his knees. He touched its face, its hands, ran his fingers over its hair. He gave a strangled sob of relief.

"It must have been a deception," Armilus said, rising, one hand clutching his wounded shoulder. "If the beast could have reached so easily from this world to ours, it wouldn't have needed me. I underestimated you, Lord Anderson. After all our struggles, in the end you were willing to sacrifice the child."

Carter put his hand over his eyes. Blood from his broken nose dripped down his palm. He shook his head. "I did what I had to."

"The Master usually does," Armilus said. "Right now, for instance, your wounded sister-in-law needs your help. And if your victory has put you in a beneficent state of mind, I would very much like someone to bind my shoulder. The bullet only grazed me, but I am losing a large quantity of blood."

"First, the key," Carter said.

The doctor looked at his hand, as if remembering for the first time that he still clutched the object of his quest. He stared at it for a long moment, and with an almost casual gesture tossed it into the void. He exchanged glances with Lord Anderson. "Best none of us be tempted."

Companions now, made so by what they had seen, the four bandaged their wounds and struggled together along the steep slope. Halfway down, one of them found voice to speak again, but did not dare mention the Face. That would be for another time.

"Why didn't you do it, Benjamin?" Erin asked the doctor.

"You had the opportunity. You could have placed the key where you wanted. You could have changed the world as you wished."

Doctor Armilus looked surprisingly embarrassed. "I suppose the question will haunt me the rest of my life. There was little time for thought. I knew the dragon feared touching the web. I suspected doing so would either cause its destruction or alert a . . . guardian. Why didn't I do it? Even if I inserted the key, the beast might have destroyed me, making my changes for naught and giving it the chance to force someone else to alter reality. But in the end, my old colleague, I was prevented by your transforming us into Living Poetry. So awful, so beautiful. What if the changes I made had taken Verse out of the world?"

And on that subject, Doctor Benjamin Armilus would say no more.

The Return

S oreness and injury forced the travelers to go slowly, but
descending from Deep Machine was quicker than the ascent,
and they were soon making their way through the strange,
twilight world of the Place of Machines. They went cautiously,
slipping among the masses of equipment to avoid encountering the
Horrid Contraption. Their concern about finding the door back to
Evenmere proved groundless, for they soon sighted a figure standing beneath a tall mechanism, waving a tube-shaped light to catch
their attention.

"Here you are," came the familiar voice of the postman. "I
heard you were in the neighborhood. Right this way. Let's be
quick."

Within moments they were once more in Mr. Carter's
homey living room.

"I'm mighty glad you made it back." The postman beamed
as he poured tea into China cups. "Mighty glad. This is an excellent camomile. Very healing."

"I should have followed your advice," the professor said.
She glanced at the others. "When I came through the first time, he
warned me to go back. If I had heeded him, I would never have
caused so much damage."

"The trouble is, we can't listen to advice we're unprepared
to hear," Mr. Carter said. "It wasn't your fault, Erin. Honest people
are the easiest to fool because they haven't any guile."

"Jormungand deceived every one of us," Lord Anderson said, gingerly touching his broken nose. "I'm still trying to put it all together. If he is imprisoned in his attic, how could he appear as the beast?"

"I'm ignorant of the various ins and outs," the postman said, "but I've read some reports about that dinosaur of yours. I can assure you, he couldn't come here in any form unless he first escaped the attic."

"How could he have?" Lizbeth asked.

"Now that I know it was he, I can supply an answer," Armilus said. "My fellow anarchists and I abducted Jormungand from his attic when we were trying to build a counterfeit house in the Outer Darkness. When our plan failed, Jormungand escaped. We assumed he was forced to return to his old prison. Apparently, we were wrong."

"But he did return," Carter said. "I saw him there immediately afterward."

"Probably pretending to still be bound," Armilus said, "unwilling to tip his hand. Biding his time. Being far-seeing, at some point he must have gotten a glimpse into the next level, seen *The Book of Verse* and realized what a terrible weapon it would make."

"But he couldn't cross the Eye Gate to reach it," Carter said. "He needed a pawn."

"Someone like me," Professor Shoemate said.

"In that case," Armilus said, "the Histian scroll that led us to *The Book of Verse* and *The Book of Lore* was probably a forgery; and the stories we were told about *The Book of Lore* must have been fabrications. Jormungand may have even written it himself. That's why it felt so foul."

"Think of the various reptiles we encountered," Lord Anderson said, "the lizards who accompanied the poets. Why, even the talking serpent I battled when I first found *The Book of Lore* in the Mere was part of the deception, perhaps Jormungand himself in another form. How he must have enjoyed the sport of that, having a sham battle, making me think I was winning the book while gloating all the while!"

"But why *were* there always lizards around the poets?" Lizbeth asked.

"Jormungand must have convinced them he had some part

in the poetry," Lord Anderson said, "and used the lizards as his surrogates to direct the poets to attack Evenmere's centers of power."

"That would be like him," the postman said. "He loves destruction for its own sake. That's what he is, you know: Tiamat, Cyclops, Dragon—a representation of every unruly force in the universe."

"But he was also trying to cover up Erin's trail to prevent anyone from finding her," Lord Anderson said.

"Are you saying the poets were merely a diversion?" Lizbeth asked. "To keep us from concentrating on the real danger?"

"There was probably more to it," Doctor Armilus said. "For one, Erin wasn't given directions to find Deep Machine, only clues."

"More than once I despaired of locating it," Professor Shoemate said.

"Of course!" Carter exclaimed, gripping the arm of the chair. "Jormungand didn't know how to get there! He needed someone to find it for him—a scholar who could interpret the signs."

"And once he knew where it was, he needed me to help slip the Black Beast past the alley guardian," Armilus said.

"I knew there was going to be trouble when I noticed the Beast hiding in the doctor's ring," the postman said.

"You knew it was there?" Armilus said.

"I can spot that sort of thing. It's a gift. That's one of the reasons I tried to talk you out of going. Other than passing the information on to my superiors, I couldn't do much else once you were past the guardian in the alley."

"To what superiors do you refer?" Armilus asked.

"Why, my bosses at the post office, though this probably went much higher up. I'm a route man, myself—don't do any of the administrative work. I leave that to those with an aptitude for it. There are servants and servants and servants, you know. My supervisor would have passed the information on."

"Yet no one did anything to help us," Lord Anderson said.

"You may have gotten more help than you know," Mr. Carter said, "but in the end the job was your responsibility as Evenmere's guardian."

"It seems an untidy way to run Existence," Armilus said.

The postman laughed. "It might, but would you really want to live in a reality where everything is easily explained? Wouldn't be much of a world, would it? I did receive word that because of your victory the Balance has been restored, and both the Inner Chambers and Shadow Valley have returned to their places. Unfortunately, poor Queen Moethus is gone; but her replacement will soon be on the job."

"I should very much like to visit your post office," Lord Anderson said.

Mr. Carter gave a friendly shrug. "They're awfully busy up there, but I'll let them know you're interested. Now if you're thinking of becoming a mail carrier, that would be different—it's a nice job. Everybody likes getting mail, except for bills, of course, and you do have to watch out for dogs, but you get lots of sunshine and exercise."

The postman glanced at the timepiece on his wrist. "Oh say, it's getting really late. I hate to rush you, but you'd better be going."

"There are so many questions," Carter Anderson said.

"And not enough books or time in the world to answer 'em," Andy Carter replied. "You've still got a job to do, Carter. Jormungand remains free and something has to be done."

The Master grew pale. "I had hoped he was either destroyed or re-imprisoned. I should have known he couldn't die."

"You've never seen Jormungand in his true, terrible form," Mr. Carter said. "You wouldn't survive it if you did. No human mind could bear it. The Black Beast was only the smallest fragment of him, like a spy sent into enemy country. When he broke the rules by touching the web, he was immediately expelled back to Evenmere."

"Do you have any suggestions for containing him?" Carter asked.

"I'm afraid not, but you'll figure something out."

The postman led the company to the backyard and let them out the wooden gate, Lord Anderson trailing thoughtfully behind.

"Ben, Liz, Erin, Carter," Andy said their names in turn as he shook their hands. "Just go straight down the alley. You won't have any trouble. The guardian doesn't bother anyone leaving. Goodbye."

They trudged along the lane. Doctor Armilus reached up and rubbed his shoulder. "My bullet wound is healed."

"So is my nose," Carter said, running his hand along the bridge.

Lizbeth touched the bandages on her left hand, then unwrapped them and said sadly, "Even the scars are gone, but whatever performed the miracle doesn't grow new fingers. What will Duskin think of me?" Her eyes filled with tears. She glanced at the Master. "Oh, Carter, what do you make of it?"

"He did say the tea was healing. I think I should consider his job offer. The position of postman would surely be a promotion from my current circumstance."

As soon as they were once more within the High House, Doctor Armilus fell a few yards behind the others and slipped down a side-passage. When Carter realized the anarchist was gone, he hurried back to survey the last intersecting corridors, but soon returned to the others, shaking his head. "Completely vanished. How can anyone that massive move so quickly?"

"I'm glad he's gone," Lizbeth said. "I could never have slept tonight knowing he might murder us in our slumber. None of us has the strength to keep watch."

"Benjamin and I are friends and colleagues," the professor insisted. "I refuse to believe he would ever harm me. I'm sorry he left. I had many questions I wished to ask him."

"Erin is right," Carter said, grimacing. "The doctor is many things, but he would never kill without good reason, so both of you were safe. Slaying the Master of the house, however, might be a different matter. I should have guarded him more carefully. He may have helped us in the end, but he has much to answer for."

They traveled that day through the Opo. That night after supper, Carter spoke the Word Which Masters Dreams and hurried to the Inner Chambers. Standing in the transverse corridor, he used the Word Which Brings Aid. To his surprise, it did not summon Sarah or William Hope as he had expected, but Jason. He wondered, not for the first time, if the Words of Power actually knew who he most wanted to see.

"Hello, Daddy," his son called, nonchalant as children sometimes are. But Carter scooped the boy into his arms, hugging him fiercely.

"Everything outside was gone," Jason said, "but it came back. Mama said it does that sometimes. She says that's why we call it Fall and Spring, because its falls away and springs back."

"Your mother is a wise woman."

"Why are you crying, Daddy?"

"Because I love you so very much."

"Aunt Lizbeth came to stay with us, but she left. We have not seen her. Have you seen her?"

"I have."

"Can we go see Mama?"

"Let's just talk here awhile."

So Lord Anderson and his son spent a happy hour, laughing and playing in the land of slumber. When at last Carter knew he must go, he asked, "Have you had fun?"

"It's been lots and lots."

"I want you to do something for me. Something very important. You see, this is another of those funny dreams you have sometimes. When you wake up, I want you to run as fast as you can to your mother, and tell her I am well and your Aunt Lizbeth is well, and I am coming home as soon as I can. Can you remember to do that?"

Jason looked very serious. "Yes."

"Do you promise?"

"Cross my heart and hope to die."

"Never hope to die. A simple 'I promise' is sufficient. A man's word is his bond."

"I promise."

Even as Carter walked the dream dimension, Lizbeth started from a deep sleep and sat upright on her bedroll, awakened by an unexpected noise. With a shock, she saw a lantern in the corridor outside the small room. She fumbled for the gun in her pack, and had it cocked and ready when a familiar figure stepped through the doorway.

"Jonathan!"

He placed a finger on his lips for silence and beckoned her into the corridor. Once there, he took her hands between his dark ones. "It is very good to see you, Lizbeth Anderson. I have been looking for you and Master Anderson, but couldn't find you until you returned to Evenmere."

"Are you well?" she asked. "You look exhausted."

"I have been . . . ill, and have traveled a long way in a short time. I'm in an awful hurry. I need to speak with you."

"I should wake Carter."

Jonathan glanced back into the room, where Lord Anderson lay sleeping. "It can't be done just now. He walks the country of dreams. You will have to tell me what I need to know."

"How did you ever find us?"

"I don't mean to be impolite, but there isn't time for your questions. I must know what happened when you stepped through the Eye Gate. You succeeded in your quest, because the Balance is changed and I haven't seen any sign of the poets, but I need the details. If you will come and sit beside me?" He gestured toward a nearby alcove.

Jonathan's eyes, suffused with an uncustomary concern, glistened as she told of the wonders of Deep Machine and the battle with Jormungand. He asked many questions, and when she was done, he rose quickly and gave a low bow.

"I thank you and bid you farewell. Tell Master Anderson I am sorry I missed him."

"But where are you going and what will you do? Why are you so desperate to know what happened?"

"It is too complicated to explain. Every minute counts."

And with that, he left her.

On the morning of the third day, the three companions reached Loft, where Carter was able to contact the White Circle Guard. There the travelers determined to part ways: Professor Shoemate to Aylyrium, Carter to the Inner Chambers, and Lizbeth to join Duskin at Lowing Hall.

"What will you do now?" Lizbeth asked the professor.

"I don't know," Erin said. "Poetry and literature have been my whole life. For it to be channeled as a weapon . . . Perhaps I can use it to somehow alleviate the harm I have done."

Carter and Lizbeth wished her luck, and she departed, accompanied by five members of the Guard. Five more would journey with Lizbeth. Two years later, the professor would be named Poet Laureate of Aylyrium. She took the post with the greatest reluctance, stating her lines were the poorest imitation of the ones she had read in *The Book of Verse*. A decade after, she would pen *Poetry as Political Force*, a volume instrumental in the historic reforms of Shyntawgwin.

Lizbeth turned to Carter. "What will you do about Jormungand, and how can we help?"

"I don't know the answer to either question. I am going to do what I can. I wish I knew what Jonathan was up to. He is being quite mysterious. I don't want to sound melodramatic, but if I fail, you may be called upon to serve in my stead."

"Oh, Carter—"

He placed his fingertips against her lips. "Hush. We will hope for the best, but you must be prepared. You and Duskin should come to the Inner Chambers as soon as you can, I think. Tell my brother . . . tell my brother I love him greatly, and am proud of the work he has done, as I am proud of you."

She hugged him fiercely and kept a brave face, but burst into tears as she watched him stride down the long corridor, alone as he so often was. She kept her eyes fastened on him until he vanished from sight.

The Last Dinosaur

Jonathan Bartholomew fell silent. Jormungand shifted his weight, making the attic boards creak. The heavy exhalations of the behemoth echoed among the rafters.

"So you rushed from your tête-à-tête with Lizbeth Anderson just to tell me this?" Jormungand asked. "Couldn't wait to spend a few hours reminding me of my defeat when victory was so close? Bad form, isn't it? Bad enough to get you vivisected."

"I told the story for three reasons. First, because the telling of tales is a part of tradition, and this is the time and place for ceremony, here in this attic on this very day. Second, because I needed to buy time, to prevent you from taking immediate revenge upon Master Anderson, which is why I was in such haste. And in the best conventions of storytelling, I will withhold the third reason until the proper moment. But there is one part of the tale I still don't understand. I believe you were the author of *The Book of Lore*. But when did you write it?"

Jormungand chuckled mirthlessly. "So even the great Storyteller doesn't know everything. Nor could you, for the book was my most carefully kept secret. Perhaps you remember a Master named Augustus Cane?"

"He wasn't Master long, and he disappeared . . ." Jonathan paused. "That's right. He vanished into the Mere of Books, his body never found. I should have remembered that."

"When he first came to my attic, I appeared in a more

pleasant guise," the dinosaur said, "more serpent in the garden than behemoth. I enticed him, turning his head, showing him sense and nonsense until the Master himself became my pupil. A most excellent jest, that, worthy of a note in a good scrapbook! At my bidding, he penned *The Book of Lore*, supposedly to depict the wonders I had seen in Evenmere. The fool didn't realize I had designed the book to bend him to my will."

"But you didn't delude him completely, did you? He caught on to your tricks and sealed the book in the cave in the Mere."

"His will was stronger than even I suspected," Jormungand said. "He was bound to the book by then, and in sealing it he paid for his heroics with his life."

"And the book remained in the cave until Lord Anderson recovered it."

"The little Masters are so easily deceived," the dinosaur said.

"I see it now," Jonathan said. "A masterful plan, executed over centuries."

"And worthless in the end." Jormungand breathed fire.

"To finish my tale, then," Storyteller said, "Lord Anderson did return to the Inner Chambers to be reunited with his wife and Mr. Hope."

"How nice for him," Jormungand rumbled. "I should have killed him the last time he was here. I let him live because I didn't want to attract the attention of Those who originally imprisoned me. That was why I couldn't operate openly."

"That's right. That's right. But there was another reason as well. You have only one nature, of which struggle is the whole part. You didn't kill him because you must always have an adversary."

The dinosaur blew a heavy breath. "He *has* proved as formidable an opponent as any of his worthless predecessors, and I do love to watch one of the Masters suffer. I wanted him to see his petty little universe brought to shambles. Quite dissatisfying. But it is the doctor who disappoints me most. He was my undoing. His lack of greed—"

"That's right. These humans show remarkable sparks of good at the oddest moments. Master Anderson is demonstrating that right now, preparing to come here to seal you in the attic."

"I knew he would." Jormungand gave a ghastly approximation of a grin. "He places his hope in the Words of Power, but even the Master of Evenmere can't contain the Last Dinosaur now that I am free. No Master ever had authority over me. Do you know what I am going to do to him? Kill him, of course, but I will do it with exquisite deliberation. I will cook him alive, minute by minute. Perhaps I will let you live long enough so you can watch. I will—"

"No, old dragon, you will not." Jonathan rose to his feet.

Jormungand breathed fire, scorching the air. "Enough of your impertinence!"

"Do you know who I am?" Storyteller asked.

"A wandering vagabond, a bit of hope in a hopeless package. Tall tales and inspiring stories for an ant hill about to be drowned by the rain."

"But we are every one of us more than we seem—you, Master Anderson, the people of Evenmere. Come closer and I will tell you my identity. I won't speak it aloud in this place."

"So much the better," Jormungand said. "It puts you in easy reach."

The behemoth leaned his great head down, and Jonathan whispered a single name into the darkness.

Jormungand sat back on his haunches. "You lie!"

"Storyteller never lies. And he has the power to put the dinosaur back in his hidey-hole."

The minstrel let his ragged coat drop from his shoulders. It fell in a heap to the floor, revealing his slender, vulnerable frame. "The third reason for telling my tale was to make you impatient, to bring out that bad temper of yours, because once begun you cannot restrain your wrath. I am here, old reptile, and you, who have but one nature, must do as it commands you."

For the space of half an hour, Jormungand raged across the attic, bellowing his fury, his heavy footfalls thundering against the floorboards, his flames lighting the darkness. Miles he traveled into the deepest recesses, so far his fires became a distant torch to Jonathan's eyes. He stomped back, shaking the entire attic, breathing so much flame the whole house would have surely gone up, had the attic not been proof against it.

At last the juggernaut stood before Storyteller again, silent with a cold and deadly hush.

"Very well," Jormungand finally said. "I do what I must. From the beginning of time, the blood-sacrifice has turned back the forces of Chaos. The blood of such a one as you, freely given, *will* imprison me once more. But understand this, old man—in thwarting me you have revealed who you are, and I, who am terrible in my defeat, will use that if I can. And I will make you suffer with a torment far greater than I would have done to Anderson. The remaining moments of your life will be an agony beyond understanding."

"Do your worst," Storyteller said, lifting his hands. "It is all I ever expected."

Stepping through the portal on his quest toward Deep Machine, Carter had feared he might never clasp William Hope's hand again, or hold his wife and son in his arms once more. To return and experience that joy had been sweet beyond his understanding. But too soon, he had hugged Sarah and Jason goodbye again, and said farewell to his friend for what might be the last time.

He thought of that as he stood at the entrance to the attic. He had climbed these steps before, wondering whether he would survive, but this was different. The Word Which Seals could not seal the entire attic, so he would try to seal Jormungand *within* the space, similar to the way he had sealed *The Book of Verse*. His intuition told him he would not prevail, but he had to make the attempt. The dinosaur could not be allowed to remain free.

He did not bother carrying weapons. His pistol would be futile against the behemoth, and his Lightning Sword lay in pieces in the Inner Chamber. Even if it were whole, it wouldn't help. As terrible as the Black Beast had been, it was the barest portion of everything that was Jormungand.

He ascended the creaking stair, lantern in hand. When he reached the top, he halted and listened, straining to hear the noise of breathing. The attic lay silent. Had Jormungand gone? Would Carter have to search for him throughout the house?

He crossed the attic, sweat beading his upper lip. The

boards groaned beneath his weight. The air lay musty and thick.

"Antsy, are we?" a voice whispered in his ear.

He turned and shouted the Word Which Seals. In his mind's eye, he saw it forming around Jormungand, a golden, growing circle. The dinosaur must have seen it too, for he snapped his jaws at it. For a breathless moment it held, then collapsed, bouncing around the attic with a sound hollow as marbles ricocheting off metal walls, unfocused and useless, sealing nothing.

A wreath of dragon-flame fountained above Carter, revealing Jormungand standing between him and the stair. The Word had failed. His only hope now lay in escape. He raised the Word Which Manifests to mind. It would not harm the brute, but might purchase enough time for him to make his exit.

"Pointless," the dinosaur said. "I see the Word flowering within you."

Lord Anderson abandoned the effort. "As always, you are infallible within your own domain."

"A pity I was less so at Deep Machine."

"I should have suspected you from the beginning." As he spoke Carter shifted his feet, edging to the right.

"No doubt you have many questions. Unfortunately, I can't provide you with a last meal—it will be the other way around—but out of courtesy for a brave enemy, I will give you the answers you seek."

Carter took another shuffling step. "The postman told us much of it. You must have enjoyed using the Poetry Men to spread your anarchy."

Jormungand blew a snort of flame. "It was a lovely plan. The poets were the perfect tools. You probably wonder why I chose forces aligned with beauty and wonder as my weapons. Not quite like me, you might say."

"I assume it was the simplest way."

"Oh no, my little gnat. Not at all."

"Why, then?" Lord Anderson took another slight step to the right, seeking a chance to bolt.

"I could have chosen a dozen other methods of causing havoc, but I picked poetry because I knew it was a power that would never be associated with me."

"But how could you . . ." Carter hesitated, feeling a faint

stirring in the back of his mind. Man and beast eyed one another through several long seconds. Lord Anderson was stalling for an opportunity to escape. Was it his imagination, or was the dinosaur also playing for time?

"How could I what?" Jormungand rumbled.

The Master kept silent, studying his adversary. Why hadn't the monster already killed him? Was this another of the dinosaur's torments, delaying the falling of the hammer? Or was something else involved?

"Perhaps you wonder why I used agents instead of acting openly?" Jormungand suggested.

Carter weighed his words carefully, any thought of escape now vanished. "Something undoubtedly prevented you."

"It was much more than that. Much more."

The dinosaur waited.

"I am sure it involved creating the maximum amount of pain," Carter finally said.

"Not at all. You've missed it completely. Not surprising, considering your limited intelligence."

Another silence fell. At last, Carter cleared his throat and said, "I have a question."

"I'm all ears."

"Are you once more a prisoner in the attic?"

The dinosaur turned with deadly speed. Carter instinctively threw his arms up to ward the blow, though he knew nothing could stop it.

Jormungand's massive tail slammed against the floor, a thundering impact that rattled the entire attic. The force threw Carter from his feet; he landed on his back on the dusty boards.

The Last Dinosaur blew flames against the roof, then grew utterly quiet.

Finding himself still alive, Lord Anderson gave a grim smile and sat up on his elbows. When his opponent remained quiescent, he stood, intentionally taking the time to brush himself off, using the seconds to steady his nerves. Still, his voice trembled when he spoke. "I believe you must answer the question, which is the second one I have asked since entering the attic."

"Jormungand, the Last Dinosaur, the Greatest Creature in Existence, is bound once more."

Carter blew a quivering breath. "You hoped I wouldn't know. You wanted me to ask more than three questions so you could slay me."

"I see nothing to my liking will come of this," Jormungand said, "except the slightest bit of revenge, a mere trifle compared to the harm you have done me. Follow me."

Eyebrows raised, still disbelieving he might cheat death, Carter paced after the brute to the nearest corner of the attic.

"See what I did to your friend."

Carter staggered as the lantern light revealed a tangled mass of flesh and bone on the floor. The face and body were unrecognizable, but the coat and hat he knew well.

"Jonathan," he whispered, the blood draining from his face. He averted his eyes, feeling faint.

"The person formerly known as Jonathan, yes. He was always nothing; I simply made his outward form conform to his true image. Shall I tell you of his agonized screams when his flesh was seared; shall I relate the details of his bloody wounds; shall I tell of his rasping, final breaths?"

Carter trembled, struggling, as the tears rolled down his cheeks, to keep from being sick. Yet even through his shock and sorrow, he was still the Master. He had a duty for the good of Evenmere to understand what had occurred. He drew a deep breath, steeling himself. "The third question. Why did you kill him?"

"Because he displeased me."

"That is an evasion! I am the Master of Evenmere and you must answer!"

Jormungand stamped a massive foot, making Carter and the attic boards jump.

"He sacrificed himself to seal me into this accursed prison."

Carter bowed his head, his hand over his eyes. "I want to take his body for proper burial."

"No. The prey of Jormungand is not to be touched. You have won, though I defeated you at every turn. I would have made the entire universe a place of undying conflict, the slain rising like the Vikings in Valhalla to battle again. It would have been despair beyond imagining, glorious beyond hope."

Carter drew a deep breath. "He was a hero to the end. I

should have known."

"He was a fly buzzing around the face of a god. If his sting momentarily annoyed me, it makes no difference. Someday I will free myself again and have my way. Now get out. And keep in mind, you worm, that you who were never anything but a diversion for me have become my enemy; and Jormungand will have his vengeance."

Carter's voice turned deadly cold. "You'll have nothing of the sort. You are the incarnation of Hate, and cannot despise me any more than you already do. You are imprisoned again and your threats are the empty bluster of a schoolyard bully."

His three questions spent, Lord Anderson would learn no more. Heartsick, knowing it was forever beyond his power to avenge his friend, he turned his back on the dinosaur and headed toward the stair, while Jormungand roared in fury behind him, his flames lighting the whole attic.

Evenmere

The memorial service for Jonathan Thaddeus Bartholomew was the largest funeral gathering in the High House in many years. For two weeks, a line of mourners stretched down the Long Corridor, as thousands came to pay their respects before the empty casket. The service was filled to overflowing. The grand rulers of Evenmere attended, but there were even more bee-keepers and burnishers, blacksmiths and housemaids, constables and firemen, the everyday people of the great house, whom Storyteller had touched.

Following the service, the Anderson family, accompanied by William Hope, gathered in the drawing room of the Inner Chambers. A fly buzzed among the seraphs and flowering festoons; Jason played with his wooden soldiers beneath the French mirrored console. Duskin, sitting beside Lizbeth, stroked her injured hand. Since her return from Deep Machine, he had kept scarcely a foot from her. The windows were open and the air was still.

Carter had experienced his share of sorrow, but had forgotten, as mortals always hasten to forget, the sheer pain of grief—the knot in the belly, the rising pressure, the need to be alone to weep. He had known Jonathan only a short time; the depth of the loss surprised him.

"I am astonished by the stories told of him," Sarah said, seated in a high-backed chair, sipping tea from a porcelain cup. "Not just from the podium. He must have been a great man. I wish

I had met him. I certainly misjudged him."

"We had only hearsay to go by," Mr. Hope said, "and what I read in the records. He was so long-lived. His passing is a great loss."

"He saved my life," Carter said. "He saved us all."

"He was a steady rock," Lizbeth said. "A lighthouse in the midst of the sea. His voice was deep and wonderful—you should have heard him speak."

"And his stories," Duskin said. "The way he encouraged the men in the Tower of Astronomy."

"One thing still troubles me," Mr. Hope said. "I can't understand how the life of even so beloved a person could re-imprison the dinosaur. Could I, for instance, have offered myself with the same result?" The butler shivered. "It gives me cold chills, just thinking of walking up those steps."

"It's one of the many mysteries of Evenmere, I suppose," Carter said. "Sometimes I worry that this is another of Jormungand's deceptions; that he isn't really bound and is biding his time before rising to do more mischief."

Together, the company spoke of the ordeal they had faced, of the poets and the anarchists, the Black Beast and the Circle of Servants, the postman and the great mechanism that runs the world. Most of all, they talked of the goodness and grace of the man who had been Storyteller.

It was a wearing day, and toward evening Carter wandered into the Yard seeking peace. As the sun set through ragged clouds fired with purple and orange, he strolled back and forth, pondering. So much had happened, much of it incomprehensible.

As the sky darkened to that point where sight becomes vague and shadows grow thick with meaning, he strolled to the northwest corner. Atop the wall, as on each of the four corners, stood a statue of an angel with a drawn longbow. Carter watched the first stars appear. He spied Venus in the east, and thought of the telescopes of Edwin Phra.

After a time, a soft humming came to his ears. He turned back toward the Yard, straining his eyes to see. The sound seemed to emanate from the porch. Was that dark shape beneath the shadows of the eaves the figure of a man?

Instinctively, he reached for his Lightning Sword before remembering it was gone. He raised a Word of Power to his mind and stepped forward. As he drew near, he realized the form was a statue of Jonathan, carved from a stone the color of bronze.

He hesitated. The resemblance was impeccable.

The stone minstrel raised his head and looked at Carter with topaz eyes. "Good evening, Master Anderson."

Carter drew back, startled. "Jonathan?"

"I have been called that." Storyteller's voice, resonating from his rock chest, was even deeper than before.

"Is it really you? Jormungand said—I saw the body. I—"

"That's right. I am very glad you escaped the old dragon's wiles. I would have warned you, but I wasn't quite myself before you reached the attic. Jormungand's entertainments are not comfortable. Not comfortable at all."

"Did you—did he really—"

"Kill me? With great deliberation. Now don't you stand there with that hangdog look, Master Anderson. We have been friends, haven't we? I'm just a little changed, a little more durable. Come shake my hand."

Laughing, half-weeping, half-afraid, Carter did so. Jonathan's stone palm felt smooth and warm. But as he gazed into the minstrel's eyes, Carter shivered at the way they never blinked.

"We *have* been friends," Carter said. "Good friends, I think. You a better friend to me. Is the dinosaur truly caged again?"

"He is," Jonathan's old smile broke through his stone features. "He most surely is."

"But how? And who *are* you, really. More than a traveling minstrel. I've always known that. The Face we saw at Deep Machine?"

"No, that was someone else. It is impossible for me to go through the Eye Gate into the next realm. Lizbeth had to tell me what happened there. My guess is the one you saw is a servant just like us, you—who are called Master—me, Chant, Enoch, the lively Mr. Hope, the members of the Servants' Circle."

Carter stared, trying to fathom, but Jonathan laughed, a sound like laughter reflecting off canyon walls.

"Let's rest our feet awhile," Jonathan said, beckoning the Master to a bench beside the stone well in the midst of the Yard.

Carter hesitated, caution overcoming his astonishment. If this were some sort of trick, the creature was strong enough to crush him bare-handed. As they sat together in the dusk, he kept the Word Which Manifests close to his lips.

"I came because you need to understand what happened," the minstrel said, "because it might help you some time in the future. Besides, I didn't want to leave you hanging without knowing the rest of the story. I do so love to tell stories."

That, at least, sounded like the old Jonathan. "Go on," Carter said.

"Do you remember the tale I told about the beginning of the High House? How Evenmere woke into a universe filled with nothing but gray mist? How time began and the earth formed beneath its foundations? How the animals and people appeared? But the house couldn't speak to them?"

"I remember."

"Do you remember what you said?"

"I said the story must be false, because if the house couldn't speak, it couldn't tell us the tale."

"And you were exactly right. But there is more to that story, Master Anderson. You see, it made the old house mighty sad to be so silent. It was all boards and stone beneath sleepy rafters. Evenmere *wanted* to speak. It wanted to understand the people living under its eaves.

"One day, a messenger came to the house, one such as the Face you saw, who knew how to talk to the house in a way both could understand. Evenmere's silent request had been heard, and it was granted a marvelous gift. A form of flesh and blood that *could* speak, that could go running around inside that grand mansion, walking inside itself, clicking his heels and talking to everybody, learning what he could about his inhabitants, giving encouragement where he might. And he learned to tell stories, Lord Anderson, stories that see into the heart."

Carter flushed. "Are you saying that you—"

Jonathan ran his hand along the edge of the well. "I have been called Storyteller, and Minstrel, and Old Vagabond, the Wanderer, Runemaker, and the Singer. But the name least used that describes me best . . . is Evenmere."

Carter stared into the statue's open, honest face. "I don't understand. A metaphor . . ."

"I am Evenmere, Master Anderson. I am the High House. You have heard the house chooses its Masters, though you haven't always believed it. Well, I was the one who chose you, as I did your father before you. I was the one who shifted my walls to guide you to the Eye Gate."

Carter struggled to marshal his thoughts. "How can a man be a house?"

"You are both a father and a son, a husband and a brother, Master of Evenmere, and a child orphaned into the world for four-teen years. I was both the house and the man. A wandering minstrel and the mansion that serves as the mechanism to regulate the universe. It is simple enough."

Carter gave an acrid laugh. "Nothing is simple! Why, if what you say is true, why couldn't you have prevented everything that happened—controlled the anarchists, destroyed the poets?"

"I am not all-powerful. I control very little. I am a house. I do what I can to protect those within my keeping, but am limited by a strict moral code. I never kill, not even to protect my own existence. I try never to cause harm, though that is more difficult. Every action has ramifications."

"You were the one who gave Lizbeth access to the Book of Forgotten Things," Carter said. "Hope told me the door was found unlocked."

"Just as I previously rearranged my passages to bring her to the Inner Chambers, where I thought she might be most needed. I feared you wouldn't survive, and at this time Lizbeth is my choice for your replacement. She is, as I told you, a remarkable woman. Whether she will become Mistress of Evenmere, only time and cir-cumstances will tell."

"We couldn't have won through without her."

"She was my one hope for the Inner Chambers when it van-ished," Jonathan said. "That was a terrible ordeal for me. Changing my passages causes me great physical pain, and I only do so in dir-est need. To have a part torn from me is like you having an arm cut off."

"Why didn't you lead me to Deep Machine earlier? You

must have known."

Storyteller shook his head. "I did not know. Mine was a dual mind, not an infinite one. There were the thoughts of Jonathan Bartholomew and those of Evenmere. As the house, I can shift my focus from one place to another, but can concentrate on only one thing at a time, just like you. I hear much that goes on within me, but not everything. Think of it this way, Master Anderson: if your elbow itches, you notice it. But a thousand things happen in your flesh and bones without your knowing. I have the advantage of being able to look into my own veins—my halls and passage-ways—but most of my thoughts are those of a house, all creaking boards and fading paint.

"As for Deep Machine, I didn't know anything about it, not even its name, until I read of it within *The Book of Lore*. Myriad are my doors and portals and I can no more know every one of them than you can name the cells of your body. Besides, people are always changing the names of things, so I didn't recognize the name of the Eye Gate. The book gave me enough clues to allow me to find it. There are many doors within me that lead Out, beyond myself. To me, they are only exits. I cannot pass through them and never know where they go."

"When did you have the chance to read *The Book of Lore*?"

"As I once told you, it seemed strange that I had never heard of a volume that had supposedly been around for centuries. My house-self began searching for it. When at last I found it, I realized I needed to examine it more closely with my human faculties. That portion of me which is a house has a wholly different sense of vision and touch, and no perception of smell; Evenmere could not see the book the same way as Storyteller. That was why I left you so abruptly at Opo. The moment I saw it, I knew Jormungand was behind it—it reeked of that wily lizard. It told how Deep Machine could be used to change reality. I had never thought even the old dragon could be that ambitious, but I knew that must be his final goal."

"But you did know Jormungand was behind it," Carter insisted. "You discouraged me from visiting him. Why, you blocked the halls and prevented my going!"

"At that point I only suspected. This had the marks of that old bag of bones. Still, I couldn't quite wrap my verandas around it until I actually saw the book. As Storyteller, I could only travel as fast as any other man, and was too far away to guide you to the Eye Gate—time was short; the Black Beast and the doctor were nearly there, so I changed my halls to lead you to it. Jormungand can never succeed forever, but had he managed to alter the nature of the universe, other, greater sacrifices would have been required at levels beyond our understanding to make it right. That would have taken time—centuries or millennia, perhaps—time when the old lizard would have wallowed in destruction."

"So . . ." A dozen thoughts ran through Carter's mind at once. "So you have lived since the beginning of the house. You *are* the house! I have so many questions. Can you tell me—"

"Do you know why I never told people who I was, Master Anderson? Why I didn't say, 'Come look at Jonathan T. Bartholomew, the man who is a house?' Because if I did, I couldn't have done a bit of my job. They wouldn't want stories that touch the heart anymore. They'd want to know what it was like in the old days, and how the house came into being, and does God whisper in my eaves in the middle of the night. Those questions aren't for me to answer, so it's better no one knew to ask."

Carter shut his mouth with an audible click of his teeth. "I understand."

"No, you don't. Not quite. There are two sides to the universe: destruction and peace. We are always following the path of one or the other. But you and I, we have our places, and that is good enough. I will tell you this: the High House is not eternal. It is very old, but like all houses, it will someday be torn down. Something new is always being put in place. That's right. Always something new."

"What will happen to you?"

"Well, Master Anderson, I don't rightly know, but there are parts and parts. Evenmere, which is me, will live on, though the High House will not. I'm not much different than anybody."

"Are you not?"

The statue grinned.

"You keep referring to Storyteller in the past tense," Carter said.

"Because he *has* passed, Master Anderson. That's right. That form was destroyed, and I will miss it. I am all house now. I will especially miss eating good food, the touch of a friend's hand, the smell of lilacs on a summer's day, a thousand things. This body of stone is one I formed at great physical effort so you and I could have our little chat. You see, through Storyteller, Evenmere finally learned to speak."

"I am so sorry, Jonathan. It's my fault. I refused to sacrifice my son. I—"

"Now you don't go talkin' that way, Carter. Master of Evenmere or no, who are you to say what would or wouldn't have happened? Who am I, with my countless rooms and chambers, to judge you? You've spent your whole life regretting stealing your father's keys, something any boy might have done. Why waste the rest of it lingering on your failures? Let's both let it go."

Carter bowed his head to hide the tears. "You are . . . very gracious. Thank you. What should I do now?"

"Have I mentioned I never offer advice? But there is always something for the Master of Evenmere to do. Some wrong to right, some battle to win. What I would do, if I were Carter Anderson, Keeper of the Master Keys, et cetera, et cetera, is walk back into the house, find my wife and son, and have a nice cup of tea."

Carter abruptly laughed.

"What's funny?"

"You have always called me *Master* Anderson, never *Lord* Anderson. You were addressing me as befits one who is my superior."

Storyteller grinned. "An old house accumulates many private jokes."

Together they walked to the door. But as the minstrel touched the knob, his form melted away, melding with the stones and timbers of the High House. As Carter stood astonished, a voice humming from the eaves said, "I will be listening for you, Master Anderson. The walls have ears, you know. They surely do."

Lord Anderson soon returned to his old life, overseeing the building of the telegraph, working with Mr. Hope, Chant, Enoch and the other servants of the house, and watching his son grow up.

He spoke often with Lizbeth, showing her much, but not all, of the knowledge normally reserved for the Master.

One day, after receiving a message from Chant, he donned his traveling boots and cast his Tawny Mantle about his shoulders. Instead of his shattered Lightning Sword, he carried an ordinary rapier. He traveled through Ghahanjhin, skirted the Mere of Books, and reached the northeast corner of Vroomanlin Wood. Among the walled gardens, he found Chant in the dusk, reciting poetry to The Men Who Are Trees. The Lamp-lighter completed the last stanzas just as Carter arrived. The strange plants gave their plaintive wails for half a minute, quieting after the last rays of the sun no longer shone on their faces.

"Why do you recite to them?" Carter asked.

Chant smiled his wry smile. "My old friend Nighthammer, the blind anarchist, asked me the same question. He assured me it was a waste of time."

Carter sat on the bench beside his companion.

"I miss him," Chant said. "We had wonderful conversations together. He was a brilliant man and an excellent poet."

"And the one who lied to you about *The Book of Lore*. Perhaps a murderer as well."

"Perhaps." Chant gazed at Carter with his rose-pink eyes. "Aren't we all soldiers, fighting for a cause?"

Carter looked down, thinking of the blood on his own hands. "Will he really come?"

"He said he would."

"The pact I made with him nearly cost us everything," Carter said. "In my fear for Jason, I almost gave Evenmere away. Armilus was *this* close to changing the universe. I measured the life of a boy against the fate of Existence and chose my son."

"Well—he's a good boy."

Carter glanced at his friend, caught the irony in his eyes. They both laughed.

"At least you decided for Evenmere at the end," Chant said.

"As a result, I alternate between feeling guilty about my first choice and my second."

"*If, chance, from fell Charybdis I escape, May I not also save from Scylla's force My people; should the monster threaten them?*" Chant recited. "We learn as we go. Throughout my life I've thought poetry the highest calling, the music of the spheres. I considered lighting the lamps a small part of that. But we almost had too much poetry, poetry not to be borne. I have been reminded that there are greater things than poetry: friendship—hope—love."

A sound behind the men caused them to rise and turn. Doctor Benjamin Armilus, dressed in his bowler hat and black greatcoat, filled the narrow opening with his bulk. In his hands, he gripped *The Book of Lore*. Carter summoned the Word Which Manifests to mind.

"Doctor," Carter said.

"Lord Anderson. Lamp-lighter," Armilus nodded his head to both of them. "May I sit?"

Carter gestured toward a bench across from their own. The seat creaked under the doctor's weight, and Carter, reminding himself that the man was more muscle than fat, placed his hand near the pocket holding his revolver.

"I appreciate you agreeing to see me," Armilus began. "Are you well?"

"Have you come to inquire on my health?" Carter asked.

Armilus gave the barest turn of a smile. "We have played a deadly game, Lord Anderson, with the highest stakes. I trust you will prove a gracious victor?"

"I have played no games, Doctor. None of it was a game. We were both manipulated. The world was nearly lost. Unless you have come to turn yourself in to the authorities, we have nothing to say to one another."

Armilus looked down, almost imperceptibly nodding his head. "I came for only one reason—to ask a question. It is about . . . I want to know about the Face we saw at the end, the one who took the beast away. Does it trouble you at night? Do you think of it?"

The question surprised Carter. "Actually, it brings me comfort."

"Who was it?" Armilus' voice grew ragged. "Do you know? Can you tell me?"

"I have recently been told that there are many servants, Doctor, so I assume it was one of those. A doorkeeper, perhaps."

"A *doorkeeper*?" Armilus pursed his lips, shaking his head. "You only make matters worse. Whoever it was, I have never seen a Face like that. I cannot get it out of my mind. Because of it, I now doubt my previous assumption of a universe of impersonal forces. If there are indeed Beings overseeing our existence . . ." He mopped his brow with a handkerchief. "I have resigned my position as Supreme Anarchist. I intend to go away for a time to meditate upon the matter."

"Will the other anarchists let you depart so easily?" Chant asked. "You still possess the knowledge from *The Book of Lore*. For that matter, I question whether we should allow you to leave here unfettered."

Armilus grimaced and set the heavy book on the ground before them. "I came under a flag of truce, and you are both honorable men. The book was a tool of Jormungand's. I know that now. It could never be turned to our purposes. That is why I brought it to you, to destroy it if you can, or to seal it back in the Mere. I informed the Council that its power was useless to us, and I believe I possess enough personal authority to assure my own safety, so long as I am not perceived as an encumbrance."

"After the way you threatened my son, surely you haven't come seeking absolution?" Carter asked.

"I came, as I said, to ask a question. Someday I may indeed seek amnesty for my crimes. The Master has the authority to grant a pardon in certain cases. But perhaps Lord Anderson has never done anything he later regretted."

Carter sat silent. Armilus rose and gave a slight bow. "Gentlemen, I thank you for your time and bid you good day."

With that, the former Supreme Anarchist departed.

"What do you make of that?" Carter asked.

"*I am down again; But now my heavy conscience sinks my knee as then your force did.*"

"Perhaps," Carter said. "Maybe he *has* undergone a change. But he is still a murderer. When he came to us, I assumed it was as the head of the Society of Anarchists, arriving under what amounted to a cease-fire. If he no longer represents them, he is merely a criminal deserving punishment."

"We can probably still catch him."

Carter studied the quiescent faces of The Men Who Are Trees. Their eyes were closed; they looked innocent as children at rest.

"Do you really think they're conscious?" Carter asked. "Are they, as some say, paying penance for a terrible crime committed long ago?"

"I only know when I read them poetry, it brings them peace."

The two servants looked at one another.

"Should we go home?" the Lamp-lighter asked.

"Let's just sit here awhile. So long as Evenmere surrounds us; we are among friends."

To find out more about Phra's story, read the short story, *The Star Watch*, for free at www.james-stoddard.com/Starwatch

Printed in Great Britain
by Amazon

17706952R00195